DeVIL's Tango

Praise for *Dance of the Assassins*

'Very dark, utterly addictive and simply brilliant.' *The Bookseller*

'This is a gloriously silly comic book of a novel which manages, in passing, to be sweet-natured, smart and flashy.' *Time Out London*

'Another thrilling read' *What's on in London*

'Victorian London, seventeenth-century Paris, Renaissance Venice and Montezuma's Mexico are the places where Hervé Jubert has choreographed his ballet, with the hand of a master . . . the result is a devilish dance which confirms the exceptional talent of its creator. Don't hesitate, join the dance . . .' *Le Monde*

'An original novel.' *Sunday Morning Post*

'It's compelling stuff, with some ingenious plotting, plenty of twists, a cast of vividly memorable characters and a number of wonderfully evocative set-pieces.' *SFX magazine*

DeViL's Tango

HERVÉ JUBERT

Translated from the original French by
Anthea Bell

A division of Hodder Headline Limited

One Heart, One Soul

'Right then, first sequence, *salida* and then eight steps forward. Ready?'

'Yes, Grégoire.'

'Off we go, then.'

The guitar echoed in the old pelota court, now a ballroom. Its walls were carved with grotesque figures. Roberta Morgenstern clung to her partner. One arm outstretched, his aquiline profile on view, he had all the majesty of a conquistador pointing to the Promised Land. The drum signalled the start of the dance. The violin and bandoneon came in, and the couple set off along the invisible diagonal of the tango.

The music, slow at first, accelerated, snapping like a whiplash above their heads. Roberta had danced the first sequence in a kind of daze. She was abruptly brought back to earth by the pause before the next movement and the half-turn into which her dancing master was guiding her as they started off the other way.

'Not so airy-fairy, Roberta. Keep your mind on it.'

The *arrabal* or city outskirts, knife fights, brothels and *milonga* dances, the wooden paving of the streets of Buenos Aires . . . Roberta abandoned herself to the strong pulse of the tango. Grégoire Rosemonde sensed that they were

I

achieving perfect unison. His partner was wild, fizzing with energy, just the way he liked her – carnivorous, incisive, very much the Amazon!

The second sequence finished. They faced each other, Roberta with a hint of challenge in her eyes, Rosemonde with the glinting glance that always disconcerted her.

'What is it?' she asked, retreating.

He took hold of her firmly again and held her close to his chest. She was a head shorter, but her air of determination made up for their difference in height. The colour of their eyes – hers emerald-green, his aquamarine – suggested that they had been made from the same block of malachite. A subtle alchemical process took place between them when they looked at each other like that.

'You're wonderful, my dear. But we mustn't keep the Devil's Tango waiting. I want you to remember the old saying *Cor unum et anima una*, one heart and one soul, and observe it to the letter.'

She was happy with the one heart bit, but was it safe to entrust her soul to him?

'Show me what you feel deep down!' he added imperiously.

The pair of them set off again in a staccato sequence, while the music of violin, flute, bandoneon and drum made the rafters, the chandeliers and the floor itself vibrate.

The Community Building was the tallest of all the ministerial office blocks. From its basement, which housed the Records Office and the tracer-manufacturing production plant, all the way to the Minister of Security's office at the very top, it stood for the vigilance and justice of the legal system that governed Basle. Major Gruber presided over the Criminal Investigation Department on the sixty-ninth floor.

And just what crimes did they investigate, he wondered? The crime rate had been in free fall for almost thirty years now. Practically nothing had happened over these last three years, not since that business of the Killer's Quadrille.[1]

'Thanks to those wonderful tracers of ours,' muttered the Major without any enthusiasm whatsoever.

The tracers were everywhere, by day and by night. Vigilant little dust-motes carried on the wind, they stored the genetic codes of the people of Basle in their memories and raised the alarm when any crime, however minor, was committed. The culprits were identified on the spot and arrested by the militia. Crime had as good as died out.

Year by year the CID had been shedding inquiry agents. Gruber kept about thirty reservists on call, including Roberta Morgenstern and young Clément Martineau, who seemed set for a fine career in Security, although he was a little too intrepid and high-spirited for the Major. Major Gruber liked the moderate, thoughtful approach – though he himself had been young at a time when there were no tracers.

Gruber slipped a hand into the middle drawer of his desk, worked the mechanism of its false bottom, and brought out a mahogany-veneered box which was still red because it had been sheltered from the light of day. Three objects wrapped in jewel-coloured velvet lay there. He set them out in front of him.

The gold dollar which came down 'heads' on both sides, a souvenir of the Silversmith, last of the famous forgers . . . His father's military decorations, fragile tinplate mementoes . . . His mirror-glass pince-nez.

He had ordered that pince-nez from Monsieur Vinay, whose optician's workshop was now in the submerged part of Old Basle. His old friends from college had thought it

---

[1] See *Dance of the Assassins*.

highly amusing. Pince-nez with mirror lenses, they had guffawed! So that you can see behind you as well as in front of you at the same time! Why not gloves with grappling irons for arresting villains?

He cleaned the lenses of the pince-nez with a chequered handkerchief and perched them on the end of his nose. He could see the room behind him in the two half-moons of mercury at the ends of the darkened lenses.

With these, you could walk straight on ahead. No need to follow your quarry, you could let *him* follow *you*. Gruber, young and therefore arrogant at the time, was planning to demonstrate his invention, patent it, and see it displayed in the main amphitheatre of the Academy, available for purchase by future investigators. In his wildest dreams whole troops of men in glasses with mirror lenses patrolled the city, followed by unsuspecting criminals. The advent of the tracers had wrecked all that, of course, and his invention had languished in the hidden compartment of that secret drawer.

He took the pince-nez off again and re-read the citation signed by Archibald Fould, his departmental Minister, and received by internal mail that morning. For good and loyal service: Medal of Merit . . . a bonus on his retirement . . . grateful Security Department . . . and so on and so forth. Age had passed judgement on him. He was being retired on the first of the following month, and no one had mentioned any successor. Perhaps they'd already decided to close the CID down entirely.

Gruber tried to imagine himself somewhere other than in the Community Building, and failed. Well, yes, he had his little house in Mimosa Street near the Palace of Justice, but he was hardly ever there. The overgrown garden had come to resemble an enchanted forest. He had spent the last thirty years in this office. The CID was his whole life.

He opened the filing cabinet containing his reports on criminal cases. Several kilos of paperwork would soon go into the Ministry archives, to lie there gathering dust . . . Gruber picked one up at random and began to read it.

'You're not paying attention, my little snowfinch,' murmured Grégoire, sweeping her away with him down the infinity of the musical slope.

The instrumental quartet was nagging away, pounding out the change of tempo. The drum echoed through Roberta's veins and arteries. Her body submitted as best it could to this infernal rhythm. The dance was a little too vigorous for her tired joints.

'Sorry, Grégoire. My mind's elsewhere today.'

'Well, bring it back here or we'll never reach the end of this tango.'

'When does the *molinete* come?'

'Now!'

Rosemonde swung his partner round vigorously to make her shimmy the other way against the beat. They were moving in time with each other, arms extended, fingers intertwined, profiles very close.

'Now, get ready to turn left to right.'

They were navigating towards a point in the room which, as they approached it, was transformed. They themselves were no longer a battering ram but the prow of a ship, heading over an ocean of pale wood towards a vast figure just emerging from the void.

'The spirit of the tango!' cried the delighted Roberta. 'It's materializing!'

The creature rose almost as high as the ceiling, about ten metres tall. Its outline was vague and silvery, with gauzy scarves of vapour wreathed around it.

'We've never achieved such precision before,' exulted Rosemonde. 'Latin American dancing is certainly full of surprises.'

'And we haven't even tried the samba yet!'

'Let's keep concentrating, or it'll disappear,' warned the Professor.

Roberta laid her cheek against Grégoire's, and a delicious shiver ran through her. Rosemonde's chest swelled and his steps grew more precise. Motes of dust swirled in the rays of light falling through the skylights. It wasn't a tango they were dancing now, it was a seismic earth tremor.

'Such power!' breathed the witch, with a thrill of pleasure.

Clément Martineau was checking that his parachute was firmly strapped on when Amatas Lusitanus, his Professor of Aerial Sciences, joined him on the University roof.

'Fine day for a good view of Basle,' said the old Professor, slightly breathless. 'A very fine day indeed.'

From east to west rose the tower blocks of the buildings housing the Ministries, the Baroque quarter with the Palace of Justice, and the enormous mass of the Municipal Mausoleum, which looked as if it might collapse on the city any moment. The dark slopes of the Black Mountain served as a backdrop. On the other side the waters of the lagoon stretched away into the distance.

Lusitanus unfolded a stool, wedged it in position on the slightly pitched roof, and sat down. 'So why did you ask me to climb all the way up here?'

Martineau wasn't quite sure where to begin. He decided to keep it both vague and simple. A practical demonstration is always better than a long speech.

'Well, I found something out about my powers.' He looked at his watch. 'You'll see what I mean in exactly thirty seconds' time,' he added, more mysteriously than ever.

'Thirty seconds? Oh, come on, tell me! That's one second gone already! I mean, I already know you have certain powers, Clément, even if you're not in perfect control of them yet.'

The young sorcerer tightened his parachute harness, put on a sleek pilot's cap offering no aerodynamic resistance, settled his goggles over his eyes, checked that his moonstone ring was firmly in place on his finger, and began counting down with his eyes on his watch:

'Ten, nine, eight . . .'

'Er . . . if I may make a suggestion?' said Lusitanus.

'Seven, six, five, four . .'

'Perhaps you could . . .'

'Three, two, one.'

'. . . explain . . .'

Lusitanus looked Martineau's way. But there was no one there. He rose to his feet, muttering.

'Oh, really, this is too much! Giving me the slip like that!'

After taking another look around with no results, he folded up his stool and made for the skylight leading down again. He supposed Clément would have some kind of explanation for him. It had better be a good one.

If he had raised his head further he would have seen the little black dot waving at him from high in the sky, just below the clouds, and he would certainly have identified it as Martineau. But the Professor merely muttered a few more cross remarks before climbing back down to the ground, where magicians, witches and flying men existed only in children's stories.

'Let's go round it,' suggested Rosemonde.

Roberta moved away from him, still keeping her fingertips in touch with his and swaying her hips like the pendulum of a clock. The being they had successfully conjured up from the void watched her in astonishment.

'It won't attack us, will it?'

'No, don't worry, it's only a spirit.'

They had made their way all round the apparition and were moving off, stepping out stiffly in time to the beat.

'Could we stop now? I'm not sure where all this is taking us.'

'I am, Roberta, and I'm not going without you.'

Raising an imperious forefinger, Grégoire Rosemonde commanded the skylights high above them to turn dark. The doors double-locked themselves. They were alone with the astral being. Its eyes were two points of phosphorescence in the dim light.

'Grégoire?'

She didn't even notice when he slipped the shoestring straps of her dress off her shoulders. The fasteners of her BodyPerfect girdle snapped in turn. All done one-handed! From what book of magic spells had the Professor of the History of Sorcery learned his technique?

'Oh, Grégoire,' sighed Roberta.

Vaclav Zrcadlo had finished reading Jules Verne's *Journey to the Centre of the Earth* a few days earlier, and he had planned this little adventure in the tunnel under the Black Mountain as a kind of epilogue.

Alone in the granite belly of the mountain . . . If a crevasse swallowed him up, if he found himself a prisoner held captive in a lost, underground world, well, he would just adopt the methods of Professor Otto Lidenbrock, or dream of the world above like the Professor's nephew Axel, and he might emerge into the daylight again somewhere near Naples.

He reached the entrance to the tunnel. It was deserted. Of course the workmen wouldn't normally be there on a Sunday night. Their tools were locked up, and no one would be dotty enough to think of stealing the rotary digger used for cutting through the rock. Anyway, Vaclav told himself, the tracers are always on watch. I'm running no risk to speak of. He switched on his torch and walked into the tunnel.

From what information he had gleaned, he knew that the tunnel had already been drilled over three hundred metres into the rock. The idea was for it to come out in the valley on the far side of the mountain range. This was one of the major civil engineering works initiated by the outgoing Mayor to allow Basle to expand. It was also a source of controversy. Digging the tunnel was expensive, and extra taxes never made anyone popular.

If he were Mayor, Vaclav would have rebuilt the Historic Cities which had been pulled down two years earlier. The quarter where the immigrant gypsies lived, built out of parts of the old stage sets of the Cities and installed on the banks of the lagoon, gave some idea of what the old reconstructions of London, Paris, Venice and Mexico had been like. Vaclav enjoyed walking along its streets, lined as they were with a medley of medieval houses, shady taverns and Mexican temples. It certainly made a change from the general monotony of the rest of Basle.

The ground beneath him was uneven now. The walls of the tunnel bristled with sharp splinters. Little heaps of granite lay about, waiting for mechanized carts to take them outside. There were particles of mica in them, like remnants of petrified mirror glass broken by some ancient spell.

Vaclav held his breath. He had heard a noise behind him. He turned round.

'Anyone there?' he asked, in a quavering voice.

An icy gust of air hit him in the face. No one. Vaclav laughed nervously. This was what he'd come for, wasn't it? To get a bit of a fright! He went on exploring the tunnel with even more determination.

The rotary digger stood in the shadows a little further on, waiting on its tracks until work began again. Its conglomeration of engines, cogwheels, flywheels and drive belts looked like the mechanism of a gigantic clock. The three rotary discs that cut through the rock bristled with triangular points arranged in spirals.

Vaclav put his forefinger out to touch one, and withdrew it at once. A bead of blood stood out on his finger. He sucked it, looking at the machine suspiciously. Then he went right to the end of the tunnel, and came up against a wall of rock with a set of interlocking circles traced on it.

Imitating Professor Otto Lidenbrock's deep voice, he announced, 'We will go no further this evening, Axel, my boy.'

A cold draught blew down on his shoulders through a shaft in the roof of the tunnel. Up above, in the middle of a scrap of sky no bigger than a quarter-dollar coin, a small star was shining. Rungs set into the rock looked as if you could climb up them to the star.

Vaclav set off on his way back – and stopped dead when the beam of his torch fell on a massive shape. A man was barring his way, standing in front of the rotary cutters of the digger. He was dressed in what looked like grey felt, and his features were blurred.

Horrific ideas shot through Vaclav's mind. But the man neither spoke nor moved. He didn't seem to mean Vaclav any harm. None the less, the teenager told himself: the tracers will raise the alarm, the militia will get me out of here. I just have to play for time.

Wind whistled down the tunnel, carrying the apparition away. Vaclav waited. For a long moment, nothing happened. His pounding heart gradually slowed down. He'd been dreaming. His imagination had played a trick on him.

'Hey!' he called, feeling braver. 'Hey, Mister Ghost! Are you still there?'

The answer was a deafening noise. The cutting discs of the digger had started rotating at top speed. They were moving towards him, sending up sparks where they touched the rock walls beside the machine.

Vaclav retreated. The shaft through the roof, he thought. But the lowest of the rungs in the rock was too high. If he stood on something . . . His eyes fell on the pieces of granite littering the floor of the tunnel.

He began piling them up, fragment upon fragment of stone. The little mound was rising as the rotary digger came implacably closer. Vaclav could see the man sitting at the controls behind the cutting discs. His outline was as vague as his face.

Vaclav took a run, jumped up on his cairn of stones, and managed to grasp the bottom rung of the ladder. The digger knocked his torch out of his hand, and it smashed into a number of sharp splinters against the rock. One of them struck Vaclav on the calf, but he still clung to the rung in the shaft. He climbed several metres, grunting with the effort. The star in the sky above was telling him he could make it.

When he finally set foot on the rocky platform above the tunnel and was out in the fresh air, the tunnelling machine had long since fallen silent. Dawn was flooding Basle with pale pink light. But he couldn't stay here. That bloodthirsty madman might be coming up through the shaft after him. A steep path led down the slope to the city. He set off along it.

The man emerged out of nowhere, right in front of him. He seized Vaclav, picked him up off the ground, carried him back to the shaft and held him at arm's length above the opening. The youth struggled, kicking at the empty air. He stopped as he heard the noise of the cutting discs, a very distinct sound rising through the vertical shaft beneath his feet. The digger was climbing up to get him.

The man let go. The youth fell into the shaft. There was a slight change of tone in the sound of the rotary cutting discs. Then they were switched off, leaving the mountain in silence.

The Good and the Bad

Roberta entered the municipal park as she did every Monday, walked up the main pathway and around the big cedar, and made straight for a thorny hedge. The sharp leaves drew aside to let her through and closed behind her again. She was in the College of Sorcery's secret garden.

Plots of ground the size of monastic cells surrounded a grove of tangled trees. Those plots that were cultivated belonged to the College professors and were used for teaching purposes. Subjects included Practical Sorcery with Carmilla Banshee, Alchemy with Otto Vandenberghe, Aerial Sciences with Amatas Lusitanus, Alchemical Cookery with Eleazar Strudel (who was also landlord of the Two Salamanders inn), Satanic Law with Suzy Boewens, and the History of Sorcery with Grégoire Rosemonde.

Our tango king doesn't take much care of his plot, thought Roberta, casting a critical eye over it.

At first glance Grégoire Rosemonde's garden did indeed seem to be full of weeds, but on closer inspection they turned out to be a rather disconcerting collection of medicinal herbs: ragwort, wormwood, saxifrage and cornflower, plants dedicated respectively to Saints James, John, Peter and Zachary.

What's up with that man of mine, Roberta wondered anxiously, is he catching religious mania?

Carmilla Banshee's plot was only a few metres away. Roberta examined it with mingled fascination and disgust. Black, viscous, hairy henbane grew next to stinking orach, plumbago, snakewood and foetid hellebore. Banshee grew species that ought to have been obliterated from the surface of the earth by the Great Flood: creeping potentilla, wild clematis, stinking goosefoot and deadly nightshade. A specimen of *Orchidia Carmilla* reigned supreme in the middle of the plot. No one knew the effects of the poison contained in its hermaphroditic flowers – or at least, no one had ever lived to tell the tale. A huge lilac with jasmine rambling through it stood guard over this nightmarish garden bed.

Roberta turned her back on Banshee's garden to go into the grove. The trees had a healthy respect for Roberta, as a witch who had a special affinity with Fire, and they showed it by moving their branches aside or burying any obstacle that might make her stumble. She appreciated their thoughtfulness, and patted the helpful trunks.

Stopping under the Martineau family tree, a hornbeam, she listened to the woodland sounds. She was alone in the grove, hearing the cracking of twigs. This was her moment – now or never. Taking her ocarina out of her bag, she rubbed it on her coat and played the opening of *Michelle, my belle*. All the little animals who lived in this secret garden listened to the refrain of the song, but no hedgehog, telepathic or otherwise, deigned to respond to her call.

What a pity, thought the witch, putting her ocarina away again.

She snapped her fingers, and a branch of the nearest oak dipped to the ground in front of her. Taking out a small embroidered cushion, she placed it on a fork in the branch.

Once she was sure she would be sitting comfortably enough she seated herself on the cushion and ordered the oak: 'Up we go. Take it slowly, please.'

The oak raised Roberta seven metres up in the air, to the branch where she had discovered the genealogical records of the Martineau family tree. Forty-one lavender-blue leaves grew along it among their bright green companions. Roberta had followed the course of the sap from the end of the branch, moving in towards the trunk. Two more generations to go, and then she would reach the original stem. The identity of the founder of the line would be revealed.

Taking an atomizer from her bag, she pointed it at the branch and sprayed a little developer on the leaves. One of them, nothing special to look at, turned from green to blue before the witch's eyes.

'Bingo!' she said.

She unfolded a sheet of soft blotting paper with her fingertips and wrapped it around the leaf, taking care not to harm it. Once the pattern of the ribs and veins on both sides of the leaf, with its delicately toothed edges, was imprinted on the absorbent paper Roberta labelled the blotting paper with the date and time of day. Then she rolled it up and put it in a copper tube, which she stuffed into the bottom of her bag.

She tapped the branch, and it took her back to ground level again. Then she smoothed down her skirt and packed her cushion away. The branch sprang up to the sky again like a catapult. Next Monday she would look into the forty-third generation. And after that the last. And then she would have the full details of Monsieur Martineau's family tree of sorcery!

Once that was done she might perhaps extend her research to the other trees, to find out which further dynasties of sorcerers and witches were related to the Martineau family.

But discovering those links among the entangled roots and making sure the data were correct would be much harder work than following the trail of magical sap along a single branch like this one. No, she decided, a simple genealogical tree would have to do.

Roberta made her way further into the grove, using her natural authority but none the less taking care to avoid the Banshee family oak, which was surrounded by dead wood. She stopped beside a mangrove tree growing in the middle of a stagnant pool. It belonged to the Barnabite dynasty, whose last representative, Hector, was the college librarian and ran the Little Prague sanctuary. Like Roberta, he had a special affinity with the element of Fire, which made them cousins.

It was Hector Barnabite who had come to break the news of her parents' death when she was just thirteen.

Roberta hurried out of the grove to go and look at her own garden plot. She picked a little love-lies-bleeding for Eleazar's infusions, and several sprigs of sensitive plant, sighing to see the verbena running wild in one corner of her herb bed. Grégoire hated it.

The Martineau plot was next to hers. It was up to the sorcerers and witches to tend their own gardens, though she rather doubted whether young Clément had ever been here. All the same, she saw that the plot contained chickweed, the airy seedheads of dandelion, and heartsease or bird's eye, all of them very suitable plants for a sorcerer whose affinity was with the Air.

And I wonder, she inquired of the cloudless sky, just where our young detective is at this moment?

A clock struck six in the distance.

'What, already?' exclaimed the witch, for Basle had changed to summer time overnight. Roberta always found putting the clocks forward a great nuisance.

I'll change my internal clock tomorrow morning, she told herself, making for the hedge.

The prickly leaves moved aside to let her through, and then twined together again in a pleasing new arrangement, closing the invisible doorway to the garden where sorcery reigned.

Martineau had discovered his talent for rising towards the Ether by chance, on a clandestine nocturnal visit to the College. He had really gone there to consult the list giving details of all the teaching staff, which was not normally accessible to students. Having quickly scribbled down the home address of Miss Suzy Boewens, he had tried taking a short cut back through the amphitheatre, and found himself sticking to the inside of the dome like a fly. Getting out of that uncomfortable position was a difficult business, and by the time he was home in his attic room he felt his brain had been turned inside out.

After working out what had happened and trying some other experiments, the young man came to the following conclusion: if he was wearing the sorcerer's moonstone ring his mother had given him, if there was no moon (that is to say, on the day before the conjunction of moon, earth and sun and the day after it), and if he was vertically above a temple formerly consecrated to Bacchus, such as the old Roman temple down in the University foundations underneath the College of Sorcery amphitheatre – then he could fly. And Clément Martineau had always dreamed of flying.

Leonardo da Vinci, Albertus Magnus, Roger Bacon, Flamel, Fulcanelli and Lusitanus had all helped him to understand the atmosphere, analyse its component parts and dismantle its mechanism, mingling on equal terms with the creatures both visible and invisible that made their way through the air.

He had spent whole nights on the bridge of the *Albatross*, once Palladio's airship,[1] now in dry dock in a hangar on the outskirts of Basle. He could have flown that fabulous vessel with his eyes closed. But he had never dared ask Gruber for permission to use it. He was almost sure that Gruber would refuse anyway.

He had immersed himself in aerophysics. The Department for the Prevention of Natural Risks had an observatory perched on top of a metal tower a hundred metres tall on the highest point in the city, behind the quarter where the Palace of Justice stood. Martineau spent most of his spare time from College and the CID there – and the CID at least had been very quiet for months.

The drifting of clouds, downpours of rain, sudden falls in atmospheric pressure – none of these held any mysteries for the hawks whose soaring flight through the air he enviously admired. The wind itself, that omnipresent force whose path could never be traced precisely, deserved more extensive study than it had yet received. Ever since his experience in the amphitheatre the young man had imagined himself swooping through the layers of the atmosphere like a meteor, hung about with measuring instruments and exploring that boundless territory.

Martineau trod hard on the brake. His car skidded, throwing up gravel at the legs of the pedestrians in the street. One of them angrily accosted him. 'Can't you watch where you're going?'

Martineau didn't so much as look at him. He had taken out a large bound street atlas of the new city of Basle, had propped it on his steering wheel and was consulting it. The furious pedestrian went on his way.

The page which interested Clément showed the part of

[1] See *Dance of the Assassins.*

Basle around the lagoon. To the west were the marshes where the Historic Quarter had been reconstructed, with Little Prague in the centre and the marina and floating market from Mexico to the east, reaching all the way to the foothills of the Black Mountain.

There was a temple dedicated to Bacchus, larger than the one in the University under the south transept of the cathedral of St John Nepomuk in Little Prague. You could see the black slate spires of the cathedral from here. But to reach it Martineau would have to cross the Historic Quarter.

He drove more slowly downhill to the gypsy quarter. Making his way through the medley of gabled roofs, geometrical terraces, domes and ornate overhanging ledges was no problem. The former curved façade of the Palace of Westminster closed off the quarter like a huge screen, with the water of the lagoon lapping at its base. On the roof-tops windmills turned their sails to the sky. Jetties made from recycled sections of bridges from the former Historic Cities reached out into the calm water. The Savoy Hotel was moored a little way off.

Martineau put his driving glasses back on, engaged the clutch, put the car in gear, honked his horn just for the fun of it, and drove through the gateway.

The monuments brought from the Cities had been erected side by side without a thought for historical verisimilitude. Notre-Dame, Paris stood next to St Mark's, Venice. Medieval houses nestled into the colonnade of the Louvre. The curving façades of Regent Street were now decorated with Aztec bas-reliefs. Venetian, Gothic and Victorian footbridges linked the upper storeys of buildings. Martineau looked at them longingly. They must give you the feeling of walking on air.

'Ocarinas, pan-pipes, whistles of all kinds!' barked out a

gypsy carrying a wooden pedlar's tray in front of him. 'This is Birds' Day! Your big chance!'

Stepping on the accelerator, the young man stopped a little further on when he reached a junction. Two of the streets running off it were too narrow for his car, but on the right he could drive down Venice Street, which ended in a beautiful fragment of a palazzo looking like a medieval illumination. On the left, Mexico Street ran off into the distance under a roof of many layers of coloured fabric. Posters announced that Paris Street would be opening soon.

Martineau crossed the Ponte Vecchio, which had been turned into an exotic menagerie. The growls and hoarse cries of the animals greeted him as he passed. Then the buildings thinned out and land appeared behind hangars full of unused façades, statues taken down from their plinths and other items of urban furniture. Martineau came out on a stretch of waste land. On the far side of it, a hundred or so metres away, stood Little Prague.

The slender roof-tops gave the impression of a small town down on its luck in the middle of a desolate countryside. There was a strong smell of rotting and drains. The main sewer of Basle discharged its contents not far away.

Martineau let out the clutch and shut off the petrol supply. The engine hiccupped and died. He consulted the map one last time, put it away in the glove compartment, got out of the car, put up the hood and crossed the waste land, avoiding the puddles of muddy water that stood there.

The streets of the sanctuary district were dirty and empty. The buildings, with their windows boarded up, looked like rotten teeth. A dark film covered the ground. Martineau felt the pulverized substance, and the tips of his fingers tingled very slightly. It had got under his nails, blackening the tiny ridges of his fingertips.

Dirty oil, he decided. As a car enthusiast he knew something about the subject.

Gusts of wind were blowing over the forecourt of St John Nepomuk. The ever-present sooty dust swirled from side to side. When there was a lull, Clément slipped into the church.

He went down the side aisle and found a spiral staircase at the end of the south transept. Climbing the spiral staircase, he came out in the Daliborka, also known as the Hunger Tower.

Iron rings were set in the concave wall of the former dungeon, tracing a spiral movement up to the dome and its fresco of cherubs chasing each other through pink and white clouds. The only furnishings were a table and a *prie-dieu* linked by large cobwebs.

Martineau looked at his watch. Almost five o'clock. He had an hour and a few seconds before the moon passed over this memento of old Bohemia. The ring was on his finger. The ruins of the temple were beneath his feet – even larger and thus surely more powerful than the ruins under the University. He must get ready and make sure he had something to cling to, before checking that he could be projected skywards here too.

A clock in the distance struck five. Martineau's heart missed a beat as he heard the sixth stroke. But surely it was only five o'clock . . . Oh no, Summer Time, he remembered. He was still keeping winter time. So the moon was entering into conjunction at this very moment.

'Oh, my stirrup leathers!' he exclaimed.

He was making for the staircase when he felt his legs rising in the air. He managed to grab the first iron ring and then, making a huge effort, to get back down to the steps. That was a close shave! At least the experiment was conclusive. No need to look for a rope or anything like that now. He might as well go back to his car and the city centre. He'd had enough drama for one day.

He was starting out for the transept when he heard the shrill voice of Carmilla Banshee echoing through the church. Hector Barnabite was with her. The two scourges of the College of Sorcery were making straight for him.

'I'd rather have seen you in College,' grumbled Banshee. 'Consecrated ground always gives me such a headache.'

'The College is far from safe.'

'Oh, Hector. Nowhere in the world is safe. Except the heart of a man vowed to the powers of darkness, since no light enters it. Very well, show me.'

'No, wait until we're up there.'

Martineau was in a jam. 'Up there' could only mean the Daliborka. He cursed himself for not reacting earlier. He couldn't escape now without passing the two alchemists. So much for discretion.

He was about to indicate his presence when Banshee uttered an exclamation that made him change his mind.

'Hector! Look! What's that?'

'A mouse.'

There was silence, a squeak, a crunch and then a munching sound that left Martineau in no doubt about what he couldn't see.

'You're disgusting, Carmilla.'

'I thought it was your job to make sure the place was empty?'

'It was only a poor little mouse.'

'Well, if I find a poor little baby here I shall treat it the same way. Are you fully aware of what we are planning to do?'

'Oh yes.' The terror in Barnabite's voice managed to scare Martineau even more than he was scared already.

'Come on, let's go up. We've wasted enough time.'

They crossed the transept and climbed the steps leading to the Daliborka. The tower seemed empty. Banshee pushed the *prie-dieu* aside while Barnabite placed an obviously heavy, ancient casket on the table. Taking a small key out of his pocket, he was about to slip it into the lock when Banshee laid a hand on his shoulder and looked round suspiciously. By now Martineau was flattened against the dome fifteen metres above their heads. He was already forcing himself not to moan, and he almost stopped breathing too.

Carmilla raised her weasel-like face. Her eyesight wasn't what it had been. What did that stupid fresco show? Clouds, cherubs, some kind of Icarus figure . . . The young sorcerer could see the trace of red at the corners of Banshee's lips. Thinking of the mouse, he started swallowing and found he couldn't stop.

'All right, we're alone,' Barnabite decided.

He opened the casket and then leaned over it, hiding Martineau's view of its contents. All he could see was the librarian's bald head and the bony shoulders of his colleague in the black arts.

'It looks dead,' said the librarian.

'Don't be stupid. Even if the clay is brittle and its limbs are broken, there's life in it. After all, you found it in—'

'Yes, yes, yes. I told you over and over again. I found it in Old School Street. The casket came from Prague with the other relics. There's no doubt about its authenticity.'

'Then the child must have the benefit of it as soon as possible.'

They closed the casket again and left the Daliborka like two conspiratorial vampires. The young man heard the sound of their footsteps dying away.

'Thanks be to St Christopher!' he sighed.

He hadn't broken any bones, but keeping perfectly still while pressed against the inside of the dome was a difficult business, and very far from the Icarus-like flight to which he aspired. He put out an arm, grabbed the nearest iron ring, and pulled on it as hard as he could. But his body, although it seemed to weigh a ton, refused to drop down.

The Major was reading the report of the last arrest he had to his credit when there were three sharp knocks at his door.

'Come in!' he called, thinking it was some civil servant lost in the Ministry corridors. It gave him a shock to see the Minister of Security enter his office.

'Not disturbing you, I hope?' asked Archibald Fould, in suave tones.

The Minister had a cloak lined with red silk over his shoulders, and was holding a cane and top hat in one hand. There was a file under his arm. He put all these things down on a chair and came over to his subordinate's desk with an inquiry in his eyes. Picking up the report, he read aloud:

' "I was following a man wearing a pale raincoat and a broad-brimmed hat when he entered a bric-à-brac establishment from Old Basle, No. 91 in the floating market, at the sign of the Old Curiosity Shop. He came out a few minutes later, still in haste, with the turned-up collar of his raincoat hiding his face. I glanced inside the shop and found the owner lying behind his counter, stunned." You should write your memoirs, Major. You've got the literary style for it, no doubt of that.'

On the defensive, Gruber did not comment.

'Assault against the person, wasn't it?' asked the Minister, turning the pages.

'Yes, sir. The man knocked out two shopkeepers before attacking me.'

'And trying to open up your skull with – with a paperweight, wasn't it?'

'With a chunk of mineral now in the evidence cupboard.'

The identification photo attached to the report showed a man of about thirty with clear eyes, a tanned skin, and a gold ring in his left ear.

'A pirate,' grunted the Minister.

'We've failed to identify him,' Gruber allowed himself to point out.

'Yes, well, anyway he won't be knocking anyone else out. Unless the next Mayor chooses to exercise his powers of amnesty and lets him loose again in the streets of our good city of Basle.'

Fould put the report down and picked up the file that he had placed on the chair when he came in. He held it out to the Major. 'There's something in there that might interest you.'

The file opened to reveal a note from the College of Mining Studies. Gruber read it, and then glanced at the aquiline profile of Fould, who was looking at the lagoon in the light of the setting sun. He was as Mephistophelian a figure as you could wish to see, with his goatee beard, hooked nose, and hair carefully tousled in a manner which might be meant to look as if he had flown here through the air.

'Terrible thing to happen to that boy,' Gruber ventured. 'But if the Mining Studies people have decided it was an accident, then . . .'

'You haven't read the rest,' said Fould.

The rest consisted of a report from Security written an hour earlier. Gruber had to read it twice before he could take it in.

'The body, or what's left of it, is still *in situ*,' Fould commented. 'Obviously we must assume that this is a case of homicide, without rejecting the accident theory out of hand.'

He picked up his cane, cloak and hat.

'I strongly suggest that you go to the crime scene as soon as possible. I suppose your two experienced investigators Morgenstern and Martineau aren't exactly overworked at the moment?'

'We haven't had a case for months.'

'Then tell yourself that this is your chance to bring your career to a glorious conclusion.'

He prepared to leave, but then suddenly turned back. His cloak swirled around his shoulders, making him look like a giant bat with atrophied wings.

'I'm counting on you to deal with this case discreetly and efficiently. As you dealt with the last one.' It was impossible to interpret his smile.

'Of course,' replied the Major.

They nodded to each with mutual understanding. Gruber was well aware what case Fould meant.

A Thousand Ways of Death

The mynah bird jumped when the phone started to ring, came down from its perch, took the phone off the hook with its beak, put the receiver down on the table and announced, in its best German accent, 'Miss Morgenschtern is out gone, but if you a message vish to leaf, pliss speak after ze beep.'

Beelzebub, Roberta's cat, had heard the phone too. He stalked closer on velvet paws, licking his lips.

'Get away!' Roberta snapped at him. 'You're quite fat enough already.' The cat made for the kitchen. 'And as for you,' she told the bird, 'get out of his reach if you want to stay alive.'

The mynah bird returned to its perch and immediately fell asleep. Roberta picked up the phone.

'When are you going to get rid of that stupid bird?' asked Gruber wearily at the other end of the line.

'Major! What a surprise!' exclaimed Roberta, genuinely pleased. But she didn't need to look out of the window to know that it was dark already. 'Don't say that your call is going to upset my daily routine!'

'It is.'

'Great!' she exclaimed.

Gruber grunted. 'There's a car waiting outside your building.'

'Good heavens, is it that serious?'

'Yes. And I'm looking for Martineau. Any idea where he is?'

'Oh, somewhere between heaven and earth, I suppose.' There was a silence. 'What's up, Major?'

Gruber replied in a voice that was both neutral and tired, and boded no good. 'Don't dawdle. I'm waiting.'

Then he hung up.

The CID had acquired a fast car some months earlier, but Roberta hadn't had a chance to ride in it yet. Nor did she think she had seen the chauffeur before, not that she could have recognized him anyway in his dark glasses and leather cap. He waited for her to make herself comfortable in the passenger seat before setting off through Basle, along those of its streets that were reasonably suitable for motor vehicles. Luckily he drove in a civilized way.

There were a few passers-by out and about. People walking in couples kept close together, and they all looked uneasy. As the car drove past the big Barometer above the Central Pharmacy, Roberta saw that the pointer was stuck on Rain.

Contrary to her expectations, the chauffeur turned after passing the University and made not for the maze of ministerial high-rise buildings but for the Museum. They drove past the Natural Sciences wing to an impressive gateway. The chauffeur honked the horn once. A porter appeared in the beam of the headlights and hurried to open the gate for them.

'The zoo?' said the surprised Roberta. 'What on earth is Gruber doing at the zoo? Has the lion murdered the lioness's lover or what?'

The chauffeur did not reply. He drove on down an avenue of giant rhododendrons, and came to a halt in front of a chain slung between two tall stones. Roberta welcomed the return of silence. This sort of car really did make too much racket. But the peaceful atmosphere around them was only relative. There were yapping, hooting, roaring, screeching sounds behind the curtain of vegetation, which seemed to be splashed with green and white as the headlights fell on it.

Was it just the rain getting the animals into that state, the witch wondered as the chauffeur turned to open the car door.

He had taken off his cap and glasses. Roberta realized that she had in fact met him before, in the CID offices. She remembered being intrigued by his delicate features.

'Are you going to tell me what's up?' she asked.

The driver merely went on ahead of her. Roberta followed, her fists clenched. The explosion of animal fury in the zoo made her feel very edgy. The birds of prey were pecking at the wire netting of the aviaries, and the big cats were flinging themselves against the bars of their cages. Terrified monkeys were chasing each other. Some of them had blood on their muzzles. It was a scene of total panic.

They passed a group of keepers trying to soothe a llama. The animal had broken a foot jumping out of its enclosure. A splendid creature with a light brown coat, it was screaming and foaming at the mouth as it lay on the ground. Even Beelzebub when she once put him on a diet for three days – she never tried it again – had been less hysterical than the usually tranquil llama.

The driver was making for a building set a little way back from the path. Roberta knew nothing about it but its name; this was the Insectarium. He opened the door of the small concrete structure. The interior was dim, sparsely illuminated by the neon lights of the vivariums arranged in a U-shape. Security tape was stretched across the opening of the U. Beyond the tape, Gruber was crouching down close to something. Two men in white overalls, inspectors from the Municipal Lab, were working on a display case against the back wall.

The insects seemed to be as upset as their feathered and furry neighbours. A tarantula was scrabbling frantically against the side of its vivarium like a hairy hand tapping at the glass. The population of the beehive was in an angry mood. The scarab beetles were united against any enemy, pincers opening and closing in time.

Gruber straightened up when he saw Morgenstern. 'Oh, here you are. Micheau was quick.'

The witch looked behind her, but the driver had stayed outside. 'You mean that deaf mute who drove me here?'

'Well, actually he really is a deaf mute,' replied the Major. 'So you're here, but we can't seem to find Martineau. The whole department's after him.' He looked down at his shoes with displeasure. 'There's something here which should interest the pair of you. You've had – well, let's call it experience.'

Feeling impatient, Roberta tried to get past the Major, but he stepped sideways to bar her way.

'What's this all about? A murder?'

'That's up to you to decide. This – er – case is on the borders of our jurisdiction, but its exceptional nature made Fould decide to hand it over to us.'

'Look, if you don't show me I'm not going to be able to cast any light on anything at all.'

Gruber sighed, and bent to raise the sheet that had been thrown over the thing on the floor. The men in white coats made haste to turn away and go on with what they had been doing.

At first Roberta thought it was a horribly mutilated animal. Then her mind admitted that this carcass had once been a human being.

'This is appalling! What happened?'

'He or she was found in that condition early this afternoon.'

'Early this afternoon?'

'It took a while for the news to get through to us. And we still don't know whose body this is.'

'You mean the tracers haven't identified it?'

'There are a few little glitches in Records at the moment. Anyway, the victim's DNA isn't on their files. It could be one of the immigrants.'

'But all the immigrants are registered, aren't they? And surely those who aren't are picked up straight away by the tracers?'

Skin and muscles had been attacked by thousands of microscopic saws. Some of the bones showed like pale patches near the surface, which reflected light from the glass cases.

'I searched the whole place outside and drew a blank. Nothing. Not a clue, not a footprint except for those the keeper made when he found the body.'

'What time was that?'

'Two o'clock. He'd done his usual check round the Insectarium a couple of hours earlier. Everything was normal then. The doors weren't closed. Anyone could have found the victim, even a child.'

Roberta gave her boss a curious look. Then she went back to the body lying on the concrete floor. 'Who on earth could have done a thing like this?'

Contrary to her expectations, Gruber told her. 'Not who, what. Amazonian ants. They live in that vivarium.' He pointed to the inspectors, who were still busy with it. 'It seems there was a fault in the rubber seal of the glass case and they got out. Then they went on the attack. According to the zoo curator, that kind of behaviour is very unusual in Amazonian ants. What's more, the victim should have been able to get away easily enough.'

'Maybe he or she was blind and didn't realize what was happening until the last minute?' suggested the sorceress.

Now it was Gruber's turn to give *her* a curious look. 'What would a blind person be doing in an insectarium? And afterwards the killer ants went home, isn't that right, gentlemen? They're back inside that case again.'

The men nodded in perfect unison. 'A few might have got lost on the way, though,' said one.

'But there doesn't seem to be any danger at the moment,' added the other.

Roberta straightened up and took a couple of steps back, feeling slightly dizzy from standing up so suddenly. She knew that Gruber was approaching retirement. Perhaps he'd decided to have a bit of fun playing on his investigators' nerves before he bowed out? She couldn't make sense of any of it. And the Major was not a man given to practical jokes in the usual sense of the term.

'Yes, I know what you're about to say,' he anticipated her, deciphering her expression. 'But I have some other unusual cases on hand too. A lad in the care of the city was cut to shreds by the rotary digger in the Black Mountain tunnel early this morning. The remains of a baker were found in his oven yesterday. Accident? Suicide? Murder? Fould wants us to find who's responsible.'

'Major, these are man-eating ants we're talking about. What do you expect me to do? Wring confessions out of them one by one?'

'Investigate exactly what happened. You can have the body. All I ask is for you to keep quiet about this business and report to me at eight tomorrow morning. Let's hope Martineau will be here by then too.'

Roberta looked at the corpse, weighing up the pros and

cons. The fact was, a little dose of adrenaline wouldn't hurt, whether there was anything to investigate or not. She could do with a nice case. It would make the tangos she danced with Grégoire even more exciting, and their after-tango sessions more delightful than ever.

'Well, I wouldn't have to take the body very far from here to get it examined by the person best qualified to give an expert opinion.'

'You mean that man Plenck?' said Gruber, looking sour. He was torn between annoyance and relief at the prospect of getting rid of this ghastly sight. 'We have very efficient forensic scientists of our own who could—'

'Yes, of course you do,' Roberta interrupted. 'But *my* forensic scientist loves little creatures like ants, and he's based here in the Museum, *and* he works at night. Do I have a free hand?' She took the Major's silence for assent. 'Get them to take the body to Room 117. I'll go ahead to let Plenck know.'

'No, tell Micheau to drive you.'

'Look, it's less than two hundred metres from here.'

'Never mind that. If there's a killer about he may still be on the premises. And you'll get there faster that way.'

Micheau had just come into the Insectarium.

'Is he really a deaf mute?' asked Roberta, looking sideways at the chauffeur.

'You think I'm having you on? The Navy sent him to us. An excellent recruit. But you can talk to him all right – he can lip-read. Isn't that correct, Micheau?' the Major said, articulating distinctly.

The chauffeur, who was looking at him, did not reply.

'There's nothing so special about that,' pointed out Roberta. 'They teach lip-reading at the College of Sorcery. It's part of the core curriculum.'

Micheau said something to her without making a sound.

Roberta uttered a peal of laughter, perhaps overdoing it a little.

'What was that?' asked Gruber, irritated. 'What did he say?'

'Oh, it was a joke! Very, very funny! I think we're going to get on well. Right, you make sure the corpse doesn't go missing on the way.'

Roberta left the Insectarium whistling a *perpetuum mobile*. The driver walked ahead of her. Gruber, watching keenly, realized that the deaf mute had suited his pace to the witch's.

It was long ago that Plenck had exchanged his sorcerer's cloak for a scientist's white coat. His forebears had an affinity with the Ether, and he still used it in his medical work at the Museum – indeed, he used it in industrial quantities, as formalin. He had a courteous nature and was always looking out for any information that would help him to explore the great mystery of creation. He also had a liking for telling stories, which didn't prevent him from being an extremely competent forensic surgeon.

Morgenstern and Micheau had had to get the car started, drive all round the zoo, and then do a U-turn in front of a road under construction, only to find themselves back where they had started. Motor vehicles were definitely not the fastest form of transport, or not in a city anyway. At least the corpse was already there when Roberta opened the door of Room 117.

'You got my little package, I see.'

'Yes, indeed. Just what I might have expected of you. It'll make a change from doing autopsies on chinchillas.'

The rabbit-hole, as Plenck called his office, was higher than it was wide. Dozens of stuffed rodents and other small mammals stared at them with shiny, expressionless eyes from glass-fronted cupboards in the four corners of the room. In the centre a large table topped with a marble slab was used for dissections and taxidermy. Beside it a trolley held Plenck's instruments, arranged by size and function, and very sharp.

A bright light bathed the corpse in a savage brilliance. The witch stopped for a moment as she saw it lying like a still–life composition under that glaring light.

Plenck put a white coat on over his city suit. Putting down her bag, Roberta copied him.

'It was ants who did it,' she told him. 'In the Insectarium.'

'Yes, I know.'

They moved over to the table, one on each side of it. 'Did the inspectors tell you?' asked Roberta.

Plenck put on a pair of latex gloves, making the ends snap. 'No, but I read their minds. One of those bad habits you pick up in the Ether. I can't seem to shake it off.'

He set to work investigating the damaged flesh. 'Well, it's a woman we're dealing with.' He moved on from the torso, turning his interest to the head, which still had some tufts of sticky hair on it. Opening the mouth, he turned the light so that he could examine it. Three of the teeth were crowns. He managed to extract one and washed it under a tap. Back in the bright light, he showed it to Roberta.

'A woman getting on a bit. Around sixty. That crown dates from before the Great Flood. Could have been my uncle who did it for her. He was the best dentist in Basle.'

He placed this evidence of the dentistry of another age on a metal tray.

Roberta came closer. Plenck was now exploring the internal organs with a sharp instrument.

'She was literally eaten from inside, almost as if by rodents. I know something about rodents . . . How long did this take to happen?'

'No more than two hours, between the keeper's two

rounds. If he's telling the truth,' said Roberta.

'That's impossible.' Plenck had taken off his gloves and was inspecting the body, looking thoughtful and rubbing his chin.

'How do you mean, impossible?' asked Roberta.

He went over to a shelf, took down a large book bound in black leather, leafed through the volume and stopped at a certain page. Roberta went over and stood beside him. The picture showed an ant in warlike armour. Its carapace was orange and its jaws were shaped like crossed sabres.

'Let me introduce you to Miss *Polyergus rufescens*,' he said. 'A real little killer in her way. Only the fact is that Amazonian ants are not known to attack human beings. Still less would they be capable of taking one apart in only a couple of hours. Particularly as this woman didn't die instantly. She must have struggled. Why couldn't she get out of the Insectarium?' He put his gloves on again. 'Help me to turn her over, will you?'

They took hold of the corpse and turned it over. It weighed surprisingly little. The back too had been gnawed, but all the same there was a patch of intact skin in the middle of the backbone, like a piece of wallpaper clinging to a crumbling wall.

'You should have started by studying the external signs, Plenck,' he reproved himself.

He examined the square of skin through a magnifying glass. It was covered with something sticky, and he removed part of this substance, looked at it through the microscope, and then came back to the corpse, muttering. Roberta took her opportunity to study the substance on the slide herself. It was certainly sticky, and it had a sugary smell. Plenck was holding the piece of skin between his forefinger and middle finger and inspecting it, standing as still as a waxwork figure.

Roberta touched the substance with her finger and tasted it with the tip of her tongue. The forensic scientist, coming back to her, said grimly, 'They used a gimlet to pierce her spinal marrow. They must have used it to let the ants out of their vivarium too. The woman was paralysed.'

The witch looked at the almost invisible hole which had been bored in the backbone.

'Of course,' added the forensic scientist, 'we may well wonder how anyone of sound mind could be capable of such an atrocity – but we do know why she didn't get away. Now we have to find out why those ants virtually ate her alive.'

'Honey,' Roberta told him.

'What?' His glance followed the witch's, which was bent on the slide.

'She was covered with honey or something like that. You can taste it if you like. It was good honey.'

'Honey, eh?' He tasted it too. 'Yes, plain honey,' he said, looking at the corpse and rubbing his chin again, 'but that doesn't tell us why the ants ate her from inside too. Let's turn her on her back again.'

They lifted the body over on its back, and Plenck tried to follow the route taken by the ants, opening up the corpse with neat, precise scalpel cuts. Roberta, watching his skilful work, could hardly follow the swift movement of the blade in his hand.

'Aha,' he said, as the first ants came into view.

They were stuck together in clumps. He stirred the mass of dead insects. The heart was quite close.

'The ventricles are normal. The blood hasn't entirely coagulated yet.'

A studious silence fell between them. Then the forensic surgeon suddenly raised a tiny metal container in the air. It had electrodes attached to it. He cleaned his find with a tissue. A red light on the container was blinking, and numbers and letters were engraved on its narrower side.

'The reply to our last question,' he said triumphantly.

'A pacemaker?' said the witch, recognizing it.

He was holding the tiny metal box, only the size of a sugar lump, between thumb and forefinger. The filaments, pulled away from the ventricles, were giving out faint electrical discharges.

'Follow me. I'll show you something really interesting.'

They left his office for the room opposite, which was a vast study area with large transparent cases placed on white ceramic lab benches. The pairs of neon strips in the ceiling gave a light almost as hard and icy as in the Insectarium.

'My entomologist colleague's den. He happens to be working on an anthill just now.'

Plenck went over to a case half full of earth and held the pacemaker over it. After a few seconds large black ants appeared, clambering on top of each other, waving their feelers towards the little electrical device that the forensic scientist was using to attract them.

'My friend is doing experiments with ants and electricity. He's worked out how to imitate the vibrations of a queen ant with a battery like this. Yes, my dears,' he whispered to the agitated soldier ants. 'You think the nasty man's got your Mummy, don't you?'

He hid the decoy in the palm of his hand and left the laboratory, leading the way back to his own rabbit-hole. 'At least we can identify the victim now,' he told Roberta happily.

He called the hospital, which gave him the information within a minute. The number on the pacemaker belonged to a retired lady called Martha Werber living near the University. Roberta phoned Gruber, expecting to find him in his office. The Major made no comment on the result of the autopsy, but simply confirmed their meeting at eight next morning.

'Poor Martha, you didn't stand a chance,' said Plenck sympathetically, looking at the ceiling as if expecting some reply. 'Don't cry! The pain's all over now, and we know what happened. You can spare us the details.'

Roberta moved very slowly towards her friend, afraid of breaking the contact between the sorcerer and his element of Ether.

'Are you really talking to her?' she whispered, ready to eavesdrop on anything.

Plenck put a finger to his lips. There was total silence.

'I'd say she's gone,' he said at last, shrugging his shoulders.

Roberta made as if to swing a punch at him, but he parried it easily. 'Plenck, you're a manipulative wretch!'

'Well, if I *could* have talked to her I'd have asked her the murderer's name and address, wouldn't I?'

Roberta had picked up her coat and now put it on. She retrieved her bag, gave the forensic scientist a hug and said, 'I'd better go. I have a meeting early tomorrow, and if I don't get my seven hours of beauty sleep the Major will have a grumpy wreck on his hands.'

Plenck escorted her to the Museum entrance, where Micheau was waiting at the wheel of the car. Roberta gave him a smile of gratitude for his patience and got in beside him. The forensic scientist, hands in the pocket of his white coat, watched the car drive away. The zoo animals were still making a great deal of noise, but it was another sound that caught his attention.

He listened, and after a while he replied. 'You can trust us. Roberta is the best. She'll find out who did this to you.'

Roberta woke at six in the morning, thinking it was seven.

Oh, this is too much, she thought crossly. I really will adjust to Basle Summer Time now.

She got up and made herself an infusion of enchanter's

nightshade, a herb that was ideal for adjusting your internal clock.

While the water was heating up, the sorceress looked out at the lagoon. Clouds had come up overnight, but they stopped at the dam protecting the city. Beyond it, a slender crescent moon lay close above the water. In clear weather Roberta could have made out the peaks of the mountains of the moon and the deep valleys between them with the naked eye, but the humidity in the atmosphere let her see only a fine curve of ashen light.

She poured boiling water on the nightshade leaves, added sugar, sipped her brew and went back to the sitting room.

'I must finish the Major's pullover,' she told Beelzebub, who was snoring next to her work-basket.

She suddenly felt that she was growing taller, floating in the air, and at the same time she fully sensed the existence of her own body, her apartment, Basle, the whole world. It was all so simple and logical . . .

The effect of the enchanter's nightshade lasted only an hour, and after that she was back at her usual weight of sixty-nine kilos and height of one metre fifty-six. But at least she would be running on the same time as the rest of the city now. Better take a bath. She ran it at once.

When the tub was three-quarters full she took a saponaria bath pearl from the big shell where she kept them and dropped it in the water. Fragrant pink foam instantly formed, rising until it covered the taps. Roberta slipped into the foam as if it were a thick quilt, letting out little squeals of pleasure. The cat came over, slightly uneasy. His mistress, her eyes closed, was smiling.

It had been last September, she remembered. She was planning to knit Hans-Friedrich a winter jumper with stitches large enough to let his prickles through. She had been taking the telepathic hedgehog's measurements when he transmitted a thought from the cat's mind to his mistress's.

Sick of tinned cat food, Beelzebub was thinking, hungry. Going to eat that stupid bird this evening. Leave feathers in prickly animal's corner. The witch will think he did it.

Morgenstern had picked the cat up by the scruff of his neck and held him in the air in front of her. 'You do that,' she had told him, 'and I'll have your skin for a pair of fur slippers.'

Roberta took some of the pink foam in the palm of her hand, moulded it into a hedgehog shape and blew it into the air. The pink hedgehog made its way slowly over to Beelzebub and exploded on his nose. The cat shot off, mewing. Then the image of Martha Werber's body came before the witch's eyes.

'Oh no!' she said. 'Please. No corpses before breakfast!'

Quickly getting out of the bath, she put on a marshmallow-coloured dressing gown, went into the sitting room and dropped into her favourite armchair. The Major's pullover, she remembered. That'll take my mind off it.

She took her knitting out of her work-basket. She had chosen very soft alpaca wool in two shades of grey, pale and dark. There was only the neck left to do. Taking her two-and-a-half size needles she knitted for several minutes, believing that her mind was a total blank.

The uneasy feeling came over her again as suddenly and unexpectedly as last time, constricting her chest as she knitted the last stitches. Her sitting room had changed, and was blurred. A memory was superimposed on reality, a memory somehow linked to Martha Werber, and it was coming from the window.

Resigned, Roberta put her knitting down and walked to the window, obeying her mind's instructions. It was a shock to see not her own reflection in the glass of the pane, but that of a young girl walking towards her. The girl was thirteen years old. She was with the Strudels. And down below in the street there was some kind of excitement.

'Death to the brute!'

'Kill him!'

'Kill the monster!' shouted the people of Basle down below, marching forward in a crowd and brandishing weapons.

There were a hundred of them, and they were making for the Museum.

Stepping quickly backwards, Roberta looked at her hands, the hands of a middle-aged woman, and then at her reflection. Yes, it was hers all right. She was home again. Why had the murder in the Insectarium brought that memory back? She stood there perfectly still, trying to put together the pieces of the puzzle scattered in her memory before the effects of the enchanter's nightshade wore off entirely.

Forty years earlier, there had been rumours arising from a series of strange accidents. The idea of a killer on the loose had taken hold of the whole city. What was it they'd called him? What name had they given the imaginary monster?

One last cry, drifting on the wind, rose to her from the street and from the past.

'Death to the Baron of the Mists!'

The Baron of the Mists, she remembered. Yes, that was it.

A serial killer with superhuman powers, a killer whose existence had never really been proved. But he had set off a brief period of collective madness. It was just after the Great Flood. One day the fantastic figure had allegedly been spotted and pursued through Basle. Roberta had seen those men pass with their weapons. The chase had ended up in the zoo, where the animals were so frightened by the frenzied people that some of them had to be put down.

Roberta opened her sitting-room window. The air was keen and biting. Day had dawned as the wind rose.

'The Baron of the Mists,' she murmured, looking at the city.

Gone with the Wind

In spite of all his efforts Clément Martineau hadn't managed to get down from his perch yet. The power of attraction was too strong, and he was wearing himself out to no purpose trying to get back to terra firma again. So he had improvised himself a harness with his belt, hitching it as best he could to the third iron ring. It was the lowest he could reach, but it was still about fifteen metres above floor level.

Strapped securely in place like this, he let himself drift off into a gentle doze which became deep sleep. In his weightless state Martineau slept like a log.

He walked into a dream. It was a house-shaped dream. He crossed patios beneath changing skies, ballrooms empty of any dancers, zigzag corridors, luxuriously furnished mirror-lined rooms, kitchens with roaring stoves and other kitchens as cold as the tomb. He went up and down staircases made of wood, stone, paper. At one moment he crossed a rope bridge slung above an indoor jungle. Overhead a stained glass window showed gods and goddesses chasing each other amidst laughter.

Martineau was well aware that he was visiting his family tree of sorcery. His moonstone ring opened all doors to him, and this way he met the witches in his ancestry. Some of them were scary, like his grandmother, who sprinkled powdered nightmare over his childhood dreams. Most of them welcomed him, reassured him, embraced him with great kindness. Others even made certain advances that frightened him more than the worst of night terrors.

One of his ancestresses, a very beautiful woman, offered to tell his fortune. Another witch was drinking with men-at-arms in a smoke-filled room at an inn. I'm somewhere near Frankfurt, he instinctively knew, just as he knew that the gold coins scattered over the table were nothing but cleverly transmuted sulphur and mercury. Later and further back in the past, he saw one woman helping another to give birth. He fell silent in the face of this mystery, greater than any of the others, and left the scene without a word.

He was coming close to the trunk now, and by the same token close to the root of the tree. The last wing but one of the house was deserted, open to the elements. He went down the longest flight of stairs he had ever seen in his life. The banisters were carved with grotesque figures. The steps, dark marble veined with bright yellow and increasingly rough and slippery, led to a black wooden door. The knocker was a metal hand, a left hand wearing a ring on the middle finger.

Martineau opened the door without knocking and found himself in a kind of low-ceilinged vault, its floor covered with sand. A fire was burning in a brazier. A silhouette outlined against the light turned towards him. And he woke up.

Dawn was casting pale light into the Daliborka. The detective wiped the sleep from the corners of his eyes, stretched in the void, braced himself against the wall and undid his belt. He clambered down, agile as a monkey, and was finally able to stand upright. That night spent between earth and sky had left his mind clear and his limbs rested, in spite of his dream with all its wealth of detail.

His car was still parked between the church and the

Historic Quarter, its hood sparkling with dew. Martineau switched on the fuel supply and turned the starting handle under the radiator grille. The engine caught at once. He got behind the wheel, put the car into gear, and left Little Prague behind.

The main road through the gypsy quarter was empty. Martineau drove along it with his foot pressed right down on the accelerator, not too bothered about waking the inhabitants with the backfiring of his engine. If he had glanced in his wing mirrors he would have seen windows opening, fists being shaken and mouths shouting at him. But why would the friend of eagles, the lord of the sky, trouble about such pathetic earthbound concerns?

He drove under the porch of the Palace of Westminister and up the slope to the coastal road. His exhilaration was far from wearing off. His tyres squealed as he drove down winding streets. If a pedestrian going for an early-morning walk set out to cross the road in front of him, Martineau made him run like a rabbit just by hooting his horn.

His route took him past the Museum, where he instinctively slowed down. Further on, the railings outside the zoo were guarded by two militiamen. He drew up beside them. One of them told him to drive on.

'Clément Martineau, police number 6373,' he said confidently. 'I'm with Security. What's going on?'

'Your card, please,' said the militiaman, taking nothing for granted.

The detective showed his identity card from the Ministry, bearing the double helix of his own genetic code. The militiaman slipped it into a scanner, glanced at the screen and handed it back to its owner.

'They've been expecting you at the CID since yesterday evening.'

'Yesterday evening?'

But the militiaman had returned to his post.

'Yesterday evening,' repeated the investigator.

A terrifying roar from the zoo sent cold shivers down his spine. Martineau trod on the accelerator as if the big cat were after him personally.

With its wooden chairs, its blackboard, and Victor the skeleton demurely seated at the lecturer's desk, the CID conference room looked like a classroom from a past age. Its ceiling was a glass roof grey with dust, looking out on a lighting shaft which went right up to the top floor of the tower.

It was not eight yet, but one of the investigators who had been summoned was already there, sitting with his legs straight, his arms crossed and his eyes closed. Roberta smiled when she saw that he was the first to arrive. She approached on tiptoe, with the firm intention of making him jump.

'With all due respect, you displace as much air as a runaway tram hurtling down a steep slope.'

Roberta stopped, bright red in the face. Martineau rose, turned round and kissed his partner's hand.

'They say you've turned into a good sorcerer, but that gives you no right to compare me to a runaway tram,' she remarked, giving him a little tap on the cheek, and then pinching it for good measure. It was Martineau's turn to go red. He was genuinely pleased to see her and would have liked to give her a hug, but he felt rather awkward and didn't venture to.

'How's Monsieur Rosemonde?'

'Fine, dear boy, just fine.' She sat down in a chair beside him. 'And by the way, I'll have finished tracing your Tree of Sorcery within two weeks. I just have to write a few more comments and then I'll deposit the parchment with the College.'

'Great! My mother is organizing a "happening" in Basle – you must come. She's always asking me how you're doing.'

'I'll tell her. But now, listen.' Roberta frowned and adopted a tone of reproof. 'Gruber had people trying to find you much of last night. It should have been possible to get hold of you. Every investigator in the department . . .'

'I know, I know. I know all about CID etiquette. But I was kind of stuck. I'll tell you later, but I can't say anything for now,' he added, with a conspiratorial air which didn't suit him at all.

'A mystery already? When our inquiries haven't even begun?' asked Roberta.

'Why has Gruber summoned us anyway? Exactly what's going on?'

'You'll soon find out.' Roberta consulted her internal clock, which had now adjusted itself to keep time for the next six months. 'The Major shouldn't be long.'

Micheau appeared. Seeing him, Martineau immediately thought of a fox. The two motoring enthusiasts looked each other up and down, noting each other's supple leather outfits. Micheau sat down at the back of the room.

'You know him?' the young detective asked his godmother in sorcery.

'The new office chauffeur. Delightful man, and wonderfully discreet.'

'A chauffeur?' Intrigued, Martineau turned to look at the other man, but Micheau ignored him. Leaning back against the wall, balanced on his chair, he was watching a ballet danced by two flies chasing each other just under the glass skylight.

New arrivals gradually filled the room, some greeting each other as old acquaintances. Martineau, who had always felt he was the only real man in the CID, adopted as haughty as possible an air. Roberta was telling herself that the situation must be really serious if Gruber had called in the whole little band of reservists he still had available.

The Major entered the room with a file under his arm. Silence fell. He climbed up on the platform, and was momentarily taken aback to see the chair behind the desk already occupied by Victor the skeleton. Finally he put his file down in front of the jigsaw puzzle of Victor's two hundred and six polished bones and looked at his audience, adopting a military pose with his thumbs tucked into his waistcoat pockets.

'Everyone's here, I see,' he said with satisfaction. 'Right, we can begin.'

Picking up a stick of chalk from the ledge under the blackboard, he started breaking it into ever smaller pieces. A break at the end of each sentence, Roberta noticed.

'Three crimes have been committed. Three crimes in under two days. And we've only just noticed.'

Three, thought Roberta. So he was linking the young lad and the baker to Martha Werber.

'And I haven't asked you here to celebrate, although there have been no murders in Basle for the last five years. I've summoned you because the tracers failed to spot anything, and from what bits of information Records will give us, our little helpers aren't about to recover from their breakdown in the next few days.'

The former detectives, now assigned to other activities for the very reason that the tracers were so efficient, shifted in their chairs. So the day of human sleuths was back! They'd show those technocrats in Security that intuition and practical work on the ground could still outdo technology and all its robots.

'Our colleague Roberta Morgenstern here has thrown light on the ways in which the killer operated on at least one of the victims.'

49

The sorceress rose so that everyone could see her. 'The ways and the means,' she corrected him. 'With the help of Dr Plenck from the Museum.'

'With the aid of Plenck,' agreed Gruber, glancing sideways at her. 'To sum up: we have three people dead. Martha Werber, killed in the Insectarium at the Municipal Zoo; Angelo Pasqualini, a baker by trade, whose bones were found in his bread oven; Vaclav Zrcadlo, a teenage boy in care – there's not much left of him except fragments of his DNA scattered round the ventilation shaft of the Black Mountain tunnel. As for Pasqualini, someone shut him in his oven and baked him. The position of the bones suggests that the poor man struggled to get out.' Gruber cast a sad glance at the seated skeleton, perhaps expecting some kind of expression of approval from it. 'In young Zrcadlo's case it was the rotary digger in the tunnel that did for him. Again, someone was operating it, and again, the tracers saw nothing and the killer left absolutely no clues behind. As for Martha Werber . . '

Gruber got rid of the now pulverized chalk, rubbed his hands, and picked up the file from the desk.

'I can only congratulate those of you who were sensible enough to skip breakfast,' he announced by way of introduction.

The Major spoke for nearly an hour, giving details of the crime scenes, the times of death, and anything else that might help them to solve the three murders. Martineau, concentrating hard, was writing in a small notebook. Some of the others were recording Gruber on tape. Roberta was scribbling notes in a diary she had bought in the Historic Quarter, fitting them in between a vol-au-vent recipe given to her by Strudel and a love poem inspired by Grégoire. Micheau simply watched the movement of the Major's lips.

'None of this must be made public,' Gruber concluded. 'If the people of Basle learned that they can be bumped off with impunity it could cast a shadow over the mayoral election. I'll see you all in turn to give you police passes and share assignments out. Roberta Morgenstern and Clément Martineau, already on active service, are excused that formality. Any questions?' There was total silence for at least ten seconds. 'Good. To work, then.'

And Gruber left the room.

'Look,' Martineau whispered to Morgenstern.

Someone had managed to pin a note saying April Fool on the Major's back.

'Well, they've got the date right,' commented the sorceress. 'Nice to see that the good old traditions aren't dying out.'

Those who had noticed the joke were wondering which of them had been dextrous enough to do such a thing unnoticed by the Major. Victor the skeleton, sitting at his desk, couldn't help smiling.

Martineau went off as soon as they had left the Community Building. There was something he had to check up on, he said in his new conspiratorial manner. He got in his car, telling Roberta he could drop her off anywhere she liked.

'I might just as well take the tram to where I was expecting to go with you,' she said, lips compressed.

The young man did not comment on this remark, called 'Ciao!', briefly honked his horn and took off at high speed, raising a cloud of dust which fell softly back on the road and on the witch's nose.

He never changed. She'd hoped he would discover the virtues of calm and patience, but apparently not. And they weren't things you learned at the College of Sorcery.

The tram took Roberta at a demure pace to the Palace of Justice, where she climbed the colossal flight of steps and entered that temple to the Law with as much self-confidence as a priestess. She passed through the waiting room, walked down galleries, along corridors and passages, and finally reached the archives of the Ministry of Security, which by some administrative quirk were situated here. Marcelin the archivist looked none too pleased to see her enter the reading room. It was empty, as usual. Few people consulted him now that the tracers and Central Filing were in charge of crime prevention.

'Well, well, if it isn't Roberta Morgenstern. May I remind you that you borrowed that street atlas of Old Basle at least two years ago? You never responded to my Overdue notices. But I still have it on record as out to you, and I'm keeping that record carefully.'

Roberta struck her forehead. 'Whatever can I have been thinking of? I'll get it back to you very, very soon. I want to ask you a favour, Marcelin.'

The sorceress had only to concentrate all her powers of persuasion in her emerald eyes for the archivist to turn meek as a lamb.

'What – what can I do for you?' he begged, in strangled tones.

'Does the name Baron of the Mists mean anything to you?'

After thinking for five seconds, Marcelin replied. 'One of the last files put together by my late predecessor. It'll probably be under T or Z.'

Roberta sat down at the reading desk and switched on the art deco lamp over it. She could hear Marcelin moving a ladder around among the huge shelves of files and other paperwork. He came back with a dusty box.

'Correctly filed under B after all. Fancy that!' He put the box down in front of her. 'Everything we have on the Baron of the Mists is in there. An interesting subject,' he continued, looking curious. 'Some kind of personal research, is it?'

Roberta's eyes turned from warm to chilly in the fraction

of a second, and Marcelin thought it more sensible to beat a retreat.

'Well, I've got work to do. Let me know if you need anything.'

The box contained a set of yellowed press cuttings dating from the time of the events. It took Roberta some time to separate the wheat from the chaff, but she found what she was looking for in an article under the by-line of one E. Pichenette for the *Lagoon Journal*, a paper once well known for its anti-municipal stance. The piece was a report on the incident of the manhunt leading to the zoo, the event that had come back to her mind only that morning. The headline read:

BARON OF THE MISTS
SLIPS THROUGH THE NET!

And the article began:

Modern Basle is the scene of strange events reminding us that in these troubled days we can fall back at any moment into the Dark Ages of medieval times.

Roberta heaved an exasperated sigh. Medieval times had been anything but Dark Ages. However, this reporter Pichenette was writing at a time of excess and ignorance. There was the threat of a war for possession of the mainland, and the wildest of notions were being taken at face value: the panic-stricken public might have followed any little tyrant who proclaimed himself a saviour. It was a miracle that the fragile Municipality had survived at all. Roberta read on.

At ten in the morning, it was reported that the notorious Baron of the Mists had been seen in the north of the city. A crowd soon gathered beneath the brand-new Barometer over the Central Pharmacy. At eleven-thirty this crowd of about a hundred men, your humble servant included, all of us armed and determined, set out to cut off the malefactor who, according to sometimes contradictory but always detailed reports, was still moving on. A strong wind blowing from the Black Mountain made our progress difficult. We reached the zoo, making the city walls echo with our shouts of indignation, which were well justified – the Baron of the Mists, remember, has been disturbing the peace of our citizens for almost six months, and the new Ministry of Security, despite its assurances and its new high-rise building, has proved unable to prevent him from going about his nefarious business [for a summary of his crimes see insert]. Our footsteps rang out as far as the Old Basle Zoo, which I must unfortunately confirm is now in a disgraceful state of decay. At a time when most of our native plant and animal species are threatened by the Great Flood, at a time when our days are numbered, we have nothing to offer the last representatives of the natural world but dirty cages, verminous fodder and rotting meat.

Pichenette, thought Roberta. Surely she'd heard that name somewhere before?

What words can I find, dear readers, to describe the scene that I now witnessed?

Roberta decided to skim swiftly over whatever words he had found. Tedious as his style was, his account summed up what she had seen and felt the previous evening. Panic-stricken animals, enclosures that had become traps, a cry for help to what might, in general terms, be called the Great Tree of Evolution.

And then at last we saw him. He was cornered. We formed a semi-circle and stood motionless. The animals had fallen silent; a racket of the kind that Noah must have heard had died down. In silence, we stared at the spectral, majestic and shocking sight of the Beast. The colossus had been carved from granite, but still looked rough-hewn. He was in human shape, but his outline was unfinished and changeable.

Roberta skipped straight to the next paragraph.

The attack began. Then a sudden gust of wind blew all round us. The Baron of the Mists had vanished into thin air, leaving our thirst for justice unquenched.

'You don't say,' muttered the witch to herself.

She quickly skimmed through the other press cuttings. The reporter Pichenette had repeated his story in the same style a good ten times. As there were no more sightings of the Baron, the rumours had died down again like a flat soufflé. The reorganization of this part of the mainland and the construction of the dam were to the forefront of everyone's mind.

Roberta studied the summary of the Baron's appearances, and noted in her diary the days and places where the inhabitants of Basle had seen him:

27 July: University quarter
28 July: foothills of the Black Mountain; the Zoo

She compared them with the notes she had taken at the CID offices:

30 March: Pasqualini cooked
31 March: Zrcadlo shredded at dawn;
Martha Werber and the ants

The dates did not match, but Roberta had a feeling that if she checked up on the times of day and the locations, the appearances of the Baron two generations later would match in some way.

The summary written by Pichenette as an insert, a small square of yellowed newsprint, said:

29 July: the Baron seen in the municipal textiles mill around two in the afternoon. One victim, Bernadette M., who survived her injuries.

Roberta consulted the clock above the door. Midday. She could come back. As she gathered up the press cuttings, a paper from the Ministry which she had failed to notice before caught her attention. It was from the then very new Criminal Investigation Department. A young investigator had been given the job of looking into the case of the Baron of the Mists. There was his name in black and white. Roberta's eyes widened as they fell on it.

My dear Major, she murmured, I'll bet my bottom dollar you've noticed how the details match too.

Closing the box, she gave it back to Marcelin. He was looking at a pamphlet with a cover adorned with a handsome compass rose, and hid it jealously when she tried to take a closer look. 'I'll bring back that street atlas as soon as possible,' she promised before leaving.

A killer vanishing into thin air, she thought as she left the Palace of Justice. Right up Martineau's street. All the same, she wished she knew just what urgent business he had gone off to check.

The observatory of the Department for the Prevention of Natural Risks perched like a golden eagle's nest on top of its tower. Three hundred and eighty-four steps led up to it. It took Martineau less than half an hour to climb them, which was quite an achievement in itself. The two staff members working up there glanced absently at him. The investigator was a frequent visitor – who else would have gone to the trouble of climbing all the way up here?

The observatory was about ten metres in diameter, with oval windows looking out on the world beyond. A work surface ran three-quarters of the way round its circumference and bore various instruments: a recording meteorograph, a hair-balance hygrometer, barometers and mercury thermometers. The pluviometer discs were lined up in vertical series. Most of the chairs at this work surface were empty, and had large closed books and weather maps in front of them.

The staff members present were entering, by hand, the data constantly spewing out of the meteorograph, so that they could work out averages and write weather forecasts for the Ministry. Martineau went over to consult their notes. The successions of indented crests on the graphs told the recent history of the air, that atmospheric ocean in which everyone bathed.

The upper line showed wind speed. It had been climbing steadily over the last twenty-four hours. During the same period the barometric line had fallen five degrees. Temperature had remained constant. However, the wind had veered erratically, changing direction three times an hour. As for the lowest line, showing precipitations, it was blank. For now.

Martineau went out on the footbridge, clung to the guard rail, and took in the vast landscape visible from the observatory. The clouds sailing from end to end of the horizon were like grey rags stitched together. The wind shredded them and sent them swirling as if to make them disgorge their contents. There'd be rain soon.

A gust of wind struck the young man in the back, impelling him towards the void. The wind-vanes and anemometers on the observatory roof were going crazy. Martineau went back inside. The two men cursed, clamping their hands down on their papers as the wind, roaring in, tried to blow them away.

'What weather!' said the young man.

'Yup, it's going to rain,' commented one of the staff members, sharpening his pencil. 'Tomorrow at the latest.'

'Nothing good ever happens when it starts raining,' the other one agreed.

'That's for sure,' agreed Martineau. 'OK, boys, there's something I have to check in the stockroom.'

He went to the cubby-hole in the small part of the observatory that faced the slope of the Black Mountain. It was used for storing records, personal property, cleaning materials and electric batteries. And it was here that the investigator kept the results of his researches on the atmosphere, in a notebook just like his CID notebook except that the CID book had a red cover, and the other one a blue cover.

He opened it and leafed through the pages of close writing with patterns marked by arrows, the outcome of long walks round the streets of Basle and his observations of the wind. He found what he was looking for at the end: three pages that he had copied from an anonymous document entitled *A Study of the Surface Winds Passing Through Basle*. He had discovered it between two out-of-date calendars in the observatory. It was a pamphlet with the engraving of a compass rose on the title page. No one knew where it had come from or who had written it.

Its author had placed anemometers around the city and spent months noting the slightest displacement of the air at ground level. By taking samples in the city streets, he or she had shown that a specific wind blew in precise areas to a rhythm that was repeated, with truly Swiss precision, at each major phase of the moon. Martineau had meticulously recorded such manifestations around the time of the new moon, but so far he had gone no further.

The wind blew first in the street where Pasqualini had

died. The next day it was howling around the slopes of the Black Mountain. And on the same day, at exactly one in the afternoon, it was unleashing its fury on the Zoo.

Martineau opened his red notebook and carefully re-read his notes: Pasqualini, Zrcadlo, Werber. The wind was there to meet them. The two sets of data coincided perfectly. It was as clear to see as it was impossible to explain.

He went back to his blue notebook. Judging by the phase of the moon, the notorious wind should be blowing around the municipal incinerator plant at about two in the afternoon. Martineau went to check in the leaflet, but he saw, with a sinking feeling, that half the documentation had been removed since his last visit.

'Yes, that's right,' one of the staff members told him when he asked. 'It's been taken to the Ministry archives. You'll find it all down there.'

He just had time to go down to the bottom of the observatory, stop off at home to pick up his gun, and then make for the incinerator plant, wondering whether he might not be doing something very stupid.

To Be Marked with a Black Stone

The Major was keeping watch on the entrance to the textiles mill, concealed behind a hoarding covered with election posters. Roberta nipped into hiding in her own turn to spy on him. She saw him put on a pair of pince-nez with mirror-glass crescents in the lenses and move out into the open, and she allowed him a little start on her before following. She expected to take him by surprise inside the factory, but he had vanished into thin air. Just like the Baron of the Mists back in the past.

'All right, so a textiles mill is a place where a lot of people mill around, but what's the idea of this?'

He had come up on her from behind, taking off his glasses. His eyes sparkled with glee.

'Why, if it isn't Obéron Gruber, otherwise the Major,' said Roberta, proud of knowing his first name at last.

The little man put his invention away in the top pocket of his jacket. 'No one's called me Obéron since the Academy,' he told her, a wistful look in his eyes.

'I've just been looking at the archives. I felt quite odd when I saw you mentioned there. You were only around Martineau's age at the time.'

Gruber, eyes half-closed, dwelt on the past with a touch of melancholy. 'Setting off in pursuit of a rumour. Oh, it was a kind of freshers' rag.' He straightened his shoulders, and the familiar steely Major in his grey flannel suit was back. 'Anyway, if it really is him again, then he's not harmless any more. Come on, Roberta! We have a date with our first really high-class killer!'

'High-class?'

'You take my word for it, this Baron character has to be an aristocrat.'

Clément Martineau had changed out of his one-piece motoring outfit and into a cotton suit which would be more comfortable in the heat of the incinerator plant. With his six-shooter in his pocket, he was driving towards the rubbish dump on the edge of the lagoon in the most remote part of Basle. No one asked him any questions when he drove into the compound.

He parked between two mounds of rubbish waiting for incineration. The wind carried the smell far and wide. Pieces of sheet metal were clanging together somewhere in the distance. He got out of his car and continued on foot.

The incinerator plant was shaped like a fifty-metre cube with a single black brick chimney rising from it. A vast sliding door yawned ahead. Putting his head round the door, Martineau called, 'Hey! Anybody there?'

No reply. He groped his way forward into the dim light. Something behind him glowed red. The heat was oppressive, and fast getting even hotter. He took off his cap. His eyes stung, and he had difficulty in breathing.

The light grew brighter, shooting blood-red flashes through the vapours. Martineau stopped. This was sheer madness. He could go no further. He'd come back better equipped and with company. He was just retracing his footsteps when a monstrous form emerged from the haze a few metres away and then plunged straight back in again.

The creature had huge, flat, glassy eyes, and a trunk for a nose. Its shell was shiny and seeping with moisture. This was no hallucination or imaginary spectre. Martineau set off after the figure, gun in hand. Now and then, when the vapours briefly parted, he caught a glimpse of the creature. Was this the criminal? What linked this nightmare vision to the wind which, after all, had put Martineau on its track?

There was a dull thud behind him, the sound of a door closing. The vapours disappeared as a vacuum device noisily sucked them in. The air cleared, and now Martineau saw the terrible trap into which he had been lured.

At the back of the huge firebrick furnace stood a cone-shaped heap of slag looking like a termite hill. Several rows of fiery sparks ran around the walls. The monster had picked up a metal rod and was turning slowly towards Martineau, who felt far from ready to confront it in this terrible arena. And in such heat too . . .

The monster came towards Martineau, who staggered. He felt he could never reach the door. He raised his gun. His adversary stopped, dropped the rod, and held out his hands palms upwards. Then he removed his helmet. The detective saw a broad, rough but undeniably human face emerging from what, after all, was only a one-piece rubber suit insulated to keep the wearer cool.

'So who are you?' asked the salamander-man. 'And just what are you doing here?' He ignored the gun that the young man, without thinking, still held aimed at him, and went over to the control panel beside the door. He pressed a series of metal knobs, and ventilators opened in the top of the furnace. The lukewarm air made the atmosphere considerably fresher.

Yes, wondered Martineau, pulling himself together, what *am* I doing here?

The workman caught some of the thin trickle of water that was constantly cooling his rubber suit in his hands and splashed it into the detective's face. Martineau was near fainting. The wind came in, howling furiously as it blew into the furnace and raising little whirlwinds of ash.

'There's easier ways to kill yourself,' growled the workman. 'And you're interfering with my work. Give me that gun.'

He tossed it aside, and then pressed a latch on the door, but the latch fell straight back into the locked position. He tried again, with the same result.

'Oh no! Now this wretched door's stuck.' The man went to use the intercom, but it seemed to have broken down.

'Is there some problem?' asked Martineau, feeling remarkably foolish.

The workman wasn't listening to him. Instead, he was struggling with the controls, which also refused to work. Suddenly he was hauled violently backwards. The ventilator louvres closed again. The light grew dim and the temperature suddenly rose, while the fiery sparks around the walls glowed more intensely than ever.

Martineau was seized from behind. Something was holding him by his legs and chest. He couldn't turn round. He could see only the dry skin of blackened hands against his chest and round his ankles.

The salamander-man was fighting some kind of giant six-armed spider. A single enormous head topped its nightmare body. The fasteners of the man's one-piece rubber suit snapped open. Its supple metal straps were undone. The workman was being undressed. His leg and arm guards, the mechanism and the hydraulic joints of his suit fell apart at his feet.

Martineau managed to grasp one side of the wheel closure that locked the door, but two more hands grabbed his wrists and twisted them behind his back.

The creature now overpowering the workman divided into two. One of the parts took human form and picked up the equipment lying in the ashes. It made for Martineau and put the suit on him, beginning with his legs and finishing with his head. The young detective and the workman exchanged glances of desperation. The creature jammed the helmet down on Martineau's shoulders and switched on the hydraulic mechanism. Cold water began circulating round the suit.

A bright fire flared at the back of the furnace. The shadowy figure strode over to its other half, which had been holding the workman captive, and merged with it again. The man was dragged half-naked towards the glowing cinder cone in the furnace. He shouted and struggled, but in vain.

Behind his tinted goggles, Clément saw the workman being lifted off the ground and thrown into the furnace. The man tried to escape, but the creature was watching, rod in hand, and pushed him back like a recalcitrant piece of rubbish. It was several minutes before the man stopped moving.

Martineau did not faint. He kept his eyes open throughout. For a blackened hand lay on his shoulder exerting a comforting pressure, as if to say: 'Watch that, my friend. See what you've just escaped.'

Roberta was in position on the catwalk above the drying room. Gruber, down on the floor below, was seated on a chair in the middle of a circle of light from a spotlight, playing the classic part of tethered goat. They were both waiting for the Baron to show up.

The foreman who met them had himself been employed

in the mill as an apprentice at the time of those past events involving the Baron. He remembered that 29th July as if it were yesterday, he said. A woman worker had her arm torn off. No, no, not by the machinery – by the monster who had been chased all the way to the zoo and never seen again! He described the monster to them in excitable terms. Four metres tall. Sharp teeth filed to points. Slanting eyes with tawny yellow irises.

'More like a wolf or more like a bear?' Roberta had asked.

'More like a wolf,' the man claimed firmly.

The place where this drama had taken place was now a drying room. The many looping skeins of wool stretched out to dry were rather attractive, but Roberta's stomach was rumbling with impatience. She was beginning to think that the Baron had never been here at all, Bernadette M. had merely been the victim of a factory accident written up by the *Lagoon Journal* as a scoop to sell the paper, and the foreman had been seeing giant wolves all over the place ever since.

Gruber, motionless beneath the octagon of criss-cross beams where the wool was draped, looked like some deity about to knit his own universe. In fact he was thinking, with his eyes closed, of Tenochtitlán and the roof of Montezuma's palace three years ago. Night had just fallen. The Killers' Quadrille was waiting for his reply. The Devil would soon appear.[1]

'Morgenstern will deal with the Devil,' Fould had assured him. 'What I want you to do – indeed, what I'm ordering you to do, if he actually does appear – is to bring back a sample of his DNA.'

Gruber had protested that he didn't understand why the Minister was asking him to do such a thing.

[1] See *Dance of the Assassins*.

'Just shake his hand and take care not to wash your own afterwards. Or sign a pact and get some of his blood – do it any way you like, but we need the Devil's DNA. The security of Basle depends on it, Major. This is an order. I'm relying on you.'

And the Devil had indeed appeared. The Major had picked up a cigarette end still damp with the satanic saliva and brought it back to Basle. Fould had congratulated him warmly on carrying out his mission so successfully. Since then the Major had heard no more. Fould had never mentioned the cigarette end again. On the sole occasion when Gruber ventured to broach the subject, the only reply he got was the two magic words, 'Municipal secret.'

The sound of breathing cut his reflections short. Someone else was in the drying room with them. A glance at the catwalk above showed him that Roberta had already left her post and gone into action.

The Major rose, stretched his arms and legs, and turned. It was difficult to make out anything much in the dim light, what with the wool draped all around the place, but he spotted the man at once. Indeed, he was about as inconspicuous as a militiaman in armour dancing the waltz at a charity ball.

There was a shrill cry. A dark, indistinct shape fell at his feet. 'Don't hurt me! Don't kill me! Please!'

Roberta stepped forward into the circle of light. Gruber gave the foreman his hand to help him up. 'What were you doing, spying on us?'

'I – I'm terribly sorry. Curiosity . . . fear . . .' He took hold of the lapel of the Major's jacket. 'The Baron of the Mists is back, isn't he? That's why you're here!'

The Major disengaged himself as best he could. In this man's eyes he saw the madness of many he had met while working on the Baron's case at the very beginning of his career.

'Cheer up, my good man,' he said, trying to keep his tone of voice light. 'There's no Baron now. He's gone. Done for. Flown the coop. No more Baron of the Mists. And keep this to yourself, will you? I'd be grateful.'

'Yes, yes,' replied the foreman, shaking with nerves. He left the drying room, looking behind him frequently. Gruber dropped back on his chair, dismayed.

'Well done, Major. You'd have made a good psychologist. Our friend will stop seeing monsters under the bed now.'

'If only you hadn't made him so scared in the first place!'

A heavy, reproachful silence fell between them. Gruber looked at the disastrous sight of the tangled wool. It resembled a trap from which some wild animal had managed to escape. His mobile rang. He answered it.

'Gruber,' he said. 'What? Stay right where you are! We're on our way.'

'Martineau?' guessed the sorceress.

'He's at the incineration plant, and we have another body on our hands.'

The female employees of the mill had stopped work and were chatting to each other. The Major didn't have to lip-read to see the Baron's name passing from mouth to mouth. The monster was acquiring new celebrity. And Gruber knew from experience that once people started talking about that kind of criminal, he liked to cultivate his notoriety.

Martineau was waiting for them in the cubby-hole where the incineration plant workers took their breaks. The walls were decorated with pictures of volcanoes, lava flows and huge fires. The investigator would have liked to go out for a breath of fresh air, but three of the workers were keeping close watch on him. It had been touch and go whether they would let him phone Gruber.

They were surprised to see a small man in a grey suit arrive, accompanied by a plump woman of around fifty with bright red hair and emerald eyes. Once Gruber had shown his Ministry of Security card, the shop steward of the plant told him what had happened.

'He followed Fliquart into the furnace room. We don't know exactly what happened then, and he won't explain.' Morgenstern, standing behind Gruber, felt sorry for Martineau, whose hunted look betrayed his embarrassment. 'Seems like the controls failed and wouldn't open the vents. Fliquart sacrificed himself – he gave your friend here his own suit.' The man cast a furious glance at Martineau. 'He had five kids, Fliquart did.'

Gruber was at least two heads shorter than this angry man, and he would have had difficulty in calming him down. However, the witch, daughter of Fire that she was, took the shop steward's hands in hers and said, 'Leave us alone with him. We'll find out what happened.'

The man was breathing like a pair of bellows, but he recognized Morgenstern's authority and nodded. 'We'll be watching the exits. Either that man leaves under militia guard or he doesn't leave at all.'

'All right, all right,' agreed Gruber, getting tired of these useless recriminations. He closed the door behind the workmen. Martineau sighed heavily.

'At last! You took your time! I thought they were going to lynch me!'

Morgenstern and Gruber each took a chair and sat down facing their pupil. All they needed was a three-thousand watt spotlight between them to make the interrogation scene perfect.

'I can't advise you too strongly to keep this clear and concise,' said Gruber.

Taking a handkerchief out of his pocket, the investigator mopped his face, merely spreading the wide tracks of black sweat already running down it.

'I saw him. The murderer. I was in the furnace room and I saw him kill that man – Fliquart.'

'Hang on a moment,' Roberta said soothingly. 'What on earth were you doing in the furnace room?'

Martineau twisted his handkerchief, wondering how best to approach this subject. Finally he folded the handkerchief and put it away in a pocket of his cotton jacket, which the heat had now turned a reddish brown colour.

'Someone wrote a study of the winds – the surface winds that blow through Basle. It was in a printed pamphlet – I saw it in the Prevention of Natural Risks observatory.'

'The observatory?' said the surprised Gruber.

'It's because he wants to fly,' explained Roberta, raising her eyes to heaven.

'Some parts of Basle are subject to very strong gusts of wind on certain fixed days and at regular times,' Martineau went on. 'And according to the author of the pamphlet, if it's as regular as that, the wind must be artificial in origin. But he failed to establish what might be causing it. To cut a long story short, the deaths of Pasqualini, Zrcadlo and Werber correspond in every detail to the places and times when the wind rises. And it was to blow over the incineration plant today. So I went there. And I was right.'

'And five children in Basle have lost their father,' Gruber reminded him. 'We're supposed to work as a team, Martineau. Now, tell us what you saw.'

The expression of annoyance on the young man's face became fixed. This was the main question he had been asking himself while he waited for his colleagues to arrive. He gave the best reply he had been able to come up with. 'A kind of solid shadow.'

'I beg your pardon?' asked Roberta and the Major in the same breath.

In a dull voice, Martineau told them about Fliquart's dreadful death, the hands holding him, the creature that had split apart and come together again before his eyes, and how he himself had been spared.

'Witchcraft!' exclaimed Gruber, and added, turning to Roberta, 'If you'll forgive the expression.'

'No offence taken, Major.'

The Major and Roberta continued their conversation as if Martineau wasn't there. 'A solid shadow,' said Gruber thoughtfully.

'Reminiscent of something, isn't it?'

'The Baron of the Mists,' said Gruber thoughtfully. 'That's him all right.'

'Baron of the Mists?' repeated Martineau.

Someone knocked vigorously on the cubby-hole door. 'We've alerted the militia,' called one of the workmen. 'They'll be here any minute.'

'Are you or are you not going to tell me who this Baron of the Mists is?' hissed Martineau urgently.

As clearly and rapidly as possible, Gruber put him in the picture about their fruitless wait in the textiles mill for the Baron. That mysterious being was from a past that Martineau's generation had never known. At least, he'd never heard of the Baron before.

'Fliquart is our fourth murder victim,' Gruber reminded them. 'So no more branching out on your own initiative. We all three follow the same trail.'

'Where else is this wind due to rise?' asked Roberta hastily. There was a good deal of turmoil on the other side of the door.

'The marina of the Fortuny Club, this evening at nearly eleven.'

'Right. I'll get our forces together and set a trap,' said the Major. 'And I don't want anyone to mention the Baron of the Mists. If the press got hold of his name . . . That poor man Fliquart sacrificed himself. He died because of your imprudence. So let a word of this get out and you're sacked, understand?'

Gruber rose to his feet and took one of Martineau's arms. Roberta took the other. The detective, rather startled by the turn events had taken, let them do as they liked. The door suddenly opened to reveal a militiaman bristling with weapons. The incineration plant workers were ranged in a solid phalanx behind him.

'We're well in control of the situation, officer,' said Gruber, showing his card, which the militiaman instantly slipped into a scanner. 'We're taking this man to the CID offices for questioning.'

And he pushed Martineau past a double line of menacing faces like any common criminal.

'This business will be thoroughly investigated!' Gruber assured the hostile crowd. 'And we'll keep you up to date with the course of our inquiries.'

They finally got away unmolested, followed by the militiamen marching in step two by two. The incineration plant workers watched the little troop move away. Their shop steward spat out a blackened quid of tobacco, which sizzled as it hit the asphalt floor in the heat of the nearby furnace.

'Wildcat strike!' he announced to the men assembled behind him. 'The fires stay out until Fliquart's been avenged.'

Gruber kept Martineau with him for the sake of appearances, and told Morgenstern to meet them at ten at the entrance to the marina. She went home to her apartment, where she found a letter from the Records Office on her round blue doormat. Apparently Administration wasn't happy: there were gaps in her records, they wanted her date of birth, her parents' professions, her present address . . .

'What a bunch of idiots!' she exclaimed. 'To think a tree was cut down so that you could print this glaring proof of total incompetence!' She consigned the letter to the same destination as her last two missives from Records, namely the dustbin. Then she soothed her nerves by finishing the Major's pullover. She embroidered a pretty motif which looked like a decoration for services rendered to the Municipality on the front of it, wrapped up her handiwork in tissue paper and went out again, intending to leave it at her boss's office.

The wind had turned, and was blowing from the lagoon. A small crowd had gathered under the big Barometer over the Central Pharmacy when Roberta passed. Everyone was talking about the approaching rain. The mercury had fallen again.

The sorceress handed the pullover to the caretaker of the Community Building, who sent it up to the sixty-ninth floor. Then she went to the Palace of Justice, planning to have a couple of words with Marcelin about that pamphlet. She ought to have remembered that Archives were closed on Tuesday and Thursday afternoons, and she hesitated to pick the lock of the door. But she could always go back tomorrow between two-fifteen in the afternoon and five forty-five in the evening . . . 'Oh, really, Admin and its fiddly timetable!' she said crossly, retracing her steps.

As soon as she put her nose out of doors again she heard that a few drops of rain had fallen on the floating market half an hour earlier. The news had already gone all round town. The people of Basle, forming small groups, were exchanging doomsday predictions. Roberta stopped close to one such group, thinking they were talking about the weather. A dignified old gentleman was addressing an audience of secretaries and clerks from the Palace of Justice.

'So the Baron of the Mists is just an old wives' tale, is he?' she heard him exclaim. 'Well, I know someone whose niece works in the textiles mill and she actually saw him – saw the Baron of the Mists this very day! No, he didn't kill anyone, but it was a close thing. Could easily have been a massacre.'

'Didn't the tracers do anything?' asked a young woman.

'Tracers? I never believed in those tracers!' said the old man firmly. 'This microscopic police force of ours – all moonshine, if you ask me. Ever seen one of those famous tracers yourself?'

The woman was obliged to admit that she had no idea of the difference between a tracer and an ordinary dust-mote. Still, she added, what was the world coming to if no one in Basle had any respect for security these days . . .?

Roberta met Grégoire at the Two Salamanders for dinner. The restaurant was half full. He was a little disappointed to hear that they weren't going on to dance in Mexico Street, as they had planned. Roberta said she had things she must do elsewhere, and that was all she could tell him. He did his best to cheer her up over dinner, but a leaden gloom was weighing down on the city. Every witch and sorcerer could feel it. People's expressions were grim, and the atmosphere was dismal.

Roberta took the tram to the marina, where she found Gruber surrounded by his reservists and arguing with the guard at the gate. The man was proving obstinate. Martineau was keeping out of the argument, leaning on his car, and Micheau had taken up the same position beside the Ministry vehicle. They were ostentatiously ignoring each other.

'I tell you, this is a police operation,' the Major repeated.

'Want me to call the militiamen to keep you company while we do our work?'

'It's not that, sir, but I'm closing the place this evening, see? On account of the wind that's going to blow. Does the same the first Tuesday of every month. And if someone goes and falls in the water I'll be held responsible.'

Roberta joined Martineau, who continued watching the scene and ignored her. He had not thought much of the way she and Gruber escorted him off the incineration plant premises.

'Nobody's going to hold you responsible for anything,' the Major promised. 'Now, are you going to let us through or am I going to take you into custody for obstructing the police in the performance of their duty?'

The guard shrugged his shoulders and retreated into his little hut without further comment.

'Ah, Morgenstern, there you are!' The sorceress saw, with surprise, that Gruber was wearing her present. 'Thank you,' he added, following her glance. 'A perfect fit. I only hope you didn't use witchcraft to take my measurements on the sly.'

'After twenty years of working with you I don't need witchcraft to know you inside out, Major,' she replied, fluttering her eyelashes.

'Oh. Er. Well. Right, reservists and militia to surround the perimeter. Micheau!' He signed to the chauffeur to come over and spoke to him, separating his syllables distinctly. 'You stay here at the entrance to the marina. The three of us will hide inside. Martineau, tell Roberta your idea.'

Reluctantly, the young man turned to speak to her. 'My parents own a boat moored in the middle of the marina. I have the keys.'

'Right. You two get on that boat, and take this mobile.' He

hesitated between Roberta and Clément, and finally handed the phone to the latter. 'Monsieur Martineau knows my number. I'll be on the pontoons myself. Very well, everyone, action stations!'

The reservists dispersed around the marina where five hundred boats of all sizes, from very small to very large, were moored side by side. Roberta saw Gruber move away over a pontoon which was swaying on a slight swell. She lost sight of him when he passed behind the slender prow of a fair-sized yacht.

'Right, follow me,' said Martineau. 'And don't get lost on the way.'

A clock struck eleven in the distance. The forest of masts was illuminated by the city lights reflected on the low clouds. The promised wind had not yet risen. Clément and Roberta were on watch aboard the *Clémentine*, a thirty-seven-metre yacht which, according to the owners' son, was equally at home on the lagoon and the high seas, though Roberta rather wondered if the pride of the Martineau fleet had ever been outside the dam.

'Did you notice? The porter knew about the wind,' Martineau pointed out for the third time. 'Oh, the hell with it! I wish I could get my hands on that pamphlet.'

'Don't worry. Marcelin is paid not to lose anything.' Roberta sniffed the air, noisily. 'When's it supposed to be going to rain properly?'

'Tonight. Tomorrow. The indicators are showing red.'

They fell silent. Roberta was trying to spot Gruber in the orange afterglow of sunset, but she couldn't see him.

'Who is he, do you think?' asked the young man.

'You mean the Baron? Oh, a dangerous psychopath escaped from a penal colony on Vega who's chosen to reproduce on our little patch of terra firma. Then he'll go back to his own gas-giant world with his progeny tucked under his arm.' Martineau was looking at her with his jaw dropping. 'I haven't the faintest idea, dear boy. All I know is that he kills innocent people, which is one good reason to prevent him from doing more harm. Not frightened, are you?'

'No. Not in the least. Never felt so relaxed in my life.'

In fact he was not entirely at ease. Having seen the Baron in action, he might well feel more anxiety than anyone else.

'It reminds me of when we were hiding in that picture of St George,' remarked Roberta. 'Remember? When they tried to make carpaccio out of me?'

'How could I ever forget? What a chase! I wouldn't mind another little adventure with you like that one.'

'Speaking of adventures, hasn't something been going on around *here* recently?' she teased him, tracing a spiral in the region of his heart with her forefinger. 'I hear you're a regular attender at lectures on Satanic Law.'

Martineau blushed, cleared his throat, and muttered something unintelligible. Roberta watched him with the expression of an entomologist waiting for the butterfly that has just been pinned to its piece of balsa wood to die. She returned to the present subject.

'The Baron is going to give us a run for our money. He'll be harder to arrest than the whole Killers' Quadrille put together. We've seen nothing yet. It's going to be some time before we can break out the champagne.'

'I like your cheerful outlook,' said Martineau gloomily.

The halyards were snapping a hundred metres to their right. They stopped talking and examined the tangle of masts. A wave had raised some of the boats, but the movement was dying down already.

'False alarm,' sighed Martineau.

As if to prove him wrong, the mobile rang. He answered

with the assurance of a man who does this kind of thing all day.

'Hello? Yes, Major. No, no. Everything's fine. You want to talk to her? We're staying put, anyway. See you soon. 'Bye for now.' He ended the call and put the Ministry's toy back in his pocket. 'The boss has gone on board that two-master over there, the one with the yellow hull. He's waiting. Like us.'

He fell silent, and sighed five times in less than a minute. Now there's a man, thought Roberta, mildly irritated, who'd benefit no end from a two-week course of *Ignatia* tablets, three grains morning, noon and night. Seeing his dreamy look, she could easily imagine who he was thinking of. She sighed in her own turn, took out the ocarina and rubbed it on her coat. If they had to kill time they might as well do it to music.

'I have an idea,' she said.

Clément made a face. He distrusted Roberta's ideas. She scribbled a few words on a blank page of her diary.

'Can you read my writing?' she asked, holding them out to him.

'Er. In English, is it?'

'I'll hum you the tune.' And Roberta hummed the very simple tune. 'OK? Just follow the ocarina. Right, here we go.'

She softly blew a long note, modulating it slightly. The detective began singing rather uncertainly. '*Julia, Julia, ocean child, calls me. So I sing a song of love, Ju-u-ulia.* Are you expecting to attract the Baron of the Mists that way?'

Roberta put her ocarina away again. It wasn't worth persisting. 'No, only a telepathic hedgehog who went missing six months ago.'

'What? You mean Hans-Friedrich has disappeared?'

'At the end of September. I'd just finished knitting him a pullover. I went out to do some shopping, leaving the sitting room window open, and when I came back he wasn't there.'

Martineau shook his head, pretending to look horrified. 'How sad!' Since he hated hedgehogs in general and this one in particular, he didn't try too hard to hide the fact that from his point of view this news was the one bright spot in a trying day. 'Did you put Lost notices in the local shop windows? "Have you seen this hedgehog? Reward offered." ' The dark look that Roberta gave him made him change his tune. 'Er – I mean – was he an ocarina fan?'

'A Beatles fan. Hans-Friedrich really loved the Beatles.'

'Oh, come on, Roberta. Don't speak of him in the past tense.'

'Ssh!'

The masts to the north-east were clacking as they blew against each other. The halyards were ringing like the cowbells on dairy cattle coming down from the Alpine pastures. The wind had risen.

'Can you spot anything?' asked Martineau. He could see nothing himself.

It was as if a giant were walking over the pontoons a hundred metres from their yacht. The boats were rearing up several metres into the air. Waves were rippling through the whole marina. The *Clémentine* began to pitch just as the wind passed directly above them. Then the air and the boats calmed down.

'Has it . . . has it gone?'

'No, that was just a foretaste. Give me the mobile. I have to talk to the Major.'

'Look!' cried Martineau, pointing to the north-east part of the marina, where the boats had now begun to pitch and sway in their own turn.

A pontoon was lifted right out of the lagoon, and fell back with a terrible crash on the prows of a dozen ships. Seen from where Roberta and Clément were, the Baron of the Mists was only a dark silhouette – a kind of solid shadow, just as Martineau had said. He moved slowly, devastating everything in his path. And he was going towards the two-master with the yellow hull, making straight for Gruber.

Roberta jumped off the *Clémentine* and ran at a tangent, hoping to intercept him. Martineau realized that she had gone only when he saw her moving over to the pontoon. His shouts were carried away by the wind that was now blowing all around the marina.

Roberta felt as if she were crossing some bumpy fairground ride. Rigging whipped in the air overhead. The prows of boats rose and fell on both sides of her like vast scythes. The wind pushed her and pulled her, tried to blow her into the lagoon. But Roberta was a tenacious woman. She reached the two-master just as the mini-hurricane was dying down. There was no trace of either the Baron of the Mists or Obéron Gruber.

'Major!' she shouted. 'Where are you?'

She heard a phone ring. Someone was calling the mobile. She got on board the two-master. The hatches gaped open. One of the masts had split and was creaking alarmingly, and the tangled rigging looked like a plateful of giant spaghetti. The mobile still went on ringing.

Roberta stepped over a broken fragment of the ship's rail and found the Ministry phone at last. Gruber's right hand was still clutching it. That hand had been neatly severed. A little further away, she spotted the pullover under a pile of debris. She pulled it off the Major without stopping to ask herself any questions. He was lying on his back, his left eye had been plucked out and a bloodstain was spreading around the area of his heart.

A voice was calling her name and the Major's. Roberta knelt down. The pince-nez with mirror lenses had slipped out of the top pocket of his jacket. One of the lenses was broken. The mirror glass had shattered, scattering tiny triangles of mercury over the little man's neck.

'Oh, Obéron,' she murmured.

She put the pince-nez in her pocket and closed the dead man's eyelids. A breath of air made her turn her head to look up at the sky. Reservists and militia were approaching. A waterdrop bounced off her forehead. Then another. A pattering sound began, swelling through the marina until it was like a million drums rolling. The rain had decided to fall on Basle at last.

Up in the Sky

Roberta and Grégoire crossed the floating market to the jetty on the eastern side and boarded one of the boats. Grégoire put a copper dollar coin into the slot at its prow. The ferryman, as the automatic ferry was called, accepted the coin, started up and carried the boat towards the place created by Basle for the last rites of its dead.

The island was half a nautical mile from shore, and looked like a set of fantastic rocks arranged in a horseshoe with a cypress grove in the middle. Abstract Cubist shapes suggested some kind of classical temple carved in the rock. In fact, the architects had taken their inspiration from a painting in the old Museum of Art in Basle. The Isle of the Dead was a large-scale fake, standing on the roof of one of the tallest buildings of the submerged Old Town, and just flush with the surface of the lagoon.

The boat moved past the opening of the horseshoe and pulled in beside the white stone jetty. Rosemonde jumped ashore and helped Roberta out. Other boats were coming over from the market too, moving at the same slow, funereal pace. The closest to the Isle had a dozen of the Major's reservists on board.

They climbed the few steps up to the crematorium hidden amidst the ash-coloured foliage of the cypress trees. You might have thought it a Gothic chapel with its little columns, open-work stone bays, and the fresco of golden stars on an ultramarine background in its domed ceiling, but there were no statues of saints and no crosses. Cremation rites these days were ecumenical and secular, and the Municipality ran them.

Plenck, who had stitched the Major's hand back in place, Boewens and all the CID office staff filled the small room. Martineau was in the front row, looking upright and dignified. The Mayor himself had come. At the appointed hour, Fould got behind the lectern and turned his gaze on the oblong coffin, wondering if Gruber might play the ultimate practical joke and emerge from it. Realizing that no such thing was about to happen, he turned to his audience and began, in vibrant tones, 'Dear friends, it is with a profound sense of loss . . .'

Roberta was only half listening to the Minister's eulogy. She preferred to immerse herself in her own memories of the good times she had shared with the Major.

'Need I remind anyone what an exemplary investigator he was? Only six months ago he caught an underworld character in the act of . . .'

A smile touched Micheau's lips where he sat in the third row. The longer Fould spoke, the more impassioned the Minister became.

'The Major died a hero on active service, struck down by the infamous being who is trying to destabilize this mainland city of ours and the authorities running it!'

Roberta roused herself from her lethargy. She felt that she was beginning to lose her temper. Fould was standing for Mayor in the forthcoming elections. He had officially announced his candidature three days ago, and now he was using Obéron Gruber's cremation to make his first campaign speech! She wasn't letting him get away with this, even if she had to distract his audience's attention by playing the ocarina.

She was sure the Major would appreciate a few bars of *Sergeant Pepper*.

As for Martineau, he was drinking in the words of the Security Minister, but a rival attraction made him crane his neck for a sight of a certain specialist in Satanic Law seated two rows behind him. The young man thought that the grave profile of Suzy Boewens was lovelier than the face of Venus as painted by the great Apelles.

'The Major fought valiantly against this new demonic threat, facing it as a heroic servant of the city. Today, others are ready to take up the torch.'

Suzy Boewens caught Martineau's eye. He looked away quickly, blushing red. Fould glared at the inquiry agent, who blushed more than ever.

'This death will be avenged. I promise you that on my honour, here and now.'

A murmur ran through the audience. Martineau's chest swelled. Roberta's fingers tightened around her ocarina. But Fould had finished. The Mayor rose, took his place at the lectern, and in a tremulous but warm voice, the very opposite of the rhetorical flights in which Fould had so resonantly indulged just now, began to read a quotation from the book he was holding, one of the Major's favourites.

'Slowly, almost pensively, he looks around him. There is much that is strange here, much that is motley. Gardens, he thinks, and he smiles. But now he realizes all at once that eyes are looking at him, he recognizes the men and knows them for miscreant dogs, and he urges his horse into their midst.'

Roberta slipped her hand into Grégoire's.

'And when all closes again behind him the gardens are still there, and the sixteen curved sabres come down on him one by one like festive jets of water, a laughing cascade.'

The words celebrating the *Life and Death of Cornet*

Christoph Rilke whirled in the air above them as vertiginously as the maelstrom of the final moment towards which all present here were moving.

The Mayor closed his book and left the platform. After a moment's silence, the ecumenical celebrant of the funeral rites took his place. As if in a dream, Roberta saw and heard the few phrases to which religion was reduced, the mechanical gestures of cremation. A mouth opened in the back wall like the way into an inferno. The coffin slid through. The metal trap shut.

The mourners rose and began going out to the boats. The Mayor leaned on a cane as he walked along the avenue followed by his Minister of Security. He stopped in front of the sorceress.

'Forgive me, you are Roberta Morgenstern, aren't you?' he asked. Roberta nodded. 'I'd known Obéron since we were at the Academy together. He was very fond of you.'

The Mayor inclined his head and left the sorceress with this last memory. Fould in his own turn stopped, looked hard at Morgenstern with his topaz eyes, and said in an imperious whisper, 'I want you to find out who's publishing that inflammatory tabloid rag the *Barometer*. That's a priority. Oh, and by the way, my condolences.'

The tabloid in question had first appeared in Basle the day after Gruber's death, littering the streets as if it had fallen from the sky. Where it came from was a mystery, but it was extremely well informed about the Baron, telling readers that the demonic creature was back in town and adding details to which only the CID had access. The discretion Fould wanted was only a pious hope: the people of Basle preferred the *Barometer* to the traditional *Home Chat* or *Mainland News*.

Roberta was looking for an appropriate reply as Rosemonde offered the Minister his hand. Going into reflex campaigning mode, Fould made haste to take it. Rosemonde did not let go.

'A fine eulogy,' the Professor praised Fould. 'I feel confident that you will win the election.'

Roberta looked at her companion, wondering what game he was playing, for at the same time Fould had turned pale, not that she minded about that.

'I . . . er, thank you . . . well, I must be going. Now!'

And Fould made for the exit. Micheau, now drafted into the Minister's service, dutifully followed. Rosemonde, frowning thoughtfully, watched them go.

'I need some fresh air,' he said.

He went down the side aisle of the chapel and out. The sorceress let a few seconds pass before setting off down the avenue beside Martineau. They allowed the movement of the small crowd to carry them towards the exit. Suzy Boewens was a few paces ahead of them. Martineau would have liked to catch up with her and share her boat back, but he stayed with the sorceress.

'There, there, there!' Eleazar Strudel, who had surprised Roberta by attending, gave his old friend a big hug. As they emerged from the crematorium they rejoined Rosemonde. Out on the steps umbrellas opened with loud clicks like a gunfire salute.

'Oh, I nearly forgot!' exclaimed Roberta, clapping her hand to her forehead. She went back into the crematorium just as the ecumenical celebrant was coming to find her, holding a copper urn. She took it and went back to the three men, who were standing to attention like members of the Praetorian Guard. Martineau gave the urn a distrustful glance.

'We can go,' she said, ignoring him. 'I don't know about the rest of you, but I'm famished!'

'Lunch at the Two Salamanders – on the house,' announced Strudel, taking the witch's left arm. Rosemonde walked on her right and Martineau brought up the rear. They strode briskly to the jetty as if participating in the kind of military charge that Cornet Christoph Rilke would have liked.

Rain was running down the steep roof of the Two Salamanders like a cascade of tears. Piles of rubbish covered the pavements. The staff of the incineration plant had been on strike for a week now, despite the Mayor's appeals to them to go back to work. Seeing that the rubbish still hadn't been collected, Strudel muttered with annoyance. He turned the door handle in the shape of a goat's head, and they entered the inn.

Martineau was hoping Suzy would be there, but he didn't see her among the regulars. Strudel went behind the counter and gave instructions to Frida, who was supposed to be his niece and who sometimes came to help out. Then he invited his friends into the back room, his personal pantheon. It was devoted to magic tricks and the great conjurors of history.

From Robert-Houdin to Nicolas Tesla, by way of Mandrake and the extraordinary Méliès, a whole throng of illusionists immortalized by the camera had their photographs fixed to the walls like votive offerings. Tickets for the Magic Theatre, the Palace of Miracles and the Electric Circus had been slipped into some of the frames. Wallace's Mondorama featured, with a copy of his last programme, although it was over ten years since the great conjuror of the lagoon had put in at Basle with his huge showboat.

Strudel collected their dripping umbrellas and raincoats. Clément, Grégoire and Roberta sat down at the little table, and Roberta put Gruber's urn down on a plate stand. Eleazar took their orders, went off to the kitchen, and came back with a glass of juniper wine for Morgenstern, a mineral water for Martineau, a spruce liqueur for himself and nothing for Rosemonde, who said he wasn't thirsty. They clinked glasses.

'I'm going to ask a stupid question,' said Clément suddenly.

'Ask away,' Roberta told him.

'Did the Major have any family?' It felt odd, he thought, to be talking about a dead person with his ashes right there in front of you.

'Apparently not,' said the witch. 'His will was deposited with the Ministry, and he'd named me sole heir. I was more surprised than anyone.'

'I have another stupid question to ask.'

'We're all ears.'

'What did he leave? I mean, I don't want to pry . . .'

'No, no, that's all right. The Major owned a little house not very far from the Palace of Justice, and a good library, and some savings which I shall give to the Ministry of Security's charity fund.'

'A house?' exclaimed the young man. 'With a garden and all?'

'With a garden.'

Although his parents were members of the billionaires' Fortuny Club, Martineau rented a ridiculously small attic room. He had always made a point of not owing his family anything financially, which was either admirable or stupid, depending how you looked at it. But many people would see the ownership of a house with a garden in Basle, where space was at such a premium, as like owning a little bit of Eden.

'How are you getting along with your inquiries?' asked the innkeeper, always keen to hear the latest gossip.

'And how are you getting along with tracing that pamphlet?' Roberta asked Martineau. 'Any news of it yet?'

The young man told Strudel his ideas about the study of the winds at ground level in the city, and how he had noted where they might blow during the days up to the time of the Major's death. The day after the tragedy Fould had summoned everyone and interviewed each of the Security staff separately. When Martineau mentioned the pamphlet to the Minister, Fould had told him to go to Archives immediately and retrieve the precious document.

Unfortunately Fate was against him. First his car wouldn't start. Then there was a traffic jam caused by a derailed tram. When he finally did reach the Palace of Justice the building was surrounded by firemen. A fire had broken out, and the Security Archives were at the heart of the blaze.

'So you found no trace of it?' said Strudel.

The young man shrugged fatalistically. 'I saw Marcelin. The Archives Department was closed when the fire broke out.'

'Considering its opening hours I'm not surprised,' said Roberta sarcastically.

'Marcelin remembered the pamphlet, though. He had just been classifying it and making out its card.'

'What bad luck!' exclaimed Strudel.

'Yes, you were really unfortunate,' agreed Roberta philosophically. 'Did you go back to the observatory?'

'Of course, but there's no one up there. It's been officially closed because of the rain.'

'Fortunately the deaths ended with the Major,' sighed Strudel.

'Yes, that's one thing. Nothing for a week now,' agreed Martineau. 'No mysterious accidents. Zero.'

'Fould is saying privately that Gruber gave the creature a mortal wound and that's why it's fallen silent,' said Morgenstern. 'Personally I feel sure the Baron is still killing, we just haven't discovered the bodies yet.' She turned to Rosemonde, who had said not a word since the end of the funeral ceremony. 'What do you think?'

'I think you're not very optimistic, my dear,' he replied apologetically.

'I expect this foul weather has something to do with it.'

'Silence from the Baron doesn't mean he's dead,' agreed Strudel.

'What really worries me is the silence of the tracers,' said Martineau. 'I mean, they're supposed to be infallible.'

Here Frida interrupted them, arriving with two large bowls. One was full of croutons fried in butter, the other was a tureen of soup from which a strong aroma of Madeira rose. She put one down on each side of the urn.

'Aha! Estramadura soup. You'll like this,' said Strudel.

Merely inhaling the fragrance of the soup made their cheeks glow. Martineau was shining brighter than a lighthouse, and Roberta's nose would have been visible from some way off on a dark night. They drank the soup in reverent silence – which in view of the presence of the urn in the middle of the table was not entirely inappropriate.

'That's better,' said the young man, mopping up the last few drops in his soup plate with a slice of farmhouse bread. Strudel rose, went out and came back with an unlabelled bottle of wine. 'My latest Flamel,' he said, filling their glasses.

Roberta thought the wine better than the previous vintage, but a little immature for her taste. Its bouquet needed a touch of myrtle, she decided.

'Heady. Perhaps a little *too* sixteenth-century,' said Rosemonde, tasting it. The innkeeper valued the opinion of a historian. 'But you're getting there. Mature it a little longer, and you'll be transporting your guests right back to the heart of the Middle Ages.'

'Real black magic!' announced Strudel, looking at the film of wine clinging to the sides of his glass. 'I must have it ready for the opening of Paris Street. I might try ageing it with ether.'

Frida cleared away and came back with the main course. A strong aroma of paprika dispelled what remained of the Madeira fragrance.

'Thank you, Frida. Onions, butter, sweet peppers, tomatoes, sausages, paprika, eggs! A gypsy in the Historic Quarter gave me the recipe. He calls it *letcho*.'

For some time nothing was heard in the back room but the sound of knives and forks on plates. Then the conversation turned to the Baron again. Who could he be?

'It's not so much a question of knowing *who* he is,' said Roberta, wiping her lips with a corner of her napkin, 'as *what* he is. What do we know that might help us to identify him? He can take many forms, he seems to be made of mist and shadow, he's fire-proof . . .'

'Could he be an astral twin?' suggested Martineau, thinking of their adventure three years ago.

'Too easy,' replied the sorceress.

'The smog that gave birth to the female Ripper – suppose it's taken on a shape of its own?' surmised Strudel more boldly.

'It could equally well be a nightmare come to life,' said Roberta, 'but the fact is that the Baron exists. As Obéron is well placed to know.'

'Could it be one of *us*?' Eleazar asked Roberta. 'One of the Family?'

'It could be everything and anything. The automatic photo we have is very imprecise. It just shows a vague figure in the dark – and we're certainly in the dark ourselves.'

'Yes, but we do know instances of entities who can change appearance or disappear in a twinkling, don't we?' said Rosemonde. The Professor of the History of Sorcery liked riddles, and it was a riddle he was asking them now. Everyone tried to think hard.

'A fakir?' said Strudel. 'Fakirs are capable of truly

phenomenal contortions. I once saw one at the Mondorama who—'

'Not as exotic as that,' Rosemonde interrupted. 'Closer to home.'

They thought again. Strudel once more tentatively ventured, 'There was that conjuror who could appear and disappear as he liked. He was an expert pickpocket too. You mean him?' Rosemonde looked at him without a word. 'Oh well, too bad.'

'You really don't make the connection?' asked Rosemonde, realizing that everyone was at a loss, even Roberta.

Strudel and Martineau shook their heads, crestfallen. The sorceress looked at the *letcho* on her plate, wondering exactly what that devilish man of hers was getting at.

'Hradcany Castle, Little Prague, the Jewish ghetto – are you sure it doesn't remind you of anything?'

'What connection could there be between the Little Prague sanctuary and a creature that no one can get hold—' But Roberta never finished her sentence. She sat there looking stupefied. The innkeeper, who had just seen the answer too, struck the table hard with the flat of his hand, almost knocking the urn over. Martineau, slightly surprised, was only just in time to catch it and put it back straight.

'But it can't be,' said the sorceress. 'The house in Old School Street disappeared when Prague was flooded. It couldn't have been brought to Basle without our knowledge. And if it *had* been brought back to life, surely the College would have heard one way or another.'

'I must be wrong, then,' said Rosemonde, with an ironic expression on his face.

Martineau looked from one to the other. He wished these brilliant minds would be a little more precise about what they meant by *it*. At the same time, 'the house in Old School

Street' did vaguely suggest something to him. He had heard of it before, although not at the College. So where and when? He was just remembering that it was somewhere high up . . .

'The Baron has clammed up on us,' added Roberta. 'But Fould is right. The author of the *Barometer* could tell us a thing or two.'

'Exactly. The latest issue appeared this morning,' said Strudel. He took the tabloid out of his pocket, unfolded it, and read out the titles of its contents.

' "The Baron, history of his first manifestations, Part Seven." "How the killer brought death to Basle marina." "A shadow in the lagoon – one more mystery to be cleared up?" Which do you fancy?'

'The story about the shadow in the lagoon,' said Roberta.

Strudel began reading out the article the sorceress had chosen.

' "As if the rain and the misdeeds of the infamous Baron were not enough to trouble our minds, it seems that the depths of the lagoon are now the scene of disturbing events. Yesterday, despite the inclemency of the elements and thanks to my good instruments of observation, I saw an oblong shape at least ONE HUNDRED METRES in length moving inside the waters of the dam. It went to ground in that shadowy zone where Old Basle is still visible, its centre marked by the cathedral spire. At this stage of our inquiries we are unable to say anything about the nature of this phenomenon. Is it animal? Is it mechanical? Whatever it may be, it was certainly there, moving rapidly and menacingly. I shall now turn my close attention to the water as well as the mainland. Fellow citizens, be of good cheer! The Robin Hood of the air is watching over you." '

'Robin Hood of the air?' said Martineau. 'That's a new one to me.'

'Sounds like Fould on top form,' said Rosemonde dryly.

But Roberta knew exactly who that bombastic style reminded her of. For the time being, however, she kept her idea under wraps. She was privately amused by the absurdity of their situation. Whoever or whatever the Baron might be, the tracers had failed to track him down – instead, some scribbler was deluging the city with high-flown prose full of fantasy and cryptozoology.

'So here we have Basle's finest reunited in this delightful spot!' said a new arrival, breaking into the thoughts of the other guests. Amatas Lusitanus had just walked into the back room of the Two Salamanders. Eleazar made haste to take his raincoat and give him his own chair. Martineau had instinctively risen to his feet.

'Ah, so the prince of the eclipse is back! I've been wondering about you for over a week. What a way to stand your Professor up! So what did you want to demonstrate? Your talent for airy evasion?'

Martineau replied without stopping to think of any consequences of his revelation. 'Well, I did it, sir. I took off like a rocket. I went up to two thousand metres above ground level. May be I should have warned you—'

Lusitanus cut these explanations short. 'Yes, all right, Martineau. Is this your new Flamel?' he asked Strudel, indicating the bottle.

The innkeeper poured the sorcerer a glass. Lusitanus tasted it in respectful silence, but contrary to everyone's expectations made no comment. Instead, he said, 'I've come from the Community Building. I checked on the Records Office system in the presence of Banshee, and our tracers are in perfect working order. Which makes their silence incomprehensible. Unacceptable, too.'

'Like the fact that we have put our own skills at the service of Security,' muttered Rosemonde, who became irate whenever the subject was mentioned in front of him.

Martineau himself had been considerably surprised to learn that the tracers were actually created by the College of Sorcery. It was up to the sorcerers and witches to maintain the system, and in exchange the municipal authorities let them do as they liked in their garden, the Little Prague sanctuary and within the University precincts. That agreement was the subject of the first clause in the famous White Charter which allowed the practice of sorcery on this part of the mainland.

'The tracers are one problem, the Baron's another,' Roberta pointed out. 'Is that the latest edition of the *Mainland News*?'

Lusitanus offered her the newspaper. The front page printed the full text of Fould's speech in memory of Major Gruber. The witch muttered crossly when she saw it. 'That man's a menace. I'd hate to see him elected Mayor.'

Martineau almost said something, but restrained himself at the last minute.

'We live in troubled times,' said Lusitanus sadly. 'And the outgoing Mayor is a tired man.' He picked up the *Barometer* from where it lay on the table. 'Have you read this nonsense? A monster in the lagoon! And a detailed account of the Major's death . . . it's not right!'

'There's nothing there we don't know already, don't worry,' replied the witch.

'No, indeed,' added Rosemonde, who was skimming the *Mainland News* in his own turn. 'But you'd better hurry up and get to know a little more. And let other people know too. The incineration plant workers on strike, the digging of the tunnel halted, all this rain . . . people are getting anxious. They're even beginning to say that the water level inside the dam has risen.'

'Well, it hasn't,' said Martineau. 'You can tell from the cathedral spire. The water inside the dam has *not* risen.'

'But we know how powerful rumour is,' sighed Strudel.

Amatas Lusitanus finished his wine, rose and put on his still-soaked raincoat. 'Well, I'll leave you to it. Good luck, everyone. And when you're free of your investigative and criminological duties, Martineau, you can explain exactly what you thought you were up to on the University roof. Goodbye, then.'

When Lusitanus had left, Roberta asked her young assistant, 'What was all that about? Flying now, are you? Taking off like a rocket?'

'No, no. Just the drink talking. I'm rambling,' he said evasively.

'Well, that's a pity. Because it's about time we interrogated the bright spark who's publishing the *Barometer*. Even if this rain isn't good weather for it.'

'You know who he is?' exclaimed Martineau.

'I know *where* he is, anyway.'

Rosemonde, Strudel and Martineau looked at her in silence. It was the witch's turn to ask a riddle, an easy one this time. 'Where does this news-sheet fall from?' she asked.

'The sky!' replied the young man at once, as light suddenly dawned.

'So the *Barometer* editorial offices are in the sky, above the clouds. And we're going to pay a call on the editor.'

'But how? I mean, if you're expecting me to fly . . .' He didn't feel able to explain about the conjunction of his moonstone ring, the moon itself and Bacchus, or not at present anyway. But Roberta had taken a key-ring out of her bag. She waved it under the investigator's nose.

'I'm in charge of the CID office for now, until Fould appoints someone more senior to the post.' An ink drawing of a seabird was attached to one of the keys. 'I believe you've been training to fly Count Palladio's old airship, is that right? Your frequent visits to the hangar haven't gone unnoticed.'

'You mean the *Albatross*?' Martineau was already on his feet. 'I could fly it with my eyes shut!'

Roberta wondered if it was really a good idea to let this weirdo loose on the controls of the flying ship. 'Be a good boy and keep them open, will you?' she replied. Then, placing one hand on the urn, she asked Strudel, 'Can you look after this? Accidents happen so easily at my place with Beelzebub around.'

The innkeeper had no objection to giving the Major house-room for a while. 'I'll put him behind the bar with my spices,' he suggested, like the good friend he was. 'Then he can listen in on the guests' conversations.'

'The living and the dead beneath the same roof,' said Rosemonde philosophically, touching his glass to the cold metal of the urn.

Roberta and Eleazar did the same, drinking a last toast to the handful of grey dust which was all that now remained of the Major. In the doorway of the back room, Clément was waiting impatiently.

The man on duty at the hangar was perfectly willing to let them on board the *Albatross*. A replica of Robur's vessel from the novel by Jules Verne, it had been in dry dock for the last three years, sheltered from wind and weather, so it looked brand new. They had gone home first, Martineau to change into his brown leather flying suit, Roberta to pick up her poncho. She was afraid of catching cold during the flight.

Martineau went to the engine room and checked that the electric batteries were charged. Satisfied, he came out again and climbed into the helmsman's glazed cabin at the prow of the ship. He turned the key Roberta had given him in the starter on the instrument panel. The thirty-seven propellers came to life, throbbing in perfect unison. Martineau revved them up slightly. The *Albatross* rose a few metres in the air.

'Wow!' said Roberta.

'Cast off moorings!' shouted Clément, purely for form's sake, since there were no moorings to be cast off. He activated the large rear propeller, which powered them out of the hangar and straight towards the lagoon.

Gaining altitude, they plunged into the clouds and lost sight of Basle. The rain made the deck of the *Albatross* a gigantic mirror. The wipers swept the glass of the deckhouse vigorously. Wind struck the hull like a battering ram. Visibility was nil. Roberta, her poncho gathered cosily around her face, was clutching the instrument panel with both hands.

'Don't worry, this ship can't take in water and it's perfectly balanced,' Martineau reassured her. He was indeed well in control of the *Albatross*.

'Why on earth did I ever think of suggesting a thing like this to you?'

'The Flamel?' the young man offered as an explanation of her momentary madness.

The light was growing noticeably brighter. A window of blue sky opened among the clouds before closing again.

'I was lying to you just now,' Martineau confessed. 'About flying, I mean. But I did tell Lusitanus the truth.'

'Go ahead, then. I'm listening – and for goodness' sake make it exciting enough for me to forget where we are.'

Martineau told her about his aeronautical experiments on the roof of the University and in the Daliborka: how the ring, the moon and Bacchus worked together, how difficult it was to explain. At the end of his story Roberta was looking at him with the same expression on her face as when she had seen him walking on air at the top of the tower of the church of Saint-Jacques in the Historic City of Paris.

'You've rediscovered the secret of transvection! That's how

witches used to fly . . . Banshee's been after it for years. She's going to be green with jealousy when she hears that you can do it.'

'Er – I'm not really flying yet. I just sort of get carried up into the sky. My degree of control over it varies.'

He was preparing to tell her about the odd conversation he had overheard between Banshee and Barnabite when the sun suddenly came out. The spectacle before their eyes left them speechless. The drops of water covering the *Albatross* were transformed into crystal beads. A landscape of white hills surrounded them on all sides. Cirrus clouds floated in the bright blue sky far above their heads. On board their sparkling ship, they were the sole masters of a velvety, brilliant world.

Martineau operated the controls to stop the *Albatross*'s ascent and keep it moving horizontally. Grazing the clouds, the ship sent great spirals of cotton wool unfurling from its flanks. Roberta emerged from the deckhouse and cautiously approached the ship's rail.

'The sun! The sun!' she sang, arms stretched wide, enjoying its wonderful caress. And to think that only a few hours earlier she had been at the crematorium, in the rain, listening to a Minister on the campaign trail!

'Roberta!' called Martineau. She went back into the deckhouse. 'There's another craft straight ahead!'

He had stopped the rear propeller. The vertical propellers would have kept them hovering and stationary but for the side wind nudging the airship over. About a kilometre away, a hot-air balloon was drifting slowly between two cloudy peaks. From their present vantage point they could see an elevator for regulating altitude, a single propeller, and a platform hanging below the oval balloon.

'You were right,' he said. 'The sky above Basle is inhabited.'

'Can you get closer discreetly?'

'I'll try.'

Roberta went to the prow of the *Albatross* to watch the manoeuvre, which Martineau carried out with great expertise. He steered their vessel into the slipstream of the balloon, and then slowly reduced the distance between them. The head-wind was in their favour: they could be seen but not heard.

The platform under the balloon was cluttered with machinery and pot plants, but there was no sign of any humans. Ropes beneath the platform went down and disappeared in the clouds. The balloon was moored, tied up to some monument on the higher part of the city. Martineau brought the *Albatross* in until its prow was just touching the platform. He adjusted the propellers to correct the effects of the side wind, and joined Roberta, looking relaxed.

'Well done, Martineau. Good work! Anyone would think you'd been doing this all your life.'

'I'm a birdman, remember. Anyway, once you can drive a car you can drive anything.'

'All right, Mister Aeronaut. How are you thinking of getting us on board?'

Taking the sorceress by the shoulders, he moved her slightly to the left. A lever came up from the deck beside the rail. He pulled it towards him. A covered articulated gangplank with a stout handrail emerged from the hull, unfolded in the direction of the balloon platform, and came gently down on it.

'After you,' said Martineau, bowing.

Roberta crossed the gangplank, trying not to think of the void that lay below its fragile wooden structure.

A tarpaulin-covered deckhouse had been constructed in the middle of the platform. There were also telescopes pointing up and out, more telescopes hitched to the superstructure and turned towards earth, a kind of periscope on a tripod straddling the deck, a portable printing press, several piles of copies of the *Barometer* and a darkroom. The deckhouse contained a kitchenette, a bed and a number of bookshelves.

The click of a typewriter reached their ears from the front of the platform. They followed it. A man was seated at a table with a scarf round his neck and a view of the sea of clouds ahead of him. Hunched over his typewriter, he was muttering and sniffing rhythmically.

'Our author at work,' Roberta whispered in Martineau's ear.

A gust of wind made her poncho snap in the air like a cape. The clicking stopped. The man turned.

His hair was tousled, his suit nondescript. From the look of him he could easily have been a doorman in the Palace of Justice, a clerk in Records, or a répétiteur at the Opera House. He narrowed his short-sighted eyes, looked past Roberta and fixed his gaze on the figure of Martineau, standing a little way behind her.

'Micheau?' he asked, squinting under his eyelids. 'Is that you?'

'Don't say anything,' whispered Roberta.

The man had risen. Very carefully, arms out in front of him, he came towards them. As he reached her, Roberta asked, 'Monsieur Pichenette, I presume?'

The author stopped and looked at the multi-coloured poncho, obviously wondering what kind of creature this might be.

'Are you from the Andes?' The sorceress went red in the face. ' 'Scuse me, but my third and last pair of glasses has gone overboard, leaving me blind as a mole, and very cross about it.'

'My name is Roberta Morgenstern, and no, I am not from the Andes.'

'Morgenstern the inquiry agent?' He turned to Martineau.

'You never told me she was working with you, Micheau.' He introduced himself. 'Ernest Pichenette junior, at present continuing the work of Ernest Pichenette senior, author of *Atrocious Crimes and Famous Murderers* . . .'

'. . . and reporter for the *Lagoon Journal* about forty years ago.'

'Well, yes. The Baron of the Mists is our family's special subject, you might say,' he said apologetically. 'Er – how did you get up here?'

'On the *Albatross*,' explained Roberta.

'On an albatross, did you say? Oh well, never mind!'

Digging his hands into his pockets, he stalked around Martineau like a vulture circling a carcass before taking it apart. Since he was masquerading as the Ministry's deaf-mute chauffeur, the young man kept quiet.

'Pleased to meet you in person, though a phone call would have done it. You don't mind about that monster story I made up, do you? I mean, we have to hold the reader's attention, and the Baron's gone quiet on us.' He stopped circling, turned on his heel, and started circling again in the opposite direction. 'It's the Baron at work, I'm sure it is. I observe the city by night through my infra-red telescope. Yes, the second scourge of the criminal fraternity to be born to the Pichenette dynasty is telling you loud and clear: there's something nasty brewing. We're only at the start of a long series of atrocities.' He took a handkerchief out of his sleeve and blew his nose with a discordant sound like bagpipes. 'As for what you wanted me to observe, I'm keeping a close watch on it, but I must admit that just now the Baron is monopolizing my attention. I need glasses, and I'll have to go down for them. Or no, wait, you can bring me up an optician. You must have an optician in your crew? I really can't see a thing without a good view of my instruments.' He suddenly turned to Roberta and shook her hand vigorously. 'Delighted to make your acquaintance!' And turning back to Martineau, he clicked his heels in military fashion. 'Well, I won't keep you. I have the second volume of *Atrocious Crimes* on the boil, and as the poets say, life is short but art is long!'

Before Morgenstern and Martineau had even moved Pichenette was seated at his typewriter again, tapping away with laudable energy.

'And next time bring me up more paper. I'm beginning to run short,' he called to them over his shoulder.

The two investigators glanced inquiringly at each other. Obviously the interview was over. They went back over the platform, crossed the gangway, pulled it up behind them, and took refuge in the deckhouse of the *Albatross*.

'Talk about eccentric!' said Morgenstern.

'Are we going to leave without doing anything?' protested Martineau, now that he could speak again at last.

'What do you want to do? Tip his printing press overboard and kill some innocent citizen of Basle down below? He's a harmless character.'

'And maybe stark staring mad too.'

'Yes, indeed. But we've found out more by keeping quiet than by putting him through the wringer. Micheau, Micheau, Micheau . . . I wonder what a deaf-mute chauffeur and a high-altitude hack are plotting together?'

The young man piloted their vessel away from the clandestinely moored balloon. 'How did you know he was a member of the Pichenette family?' he asked, not best pleased. As a great fan of the works of Pichenette senior, he felt he ought to have realized that himself.

'His literary style, dear boy, his literary style.'

They plunged into the clouds, and the light suddenly grew dim. Rain lashed the deck and the glazed cabin. This grey light reminded Martineau of the lunar atmosphere in the Daliborka.

He remembered every word of the conversation between Banshee and Barnabite. He could see the two sorcerers again, bending over the mysterious casket and talking about some house or other in Old School Street . . .

A sudden surge of heat brought a red flush to his face when he made the connection between this memory and the riddle Rosemonde had asked in the back room of the Two Salamanders.

'Er . . . there's something I ought to tell you,' he began in a very small voice.

'What, one revelation on the journey out and another on the way back? Such generosity!'

But this time the effect was not so good. Roberta's expression grew fixed as Martineau told her about the scene he had witnessed, stuck to the ceiling of the Hunger Tower a week earlier.

'Do you think it's important, Roberta?'

From the black look she gave him, he gathered that this business of the broken shards of clay did indeed have a certain significance. He decided to revert to his role of mute pilot, guiding the *Albatross* home to its hangar without a hitch. The airship was back in dry dock. The thirty-seven propellers slowed down and then stopped by fits and starts. Martineau gave the key of the *Albatross* back to Roberta, who put it in the bottom of her bag.

Night was falling. It had been a long day, and Roberta was tired, but she had to talk to Grégoire as soon as possible. She asked Martineau to drop her off at the block of flats where Rosemonde lived. They drove there to the sound of rain drumming on the bonnet of the car and the swish of the windscreen wipers. Before they parted, Roberta told the young man, 'Meet me in the tea-room of the pagoda in the Historic Quarter at midday tomorrow. And meanwhile don't say a word about any of this to anyone.'

Once he was alone again Martineau, hands on his steering wheel, began thinking hard. After some minutes spent racking his brains, he inquired of any spirits who might be listening, 'Just what is it she doesn't want me to say a word about?'

He still didn't know what she had meant by *it* or *any of this*, or what terrible secret the house in Old School Street could be hiding. And the spirits were no great help, for none of them went to the trouble of enlightening him.

Earlier, two men had been observing the mainland from the top of the old cathedral spire where it emerged from the lagoon. The Münsterkirche had once had two spires, but a barge had collided with the smaller one a few years earlier. The men wore colourful outfits which would have struck the sober inhabitants of Basle as very extravagant: baggy trousers with yellow and blue stripes, jackets trimmed with braid, broad-brimmed hats suitable for keeping off the tropical sun. One wore a sword slipped into his belt, the other had two revolvers crossed over his stomach.

'Not too hot here, eh?'

'Too right. I could do with a tot of rum.'

'Not while we're on watch. The cap'n don't hold with that kind of thing.'

'Cap'ness, more like! Fancy being commanded by a female . . . I've seen everything now.'

'No you ain't, that's just it,' said his companion angrily, lowering his binoculars. 'You ain't seen her in a fight. A right lioness then, she is. None of us handles a sword like she does.'

'Fair enough. We'll see when it comes to a fight.'

They returned to their watching.

'What in the name of thunder is that?' asked the sceptical character.

A boat bristling with masts but no sails was coming down out of the sky above the city. It reached the level of the water and disappeared behind the tower blocks of the Administrative Quarter.

'Looked like a boat.'

'A flying boat.'

'Has the world turned upside down?'

'Not yet, but it's a good start.'

In Law and in Fact

The pagoda had once stood in Kew Gardens, the former botanical gardens in London, and was built in 1762 for Princess Augusta, the mother of George III. Long before the Great Flood it had been dismantled, crated, labelled and taken to a repository in the high mountains of Wales for storage. Like most of the rest of the British Isles, Kew Gardens had disappeared beneath the water some years earlier.

The crates had been rediscovered by Count Palladio's stage designers, but it was the Queen of the Gypsies who had had the pagoda rebuilt in the Historic Quarter, making it only one floor lower than the original ten. Its entrance was guarded by two Venetian clockwork figures. There was a tea-room on the third floor. The wording over the pediment of the entrance said:

THE GODS LOVE ODD NUMBERS

Roberta Morgenstern thought the view from the tea-room fascinating. Although a fine rain was steadily falling, gypsies were working on the scaffolding of Paris Street. Cables had been thrown out from the pagoda to various points in the area, to allow a velarium to unfold like a vast umbrella. The sails of the windmills mounted on the roof-tops were turning all the time.

Martineau was fidgeting. Rosemonde was doing a drawing of the dance figures that he and Roberta had just been performing in Mexico Street, noting their power of incarnating the spirits of the dance with choreographic precision. The waiter brought their tea.

'This Fu-chong is even better than the Darjeeling we had at the Savoy,' exclaimed the sorceress happily. She poured the tea, her wrist supple, her elbow elegantly raised. 'Under Palladio the gypsies did the most menial tasks in the Historic Cities. Nowadays they run the whole Historic Quarter, they're received by the Mayor and –' here she sipped her tea, crooking her little finger – 'and they're the best importers I know of such products as this. Well, carry on, Martineau. Tell us about your adventure in the Daliborka.'

Rosemonde put away his notebook and listened attentively to the investigator, although Roberta had already told him all about it the evening before. He did not interrupt Clément's tale.

'Barnabite and Banshee,' he muttered when it was over. 'Yes, they'd have been perfectly capable of bringing it back to life.'

'Bringing what back to life?' asked Clément impatiently. He had spent part of the night trying to find an answer to the riddle. Rosemonde looked at him with an expression that was definitely less than friendly. There was a buzzing in the young man's eardrums, but he stood up to the inquisition.

'Little Prague is forbidden ground, Monsieur Martineau. It's a sanctuary. I could have you expelled from the College for going in without authorization.' Rosemonde looked rather less forbidding now, but there was nothing reassuring about his smile. 'All the same, but for your spirit of enterprise we'd have no idea what's cooking over there now.'

He had only to turn slightly towards the east to indicate what he meant by 'over there'. Little Prague was scarcely five hundred metres away. The view was blurred by the rain, and it looked like some dark, indistinct mass of buildings washed up on the shores of the lagoon. Martineau was feeling reckless, and he really wanted to know.

'What *is* cooking?' he persisted.

Rosemonde looked inquiringly at Roberta, who only fluttered her eyelashes. She was leaving it to him. He took several sugar lumps, built them into two doorposts with a lintel over them, and arranged a double row of little lopsided pillars like open doors.

'Tell me what you know about the sanctuaries.'

'Well, they date from when the waters rose. The Council of Witches, Sorcerers and Magicians organized an emergency plan to save ancient monuments and sites that . . . that . . .'

Martineau was in trouble. The History of Sorcery was not his strongest subject.

'Can you tell me five of them?'

'Little Prague. Wallace's Mondorama with its Robert-Houdin Theatre. Stonehenge rebuilt in Kashmir. Delphi moved to . . . to . . . ?' Martineau looked at Morgenstern for help, but she just smiled benignly. 'Delphi moved to Bogota?'

'La Paz,' Rosemonde corrected him. 'But the list of sanctuaries isn't so important. It's their role that interests us. Why have they been preserved in spite of all objections?' This time Rosemonde didn't wait to see the young man floundering. 'I'll tell you: it was to save certain forms of magic which risked being lost for ever outside the environments where they came into being, and where they had been practised since time immemorial.'

'A bit like the preservation of species?' Martineau suggested. 'Outside their own environment they won't survive.'

'Or like this Chinese tea which wouldn't be so good drunk anywhere but in this authentic Chinese-style pagoda,' agreed Roberta.

'Our surroundings leave their mark on us. Palladio was right about that. And you're the living proof of it, Martineau, attracted as you are to the moon every time it's occluded.'

'That's right,' added Roberta. 'You wouldn't be the same man if your affinity was with Fire or Earth. And I won't even mention the Ether.'

While Martineau took in her allusion, Rosemonde went on with his explanation. 'Little Prague was rebuilt in Basle so that the Kabbalah could continue to exist. On certain terms, of course, in line with the undertakings of the White Charter. No black magic, no invocations, no domestic hauntings and no resurrection of ancient demons.'

Rosemonde flicked one of the sugar lumps, and his sanctuary collapsed like a set of dominoes. He picked up the lintel, stirred it into his tea, sipped, and concluded his demonstration with two basic pieces of information. 'Barnabite runs the sanctuary. As a visitor to it, Carmilla Banshee is bad news.'

'What have they been doing?'

'Haven't you read *any* of the titles on the third-year reading list?'

'Well, I – er – I was thinking of getting down to them pretty soon.'

'Does the Talmud mean anything to you?' asked Rosemonde, giving him the first clue.

'That being created from a combination of letters?' added Roberta helpfully.

'Rabbi Judah Loew ben Bezabel?'

'The house in Old School Street and the room with no door?'

'The clay figure kept in the synagogue in Prague? And but

for that accursed house it would never have had a chance of seeing the light of day again.'

Rosemonde had just dealt him his last card. 'The golem!' cried Martineau.

'Now we're getting somewhere,' sighed Morgenstern. 'You're not completely lost to science.'

'The golem,' repeated Martineau, more quietly. 'You think the Baron of the Mists is really the golem?'

'You've heard of slipware pottery, haven't you? It stands to reason that a creature made of pottery can slip in anywhere,' pointed out Rosemonde. 'And this one has already shown a certain gift for indiscriminate, pitiless murder.'

The Professor stretched his legs, put his feet up on the cushions, and looked at the low clouds. A long form was drifting above the lagoon, echoing his own relaxed position. Perhaps it was all that remained of the spirit they had so brilliantly conjured up, now still lingering in the atmosphere? Roberta, rising, brought him out of his reverie.

'Come on, we're off,' she told Martineau. 'We have a date to meet someone you're fond of. Someone who apparently has some grave news for us.'

The young man unwillingly rose to his feet. 'About the golem?'

'About the Baron. We still don't know if the golem and the Baron are one and the same.' She picked up her bag. 'See you this evening!' she said softly to Rosemonde.

Then she made for the stairs. Clément thought he would rather have explored Little Prague, even if midday was not the best time to pass unnoticed. After all, he was the one who'd put them on this trail, wasn't he? Just as he'd put them on the trail of the wind and its meaning!

Morgenstern stopped at the top of the stairs, turned round and saw that he hadn't moved an inch.

'On the other hand, if you have better things to do I'll go

on my own,' she told him. 'It would be a pity, though. Suzy Boewens really did sound as if she wanted to see us.'

'She lives at 18 Roses Street,' Roberta told him.

Martineau was doing his best not to drive through the large puddles of water and splash pedestrians, which wasn't at all like him.

'Do you know where to find Roses Street?' the sorceress teased him. 'It's rather small.'

He could hardly admit that he had spent whole evenings in Roses Street, lurking behind a street light and hoping to see Suzy close her shutters.

'Look in the glove compartment,' he said.

Roberta took out the street atlas of the new city. 'How funny,' she said. 'I have the other volume – the map of the Old Town now under water. Well, at least these two volumes have escaped the fire in Archives.'

'I know it by heart. That's how I know where to find Roses Street.'

'I see. Excellent. If the CID closes down you can always get a job as a taxi driver.'

Here their conversation stopped, since they had arrived. Martineau parked the car in front of a small house of dark brick, typical of this part of the city. It had once been a working-class quarter and was now the preserve of high-up civil servants. The house that Gruber had left in his will was a couple of blocks away. Suzy Boewens opened the door before they had time to ring the bell. She looked tired, but the young man, standing behind Roberta, was dazzled.

Suzy wore pink mules and a lilac silk dressing-gown. At last he could admire her ankles, delicate and white as alabaster, and her Achilles tendons, which he thought equally ravishing.

'I'b terribly sorry,' she said as they came in. 'I'b inherited an affinity wib the Ether from my mober. It makes be clubsy. Cobing back from the crebatoriub yesterday I—'

She sneezed energetically enough to split the primordial elements of matter. Then she blew her nose noisily. The angels blowing their trumpets in paradise would not have sounded sweeter to Martineau.

'Cobing back frob the funeral I fell in the lagoon,' she finished, 'and now I'b caught a cold.'

They followed her into a room with a large bay window looking out on a garden. Shelves full of books and souvenirs of Old Basle lined the walls. A stove was enthroned on a hearth with a low hood over it.

'Nice place,' said Roberta.

Boewens sneezed again. The floor shook under their feet.

'I hope you're looking after yourself?' said the witch.

'I'b taking asbirin.'

'Aspirin! Huh! That's the Ether for you! Can I take a look round your jungle out there?'

'Yes, ob course.'

Roberta put the hood of her raincoat over her head and went out into the tall grass and herbs in the garden. Martineau's heart was thudding. Here he was, alone with Suzy in her house!

'Hot milk with honey is good for the throat,' he said, imitating the quavering voice of an old man, but looking like a cheeky ten-year-old.

Boewens wasn't listening. She was trying to take a book off one of the top shelves of her little library. Martineau was hurrying to help her when two volumes of a large, heavy dictionary fell on top of her. When Roberta came back into the room she found Martineau trying to clear up after the accident, while Suzy, sitting in an armchair, was rubbing the top of her head and groaning.

'Didn't you think our legal adviser was in a bad enough

way already?' snapped the witch. She had handfuls of herbs stuffed into her pockets.

'I – er – um – I,' stammered Martineau, looking at his feet.

'Where can I boil some water?' asked Roberta.

Suzy led her to the kitchen. Martineau followed, making inarticulate sounds in his throat. Roberta took a saucepan, filled it, and put it on the gas, which she lit by clicking her fingers. Suzy, feeling weak at the knees, decided to sit down, and went on talking to Martineau while Morgenstern prepared her infusion.

'How are you gebbing on wib the thirb year work?'

'Oh, it's all right, yes, fine, very interesting, I really like it.'

'I wab going to cobgrabulate you. You'b been abong by best pubils. Your last essay on the Debils of Loudun wab very goob ibdeed. *Sniff*. Urbain Grandier woulb hab escaped the stake if you'b been defenbing hib.'

Her pupil . . . that was the last way Martineau wanted her to think of him. Noticing his downcast expression out of the corner of her eye, Roberta decided to lend him a hand.

'Clément is not just a good pupil but an excellent investigator too. And guess what – he's rediscovered one of our lost powers.' She stirred the leaves of mallow and wild thyme she had picked in the garden into the pan. 'Transvection. Young Martineau here can fly. Only in certain conditions, apparently, but he can fly.'

'Thab's great!' said Suzy enthusiastically. 'You bust show be!'

He wanted to reply eloquently, 'I am entirely at your service. Let us fly together to the gates of the Venusberg. I love you!' But all he actually found the courage to say was, 'Any time.'

Roberta poured her infusion into a cup, added sugar, and waited for Suzy to come to the end of another salvo of cataclysmic sneezes.

'Got a drop of the hard stuff about the place?'

'Ubder the sink. My farber brought be a bottle of brandy.'

Roberta laced the infusion generously from the bottle, and Boewens drank it. She sniffed once, blew her nose, rose to her feet and found that she no longer felt shaky.

'Wow! That was great.' She suddenly seemed to realize that she was in dressing-gown and slippers. 'Oh dear. Just wait here. I'll be back in a minute.'

Several minutes passed, during which the young man, misty-eyed, stood as motionless as a statue carved from solid marble.

'Martineau!'

He jumped. Morgenstern was handing him a small glass of Suzy's father's brandy.

'What?'

'Drink this. It'll give you the courage for what you have in mind.'

He gave her a grateful smile and drank. Then he felt his teeth with the tip of his tongue to make quite sure the enamel was still on them. That brandy was strong stuff. Suzy reappeared. She had her hair up in a chignon now, and she had taken the time to apply lipstick. Roberta had to admit that she looked charming.

'Well, now we can get down to serious business,' said the lawyer. 'Come with me and I'll show you how the Baron of the Mists operates.'

Looking inquiringly at each other, the two investigators followed Suzy back into her sitting-room. She took a book off the shelves, this time without causing any accidents, and put it on her desk. The investigators went over to look. She opened the book at the first mark she had put in it, to reveal an engraving showing a flight of steps carved into the side of a cliff. Vultures were perched on the steps. At the bottom of the gulf below, sharp stakes awaited victims who were being thrown off the cliff-top by armed men. A classical temple with an ornate roof could be seen in the background.

'The punishment known as the barathrum,' explained Suzy. 'In ancient Greece, they dug a pit and filled it with iron spikes as a method of execution for traitors, spies, and people who committed sacrilege.'

Once she was sure that they had had a good look at the picture, Suzy moved on to her next bookmark. The second engraving was even nastier than the first. It showed a naked woman tied to a stake with her hands and feet bound. A swarm of insects covered her body.

'Cyphonism. A punishment used in several countries in ancient times for disobedient slaves. The person condemned to death was covered with honey and left to be eaten by climbing or flying insects.'

'Martha Werber,' whispered Martineau.

'And Vaclav Zrcadlo before that,' added Morgenstern.

Suzy went on escorting them through her little horror show. The third engraving showed a public square in the Middle Ages, full of people who had come to watch an execution. The executioner wore a leather hood and mask. The victim had just had one eye put out and his right hand cut off, and the executioner was preparing to hammer a stake through his heart, as if destroying a vampire.

'Eye, hand and heart. The trio of punishments imposed by Carolingian courts as a method of execution for persistent offenders.'

'Obéron,' breathed Roberta.

Suzy closed the book, but kept her hand placed on it. With a pair of scales in the other hand and a blindfold over her eyes, she could have posed for the allegorical figure of Justice.

'As for Pasqualini and Fliquart – well, executions by fire have always been so common that it's difficult to link them to any precise period. But to sum up what I'm trying to say, the Baron of the Mists is using the methods of executioners of the past.' She put the book back in its place on her shelves. 'After the Historic Cities, a killer in historical costume . . . anyone might think the past had it in for you.'

The rain was falling twice as hard now. All three turned to look out at the garden.

'When on earth is this going to stop?' sighed Suzy. No one, not even Clément the budding meteorologist, felt bold enough to answer that question.

'I must tell Fould what you've found out,' said the sorceress. 'Even though we've heard nothing of the Baron for more than a week. And we have to pay another call on Pichenette,' she told Martineau.

'Pichenette?' asked Suzy. The name meant something to her.

'The man who writes the *Barometer*,' explained the investigator. 'He's living in a hot-air balloon above the clouds, and I very much suspect that his balloon is moored to the observatory.'

Suzy, her arms crossed, was looking from one to the other of them. 'Well, I'm not too busy at the moment. In fact my only case is one involving Siamese twins, and it was giving me a nasty headache even before I caught that cold. So if I can help you in any way?' Here Martineau nodded vigorously. 'But listen – I can't advise you too strongly to be discreet and keep this business of historical executions quiet. People who have an affinity with the Ether pluck all sorts of things out of the air, and I can tell you there's fear abroad in this city. If the people of Basle learn that the Baron is using historical methods there's a great risk that they'll turn on the gypsies.'

'Everyone in the Security Building will keep silent as the grave,' the young detective assured her. 'And Archibald Fould is the man to deal with the situation. He'll make all the decisions.'

That's exactly what worries us, thought both witches, but they kept this observation to themselves. Roberta, Martineau and Suzy parted, promising that they would all keep in touch. But once back in his car, Martineau showed no sign of driving away.

'Suzy's a good girl,' said Roberta. 'She's right about the gypsies too.' Realizing that the car was still stationary, she added, 'Want me to get out and push?'

Unexpectedly, he got out himself, ran back through the rain to the steps leading up to Suzy's door and rang the bell. Suzy opened the door. Their conversation was brief. He gave her something, came back, turned the starter handle of the engine, and got back into the driving seat with a radiant smile on his face.

'So what are we going to do about these revelations Miss Boewens has made?' he said. 'I mean, a killer acting like an executioner – rather serious, don't you think?'

Morgenstern wondered what had come over him, and then told herself that Martineau was a lot younger than she was, and obviously in love.

'Fould's summoned everyone to a meeting at eight tomorrow morning,' she reminded him, in part to calm him down. 'We'll bring him up to date and then assess the situation.'

'Bring him up to date about Pichenette and Micheau too?'

'I'd rather we kept Pichenette and Micheau to ourselves.'

'But the Minister of Security did ask the CID to find out who was behind the *Barometer*!' objected Clément the model civil servant.

'However that may be, we have a free hand until tomorrow morning. So let's take advantage of it. I have a kind of feeling that events are about to speed up pretty soon.'

'Great! Where shall I drop you off?'

'At the Museum. I have to print out the last leaf of your family tree. Well, that really means the first leaf.'

'Brilliant!'

But the imminent revelation of the identity of the witch who had founded his line passed right over the young sorcerer's head. He drove towards the Museum whistling. Roberta guessed that where everything had looked grey so recently, he was now seeing blue and green, brightly coloured rainbows and little birds singing.

'By the way, I do hope you're coming tomorrow?' he suddenly asked.

'Coming where?'

'To the happening! My mother's organizing a tea-time happening!' He cheerfully honked his horn to announce this good news to the entire city. 'Didn't you get her invitation card?'

'I never went home yesterday. A tea-time happening? Perfect. I don't have any engagements at tea time. I'll be happy to accept. And I can bring your family tree of sorcery and show it to you.'

Martineau managed to keep quiet for at least a hundred metres along the road. Then he confided, in a whisper, 'Suzy's coming too. She said yes.'

Ah, that's it, thought Roberta. Judging by the young man's exalted expression, she decided there was no more to be said.

Martineau dropped Roberta outside the Museum railings. Before leaving the young man to his dreams, she advised him, 'Keep your eye on the road, won't you, Romeo?'

She watched the car move off at the demure pace of a trotting pony, which in itself was a good sign.

★ ★ ★

After finding the forty-fourth leaf of the Martineau family tree the witch picked a few sprigs of tarragon from her own garden. Grégoire wanted them to flavour the scallops he was cooking for dinner that evening. Then she went home, braving the rain and the pedestrians marching towards her, heads bent, without any thought for small women like Roberta who might be crossing their path.

New posters had gone up in large numbers on the election hoardings, covering the faces of Fould, the outgoing Mayor and the other candidates. They were ads posted by the citizens of Basle, asking for information about missing persons. Roberta counted a dozen different appeals, with photos and phone numbers. These cries for help augured no good.

They made Roberta decide to stop at the Central Post Office near her home. She sent Fould a telegram about Suzy's discoveries, then picked up her mail and climbed the six floors to her flat.

The mail included her invitation to the happening next day with a note from Clémentine, a large legal envelope containing a copy of Major Gruber's will, the keys to his house in Mimosa Street, and a form to be signed and sent back. The Records Office was still after her, wanting to know her address yet again. Roberta decided to keep this letter. One day she planned to open a museum of Public Inefficiency. Framed and prominently displayed, the letter asking for her address would make a good exhibit.

But the best item in her mail was the last: the spring to summer BodyPerfect catalogue. It was fat, heavy, full of new products, and printed on glossy paper in full colour.

Special self-adjusting pregnancy girdles, what a brilliant idea, she thought as she stopped at her front door. Whether she herself would find a product useful made no difference to her admiration for the Norwegian firm that made the girdles. Its address was a fjord with an unpronounceable name. In Roberta's view BodyPerfect had done as much for women's lib as the right to vote and the Pill together.

She dropped the catalogue on the sofa. The mynah bird had no messages for her. Beelzebub was looking gloomily out at the rain. She filled his bowl, threw some toilet articles and a change of clothing into her bag and then prepared to go out again. Her eye fell on the catalogue, which had opened at page 54.

'Thanks to its revolutionary integrated waterproof electro-vitalo-stimulant system, the Electrum girdle will restore your figure to what it was at the age of twenty,' she read. 'The frequency and intensity of the pulsations can be regulated. Only 399 dollars, postage and packing included. This product is sold with the BodyPerfect guarantee: "Money Back If Not Completely Satisfied". Wow!' she added.

She slipped the catalogue in her bag as if it were the most precious of rare volumes. Then she locked her door, went two floors down, stopped, and re-opened the catalogue at the page showing the Electrum girdle.

'I must have it!' she announced firmly.

Grégoire Rosemonde lived in one of those blocks hastily built to solve the housing problem after the Great Flood. His flat was small, simple, functional and had no view, but the Professor had furnished it with good taste. The silver kitchen, the red sitting-room, the blue bedroom – visitors who went through them in that order were making a chromatic journey along the path traced by Dante and Virgil, from the first circle of Hell to the last of Paradise.

The scallops, accompanied by Roberta's tarragon, were waiting to be cooked. The music system in the bedroom was playing what Bach had written for the apostle Matthew to sing. The Sinhalese demon mask, the only decoration on the wall of the sitting-room, grinned as it looked down on

Rosemonde seated at his architect's table. He was unfolding the sheet of blotting paper that Roberta had brought him. The witch watched him, perching on a stool with a glass of Lachryma Christi in her hand.

'How's Beelzebub? Not too cross with you?'

'He's been grumpy ever since I took him off the dry cat food. He doesn't fancy a health food diet, but it won't do him any harm.'

Rosemonde opened the *Liber genealogicum* at the page headed 'Charms', compared the leaf imprint on the blotting paper with the pictures in the book, took a narrow strip of parchment, entered the signs indicated by the *Liber* on it, closed the book, rolled up the blotting paper and the parchment together, and tied the whole thing with a red silk thread.

Opening a wall cupboard with uprights shaped like bodies twisted in agony, very much in the same spirit as the mournful aria coming from the bedroom, he put away the *Liber* in the cupboard and picked up a blue glass jar of Byzantine design.

Fragments of bark lying on a pale felt cloth in one of the long, flat drawers in the lower part of the cupboard looked like votive offerings or Sumerian hieroglyphs. Rosemonde picked one up, closed the drawer and then the cupboard, and went back to his table. The jar was half full of cloudy liquid. He placed the piece of bark over the open neck of the jar, with the little roll of parchment and blotting paper balanced on top of it.

'Over to you, my dear. I'll go and see to our mollusc friends.'

Morgenstern let him go off to the kitchen and sat down in his place. She traced a series of signs of Fire above the little pile of objects on the jar. The bark and the parchment caught fire as suddenly as camphor, falling into the jar in incandescent scraps. She quickly closed the jar, shook it, then left it to settle and went to join that master of sorcery Grégoire, who had an apron round his waist and was frying the scallops over a hot flame. He turned off the gas and put the scallops on their plates. Roberta fetched the bottle of wine and a second glass, and they sat down at the architect's table, drinking to each other and clinking their glasses against the jar, just as they had with Major Gruber's urn.

'To the Martineau line whose founder will soon be revealed to us,' said Rosemonde, proposing a toast. 'Eat it while it's hot.'

St Matthew was climbing Golgotha. The scallops were delicious, the Lachryma Christi smooth, dark and strong. Roberta held back on the amount she was drinking when she felt her head about to float away from her neck.

Rosemonde half-opened a window and lit a cigarette. One elbow on the table, the white tube between two fingers, little imps dancing in his eyes, he spent a few moments making a big performance of being enchanted by Roberta, who was grateful for this delicate attention. But the witch's thoughts were full of the executioner, and she couldn't wait to find out what the Professor of the History of Sorcery thought about it all.

'So the Baron of the Mists thinks he's the famous executioner Monsieur de Paris?' he murmured, tapping his cigarette on the edge of an onyx ashtray. 'That doesn't fit the golem theory, not at all.'

'That's what bothers me. Could we be dealing with *two* entities? I don't even know what I'm supposed to be looking for.'

'So far as the golem's concerned, we have all the literature anyone could want on the subject in college.'

'Did you see those ads asking for information on the hoardings?'

'About missing persons? Hm, yes.'

'This stinks like smallpox blisters. It really stinks.'

'Not a bad simile. Have some cheese?'

He finished the bottle, cleared away, and came back with a plate of cheese and a second opened bottle.

'I warn you, I'm not getting tipsy. I have a meeting tomorrow morning,' said Roberta.

'Then you can stay sober for both of us,' he said, refilling his glass.

Roberta hesitated between the Saint-Marcellin and the Pont-l'Évêque. In the end she opted for a little of both. 'Did you buy them in the market?' These cheeses, like the wine made from grapes grown on the slopes of Mount Vesuvius and the scallops themselves, were normally rather difficult to find in Basle.

'I get them delivered direct,' replied Rosemonde.

The Professor of History's wonderfully efficient way of getting supplies, like his strong head for alcohol, was a secret that Roberta had never managed to fathom. She forgot her good resolutions and poured herself another glass, drinking to the health of this enigma in human form.

'All the same, I wish I knew why Barnabite and Banshee have resuscitated the golem,' she said.

'*May* have resuscitated the golem, my dear. At the moment we have nothing to go on but our friend Martineau's evidence. I feel that a courtesy visit to Hector Barnabite is called for if we're to get confirmation.'

Roberta said nothing.

'I don't mind doing it,' he offered.

'No, no. Hector's my cousin. I shall look forward to seeing him again,' she added with a rather forced smile, emptying her glass to give herself courage. 'A baron, an executioner, a golem – there's something wrong about all this.'

'I'm quite sure you'll know more about it very soon.'

Roberta saw the grinning mask and Rosemonde's face seem to merge, and gave the nerve inside the crook of her elbow a hard pinch to sober herself up. The sensation sent her giddiness down from her brain to her liver, where it settled like an evil genie which ought never have been allowed out of its lamp. She gently pushed her glass away. Finito. Quite enough wine for this evening.

'I made you some soufflé fritters,' announced Rosemonde, going into the kitchen with the empty cheese plates.

'You're an angel!'

'Only a fallen one, I'm afraid,' he said, coming back with the little desserts.

The soufflé fritters went the same way as the scallops, and then Rosemonde took a roll of parchment out of the cupboard and laid it flat on the table, holding it down with large stones. The Martineau tree, like all family trees of sorcery, showed branching alchemical imprints linked to each other by flexible, fine arcana. There was still one place to be filled in, down by the root.

On the Bach recording, the prophetic magician was appealing to his father for aid. His father was not responding.

'No proper family feeling,' said Rosemonde critically, raising his eyes to heaven.

He stubbed out his second cigarette in the ashtray, crushed it between two fingers, shredded the paper and separated the fibres of the filter to make the butt unrecognizable.

'I found nothing fundamentally new in the Martineau tree,' he began, once he had finished his methodical work of destruction. 'You can count the ancestors who are anything really out of the ordinary on the fingers of one hand. Here's the woman who was assistant to Klettenberg of Frankfurt, alchemist at the court of Frederick I. Here's the merry widow of Zachaire. Any number of midwives, of course. The sibyl of Saint-Aignan who lived in Denbigh and was said to be very beautiful. The lady of Lake Cybele near Mount Aubrac. Not much is known about the rest of these women. Most of them were married. None of them died at the stake.'

'Did you solve the mystery of that cross?'

Roberta was referring to the figure of an X with its ends bent back which came up generation after generation. Despite all his expertise, Rosemonde too had failed to make anything of it.

'It could be a lunar sign. It's like the ends of those tie beams that builders use to hold façades in place.'

'Or the marks that used to be put on criminals in the past.'

'Brands, you mean?' She nodded. 'A brand,' he said, thoughtfully. 'Was there anything in the Martineau family to be ashamed of? Could there be some curse written into their family tree of sorcery? Clément's imprint gives it prominence. Look.'

'Oh, I'm sure he has something very serious on his conscience,' said Roberta, jokingly. 'Right. So can we now bring the witch who actually founded the line out of the void, then?'

Rosemonde opened the jar, dipped a pipette into it and drew up a little liquid. He moved the pipette to the bottom of the parchment and let a black drop fall on the blank space. The liquid spread, forming the shape of the imprint of the founder of the line. The strange X reappeared. So the brand, if that was really what it was, went back to the very beginning of the Martineau dynasty.

Rosemonde took his time over finishing his wine, relishing the last drop as the St Matthew Passion ended. He rubbed his right thumb and forefinger together. 'One of these days I must show you how to do a direct reading. Then you'll see the hidden meaning of words – what goes on behind the written characters. It's fascinating.'

'I'm too old for those little games. Just tell me what the imprint says.'

Rosemonde placed his forefinger on the first sign, which was a crescent moon, and closed his eyes. He did not have to wait long for the ridges on his fingertip to find the key to the drawing. Taking a deep breath, he plunged down into the mystery, leaving Roberta on her own, alone on the other side of the world.

He saw a cavern with a sandy floor and bare walls. There was a faint odour of bitumen in the air. A flame was burning behind a pillar, casting bright, flickering orange light on the scene.

The direct reading process left you with only a very restricted field of vision, but Rosemonde could still crane his neck to see what the pillar was hiding. He did. Flames were twisting and turning in the heart of a brazier. He saw a black doorway and a man in a toga.

'Is that you?' Rosemonde recognized that the man was speaking ancient Coptic. 'Why did you run away? I need your hel—'

The Professor stepped hastily back and was in his sitting-room again with Roberta while the rain went on falling outside. He looked at the tip of his forefinger, which was stained black.

'Grégoire,' said the witch, looking at him hard. 'Clément's print . . . it's the same as the print of the founder of the line, but in reverse. Look.'

Rosemonde didn't need to look. He already knew that Roberta was telling the truth. 'Yes, I've just seen the founder,' he said.

'You have? The witch who founded the dynasty?'

'The sorcerer who founded it.'

'You mean it was a man? Oh, can't the Martineau family ever do anything like other people?'

'He had Clément's face,' Rosemonde went on. 'You'd have taken him for Clément himself.'

'What? Are you sure?'

Roberta looked at the family tree, the window, Rosemonde . . . She refilled her glass and tipped it straight down her throat, contracting her abdominal muscles. The demon drink kicked her in the liver a couple of times, but it stayed put there.

'*Was* it him?' she said, stressing the point.

'Ah, that's the question.'

'The beginning and the end. The alpha and omega of sorcery. This has never been known before, am I right?' she asked, not a little proud to have unearthed such a thing.

Rosemonde rubbed his forefinger on his napkin as if to erase the image of the signs. 'No, it's never been known before.' He rolled up the tree of sorcery and wedged it between two stones. 'I shall have to study this more closely.'

'Yes. Right. Meanwhile I've had quite enough mysteries for one evening, Professor. I'm going to bed.'

'I'll join you soon,' he said, lighting a last cigarette. As he smoked it, he watched the rain tracing vertical rivers at random down the sitting-room windows.

'Grégoire!' called Roberta, after a good ten minutes. 'Come here! I want to show you something.'

He opened the window to throw out his cigarette end, but then thought better of it, deciding to crush it out in the ashtray instead and destroy every trace, even the very last scrap of the filter tip.

'Yes, we've had enough mysteries for one evening,' he agreed, closing the window.

He put out the sitting-room lights. Roberta was lounging on the bed fully clothed, with an open catalogue on her knees.

'You wouldn't believe the amazing things those Norwegians think up.'

The underground stem emerged into the air. It coiled around one of the pillars of the observatory, used it as a stake, and five minutes later had twined its way up to the external gallery above the three hundred and eighty-four steps of the staircase. It then leaped on to the roof, bypassed the measuring instruments, and coiled around the cleat holding the rope of the balloon in place. It tested the link, felt the great force latent in the rope and became secretly wedded to it, making its way towards the sky in long spirals and moving faster than ever.

Pichenette was dreaming that Volume Two of *Atrocious Crimes and Famous Murderers* was a runaway best-seller, translated into languages he hadn't even known existed, when a dull sound woke him. He lit the little storm lantern on his bedside table. Another thud. He went out on the platform in the light of the moon, which was just past the half-moon phase. He was armed with a paperknife, the only weapon within reach.

The sound came again, behind him. Pichenette skirted the deckhouse, more intrigued than afraid, and bumped into something in the very middle of the deck. He bent down. His myopic eyes recognized a very large pumpkin. The twining stem that had brought it up here was now coiling over the deck from the front.

'What do you think you're doing here?' the writer asked the plant in reproachful tones.

Boom! Boom again! *Boom, boom, boom!* Pichenette walked forward, tracing a zigzag course between the pumpkins littering the deck. One of them rolled past him. The writer stopped beside his desk.

The sight he now saw was both blurred and fantastic. The

front of the platform had disappeared beneath a mountain of orange globes disgorged by a stem gone crazy, thick as a tree trunk and rising from beneath the balloon. Its spiral ends coiled and uncoiled to let pumpkins roll free. They kept piling on top of each other at an astounding pace.

Surely this isn't Hallowe'en, thought Pichenette, feeling he must still be dreaming. It was only when he heard the platform creak that he thought of the practical side of his situation and began to worry.

A giant pumpkin crushed the deckhouse. Another tore away part of the rail before disappearing overboard. The writer flung himself on the stem with his pathetic paperknife. All he did was lose the knife, flinging himself rapidly to one side as a gourd weighing nearly fifty kilos almost smashed his skull.

The ropes holding the platform to the balloon gave way, unable to support the weight any longer. The deck dropped through the clouds, breaking up as it fell, while the balloon flew up towards the stars. As for the pumpkin vine, its leaves, fruits and stems were scattered to the winds above Basle, imparting a faint smell of pumpkin soup to the rain as it fell on the city below.

The Terror of Unknown Dangers

The news spread like wildfire: a hot-air balloon, origin unknown, had crashed between Little Prague and the Historic Quarter in the middle of the night. The impact, churning up a large area of muddy ground, had uncovered a charnel-house. Eleven corpses of men and women had been found under a metre of mud, their torsos and heads entangled in fishing nets.

The conference room in the CID offices was crammed. About a hundred militia in civilian clothing had come to reinforce the ranks of the reservists. Fould's men all had the same faintly sinister look about them. Scattered among a crowd they passed unnoticed, but when they were all together the impression of contained violence emanating from them weighed heavily on the atmosphere. Roberta was trying to spot Micheau in the throng of inquiry agents. Pichenette's body had not been found, and she would have liked a word with the chauffeur about it, even if he was a deaf mute. But she couldn't see him. The boss flung the door open, strode to the speaker's platform and launched straight into his harangue.

'Sixteen murders! How many more before this killing stops?' His eyes fell on some poor fellow sent by Records who was fidgeting nervously in his chair right in front of the speaker's lectern. 'And why have the tracers failed to warn us of such atrocities?' Fould asked him. 'According to the forensic surgeon the first of the victims were buried alive over a week ago. Well?'

'We think the problem's in Central Filing,' the civil servant replied, breaking the deathly hush. 'It's possible that a breakdown in—'

'Spare me the technical details. Find the cause of this breakdown and repair it! Or we shall use all requisite sanctions to rid this Ministry of the dead wood cluttering it up.'

A murmur of discontent ran through the reservists, but none of them dared protest openly.

'The Baron of the Mists exists all right,' continued Fould. 'That's no rumour. So we can prevent him from doing further harm.' As no one could think of any comment on that, he continued, 'And recent events have cast light on his mode of operation. Miss Boewens, please. We're listening.'

All heads turned towards the back of the room. Suzy had turned up, as requested, but she wasn't expecting Fould to ask her to explain her theory in public. That went right against the principle of confidentiality and discretion which she had recommended to Morgenstern and Martineau.

'It's possible that the Baron is imitating some executioner of the past,' she began, reluctantly. 'The eleven people found in the waste land drowned in the mud of the marshes with nets around their heads. They suffered the fate inflicted on cowards and prostitutes by the Germans of the late Middle Ages. I was thinking of writing a memo on the subject, and on the previous victims—'

'Thank you, Miss Boewens,' Fould interrupted. 'We shall certainly read your memo.' He placed his hands flat on the top of the desk and looked at the audience. 'I want you to observe, investigate, and track the criminal down, since it appears that Records isn't up to the job. Search every nook and cranny in Basle. Find this – this executioner. I am personally taking charge of the inquiry. A new flow chart has been drawn up. Ten departmental heads have been appointed, one for each part of the city. It's all pinned up in the corridor. I want results, is that understood?'

'Yes,' replied the militiamen with one voice. The reservists were more restrained. But Fould was right: the serial killer must be rendered harmless, and this was no time for half-measures.

'What about the wrecked balloon?' asked one reservist. 'We haven't found the pilot's body, and—'

'The authorities responsible will see to that part of the problem. For the time being the Baron is your sole priority.'

Fould strode out fast. Everyone rose, and there was a great deal of noise. Victor the skeleton, sitting in the corner of the platform to which he had been moved, told himself that the living appeared to be in an uncomfortable position. He thought himself rather lucky to be dead already.

Empty offices had been occupied in haste. Phones rang all the time, and there was constant coming and going in the corridor. Martineau and Morgenstern had taken refuge in Major Gruber's old office. Roberta had never seen so much activity on the sixty-ninth floor of the Community Building. She didn't like Fould or his militia, but she could hardly accuse them of being lax.

Martineau was standing at the window in a pose borrowed from Fould himself, one leg straight, the other bent, hands crossed behind his back. Suzy was pacing up and down. Roberta had asked to see all the data on the victims. While she waited she filled in an order form and made out a cheque for 399 dollars to BodyPerfect, Øksfjordøkelen, Norway.

'If only we had that pamphlet!' muttered Martineau for the umpteenth time. 'And I actually had it in my hands!'

Roberta put the order form and her cheque in the pre-paid BodyPerfect envelope, and carefully licked the flap.

'The missing pamphlet, the tracers failing to pick up anything, Pichenette crashing. You'd think someone had it in for us.'

'You would indeed,' agreed Suzy, 'and it's worrying.'

There was a knock on the door. Sixteen civil servants came in to leave a small pyramid of sixteen cartons in one corner of the office. As soon as they had left Roberta dug into the first.

'Good, they haven't done things by halves,' she said, pleased. 'We even have the DNA codes here.'

Boewens crouched down beside her. Roberta passed her an X-ray print of Vaclav Zrcadlo's DNA sequence, with the Records Office stamp on the back. Suzy went over to the window and held the print up to the light. The DNA code was made up of black and white squares, a set of 0s and 1s adding up to a very precise image of what the youth had been. There was nothing random about their disposition. This was the picture of a complex, mysterious life brutally cut short.

'Did I tell you about my Siamese twins?' she asked.

'Yes,' replied Martineau, eager to please. 'At your house. The case that was giving you a headache.'

'That's right.' She handed the print back to Roberta. 'They murdered their lodger. Or one of them did, because it took just a single stab wound to go through the poor woman's heart. Only the thing is that the Siamese twins are joined at the chest, and they have just the one set of DNA between them. So one of the brothers is perfectly innocent. But of course all the tracers see is a single person.'

'They could both be guilty,' suggested Martineau. 'Perhaps one of them held the knife,' he added, miming it, 'and the other gave the order to kill.'

'I'd rather not contemplate that possibility,' admitted Boewens. 'But it's the first time in my brief legal career to date that a DNA code has been no use to me at all.'

'Separate the twins,' went on the investigator enthusiastically. 'Then you could confront them with each other.'

Suzy, who was shorter than Martineau, looked up at him from below. He could feel her breath on his neck and see the irises of her eyes in close-up. They were like green silk delicately pleated around the pupil.

'Oh, Clément,' she sighed, 'if only things were that simple. But they aren't.'

And she turned brusquely on her heel. The effect on the captivated Martineau was like an electric shock. She picked up her raincoat and umbrella.

'I'm off. I have to be in court in two hours' time. And I must write that so-called confidential memo about the history of capital punishment for Fould.'

'What line of defence are you going to take over the Siamese twins?' asked Roberta.

'A technicality,' replied the lawyer, eyes sparkling with glee. 'They can't be defended so they can't be found guilty.' She opened the door.

'By the way – excuse me, can I still expect you?' Martineau ventured to ask. 'At my mother's happening at five o'clock?'

'I'll be there,' she promised.

The young man could have taken off into the air without any lunar assistance. Roberta quickly brought him down to earth.

'Come on, Martineau. We'll take up our inquiries where we ought to have begun in the first place. Let's look for matching factors. We want to find out whether the Baron is acting purely at random, or whether, like the tracers, he obeys some mysterious fate imposed on him by those who preside over our miserable existence.'

★ ★ ★

They had immersed themselves in the private lives of Vaclav Zrcadlo, Martha Werber, Angelo Pasqualini, Georges Fliquart, Gustave Lherbier, Simone Vespare, Ang Chou, Wilhelm Vogt and the rest of the victims. They had sorted through all the information in case they could find some point in common. The carton containing Gruber's data was still closed. Up to now Roberta had preferred to leave it aside.

'Well, let's sum up,' she said, pinching the bridge of her nose. 'What professions do we have?'

'Baker, incineration plant worker, roofer, cashier, two dockers.' Martineau counted them up, tipping his chair backwards and keeping it in equilibrium. 'Three minors due to come of age in less than six months. Two recently retired people. One civil servant in the War Ministry, one Line 8 tram driver, a caretaker, a wholesaler.'

And the former head of the CID, he added to himself. He brought his chair back to stand four-square on the floor.

'Wholesaler in what?'

Martineau looked at his notes. 'Umbrellas. You could say he had a weather eye open for the main chance.'

'True, and the *Barometer* fell,' she joked, and then rose, stretching her arms. 'We're not getting much further, Martineau. No, we're not getting much further.'

Outside, the rain had turned into a kind of drizzle which made the high-rise Civil Service blocks look like mirages swollen with water.

'I found out some more about Micheau,' said Martineau. 'He goes everywhere with the Minister, but you can never find out just where he is at a given time, because Fould's movements are protected by municipal secrecy for the sake of security.'

'Never mind. We can question him later.'

A dozen files were scattered over the desk, giving details of addresses, habits, medical records, hobbies. But the shared features they had managed to dig out of these fragments of human identity were very few. The tram driver and the civil servant had first seen the light of day in the same maternity hospital. Martha Werber and Fliquart both owned the complete twelve-volume collection of *The World and its Secrets*. There were no grounds for thinking that anything linked all the victims of the Baron of the Mists together.

None the less, they had been condemned to death, and their sentences had been carried out by the executioner. Why had he spared Martineau the incinerator furnace if he had been acting at random? Either that or they were dealing with a particularly perverse killer.

The young man had made a discovery that seemed so minor he hadn't mentioned it to Roberta while she was filling in her files. Now he did. 'They all had a letter from Records,' he said, picking up the bundle of letters he had set aside and opening one. 'Werber hadn't filled in the nature of her professional occupation for the last three years. Not surprisingly, since she was retired.' He picked up another. 'This was Lherbier the caretaker. According to his date of birth as recorded in Central Filing, he was 257 years old. They want him to confirm that this information is correct, in which case "the authorities responsible will look into the matter". Have they lost their marbles or what?'

'Let's see.' Roberta consulted these pearls of bureaucratic wisdom, which were on about the same level as her own letter. They could be reflecting the last word in stupidity, confirming that Records had broken down as reported by the civil servant, or they could point to a trail as yet unexplored.

'I had a letter of the same kind myself,' said the young man. 'It seems that the Clément Martineau who holds a driving licence isn't the one who works in the CID or the one whose family owns Martineau Cement Industries. There are three of me around this city. Weird, eh?'

'If you have a complaint to make to the civil service, you'd better put it in writing,' Roberta gravely advised him.

She opened the Major's carton, dug out his correspondence, and found a letter from Records. They were asking Gruber to say how many years he had been in the civil service, having in fact entered his dates in black and white two lines earlier in the same letter. Roberta gathered these missives together and put them in her bag. 'I have to go and see them about you anyway,' she said, and seeing Martineau's inquiring look, added, 'When your family tree of sorcery is deposited at the College it has to be followed by a declaration to Records. It's among the privileges we acquired after the signing of the White Charter. You are a *bona fide* sorcerer, so you fulfil condition K21 and you get the benefit of tax allowances, theatre and travel concessions—'

'Great,' he said, without enthusiasm, and pointed to the rolled tubular shape in her bag. 'Is that my family tree?'

'Yes, but I have to show it to your mother first.'

'That's all right, I'm not stupid, I know the etiquette,' he said with some annoyance.

Roberta looked at him, thinking once again of the way his dynasty went full circle. Grégoire had taken it into his head to identify the spouses and partners of all the witches on the family tree. To perform this great labour he would not, as they did here, have all the genetic codes of—

The witch's mind halted this train of thought. She looked at the Major's DNA and arranged it on the desk with the others, making a chessboard with sixteen squares on it. The truth, she felt sure, was hidden in that magic shape. But in which square? What were they looking for?

'The victims would have made things a lot easier for us if they'd all been members of the same family,' complained Martineau. 'Then our suspects would be the survivors.'

He had just put his finger on the elusive idea she hadn't managed to pin down.

'We're all part of the same family,' she reasoned out loud, reassembling the DNA sequences and arranging them like large plastic playing cards. 'All of us, however many we are. You and I have a link, distant as it may be, with any one of these dead people.'

'Are you feeling all right?' asked Clément anxiously. 'Perhaps we should have stopped for breakfast.'

She held the prints close together, held the transparencies up to the window and looked at them just as Boewens had looked at Zrcadlo's print a few hours earlier. Once they were all superimposed the DNA patterns appeared blurred. Except for one chromosomal locus, which was extremely clear. Roberta placed it over each print and then tried the superimposition experiment again. Each code was unique, but that particular gene occurred in them all.

'It's — it's like a trade mark,' suggested the inquiry agent when she showed him her discovery.

Or a black window, thought the sorceress, and all we have to do is open it and see what's on the other side.

A clock struck four out in the corridor.

'Good heavens!' exclaimed Martineau. 'Time to go to my mother's!'

Martineau senior had built his fortune on cement. The Community Building and most of the towers in Basle were his firm's work. So was the reinforcement of the old city of Venice for Count Palladio. Clément's mother put much of her energy into being a patron of the arts; the more prosperous citizens of Basle had always been keen art collectors. Probably because of her affinity with the Ether, Clémentine Martineau liked happenings best. Roberta had already been to several of these fascinating artistic events.

She had seen naked women grappling with each other in a gigantic dish of spaghetti (this happening was called Heinz Body Art), she had watched twelve grand pianos being dropped from the terrace of the Martineau penthouse (the Catastrophic Sound Experience), she had attended a spiritual sculpture séance from which she herself had emerged with a blue, gelatinous item shaped like a turd and supposed to be a three-dimensional image of her aura. She left it on the pavement outside, making people think that some kind of space dog had been that way.

'Roberta, darling!' cried Clémentine Martineau, seeing her emerge from the private lift. They kissed without actually touching, in the style of the fashionable Fortuny Club. 'What a surprise! Clément?' She stepped back on seeing her son behind Roberta, one hand theatrically placed on her heart. 'You here too?'

Taking them by their arms, Clémentine led them into the three-floor apartment, which was full of high society and intellectual conversation.

'The happening I have for you is by a won-der-fully gifted artistic company. I'm so glad you could come. You'll love their performance, Roberta dear.'

'There's another thing – the family tree of sorcery is finished,' the witch made haste to tell her. 'I came to show you that too.'

All Clémentine had done was pass on her ring and her power to her son. To be reminded of her roots in witchcraft, which she had always more or less ignored, made her a little uneasy. Particularly if there were members of the Club around – and just now they were all over the place.

'I invited Suzy Boewens,' added Clément, taking advantage

of his mother's confusion to disengage his arm. 'You remember – the lecturer in Satanic Law?'

Clémentine did not seem to have heard what her son was telling her. Looking slightly distracted, she told Roberta, 'Robert is out on the dam. The water level in the lagoon has the Municipality worried. The dam will have to be raised higher as an emergency measure.'

'Father doesn't have to be here,' interrupted Clément impatiently. 'Miss Morgenstern has to show *you* the tree. Well, you and me. No one else.'

A strange figure in a robe of pale brown velvet embroidered with flowers in gold thread came and whispered a few words to the mistress of the house. He had a pudding-basin haircut, a straight nose, a haughty mouth and bright eyes. He moved away without so much as glancing at Morgenstern, although she herself was watching him closely. She had seen him before, and she remembered where. But she couldn't accost him here and now.

'One of our performers,' Clémentine explained. 'Let's go to Robert's studio and look at the tree.'

They went down a corridor lined with engravings of the ruins of ancient Rome, which Martineau senior was sure he could have restored if the Great Flood hadn't prevented him. His studio was full of plans, models, reductions of projected and fragmentary cities. The largest plan showed a conglomeration of deserts, ice floes, gulfs, tropical islands and virgin forest. A few isolated buildings were dotted about here and there: a lighthouse, a viaduct, a metal tower, a huge cannon.

'The Jules Verne City project,' explained Clémentine. 'The Fortuny Club has accepted the commission and will carry it out. Now that Tenochtitlán has been demolished, you see, we have no second homes, and we're all of us absolutely exhausted by life here.' Roberta realized that 'all of us' meant the super-rich citizens of Basle. 'So we are financing the project and Robert is drawing up the plans.'

'Are the gypsies in on it too?' asked Roberta in surprise.

'You must be joking! We have quite enough of the gypsies down in the Historic Quarter already!' She shook her head in dismay. 'How on earth could the Mayor let them settle in Basle? Sometimes I don't understand that man.'

Roberta could hardly believe her ears. Clémentine was an aristocrat, but she had never shown herself openly xenophobic. Clément didn't react. Roberta hoped he hadn't heard.

She took the family tree out of the tube and unrolled it on an architect's table very much like Rosemonde's. Rather hesitantly, the young man moved closer to the parchment. Clémentine had put on a pair of half-moon glasses, and was examining the tree, clearing her throat. The signs translating over two thousand years of her secret genes into images could have been Tibetan as far as she was concerned, and she frankly said so.

It was Roberta's job to explain the tree to them, so she did, ending with the story of how the Professor of History had taken the founder of the line by surprise in his cell. She left out only the fact that the first and last figures on the whole family tree had the same face.

'Very interesting,' said Clémentine.

Clément, who was more directly affected than his mother, ventured a question. 'What's that sign that keeps showing up all the time?'

'We don't know yet, but Grégoire Rosemonde is working hard to find out.'

'And that one's my leaf on the tree?' asked Clémentine.

'That's right.'

'Just below my son's! I'm proud of him, you know. The Minister of Security predicts a brilliant future for him. You'll do great things, poppet. Your mother always said so.'

The door opened, and a woman with a wonderful figure and red hair put her head round the studio door.

'I must go,' Clémentine excused herself. 'The happening is about to begin, but it will go on for a good hour, so you can take your time over joining us.'

She closed the door gently behind her. Once they were alone Roberta dug Martineau in the ribs. 'Poppet! Did you know that's what I called Hans-Friedrich, my hedgehog?'

Martineau, glowering, was about to reply when Suzy Boewens entered the studio. 'I'm so sorry I'm late. It was those Siamese twins – I was asked to enter two pleas instead of one. Result: one twin found guilty, one acquitted. So the score's one all, and I'm totally wrecked.'

'Exactly how are they going to sentence the guilty party?' asked Roberta.

'Oh, that's not the court's problem,' said Suzy. 'Security will have to sort it out.'

In her haste the young woman caught her feet in the rug and toppled head first towards Clément, who caught her gently in his arms. Suzy recovered her balance and thanked him, smoothing her slightly crumpled blouse. 'So clumsy of me. Thank you, Clément.'

'D-d-don't m-m-mention it.'

He felt he had just been hit over the head with a soft pink hammer. Suzy was distinct, everything else was blurred.

'Is that your tree of sorcery?' she asked, going over to the table. She noticed at once that the first and last imprints were as like as two peas in a pod. 'It's the wrong way round, isn't it? Oh well, I never did really understand genealogy. Have you two got anywhere with the Baron?'

'Yes and no,' replied Morgenstern.

Suzy narrowed her lips, raised one eyebrow, and decided to leave the sphinx-like Roberta to her mysteries. 'Appearing in court makes you really thirsty. Let's go and drink your health, Clément. In a way it's your official acceptance in the world of sorcery we're celebrating today. Welcome to the Family!'

She kissed the young man's cheek, slipped her arm through his and led him towards the corridor. Roberta followed them, wondering if the soles of the sorcerer's shoes were still on the floor. Everything in his expression suggested that he was floating on air.

Clément and Suzy had slipped away. Most of the party guests had scattered, no doubt to see the happening. Roberta was nibbling petits fours without much enthusiasm. It was time for her to visit her closest relation, Cousin Hector, the last scion of the Barnabite clan. And thinking of her surviving family always spoiled her appetite a bit.

Before going to the Little Prague sanctuary she must stop off at the College to deposit the family tree, which at the moment was still in her bag in Robert Martineau's studio. She went back along the corridor with the engravings, but all the doors looked the same. Opening one at random, she entered a room half plunged in darkness.

At the back, however, on a brightly lit stage, the man with the pudding-basin haircut was kneeling in front of the red-headed woman, whose dress, garnet red trimmed with gold braid, fell in straight and stiffly angled folds as if it were carved in stone. A plastic baby doll lay on her knees, and an angel was holding a crown above her head. A backdrop showed three arches opening on the view of a luminous townscape. Clémentine Martineau's guests were contemplating the happening in silence. The scene reproduced Van Eyck's picture *The Virgin With Chancellor Rolin*. It had been a favourite of Roberta's mother.

Someone coughed. The man playing the part of

Chancellor Rolin moved his head very slightly. The Virgin sighed. Roberta retreated to the back wall and reduced her field of vision so as to immerse herself in the illusion better.

Clément Martineau was just finishing an account of his father as a true hero of the Municipality, hinting that he had inherited many of Robert's wonderful genes himself.

Suzy was only half listening to the enthusiastic young man. She was hoping that he would train to do some practical work on ways to master the Ether, but Martineau had moved on to another subject that fascinated him: cars.

'Ever been in an Intrepid? Four-cylinder engine, Bounder brand tyres. Goes like the wind! I could take you for a drive if you like.'

Suzy suppressed a yawn. She rose to her feet, went round behind the young man and put both hands on his shoulders. He immediately fell silent.

'I've got a favour to ask you, Clément,' she said softly.

'Anything you like,' he replied, his breath coming short, his heart thudding and his mouth as dry as sandpaper.

'I want to hypnotize you.'

'What?'

'Well, not exactly hypnotize. When you're initiated into the Ether, one of the tests you have to pass is taking someone else there with you. I'd only have to find your aestheteria, discover how to control it, and that would be it.'

'My aesthe-what?'

'The place in your body where all your sensations come together. Would you mind being a guinea-pig? Do say yes!'

All right. So Clément Martineau wouldn't be the one taking Suzy up above the clouds. Suzy would be the one to transport Clément Martineau into the wonderful world of the Ether. 'Yes,' he said in his firmest, most masculine voice.

'Good. Then don't move.'

She sat down opposite him, scrutinized first his face and then his neck. 'Take your jacket off.'

He did so with alacrity. He was wearing only a vest under it, which made Suzy's research easier. Her eyes wandered over his torso, moved up to the left shoulder and rested on a point on his shoulder-blade. Her eyes narrowed.

'Found it! Now I'm going to try to numb it from a distance. When you begin to feel you're floating on air let me know.'

He had felt he was floating on air for over an hour, but he didn't say so. Suzy stayed perfectly motionless. She closed her eyes. Her face relaxed. Martineau waited for a couple of minutes. A barely audible little snore roused him.

'Miss Boewens?' No reply. 'Suzy?'

He put his jacket on, sighing. This was Sleeping Beauty syndrome. He couldn't leave her sitting in that chair. Picking her up in his arms, he carried her over to the sofa. She didn't move, she barely murmured. Legs curled up, mouth open, calm, breathing deeply – she was even more desirable like this than awake, he thought.

Martineau knelt down beside his beloved, bent gently towards her face millimetre by millimetre, watching for the slightest reaction, scrutinizing the movements behind her eyelids. He kissed her.

The door of the studio was suddenly opened. Martineau leaped to his feet. Roberta Morgenstern marched in like a sergeant-major and stopped, looking down at the young woman. Suzy was smiling in her sleep. Martineau was crimson in the face.

'She's asleep,' he said.

The witch picked up the family tree and her bag, and then planted herself in front of her partner, looking him up and down. 'Then let's leave her to sleep. You can drive me back to the College and then to the sanctuary. Unless you have something more important to do, of course.'

'Oh, no. Let's go! We mustn't wake her up.'

Leaving the studio Martineau caught the sleeve of his jacket on the door handle, and once they were out in the corridor he dropped his driving gloves three times.

If he drops them again, thought Roberta, I shall suspect him of sampling the Ether himself.

'Oh, bother!' she heard him exclaim behind her back.

The detective, suddenly so clumsy, picked up his gloves and hurried to catch up with her. He trod on his untied shoelaces and fell head first into the lift, where Roberta was waiting with one fatalistic finger on the button that would take them down to ground level.

He had knocked his knee hard on the handle while starting the engine, he had pinched a finger on the fuel inlet, and he had almost slammed the door on his own ankle. Martineau drove chaotically, braking and accelerating for no good reason, driving into any potholes or over any bumps in the road that came anywhere near his tyres.

'You didn't kiss Suzy Boewens, did you?' said the sorceress, keeping an eye open for passing pedestrians.

'No, of course not. She was asleep, I told you.'

'Because if you had, her clumsiness would have infected you. When people have an affinity with the Ether that kind of unwanted side-effect is passed on through the breath.'

They were reaching the University, which spared Martineau a reply.

'I won't be a minute,' she said.

Roberta crossed the Great Court, climbed Staircase F, and went through the School of Practical Studies to reach the College of Sorcery. She deposited Clément's family tree in the genealogical cupboard. A glance into the library told her that Barnabite wasn't there, so he must be at the sanctuary.

Searching in the apothecarium, she found the tube she was looking for. Roberta left the College again, went back through the University and found Martineau still behind the wheel of his car. He hadn't moved, perhaps for fear of injuring himself. His forehead was adorned with a bump like a mauve quail's egg where it had hit the wall of the lift, and the finger he had pinched was scarlet. Roberta told him to lean forward and felt the bump.

'Ouch! You're hurting me!'

'Cry-baby! I've brought you something that may come in useful over the next few days, because if it turns out that you've caught clumsiness then you'll stay clumsy for a while.'

She unscrewed the top of the tube she had taken from the apothecarium and dabbed some brown ointment on his forehead. Martineau waited a few seconds before touching his skull.

'Hey, I don't feel anything any more.'

Smearing some of the ointment on his finger, he managed to bend the joint without groaning.

'I'll leave you the tube. I'm not sure you could find this in the shops. Now, would you drop me off outside the Historic Quarter, please?'

Ten minutes later Martineau drew up outside the entrance to the Palace of Westminster. The banked edge of the lagoon was barely visible; the water was approaching the foot of the ramp, licking at it with long, brown tongues.

'If this rain goes on the gypsies will have to leave,' said Roberta.

'They're used to it!' commented Martineau. 'They're called travellers, aren't they?'

She gave the sorcerer a look which was both piercing and regretful, but Martineau, apparently pleased with his little joke, just applied another layer of the miracle ointment to his forehead.

'If you run out,' said Roberta, 'go to the apothecarium in College and ask for castorium ointment.'

'Castorium? I never heard of that before.'

'No, it's an old wives' remedy. Nothing better than beaver shit for everyday scratches and bruises. Ciao, Martineau.'

He was still looking at the tube with an expression of disgust as Roberta passed under the porch of the entrance to the old Palace of Westminster, folding up her umbrella. The giant velarium had been spread above the Historic Quarter, thus making it, paradoxically, both the lowest-lying and the driest part of Basle.

The rail of the balloon's platform was planted at a lop-sided angle in the waste land. Security tape marked off the zone of mud, and a path of planks around it led to Little Prague. Roberta went along the path, getting the hem of her dress muddy and ignoring the citizens of Basle gawping at the site of the mass grave from the coastal road above it.

The sorceress made straight for the only inhabited house and scraped the mud off the soles of her boots as she climbed the steps. The grey powder all over the streets had congealed into a sticky mass and stuck to her boots like a kind of elastic treacle. The front door wasn't locked. She opened it without announcing herself.

She hadn't visited Barnabite at home for a long time, but here was the same crooked little house with its peeling walls, giving off an unpleasant odour of humidity. However, the corridor was not as tall and narrow as she remembered it.

Sounds rose from the cellar. Roberta left her umbrella in the hall. Broken retorts and alembics were heaped on the steps leading down to the basement, along with piles of books thickly covered with cobwebs.

Making no noise, Roberta went down to the alchemist's crypt. It was full of tables and chests, themselves laden with instruments, jars and books of spells. A furnace of the kind known as an athanor was purring away in one corner, generating a pervasive green haze. A copper pipe rose from the athanor to a window and turned in the direction of the garden.

Hector Barnabite was leaning over a table, singing quietly to himself as he took the ingredients set out in front of him and mixed them into cheerful explosions of colour.

'Here we have the Sun for gold, quicksilver's Mercury, we're told. Old man Saturn stands for lead, Venus stands for brass, 'tis said. Silver to the Moon is kin, Jupiter is known for tin. Iron, says the ancient lore, stands for Mars the god of war.'

Roberta recognized the old rhyme about the transmutation of metals. Could he still be working on that crazy attempt to find the philosopher's stone? For all his deep knowledge the little man, desiccated by too much contact with books, was a mass of the obsessions that had killed more than one alchemist in their time. By now the witch felt pity rather than revulsion for him.

When Barnabite was not working as librarian of the College of Sorcery, he spent his time dissecting newts, mixing sulphur and the universal solvent alkahest, experimenting with methods of divination or examining ordinary pebbles in search of any trace of such legendary stones as horminod and molochite, minerals that were supposed to have unlimited powers ranging from ordinary enchantments to the gift of immortality.

The alchemists Barnabite most admired were Robert Boyle, Edward Kelly, Lascaris, Sandivigius, Seth, Flamel and Paykhül. He had immersed himself in their writings. He had revived forbidden secrets, tested charms and spells, and invoked the Devil more often than that legendary poisoner La Voisin herself. Had Old Nick ever responded? Roberta had no idea. She hoped he had, at least once, so that Hector's efforts would not have been all in vain. One thing was certain: he lived for black magic, and black magic would kill him in the end.

'Now, my little phosphorus, will the furnace do for us?' sang old Hector.

A white light flared in the crypt. Evidently satisfied with the result of his experiment, Barnabite was vigorously crushing something which was unfurling long, milky filaments over the trodden earth floor. Roberta recognized the garlic aroma of phosphoric acid and went several steps back up the stairs to get away from its poisonous fumes. Only if you lived permanently with these noxious vapours could you avoid feeling their effects!

Hector tipped the contents of his mortar into the athanor. When he had put it back on the table, Roberta coughed. The alchemist turned round, saw her, and went pale.

'*Milostpane!*' In Czech, that meant, *Good Lord*! 'Cousin Roberta! Well, obviously I must have left my door open, but I'm afraid you find me very busy with some abstruse alchemical experiments!'

Exactly what I had in mind, thought Morgenstern, forcing herself to look apologetic.

She had known at first glance that Barnabite was hard at work. The state of his skin showed how deeply he was involved in any project: if it looked dirty and unhealthy, then the alchemist was hot in pursuit of something. Today his face was ravaged by what looked like a nasty attack of pruritis. But there was no golem to be seen. The only traces of clay in this gurgling jumble of items had been brought in by the witch herself, on her boots.

Barnabite saw his cousin glancing curiously around and made her climb the steps again. He locked the door of the cellar with a large key dug out of the bottom of his pocket. Then he took her into the little kitchen where grey window panes looked out on the garden.

'So to what do I owe the pleasure of your visit? By St Wenceslas, you don't call on a distant relation once in thirty years or so just to drink a glass of punch. Would you like some punch, by the way? I've just made some.'

'Why not, Cousin Hector?'

While he found glasses and the bottle, Roberta cleaned a dirty pane with her sleeve to look out into the garden. It was divided in two by a positive rampart of lilac and jasmine. The copper pipe emerging from the cellar went on across the flower beds and towards a small observatory, with a verdigris dome that shone slightly in the rain.

The occupant of Barnabite's house had once been the alchemist Curtius when he lived in Prague – Curtius, who gave shelter to the great astronomer Tycho Brahe when he was expelled from his property of Uraniborg by the ignorance of a sovereign who could not believe that the stars sang.

'Do you still use the observatory?' she asked, taking the glass he was handing her. It was almost as dirty as the window panes.

'In this weather? You must be joking.' He opened the window, breathed in the air of the garden, heady with intoxicating scents, and spat outside before closing it again.

'So you're into phosphorus at the moment?'

'What I do in my cellar is my own business,' replied the alchemist tartly. 'And as it happens it takes all my time, so I'll ask you to keep this brief.'

'Of course.' Roberta put down her glass and took a chair, but on hearing it creak changed her mind about sitting in it.

'Right. In spite of your liking for seclusion, you must have heard about the Baron of the Mists?'

'Yes. What about it?'

'I was wondering if there wasn't some connection with the alchemist Richthausen. I believe you've studied his work.'

The scholar's face wore an expression as much as to say: oh, is that all it is? 'Ferdinand III may have given him the title of Baron of Chaos, but that doesn't mean he can be associated with this ridiculous "Baron of the Mists" business. Richthausen was a great alchemist, but he's well and truly dead. I've even been privileged to handle a few ounces of his ashes.'

Roberta looked at the kitchen – very much the kitchen of an old bachelor. A casserole of something cold was standing on the gas stove.

'Goulash,' said Barnabite. 'Would you like to share my modest dinner? I have a bottle of Melnik which would go nicely with it.'

'Beef in paprika sauce doesn't agree with my digestion,' Roberta excused herself. 'And Czech wine – er, it always gives me a migraine. Do you have any cucumber juice? That's what I'd really like.'

'Yes, yes, here we are. Don't move.'

He took a bottle full of thick, green liquid out of his fridge. Roberta drank a little without great enthusiasm, and then thanked her cousin for his help, the punch and the cucumber juice. She retrieved her umbrella, which had left a puddle of water in the hall, and said goodbye, secretly exultant. Her little visit had paid off.

Roberta was pleased to be back in the Historic Quarter despite the uneasy atmosphere there. She wasn't sure what was up. The gypsies had gathered in the main street, their expressions grave and determined. Grégoire was on the watch for her at the end of Mexico Street, outside the pelota court where they'd been planning to dance. He welcomed her in under his umbrella.

'I thought you were never coming. The ballroom's been requisitioned. The Queen is assembling the whole clan.'

'What's going on?'

He showed her a special edition of the *Mainland News* with a large headline announcing, 'The Baron of the Mists is from the Historic Quarter!' The journalist had seized upon Suzy Boewens's theory, and he didn't mince his words. If the killer was acting like an executioner, claimed the article, then he must come from the gypsy colony. As a relic of the Historic Cities network, it was the cause of all the trouble. Hadn't the victims in the mass grave been discovered only a few metres away?

'The people of Basle have organized a demonstration,' Rosemonde explained. 'They're blocking the main entrance. The militia are there, but they're not intervening. That's the status quo, for now anyway.'

The worst is yet to come, thought Roberta.

'Did you see Barnabite?' asked Rosemonde.

'Yes, he was working in his crypt, manipulating phosphorus. I couldn't really make much of what he was doing, but there's something strange around that observatory of his. It's protected by plants like lilac and jasmine – witchcraft plants. Banshee's behind this somewhere. In any case, Gustav Meyrink's novel *The Golem* is on his bedside table.'

'You went into his bedroom?'

'Good heavens, what do you take me for?'

'Then how can you be so sure?'

'Well, you know Barnabite and his love of books – when he was studying the hidden meaning of the Bible he lived like an Old Testament prophet, he dreamed and spoke in Aramaic. So now he's swearing, eating and drinking like

Athanasius Pernath in the fable. He even had cucumber juice in his fridge!'

'Yes, I see. Who but an alchemist of Prague would drink anything so disgusting?'

'I didn't see the golem, but I bet you anything it's there at my cousin's – I swear it is. Cross my heart and hope to die!'

'Oh, don't do that, my love. I couldn't do without you,' protested the seductive Rosemonde. Roberta was just standing on tiptoe to kiss him when a young gypsy emerged from the pelota court.

'The way's clear,' he told them. 'Follow me!'

They made their way down a narrow, winding corridor to a Parisian carriage entrance adorned with carved heads of gorgons ugly enough to keep away any kind of parasite. It stood behind a pillar taken from the Palace of Westminster, a hundred metres from the main entrance to the Quarter. Rosemonde and Roberta skirted the crowd of citizens of Basle unnoticed. Behind them, they heard the angry demonstrators shouting, 'You've got the killer in there! And we've got the militia out here!'

'I wish I knew why your cousin came to see you!'

Barnabite made sure that the phosphorus was doing all right. In the matrix, the fine mother-of-pearl loops now forming suggested the birth of a star still imprisoned in its cocoon of heavy gas. But the project was still unfinished. For now, it was impossible to have even an approximate idea of what the end product of this black magic would be.

'You shouldn't leave your door unlocked so that just anyone can come in,' said Banshee.

'I've already told you why Morgenstern came,' grumbled Barnabite. 'To question me about Richthausen.' In this cross mood, he thought, Carmilla was ruining his daily session of black magic. 'She's a snooper, you know that as well as I do. Locking my door against her would only have put ideas into her head.' Aware that he had scored a point, he added, 'She's only a little third-level witch, anyway. She could never have got past the traps you've set in my garden.'

'Your entire garden is a trap now that I've seen to it,' Banshee corrected him, with an ominous smile. But this argument was getting nowhere. She went over to the matrix. The swirling traces of energy were coming together as a concentrate in the depths. So far they had succeeded in producing a nebula. It was a good start. 'How are we doing for the elements?'

Barnabite consulted Dalton's heavy tome and counted them up. 'We have the five gases – oxygen, hydrogen, nitrogen, chlorine, fluorine – and one solid, phosphorus. Good quality stuff too. You could say the Baron has made things easier for us with his graveyard full of corpses.'

'When shall we have all thirteen elements?'

Barnabite shrugged, scratching his itchy face. 'Well, that depends on our supplier. If he carries on providing one corpse a day, which is how it looks, I'll soon have enough carbon. And then for sulphur and the metals! I can't wait!' he said, rubbing his hands.

Banshee's mind was elsewhere. She was thinking of her phone conversation with the Minister. He was beginning to get her down. He was not pleased that the balloon had crashed on the graveyard. So what? The object of the exercise, after all, was for it to crash, and her magic pumpkin had done the job rather well.

What was more, it seemed he was in a hurry. The ignoramus had no notion how much magic they were working on his behalf. She'd open his eyes later, one way or another.

'Did he phone?' asked Barnabite, deciphering his

colleague's black look. Banshee nodded. 'When am I to prepare the golem?'

She meant to caress the vessel of the matrix with a tender, maternal gesture, but all she did was scratch it. 'You'll soon have your sulphur,' she promised the young embryo inside it. Then, turning to Barnabite with a doom-laden air, she told him, 'The golem has another date with death. The Baron of the Mists will strike at noon tomorrow. Under the Barometer.'

The Known and the Unknown

The rain had stopped falling at dawn. You could see patches of blue sky big enough to make a sailor a pair of trousers here and there among the grey clouds. The Number 4 tram (the Coastal Road – Black Mountain – Coastal Road route) was going up the slope leading to the Municipal Mausoleum. A ray of sun bathed the vehicle in pleasant warmth. Roberta looked up from her newspaper to enjoy it, her eyes half-closed.

She had bought the *Mainland News*. Like most of the people of Basle, she looked at the weather forecast first. The Prevention of Natural Risks office gave warning that the clear spell wouldn't last. Another depression on its way from the British Isles would soon replace the depression from the Ile de France. The Barometer wouldn't tell them what the sky really had in store until the middle of the day.

But the first flood warning had already come into force. The water level in the lagoon outside was now higher than the level inside the dam, which could hold no more. When the rain began again the level would start inexorably rising.

The newspaper had kept its headline for the unprecedented manhunt launched by the Minister of

Security to arrest the Baron of the Mists, or the executioner from the Historic Quarter, if that was what you preferred to call him. Fould announced that their inquiries were 'making great progress', and 'significant results' would soon be published in the press. A long article listed the methods of execution so far employed by the malefactor, with many details. It could have been illustrated by the engravings in the book that Suzy Boewens had shown them.

Yesterday's demonstrators had dispersed without further incident. But the Basle Action Group 'spontaneously formed to combat the threat from within, and to remain vigilant in the face of mounting insecurity', was calling for more meetings outside the Historic Quarter, to continue until the killer was arrested. Fould, who was evidently here, there and everywhere, had apparently listened to 'the legitimate concerns of his fellow citizens', and was studying ways to isolate the gypsies from the rest of the city 'for their own protection'.

For a better chance to keep watch on them, more like, thought Roberta.

Page 3 described, ludicrously exaggerated and denounced various gypsy traditions and customs. For instance, who ever said they could have their own calendar? Children's Day. Birds' Day. Travellers' Day – why not a Baron's Day or a Premeditated Killing Day?

Roberta didn't have to consult the calendar to know that this was St Cretin's Day, and Basle had acquired three more minutes' worth of hate-filled idiocy.

The tram stopped at the Great Men station, and set off again along the straight part of the line which would take it to the Ministries.

The *Mainland News* reported on the incineration plant workers, now entering upon the tenth day of their strike. Their demands were still the same: arrest the Baron, bring him to justice, and then we'll go back to work. The streets of Basle were full of unemptied dustbins, and the textiles mill workers were threatening to follow the example of the incineration plant men, along with the bakers, the schoolchildren, and the bridge-playing ladies of the University Patriotic Club. Martha Werber had been a member.

Another subject of burning interest was the first round of the elections, to take place in just over a week's time. Out of the ten or so candidates only the outgoing Mayor or Archibald Fould could emerge victorious, since the opinion polls credited each of them with half the votes. The reporter did not fail to add that the affair of the Baron of the Mists and the resolution announced by the Minister of Security would have considerable influence on the degree of confidence felt in him.

There was nothing explicit about the now defunct *Barometer*, but Pichenette was still around if you read between the lines of the municipal newspaper. Roberta re-read the ad she had spotted and circled with red pencil on page 24, in the small ads section among House Clearances Undertaken and the lonely hearts: 'Is your life going nowhere? Are you in the dark? Do you need a *Barometer* of public opinions? Then come to the Barometer at midday.'

The tram pulled up at the Ministries stop, rang its bell and set off again. The high-rise ministerial office blocks lined the street, as gloomy and grey as their model the Community Building, which stood out against the horizon with its monumental flight of steps and colossal bronze door.

Roberta placed her hands on her stomach, feeling the electric caress of her girdle. She hadn't been able to believe her eyes when the BodyPerfect parcel arrived that morning at eight a.m. on the dot. Less than twenty-four hours after she sent off her order form from the CID office! Furthermore, the Electrum version of the famous girdle, size medium by Norwegian measurements, was everything the catalogue had promised.

Roberta had set its frequency to a pulsation of medium intensity every thirty minutes. Each time she felt herself melting like a piece of Turkish delight in a bath of warm caramel. Slipping her hand under her dress, she pressed the programming button, adjusting the frequency to every fifteen minutes. She didn't really expect to regain the slim figure she had at the age of twenty, but if you had to begin the day with a visit to Records you deserved a little comfort.

The lobby of the Records Office took up almost as much space on the mainland soil of Basle as the site occupied by the Community Building. It bore a slight family likeness to the headquarters of the Fortuny Bank, except that here they dealt not in nickel, copper or silver dollars but in identities.

Borne up by her girdle, Roberta crossed the lobby with a step as close to the tango as possible. The acoustics were amazing. Her heels echoed on the mosaic floor portraying a DNA double helix. The chandelier in the ceiling above gave the whole place an undeniable air of grandeur.

Two armed militiamen were guarding access to the underground manufacturing plant. A civil servant was sitting behind the central desk. Otherwise the place was empty. Roberta handed her card to the man at the desk, announcing, 'I've come about a profile modification.'

The man slipped the card into a scanner to make sure that this middle-aged redhead wasn't telling him a tall story. Having verified her ID, he pressed a button and prepared to emerge from behind his desk and escort her.

'Don't worry,' said Roberta. 'I know the way.' And she went over to a round, armoured door, which opened slowly as she approached.

The filing cabinets in the Records Office strong-room contained the many thousand paper files recording details of the inhabitants of Basle. A wooden table, two chairs, writing materials and a pile of blank forms awaited authorized visitors. Roberta put her bag down, opened the section of one cabinet marked Mart–Mort, found Clément's name, undid the catch slide securing his file, took it out, picked up one of the Records forms and sat down at the table to fill it in.

This part of her labours on his family tree of sorcery was a rather tedious piece of paperwork. Give Martineau's identity number, calculated on the basis of his date of birth, address, profession and other items of information. Tick Box 21 requesting modification. Enter a plausible reason for modification. Roberta resorted to the time-honoured plea of intradepartmental promotion, a little far-fetched given Martineau's youthful age, but she didn't feel like racking her brains for something new.

And anyway, wasn't the investigator high in the Minister of Security's favour? According to his mother, he'd been promised a brilliant future.

However, she couldn't find the other form, the one for Central Filing, where the DNA codes of the people of Basle were kept. Filing and Records worked together but had never been really close to each other, at least as far as she knew, which meant that every operation, however minor, had to be carried out twice. It would be amazing if Admin ever got those two departments to work together efficiently, she told herself on her way back to the reception desk in the lobby.

The civil servant took the form, checked that it was properly filled in, rubber-stamped it vigorously, rolled it up and slipped it into a shuttle which the pneumatic network sucked up, whistling. At that moment the floor throbbed. The vibration made the chandelier tinkle faintly.

The plant for manufacturing the tracers was just beneath their feet. Access to that part of the building was strictly limited, and in spite of her double status as civil servant and witch, Roberta had never had permission to visit it.

'Excuse me,' she said. The civil servant evidently thought he had finished with her, and was planning to go back to reading his *Lagoon Journal*. 'Don't I have to fill in *two* forms for a profile modification?'

He looked at her with disfavour, but evidently decided that her question deserved a reply. 'Filing and Records have merged,' he told her. 'It's not been officially announced yet. All these murders, you see. We can't really be said to be getting good results.'

So the genetic and biographical records had merged? That must have been a major undertaking. And Fould hadn't told the press?

The floor shook again. The civil servant, who was used to it, didn't bat an eyelid.

'Well, as a matter of fact I'm working on those murders,' she confided in her turn. 'It seems that all the victims had the same kind of letter from you. From Records, I mean.' She took the packet of letters out of her bag and put them on the desk. 'And the dead people aren't in Central Filing any more. Can you by any chance explain that?'

She felt sure that an army of engineers was working hard, at Fould's behest, on the tracer breakdown. But she had often found ordinary clerks like this man very useful. You had to start at the bottom: her father, a keen mountaineer, often repeated that maxim.

With the letters spread out in front of him, the civil servant tapped away on a small machine hidden under the counter. After five minutes spent consulting the files,

162

he told Roberta, 'The identity numbers of these people were in the process of being updated when they died. For various reasons. Martha Werber was going to move into a retirement home. The profile modification comes from the Third Age Department, twenty-first floor. Vaclav Zrcadlo was about to reach his majority, when he'd be out of care. Profile modification from the Registry Office, forty-fifth floor. Georges Fliquart had the bailiffs after him, and there'd been an application to freeze his assets. Modification from the Fiscal Recovery Office, thirteenth floor . . . do you want me to go on?'

'No, thanks, it won't be necessary.'

The civil servant gave her back the letters, took off his glasses, and sucked the ends of them. 'There were some glitches when Filing and Records merged,' he said. 'We had a breakdown, and it's still affecting operations now and then, particularly in updating. Hence these letters. They go out automatically, you know. I can't say I'm surprised.' Evidently there was a question on the tip of his tongue. 'There are rumours that the tracers didn't see anything – not the victims or the killer.'

The civil servant himself was well placed to know, but the failure of the tracers to respond had been one of the best-kept secrets of this inquiry – better kept than the nature of the Baron's methods, anyway.

'You're right, they didn't see anything.'

'I knew it, by St Babbage!' He was folding and unfolding his glasses frantically. 'If our identity numbers didn't match the DNA codes in Filing any more, it makes sense that the tracers didn't see anything! You see, from our point of view those people didn't exist!'

'When did the merger of Filing and Records take place?' asked Roberta.

'About two weeks ago.'

Just before the murders began, then. 'How many people are involved in these updating problems?'

The sorceress herself, she reflected, was one of them, since she was still getting those letters from Records. So was Martineau. And so were the murder victims.

'A quarter.'

'A quarter of what?'

'A quarter of the city. It's going to take months to straighten everything out.'

The throbbing in the floorboards came again. The chandelier chinked. Roberta wanted to see the underground plant for herself, but the militiamen would never let her through, even if she gave them a smile warm enough to defrost the Spitzberg.

'Is there a Ladies over there?' She pointed to a door behind some pot plants.

'Yes, that's right.'

Roberta crossed the lobby and closed the door behind her. So it was true, thought the clerk, devastated. The tracers really were out of action. The whole Records Office could have been prosecuted for failing to render assistance to persons in danger.

The door to the Ladies opened. A pink bath pearl rolled out and over the mosaic floor to the reception desk. The man hoisted himself up on his seat to get a better look. The bath pearl crackled, giving off several discreet little pops and turning into a small amount of fuchsia-pink foam.

'What on earth . . . ?'

The foam rapidly increased in volume, rose to the clerk's desk, and then set off onwards and upwards in the direction of the chandelier.

'Oh, really!' said the civil servant indignantly, retreating from his desk to the exit.

The militiamen had left their posts and were advancing

hesitantly towards the invasive foam. No one saw Roberta take advantage of the diversion to skirt the wall and make her way to the corridor down to the basement. She found herself in a cloakroom where insulated white rubber suits with red visors were arranged on coat hangers.

This is going to lose you all your retirement privileges, she told herself severely, getting into one of the suits.

Three airlocks swept her clean of any particles coming in from the outside world. The third opened, with a hissing sound, into the holy of holies of Security.

The access catwalk had a panoramic view of the magical assembly line that produced the tracers. Complicated machinery was involved, but at least in principle Roberta knew how it worked.

The process began in large settling tanks, into which complex nutrient solutions were fed. Next the tracers were calibrated, filtered, and dried. Then they were put through the machine known as the statistician, a vast steam-powered device which required the permanent attention of the engineers, whether sorcerers or lay people, who worked here in the basement watching it and noting its reactions.

The statistician bristled with perforated file cards directly linked to Central Filing and Records. The new tracers were thrown into it and saturated with data in the form of electric charges. Now that they knew everything about the inhabitants of Basle and the text of the legal code, they were moved to the five large boilers which propelled them into the outside world through ducts, five pipes of wide diameter driven through the thickness of the wall.

As life forms, the tracers were enigmatic in many respects. Arachnids, aerial jellyfish, thinking dust-motes – they had fabulous memories despite their microscopic size. They were sometimes called Selenes, from the Greek name for the goddess of the moon, because their cycle of reproduction corresponded with the lunar phases. The imminent full moon would see the next generation of tiny informers born, and the engineers were just carrying out the final checks in preparation for that event.

'Start the simulation!' crackled a loudspeaker.

The tanks simulated bubbling, the statistician simulated clicking, the boilers went round in rapid succession. The five-fold roar of the virtual propulsion of tracers into the city shook the catwalk.

'More presure on duct number three!' ordered a engineer.

Roberta went back to the changing-room, took off her rubber suit, picked up her bag and returned to the surface. Here she stopped, taken aback. The saponaria foam had completely filled the lobby. A pale rectangular patch in the distance showed roughly where the double door was. Both sides of it were open, and vague forms were moving in the foam. The ground floor of the Records Office was pink from floor to ceiling and smelled delicious.

The sorceress plunged into this effervescent, pearly, unreal stuff. She felt as she had when Summer Time began, removed from reality, highly intuitive but as if her reactions were suspended. She slowed down to prolong her passage through the saponaria foam on which she had cast a spell in the Ladies. You don't get the chance to enjoy a foam bath as high as a ten-storey apartment block every day of the week.

She stopped in the doorway. Large bronze letters set into the paving announced the motto of Security to visitors. *Jure et facto*. 'In law and in fact,' she translated.

The laws and their application, the judges and the executioner . . . The floor boomed. Her legs shook.

A sudden flash of intuition struck the witch like a

thunderbolt. She quickly emerged from the foam. The firemen were bringing in a pump to suck up the invading bubbles as they slowly rolled down the steps to set off and attack the city.

I must get this clear in my mind, she told herself, rounding the Community Building.

She was looking at the outside of the Security block. Five vast structures like the funnels of a steamer emerged from the concrete foundations, turning in five directions towards Basle.

A booming sound was emerging from the entrails of the Records Office. There was a shrill whistling too. No grey matter was being pumped out into the atmosphere, but Roberta could feel the violence of the blast of air even though she was a long way from it.

'The wind,' she murmured. 'This is where it comes from.'

Her Electrum girdle pulsed, as if to assure her that she wasn't dreaming and her intuition was not pure delirium.

She went back to the tram stop, feeling dazed. A tram was coming up behind her, and the driver rang his bell to make her get off the tracks.

'It's impossible,' she tried to convince herself as she boarded the vehicle, showing her civil service pass. 'The tracers protect us.'

She sat down and went on thinking out loud, ignoring the odd looks the other passengers gave her.

'You'd better go and see Plenck. Ask him about that mystery gene. One thing at a time, Roberta.'

But she couldn't help trembling. For if she was right, then the safe, secure city of Basle had now become one of the most dangerous places on terra firma.

And whatever the good Mr Fould may say there'll be hundreds of deaths, she added to herself, as the temple of Security disappeared in the distance.

Roberta found Plenck bending over his dissecting slab. One of the lab cupboards was wide open. Apart from that detail the scene hadn't changed since the post-mortem on Martha Werber.

'You're in a bad way,' the forensic scientist was muttering. 'Now what are we going to do with you?'

Roberta, who had entered without knocking, couldn't see the legs or the head of the corpse he was working on. Was he carrying out a post-mortem on a child?

'Your tail's all ratty too. Was it the tracers left you in such a state? They're certainly a sinister influence.'

The sorceress felt it was time to make her presence known. She coughed.

Plenck turned round, saw her, and a wide smile lit up his features. One of his stuffed animals was lying on the slab. A badger, judging by the nose, and preserved in the act of burrowing, not that Roberta was very knowledgeable about furry mammals.

'You know something? I'm the last taxidermist in Basle, and that damn Baron doesn't leave me a free moment,' complained Plenck, taking a brush to the animal. 'I almost regret the chinchillas, although they're trickier to clean than anything else.'

He put the badger away in the cupboard and took out a sable which looked like a kind of coypu but was white as snow, snarling at the hunter who had obviously killed it in the end.

'I finished the post-mortems in the small hours. Devil take these serial killers! What do they think they're doing to the union agreements we had so much difficulty getting our employers to accept?' He put the sable down and turned it around on its stand. 'Look at that.' The fur was rippling beneath the movement of his fingers in magnetic waves. 'My little friends get all stressed out by the tracers. See? They leave the fur full of static electricity.'

Roberta sat down and twisted a curly strand of her long red hair into a ringlet between two fingers. Plenck continued his monologue, vigorously brushing the back of the sable and trying to restore order to its fur.

'I analysed the material that was covering Martha Werber,' he went on, still working 'It was honey all right. Ordinary honey, but one hundred per cent natural and organic. You don't find that kind of thing very easily in Basle, so the few people who do sell it will probably have had a visit from our friends in the militia.' Blue sparks fleetingly appeared in the sable's fur under his energetic brushing. 'And the murder victims in the mass grave were slowly drowned. A terrible end.'

He twitched a tuft of fur into place and affectionately patted the sable's head. It was looking good again. Putting it away in the cupboard, he hesitated between a porcupine and a baby armadillo, decided on a flying squirrel with its membranes unfolded, and then stopped and stood motionless halfway down the side of the dissecting slab, squirrel in one hand, and looked at her.

'Did you just drop in to pass the time of day, or do you have any new surprises for me?'

'I want you to tell me all about genetics. And quickly. I have to meet someone under the Barometer in an hour's time.'

Plenck put down the squirrel and stared at her, arms crossed, half perching on the table. 'All about genetics? I suggest you put that question to the first god you happen to meet. And come back and see me afterwards. I'd love to know the answer myself.'

'The gods are dead,' Roberta reminded him, 'and I'm asking you.'

She took the sequences of DNA codes out of her bag, put them together, checked that the mystery gene still showed up clearly and placed them on the slab beside Plenck, who sighed, picked up the prints and counted them.

'Sixteen,' he said. 'The least original of numbers at present.'

He studied the transparencies under his projector, one by one and then superimposed. The oddity did not escape him. Roberta watched him, her hands clasped in front of her. Was it the effect of the saponaria foam, her girdle, or the reassuring atmosphere of Plenck's hideout here? She felt incredibly relaxed.

'Could it be coincidence?'

'The people in Central Filing take five samples before building up these photos. A gene in common is statistically impossible.'

Roberta made a face, and reminded him, 'That's why I'm here. To find out what this means.'

Plenck didn't have to dust off his neurones in order to talk genetics. It was one of his favourite subjects. 'Well, let's take the technical aspect of the problem first,' he began. 'The genetic code itself is common to all living things, amoebas, protozoans, viruses, mammals, and so on. It's the key to the transmission of heredity. But the composition of every individual's deoxyribonucleic acid is peculiar to that individual. It consists of what are called the variable areas – you can use the term genes if you like – that make us different from each other, allow the tracers to identify us, and are shown on these prints. Shall I go over that again for you?'

'No, don't bother,' said Roberta.

Plenck continued. 'That was rather a brief definition, but you got it from the Museum's forensic surgeon. Now I'll give you a definition as provided by a sorcerer who has an affinity with the Ether.'

Cracking his finger joints, he paced around the dissecting slab like a doctor round a specimen in an imaginary anatomy theatre.

'We are made up of movement,' he said. 'Our organs interact with each other, and with organs outside ourselves, and with the elements. The environment has a long-term effect on us, and so do our daily experiences and our feelings, and millions of other factors.'

'I wasn't asking for a course on sympathetic effects,' said Roberta.

She had interrupted him. He gave her a piercing look. 'Why do you take size four shoes?'

'My mother had small feet,' replied the sorceress, slightly annoyed.

'And where does your pigheaded obstinacy come from?'

'You should have met my father!'

'Last question: did you dream of making love when you were still a virgin?'

Roberta did not reply to that one. She could still remember how confused she felt on finding that the reality was very like what she had imagined. She had not felt as if she were discovering something new, just continuing along the same line. Even though a door of some importance had opened for her.

'Your mother's shoe size, your great-great-uncle's hair colour, recognition of the sound of the sea, animal instincts, fear of the dark or of spiders or snakes, your internal clock, your feelings, your character, what you think about death . . .' Plenck took a deep breath. 'All that is stored in the DNA in every single one of your cells.' He picked up a print at random and waved it about like irrefutable proof of his remarks. 'Think of these prints as paintings. The visible surface, the image, shows a life. But there are previous lives beneath that top layer, going right down to the canvas and the frame on which it's stretched.' Plenck assumed a grave expression. 'As a forensic scientist I can't explain that mystery gene. So here the sorcerer takes over and says: 'The gene could be a record of an experience shared by all the victims, something traumatic enough to leave a mark on the visible part of their genetic codes. Like a physical accident happening to the surface of the painting, piercing it to a greater or lesser extent.'

'But we didn't find anything,' Roberta objected. 'Nothing they shared in common, nothing exceptional – apart from a violent death in each case.'

'The investigator has done her work and the Minister congratulates her,' said Plenck, imitating Archibald Fould's voice. 'But now here's the sorcerer asking the sorceress: has she looked elsewhere? Has she explored the past of these good folk?'

'The – the recent past?'

'No, the distant past. Their ancestry.'

At last Roberta saw what Plenck was getting at. His view of genetics wasn't so very far from the work she herself had done on the Martineau family tree, in casting light on the transmission of powers from one generation to another.

'The killer's using historical methods, isn't he?' said the forensic surgeon. 'And there's no faking it – the executions are carried out? I'll tell you one thing, my dear: that gene isn't just something they have in common. It amounts to a death sentence.'

'Like a hereditary disease,' she suggested.

'I'd call it a physical memento, the genetic engram or memory trace of an event back in the past, but one for which a later generation has paid the price. Yes, a genetic engram.'

Roberta thought of the X sign that showed up on every imprint of links in the Martineau family tree, passed on down two thousand years of history. Grégoire had used a certain term for it, but what it was she couldn't remember.

'There *is* someone who could tell you more,' suggested Plenck. 'The question is, would she agree to see you?'

She knew that he meant Ragnetrude the Earth Spirit, the perfect source of information for any in-depth study of origins.

'Didn't you say you had to meet someone?' Plenck added.

'Yes, at midday under the Barometer.'

'Well, it's twenty to twelve now.'

'Oh, my word! I must be off, then,' said Roberta.

Plenck helped her on with her coat. 'And before you go, I wanted to tell you there was something odd about the bodies in the mass grave.'

'What?'

'Well – how shall I put it? They were missing certain . . . elements.'

'How do you mean?'

'I've never seen anything like it before. One body contained no phosphorus, others no fluorine, carbon or chlorine. Obviously that's something no one but a sorcerer would have noticed. But I've done some complementary analyses.' He shrugged. 'Do you see what I mean? It's like the traffic in human organs, but applied to the very essence of human nature. What's the world coming to?'

'Did you say phosphorus?'

In her mind's eye Roberta saw Hector working frantically away in his enchanted crypt.

'I drew up a detailed list. I'll let you have it.'

'Did you put this in your report?'

'Sorcery is not the Ministry's business, or not as far as I know.'

Roberta had to go. She kissed the forensic scientist and

left him to his flying squirrel and his own faintly deranged obsession.

Why would Barnabite be tapping bodies to extract those elements? Was he linked to the Baron of the Mists in some way? What terrible inheritance did that gene represent, wondered Roberta, and would Ragnetrude agree to speak to her? Her mind was working overtime as she left the Museum. The Number 2 tram was moving slowly away towards Basle city centre. The sorceress didn't dither any longer, but ran to catch up with it. All those questions could wait.

Half the city had decided to meet under the Barometer at midday. Everyone's worst fears were confirmed. According to the pointer of the meteorological monument marking the theoretical centre of Basle, it was about to start raining again. Opinions were freely exchanged. The crowd milled vaguely around, grew ever larger, and the sorceress wondered how she was ever going to find Ernest Pichenette in all this chaos.

She went into the Central Pharmacy, climbed to the first floor, and found herself a place on the balcony where a photographer stood taking pictures of the crowd. The upper part of the Barometer sign hid her from view herself, but almost all heads were turned her way to see the photographer, so she was in an ideal position to spot Pichenette.

Instead, she saw Martineau trying to make his way into the crowd at the wheel of his car. Finding himself hemmed in, the young man continued towards the Pharmacy on foot. Another bump, larger than the first, adorned his forehead. Obviously his clumsiness had not cleared up yet and he had exhausted his supplies of castorium.

Roberta stayed in hiding. Martineau's comments on the gypsies had made her feel a little cool towards him.

Furthermore, you don't take advantage of the fact that a woman is asleep to kiss her. He hadn't raped Boewens, of course, but Roberta had fixed ideas on the subject: those who play about with dangerous weapons have often begun with toy pistols.

The clock of the City Hall, a long Baroque building along one side of the square, chimed twelve. On the twelfth stroke the wind rose. Hats flew into the air. The weathercock on the Barometer turned round and round with a hissing sound before settling to point north. Roberta felt the tension in the atmosphere. This was exactly how the Baron of the Mists would have planned to prepare his audience if he wanted to appear at that precise moment.

Suddenly the crowd in the middle of the square retreated, clearing a space around a massive column of grey dust. A human form around two metres tall stood there like a totem. The features of this apparition were blurred but ever-changing. From where he stood, Martineau couldn't see it. He went on towards the Pharmacy. But Roberta let none of the details escape her.

The Baron of the Mists, like some fabulous illusionist, was waving a shadowy whip above his head. He cracked it four times. Four grey horses appeared out of the void and pirouetted around him, making the crowd withdraw a little further. There were gasps of admiration. The photographer immortalized the moment. Some of the spectators applauded, although they should all have been running for their lives. Clearly Basle had gone mad.

The Baron approached the crowd and laid one hand on the shoulder of a man in a green raincoat.

'Martineau!' shouted Roberta.

The crowd was beginning to understand. The effect of the first hallucination was wearing off, and fear took over. Clément saw the sorceress on the balcony of the Pharmacy, but he was pushed to one side. The man in the raincoat was struggling. The Baron threw him down between the horses. Ropes unfurled from their hindquarters and coiled round his arms and legs. The Baron cracked his whip once, and the unfortunate man was raised horizontally above the road. A second crack of the whip sent the horses galloping off in four different directions.

The screams of the man being torn apart set off panic which spread like a shock wave through everyone in the square. They were all pushing and kicking each other, uttering screams. But a kind of sacred precinct was left free for the executioner to do his work. Martineau had disappeared.

The horses, the ropes and the whip vanished into thin air. The Baron unclothed and cut up his victim. He put everything into a large sack which he slung over his shoulder. Then, feet together, he jumped in the air and took off towards the sky. His grey cloak unfolded, snapping like a topsail. He flew over the crowd, landed on the pediment of the City Hall, and took off from it again, flying eastwards fast.

Roberta saw Martineau trying to reach his car. The Baron was now moving away over the roof-tops with great lunar leaps. Human bodies are bound to the Earth, which is bound to the Sky, which is bound to the Ether, she reminded herself. Her Electrum girdle was urging her to do something. The only way to pursue the creature was to merge with the elements. There was only one means of doing that, and as it happened it was within her reach.

She hurried into the Pharmacy. The first floor was almost empty, and no one took any notice of a small woman slipping into the stockroom. Swiftly, she inspected the shelves full of jars covered with decorative tin lids. She ignored the boxes of sticking plasters and bundles of liquorice sticks; she was looking for a dangerous item bound to be kept under lock and key. She stopped in front of a padlocked cupboard.

The padlock gave way to the pressure of her fingers. Inside she found a fine collection of poisons: strychnine, opium, arsenic, all kinds of cyanide. Roberta put her bag down beside some precious musk which was giving off a powerful scent.

She soon found what she was looking for. Taking the jar of white powder out of the cupboard, she dipped five greedy fingers into it, took them out covered with the substance and sucked them, fighting off nausea. She repeated this operation three times and then returned to the balcony, pushing aside a little man barring her way with a single movement of her shoulders.

Martineau had started his car, and managed to perform a complicated manoeuvre to extract himself from the chaos in the square. Roberta watched him as she felt the transformation take place. The white copper sulphate (also known as Sympathetic Powder in the apothecarium of the College) was beginning to take effect.

The sorceress prepared to put theory into practice: the theory of the interaction of her organs with the elements as described by Plenck an hour earlier. The fluid in which her own little cells were now bathing was attuned to the atmosphere above the city: the air carrying the bloodthirsty form that was the Baron of the Mists.

Her vision changed, and now she saw imponderable forces – calorific, magnetic, nervous, universal – like long, luminous tracks of pale colour. The people of Basle were leaving behind them filaments of energy and fear, traces that mingled, crossed and broke, and took off into the atmosphere like lazy gossamer threads. In the middle of the square a grey, net-like structure was turning slowly and rising to the roof of the

City Hall. It was the trail left behind by the Baron of the Mists.

The photographer had left; the square was almost empty. Keeping both feet together, Roberta jumped up on the wrought-iron balustrade and balanced on the toes of her boots in an unreal, weightless state. She plunged into the void and let herself drift towards the grey whirlwind, which seized her and flung her up to the sky. At the last minute she caught hold of the lightning conductor on the City Hall and stopped herself. She hadn't been expecting anything quite so violent.

The roof-tops of Basle stretched below, all the way to the lagoon. The Baron was out of sight, but not the wake he had left behind him. The sorceress took off, using as her guide its huge and undulating line, accelerating the pace of her increasingly long strides. The streets slipped by beneath her feet, fast as a breath. Roberta leaped from gables to roof ridges, from roof ridges to chimneys. She was running and flying at one and the same time.

The trail plunged down between two apartment blocks. The Baron had come to earth again here. Roberta followed it and landed on the road thirty metres below. Crouching down, hardly even breathless, she saw Martineau's car making in her direction. He braked hard. Stretching her legs, she leaped up on to the roof of a large store, where she clung to the shop sign, one hand shielding her eyes, and studied the new hunting grounds opening up before her.

The Baron, his sack still over his shoulder, was running through the air again two hundred metres away. He seemed to be swirling to the point of dissolution and reconstituting himself. Then he plunged down once more. Taking up the pursuit, Roberta joined his grey shape between the tall buildings in a narrow street.

They moved along it at pavement level, dodging between

the pedestrians in zigzag movements. Fifty metres separated them, then thirty. Shutters slammed as they passed. Bystanders pointed at the dark being and the creature with the fiery red crest pursuing it. To Roberta, nothing existed except the Baron out there ahead of her. She was sticking close to the track he left behind him.

Run as fast as you like, she thought, I'll catch up with you.

Madame Gravila was a well-known medium who always observed the proprieties in her work. A black curtain had been drawn over her window, which itself was left open so that the spirits could visit her. The big mirror had been turned to face the wall. A glass of sherry, intended to revive her after the stress of contact with the spirit world, stood on a Chippendale pedestal table to her left. Meanwhile the participants in the séance were concentrating hard, and fortunately they were gullible. The old aunt whose spirit they wanted to call up had hidden a small fortune in municipal bonds somewhere in her flat, and so far they had failed to find the bonds.

'Let us join hands and open our minds,' intoned the medium.

They formed a circle, fingertips touching. Madame Gravila closed her eyes and called, 'Gertrude! Gertrude! Tap once if you can hear us!'

She spoke in a loud voice, since the aunt was slightly deaf and she had other séances to hold that day. Mentally she counted to fifteen, and told the heirs, with a confident smile: 'We have a good connection. I can sense her coming.'

The Baron turned into a street on his left. Roberta followed, but she was taken by surprise when his trail suddenly rose, climbing to the sky again. Roberta flew towards the façade of a building, bumped into a carved lion's head, crashed into a set of flowerpots which broke under the impact, and set off again the other way. She lost the trail and made for a window with a black velvet curtain over it.

A kind of dark meteor bounced off the oak table and fell heavily to the floor. Madame Gravila and her three clients were transfixed. The dark form, grumbling, struggled out of the curtain. They saw a small woman with red hair, a Fury in a flowered dress.

'What the hell, he's trying to throw me off the track!' she complained, staggering slightly.

In a fluting voice that shook slightly, Madame Gravila inquired, 'Er – are you Auntie Gertrude?'

The witch saw the glass of sherry still standing on the table, intact, and tossed it straight down her throat. After the nasty shock her organism had suffered the wine had a reinvigorating effect.

'No, I'm Cousin Roberta,' she told the medium. 'But I'll say hello to her for you.'

And with two bounds she had jumped out of the window and seemed to be sucked up towards the sky. The three members of the bereaved family stared out of the window for some moments.

'But we never had any Cousin Roberta,' the eldest of them told the medium, in tones somewhere between reproach and incredulity.

The sorceress was racing over the roof-tops again. The Baron had increased his lead, and she felt her strength fading. The copper sulphate had drained her energy. She couldn't keep up this pace for very long.

'Run as fast as you still can,' she hissed between her teeth, taking short breaths and panting so as to maintain her speed.

But then she had to stop, and she had been moving more slowly anyway. Further off, the Baron reached the edge of the lagoon and flew across the water separating Basle from the Isle of the Dead, his cloak flying. Roberta could see him distinctly in the clear air. Her senses, stimulated by the Sympathetic Powder, enabled her to perceive him as if in a prism.

The Baron landed gracefully on the flat roof of the crematorium. He bent down, emptied part of the contents of his sack, slung it over his shoulder again and raced off in the opposite direction to return to the air over the market. He was going west now, still taking giant airborne strides. Roberta assessed the distance between them, visualized the trajectory she must take to intercept him, summoned up her strength and made for the killer with the energy of a red-hot cannon ball.

Her flight lasted scarcely ten seconds, but her aim had been good, and she struck the Baron of the Mists head on. Or rather, she went right through him head on. Braking, she examined the results, her breath coming fast. The Baron was continuing on his way without turning back. She'd have got the same result from trying to tackle a ghost.

'So I . . . was . . . right,' she gasped, spitting out chalky saliva.

Then she let the air carry her to the crematorium, drifting above the market and the lagoon like a balloon in the wake of the killer whom she had failed to stop. She made a soft landing on the roof of the little Gothic edifice.

There was a cremation going on. Roberta could hear the thoughts of the mourners, tearful, devout or bored, right beneath her feet. In the middle of the multiple whisper of their minds there was a great silence, an empty hole, like an eye without any pupil or iris. It was the presence of the dead person whom the flames would soon return to the void.

The Baron had arranged the limbs of his seventeenth victim in the shape of a cross. A macabre compass rose, thought Roberta. She turned to look west. Her view of the horizon was blocked by the hill where the Municipal Mausoleum stood. If only she could gain height . . . She looked up at the chimney of the crematorium, from which thick white smoke was beginning to billow.

Below, the mourners' thoughts united, accompanying the dead man on his last journey. They passed through the roof, winding around the chimney to mingle with the smoke. Roberta cautiously approached this haze, which was shaped like a staircase, and set foot on it. Sorrow, compassion, fear, memories, regrets raised her in a slow spiral movement to that point in the sky where the thoughts of the living abandoned the dead man, falling back to Basle in a cascade of resignation.

Roberta saw the Baron, a minuscule grey dot, emptying his sack on top of the most distant tower of the Fortuny building. Then he set off in a new direction, making for the south of the city this time.

She let herself fall back to earth at a tangent that would bring her down in the floating market. From there, she reached the first street on terra firma. Martineau's car, backfiring, was just driving down it.

'Here comes the cavalry, on its own and late,' noted the sorceress, in a hoarse voice.

She launched herself into the air, but miscalculated and dropped like a stone into the front seat of the Intrepid. Martineau drove past a mountain of dustbins before stopping with a squeal of tyres.

'You!' he exclaimed, taking his cap off.

The witch's hair was standing on end, her face was waxen, her eyes hollow, and her body was trembling spasmodically. 'Hello, dear boy, everything OK?' she asked. 'Had another bump on the head?'

He glanced alternately at the sky and his CID partner,

sitting beside him and looking rather groggy. 'So I wasn't dreaming! You did bounce past my nose just now.'

Roberta opened the glove compartment, took out the city street atlas and tried to consult it – but waves of hot and cold were running through her. She was exhausted.

'You need a pick-me-up,' said Martineau. Taking his grandfather's flask out of a pocket of his driving suit he carefully opened it, filled the tiny cup from the top of the flask and offered it to his passenger. She ignored the cup, took the flask instead, emptied it in a single greedy gulp and threw it on the back seat. Some colour returned to her cheeks, making her look like a slightly demonic doll. Martineau drank the contents of the cup and tossed it into the back of the car to join the flask. Roberta had picked up the street atlas again. Her hands were no longer trembling.

'What's the most southerly point in Basle?' she asked in a steady voice.

'Er – the lighthouse at the end of South Point, I think.'

'Then put your foot down.' She found the page in the atlas showing where they were now. 'I'll pilot you. And if I catch you running over any hedgehogs I'll turn your wheels square. Off we go! Home, James, and don't spare the horses! Turn half right here!'

Martineau wondered whether a map and a woman were compatible in a car together. He turned half right, sending several more innocent dustbins flying.

'Now second on the left. That'll be the quickest way to get back to the coastal road.'

He tried and failed to find an answer, so he put the car into gear, trod on the accelerator, and followed the witch's instructions.

The Electrum girdle, which Roberta had programmed to give one pulsation a minute, electrified her five times and to some extent recharged her batteries. No one could ask her to race across the roof-tops again, but she'd be able to walk like any normal biped.

Martineau was pestering her with questions. He wanted to know what magic had enabled her to fly through the air like that, but she refused to tell him. Sympathetic Powder was a well-kept secret of the College. A daredevil like Clément would be perfectly capable of over-indulging if he found out about it, and then he might become addicted.

They reached the South Point jetty. Martineau drove along it at snail's pace. The surface of the water, close and menacing on both sides, was fringed with curling foam.

'Go right to the end,' she said.

They drove to the lighthouse. 'There's no one here,' pointed out the investigator, switching off his engine.

But Roberta knew that the Baron *was* there. His trail, as clear as the wake of a ship crossing a calm sea, went round the lighthouse, along the jetty, and disappeared into one of the crevices in the rocks level with the waves.

'Follow me,' she told Martineau, and started without waiting for him. He watched her go back along the jetty. What did she hope to find in the jumbled shoreline apart from crabs and fragments of mildewed wreckage?

She slipped through an opening among the rocks, and he joined her, grumbling.

The cave inside smelled of low tide and echoed to the sound of thousands of lapping waves. Lying flat on her front on a sloping concrete surface, she pointed to a rectangular opening looking down on another cave below. Martineau lay down too, working his way over to her.

'I get the idea,' he whispered, sarcastically. 'The Baron of the Mists is a pirate, and this is where he keeps his buried treas—'

But the Baron was indeed in the lower cave. He was

motionless. The murdered man's head, its mouth still open in a scream, was placed on the concrete between his feet. Roberta felt a new agitation in the atmosphere – and it didn't come from Martineau's teeth, which were chattering like castanets. 'There's something coming,' she told him.

A massive creature, as big as the Baron himself and roughly fashioned from some kind of red clay, entered the cave with a mechanical step. Clément had stiffened on seeing the monster. Roberta placed her hand over his to reassure him.

'The tenant of Old School Street,' she explained. 'The golem. The creation of the Kabbalah.' Roberta was as fascinated as Plenck might have been to discover white sables still living somewhere on the mainland. She saw the astral forces that gave the legendary being life escaping like blue filaments from its mouth and forming a trail like sparkling gemstones.

The golem turned its massive head and stared at the witch from empty eye sockets. Morgenstern squeezed Martineau's wrist, indicating that he must not move.

Seeing only motionless forms, the golem did what it had been created to do. It bent down, picked up the severed head in both hands, raised it level with its own head, and inserted its thumbs into the murdered man's mouth to separate the jaws a little further. A quicksilver flash of light passed from the human's throat to the golem's and lodged in the creature's clay chest. The golem put down the head, grunted, and withdrew. The Baron dematerialized, leaving no trace behind.

It took Martineau a few seconds to realize that the two monsters had disappeared. He rolled over on his back and tried to breathe calmly, but he was trembling all over. Roberta gave him her hand to help him up.

'OK?' she asked.

'In a minute.'

They left through the crevice and took shelter behind a rock almost level with the road. The golem was moving off towards Little Prague with a heavy step, its clay feet sinking deep into the mud. As for the Baron, he had resumed human form and was returning to the city.

'Which will you take?' asked the witch, perfectly recovered by now. She was looking avidly at the Baron, her prime quarry. Perhaps the golem's clumsy gait reassured Martineau.

'The brown bear,' he said, putting a brave face on it.

'Then I'll tackle the grey wolf.'

Not that she'd have left him the choice anyway.

The treacherous, sticky mud wasn't made for beings of flesh, bone and muscle like Clément Martineau, but the golem was in its element on this spongy terrain. When the investigator set foot on the surface of the waste land, soaked as it was by rain, he recoiled, feeling his ankle being swallowed up with a sucking sound. He made for the safety of the nearest block of concrete, and stayed there watching the golem until it disappeared from sight into the Little Prague sanctuary.

The Baron of the Mists had lost substance and size in order to mingle with the crowd. His voluminous, dirty grey felt cape made him look like a beggar, particularly with his sack, now almost empty, thrown over his shoulder. The people of Basle either avoided him or crossed to the opposite pavement when they saw him coming.

Roberta followed him to the central square. The militia had cleaned it up, and large circular patches of white sand lay where the blood had flowed. The Baron made for the Central Pharmacy and leaped up on its balcony. In her now enfeebled state, Roberta didn't even contemplate copying him, but she could do as everyone else did and go through the front door.

A hand on the latch, and she was in the Pharmacy. Footsteps echoed from the first floor. Roberta listened, eyes riveted to the ceiling. They stopped when she reached the bottom of the staircase.

She climbed it and came upon the Baron from behind. He was at the bench where the dispensers usually worked. He had lit a stove, and the fire was roaring away in it. The sack made out of dust was beside him. It disintegrated and revealed the last of the murder victim's body parts. The Baron simply threw them into the fire.

Roberta was telling herself that, having completed his task, the Baron would disintegrate too when a whiplash coiled around her throat and threw her on the floor. A hand felt her neck. She felt a pricking sensation which made her grimace.

The Baron seemed to be tasting something on his fingertip. It was a tiny sample of Roberta Morgenstern's DNA, and he was analysing it, she knew, to find out if there were historical reasons for executing her. He must have been satisfied, for a smile appeared on his stony features.

He looked at the stove and at the woman whom he meant to execute. The witch read his train of thought. You must burn, but all I have available is this pathetic little fire. All the same, the execution will take place. We mustn't keep Dame Justice waiting.

I shall begin with the head, he thought, and burn the rest bit by bit – yes, that's the best way to do it.

He took hold of her chin and raised her from the floor. Roberta tried to shake him off, but the Baron of the Mists never left a job unfinished. And he did not fear fire, as he had already shown in the incineration plant.

Then the Electrum girdle pulsed. The hand let go of Roberta. She fell on the floor again and scrambled to get back into safety. The Baron's arm had been reabsorbed up to the shoulder. For several seconds he did not react. Then he made for the sorceress again.

She had lost no time in putting her hand inside her dress to adjust the programming button of her girdle. Maximum intensity, manual mode. One finger on the switch, she waited for the executioner to fling himself on her.

The electric impulse went right through her body and into the creature before her. The legs of the Baron of the Mists gave way. His torso exploded into millions of particles which were scattered around the pharmacy. His head seemed to be dissolving. She had won.

'Baron nil, BodyPerfect one,' announced Roberta, in a quavering voice.

She got up, and took her time over deciding what state she was in. Apart from a few bruises and a nasty fright, she had come out of it unscathed. She switched the Electrum girdle over to standby. She'd had quite enough shocks for one day.

She went back to the stockroom, feet dragging, opened the cupboard of precious substances and retrieved her bag, which was giving off a distinctly enchanting smell of musk.

Roberta consulted herself on her next step. 'We shall go back home. We shall pretty ourselves up. And we shall throw ourselves into the arms of our beloved Grégoire,' she decided by a large majority.

Then she noticed a movement behind the shelf of medicinal herbs. Someone was hiding in the stockroom. She had only to move to one side to see the outline of a small man. Recognizing him, she smiled. She went over to him without a sound and tapped him on the shoulder. He jumped, turned round, and immediately warned, hands in front of his face, 'You can't hit me. I'm short-sighted.'

'Pichenette,' said Morgenstern between her teeth. 'So you did come to the meeting place.'

The writer moved as if to adjust an invisible pair of glasses on his nose. That voice meant something to him. 'Morgenstern?'

'No, some creature from the Andes.' But on seeing his baffled look, she decided to limit herself to straight questioning. 'Yes, Roberta Morgenstern. Of the CID.'

'Let's get out of this horrible place,' he begged, looking frantic.

'By all means. That's certainly our best course of action,' agreed the witch.

Her own flat wasn't safe any more, or Grégoire's, or any of the places to which she usually resorted. But she had another card up her sleeve. They left the Pharmacy and moved away from the central square towards the Palace of Justice.

'You seem to know where you're going,' Pichenette noticed.

'42 Mimosa Street,' said the sorceress.

The address meant nothing to the journalist, but Morgenstern could hardly have been more precise about it, so he decided to follow her without asking any questions. He told himself, after they had been walking for several minutes, that this woman's perfume was extremely disturbing and – well, evocative.

'Funny smell, don't you think?' he tried in a low voice when they reached a tram stop. Morgenstern did not reply. 'It kind of gives me ideas.'

He had only to close his eyes to see a four-poster bed, large mirrors on stands, a sea of cushions . . .

The tram was coming, ringing its bell. They boarded it and sat beside each other. The writer realized that his imaginary stage setting had acquired a tenant: Mata Hari, lying on the bed and wearing a delicious pink silk baby-doll nightie, was beckoning him over to her.

Rain pattered down on the canvas roof of the tram. Of all

the passengers, Roberta was the only one to notice that it had started again. The others, men and woman alike, had their eyes closed. All their faces wore Mona Lisa smiles.

The Punishment Follows the Crime –
Long After the Event

The last stage of the journey was quite an ordeal for Roberta.
The Sympathetic Powder had taken its toll of her. The writer
supported her until they reached Major Gruber's house, then
searched her bag for the key of Number 42, opened the door
and sat her down on the bottom step of the stairs.

'Telephone,' she breathed. With her last conscious breath,
she told Pichenette Rosemonde's number. Then she fainted.

When she woke up it was night. She was lying in a bed,
with the Professor of History sitting beside her.

'My Prince Charming,' she sighed tenderly.

'What on earth have you been doing to get into such a state?'

'I took a little Sympathetic Powder to help me chase the
Baron. Just one finger. No, wait, five fingers. No, let's see,
fifteen fingers.'

'Are you out of your mind? Copper is fatal in high doses,
even to witches of your calibre.'

But Roberta changed the subject. She told him about her
pursuit of the Baron, his meeting with the golem as witnessed
by herself and Martineau, and her confrontation with the
killer himself.

She wanted to sit up, but when she tried she felt her head
floating towards the ceiling and her limbs reaching out to
the four corners of the room.

'That's funny – I feel as if I were moving huge tentacles instead of my fingers,' she observed in surprise.

'Don't move,' Rosemonde told her. 'I'll be back in five minutes.'

He found the ingredients he needed in the kitchen. Pichenette, who had dozed off in the sitting room, was woken by the noise. He looked in through the kitchen door. His myopic eyes showed him the indistinct figure of a man who, judging by the noisy explosions, must be making a model of a city during an air raid on the kitchen table. He decided to retreat to the sitting room again without making his presence known.

Rosemonde went back up to the bedroom carrying a tankard with the arms of the old city of Munich on it. Roberta, who hadn't moved an inch for fear of turning into something soft and sticky, sniffed the brew he handed her. It was difficult to tell anything about its smell, colour or texture. *Liquid rock* was the most appropriate term she could find for it.

'The best remedy I know for the after-effects of Sympathetic Powder. Isis invented it when she was putting her dismembered husband together again. Drink up.'

Roberta made a face, but she swallowed every last drop of the potion and felt her constituent elements, both physical and mental, slipping back into their old grooves. The process finished at her head, and at last she felt more like herself. She rose, took several steps, and jumped on the bedroom floor with both feet together.

'I'm back in one piece again,' she said, relieved.

Sitting on the edge of the bed, she spent several minutes disentangling her thoughts, which were seriously confused. 'What's the time?' she asked, at the end of this laborious process of readjustment.

'Four in the morning.'

She put on her boots and went to the bathroom to check that her reflection in the mirror was still true to the original. Reassured on that point, she felt a pressing need to clean her teeth. Some friendly hand had put her spongebag beside the basin.

'Is Pichenette still here?' she asked, squeezing ginseng toothpaste on her brush.

'Asleep downstairs,' replied Rosemonde from the bedroom.

'Good.' She began brushing her teeth vigorously. 'Thereshashecondpershon Ishlluvtoqueshtion.'

The Professor of History, who spent most of his time deciphering the indecipherable, translated this mentally and replied, 'So who is this second person you have to question, my love?'

Roberta spat into the basin three times. He thought he heard her say, 'Ragnetrude.'

When she came out of the bathroom Rosemonde was looking upset.

'Even if she can't actually be called a person,' added the witch, defiantly.

Familiar as he was with his companion's opinionated nature, the Professor of History told himself that any attempt to reason with her would be useless. He contented himself with heaving a sigh of resignation.

Sleep had eluded Pichenette, so he was thinking instead. The situation was puzzling, to say the least. Micheau had not been at the meeting place under the Barometer. Neither this woman Morgenstern nor the man who arrived in response to his phone call looked like being the kind of Good Samaritan he needed to get him out of the city. He wondered whether, all things considered, he hadn't simply jumped out of the frying pan and into the fire.

He heard them come downstairs, and then saw their blurred shapes enter the sitting-room. Morgenstern took a chair and sat down facing him. The man began pacing round the room like a militiaman on patrol. In fact Rosemonde was studying the Major's library.

'Are you feeling better?' Pichenette asked Morgenstern, hoping to placate her.

'Who is Micheau?' she asked point-blank.

So he was going to be put through an interrogation. Very well: he would reply to any questions he was asked, giving only small fragments of the truth to start with.

'The Ministry of Security chauffeur,' he said, truthfully. 'You know that as well as I do. You came to see me with him, didn't you?'

Roberta remembered that Pichenette had taken Martineau for Archibald Fould's chauffeur. 'No, I wasn't with Micheau. I was with a CID investigator. If you hadn't lost all three pairs of glasses you'd have realized that at once.'

'Oh no!' said Pichenette, feeling himself shrivel up in his chair. This woman was one of the militia in civilian clothing, a member of the Security staff. They were going to make him pay for his amazing aerial audacity.

'*The Critique of Pure Reason*,' said Rosemonde, picking a book out of the bookcase. 'Ever read it? It's even more abstruse than St Anthony's last vision. Enough to make you tear your hair out.'

Obviously the man was speaking in veiled terms of the atrocious tortures they were planning to inflict on him . . . Roberta attracted the short-sighted Pichenette's attention by taking hold of his chin.

'What were you doing up in that balloon? Who were you distributing that tabloid rag the *Barometer* for?'

She had just insulted what he held most dear: the pen and ink that did duty for his brain. The chest of Ernest Pichenette junior swelled as he once again became the worthy heir to Ernest Pichenette senior.

'It's not a rag, it's an organ of investigative journalism! And I don't work for anyone! I'm an independent freelance, madam! I'd have discovered the identity of the Baron of the Mists if those magic pumpkins hadn't attacked my balloon!'

'Magic pumpkins?' repeated Grégoire and Roberta in unison.

Pichenette gave them a rough outline of the incident, or anyway of what he had been able to see of it. 'It so happens that I walk in my sleep, I've no idea why. So in case I take a nasty tumble I sleep with a lap-pack parachute. On my back,' he explained.

'You're a lucky man,' remarked Roberta.

'No, I'm a provident man.'

'Aha,' said Rosemonde, who had returned to his exploration. 'The pestiferous Schopenhauer's *Magical Library*. Gruber was definitively a man worth knowing.'

Roberta went on with her interrogation. 'What was your connection with Micheau? And don't try wriggling out of it this time.'

Pichenette was sorry to see the militia back in action. He decided to add rather larger fragments of the truth to his replies. 'He was feeding me information. For the *Barometer*, I mean.'

'And?'

'And what?

'What did he want you to do in return for his information?'

This was a woman who would show no mercy. 'I was to keep watch on the municipal jail,' he admitted in a small voice.

'Oh, was that all?' exclaimed the witch. 'I suppose you know that Basle has buildings less sensitive than the jail?'

Why, the writer reproached himself, why had he ever agreed to help that lagoon pirate? Well, because Micheau had revealed that the Baron of the Mists was back in Basle. Because Pichenette junior wanted to finish his father's work. If he hadn't fallen straight into that trap he'd still have his balloon and his life wouldn't be hanging by a thread. A fraying thread at that.

'What are we going to do with you?' the sorceress wondered aloud.

Probably bury me alive in the cellar or the garden, thought the writer, but he kept that reply to himself.

Roberta rose to her feet, went to the window, opened it and breathed in the night air. It was pouring with rain. The light from the sitting room bathed the garden in pale yellow. Had Gruber ever set foot in his little realm of weeds? At least she was more or less certain to find an extension of Ragnetrude there.

'Are you going to question her?' asked Rosemonde, who had joined her.

'She may know about the gene.' Roberta leaned against the Professor of History's shoulder for a bit of comfort.

'Promise me not to anger her,' he demanded.

'*You* promise *me* not to frighten Pichenette any worse than he's frightened already.'

'I'm not a monster, you know! I was thinking of giving him a better idea of what we really are. What do you think?'

'If he's been attacked by a magic pumpkin I expect it's only fair.'

Roberta moved away, and Rosemonde took her place on the chair facing Pichenette. So this one's sticking to me like a limpet now, thought the writer, sure that his last hour had come. A leaden silence fell. The Professor cracked his finger joints. Then he told Pichenette, 'You like scoops. Well, I have a sensational scoop for you.'

The writer swallowed noisily. 'I'm listening. Since I can't really see you.'

'Witches, dragons and magicians really do exist.'

'Oh, puhlease!' For goodness' sake, thought Pichenette, not mental torture too! He'd tell the man everything. He'd invent more if he had to. He tried to speak, but his mouth wouldn't open. Panic constricted his chest.

'I can also turn you into an earthworm and cut you up into tiny pieces if you don't pay attention. And believe me, invertebrates do experience pain.'

Pichenette curbed a gesture of revulsion and shook his head. Feeling quite sorry for him, Rosemonde passed his hand over the writer's face, restoring his eyesight and his power of speech. Pichenette widened his eyes. He could see perfectly now, even without glasses.

'Huh – huh – huh!' he coughed, astonished by the miracle.

Rosemonde pointed to the fireplace. Mauve, purple and yellow flames were flickering on the hearth. Let's keep this simple, he told himself. We'll begin at the beginning with my introductory lecture on the History of Sorcery. He rose and rested his elbow on the mantelpiece. The fire lit him from below, giving him a Satanic appearance.

'Once upon a time . . .' he began in a deep voice.

Very few people had ever met Ragnetrude. Her reputation didn't exactly invite them to try. She was known to be deceitful, devious, gifted in evil. Her priorities were her own, and they were secret and subterranean. Instead of replying to the questions people asked her she would revive bad memories, or create others to accompany them all their lives as night terrors. Or alternatively she might simply content herself with lying.

Ragnetrude was one of the Founding Sisters who made up the Club of Five. No one in the College of Sorcery was quite sure about its origins. It was as old as the world, or so at least it claimed. Ragnetrude, the incarnation of the Earth just as her sisters were the spirits of Air, Water, Fire and the Ether, took no interest in human beings.

But like every immortal worthy of the name she hated solitude, and when she hadn't had a visit from anyone for a long time it made her ready to talk, coaxing and caressing – in short, in the state of mind in which Roberta hoped to find her.

The sorceress picked up her bag, took off her boots, and went out into the garden barefoot, sheltering under her umbrella. The grass of the lawn soon turned to corn-cockle, couch grass and wild poppy. Thistles pricked her ankles. Nettles stung her. However, she went on walking towards the bed of convolvulus in the middle of this little jungle.

Once among the tangled, wild stems, she projected her appeal downwards. She must direct her thoughts to the plants at her feet, let them penetrate the earth, wait for Ragnetrude to show up . . . I suspect all I'll get out of this is a heavy cold, she told herself after five minutes of this fruitless exercise.

She was just about to return to the house when a convolvulus stem coiled around first one of her ankles and then the other, forming a figure of eight and hobbling her legs. Roberta had the strange sensation of hearing a toneless voice speak through her heels.

'You want to talk to me?'

Yes, or I wouldn't be freezing to death out here, thought the sorceress, not bothering to hide her annoyance.

The convolvulus tightened its grip, forcing her to move her legs closer together. Roberta regretting not having armed herself with a sharp knife.

'Close your eyes.'

Roberta did as she was told.

'You can open them now.'

It was a shock to see the kitchen of her parents' house. Sunlight came flooding in through the window. Pigeons were cooing in the gutter. Her mother, with her back turned, was chopping something on a work surface. Roberta almost called out to her, but stopped herself at the last moment.

Ragnetrude turned to face her. She tied her hair back in a pony-tail, a gesture familiar to Roberta, and sipped some Madeira before putting the sliced peppers in a casserole heating up on the gas stove. 'Hello, my dear.' Ragnetrude took a mixer out of a cupboard, switched it on and liquidized a piece of raw meat. Through the window Roberta could see the railway station, Basle and the blue sky, or at least the illusion of them. The mixer stopped and its contents were tipped into the casserole. Roberta remembered why she had come. She was putting her hand in her bag to bring out the DNA codes when the entity said, 'If you want to know what the gene means, keep looking out of the window.'

One of the panes no longer showed Basle, but a landscape of hills covered with olive trees. Peasants were coming and going in the yard of a white-walled farmhouse. Ragnetrude came over to Roberta and looked at the moving picture, wiping her hands on a cloth. She placed a finger on one man who was speaking angrily to another.

'Meet Demetrius, a Corinthian landowner of the fourth century AD. He's angry because one of his slaves has escaped. Tomorrow Demetrius will go to the city and lodge an accusation. If the runaway slave is found he will be smeared with honey and exposed to be eaten by insects.'

Another scene appeared in a second window pane: a battlefield covered with corpses, and a trireme on fire at sea on the horizon. It was not very far from the first scene, and the devastation and the vultures were similar too.

'Salamis, a few years earlier . . . ah, there's our deserter.'

A Spartan who had been playing dead rose from the ground with the greatest of care. He threw away his helmet, greaves, breastplate and shield, and set off at a run without turning to look back.

'He wasn't called Zrcadlo yet, but he was found guilty of cowardice and treachery *in absentia* and condemned to die by the barathrum – you know what that was: tortured to death by being thrown into a pit full of sharp blades.'

The food mixer started, illustrating Ragnetrude's account. A third scene appeared in the window. This one was difficult to date. Armed men were feasting and making merry in an inn. Women came and went. There was a dark, violent atmosphere.

'Those Germans didn't do things by halves!' exclaimed the entity. 'You've no idea how many of the good people of Basle are descended from the prostitutes who were forced to go into exile if they didn't want to die slowly, buried in the mud. Of course, there was no Pill in those days. How many *were* there?' She began counting on her fingers, and then gave up. 'Well, at least as many as those found in the mass grave.'

Ragnetrude tapped a blank pane with her fingernail, and the nightmare picture show acquired a new scene: a medieval town square. A herald on a platform was holding an unrolled parchment scroll in front of him. A dense and colourful crowd was either listening to him or going about its own business.

'Hear ye, hear ye! For Papist connections and plotting against the Crown of England, Clan Chief MacMachin is condemned to be quartered. His limbs, his head and his guts shall be exposed in different parts of town, and his private parts shall be thrown into the fire so that his foul line shall be wiped out!'

Ragnetrude returned to her cooking as new scenes continued to replace their predecessors. Captions accompanied these little silent films: 'A Scythian camp'; 'The soothsayer reads the entrails of a bird while the military commander listens'; 'He predicts a victory over the enemy tribe'; 'After the defeat'; 'A pyre is built'; 'The soothsayer escapes, making for the mysterious region of Bactria'.

That little scene could relate to either Pasqualini or Fliquart. Another took over.

'Aix-la-Chapelle in the time of Charlemagne'; 'The outskirts of the city at night'; 'Highway robbers'; 'A merchant is attacked'; 'Men at arms lie in wait;' 'Interrogation in the dungeons of the imperial palace'; 'They give the name of their leader'; 'The Emperor orders him to be found'.

So Obéron Gruber had a highway robber among his ancestors, thought the witch, with a private smile.

The historical scenes disappeared, and Basle in the recent past showed through the window again. Roberta had remembered the term used by Rosemonde for the inherited mark that they had seen on the Martineau family tree.

'So the mystery gene is a brand,' she said.

'A legacy of shame written into the genetic code. Sentence was passed on these people but never carried out. The modern citizens of Basle were guilty without knowing it. Each of them was born with a little sword of Damocles hanging over his head – or her head. Our executioner, the Baron of the Mists, is only finishing the job.'

'Hello, my dear girl!' Roberta's father had just entered the kitchen. He gave his daughter a hug. 'Had a good day?'

'You know quite well that Roberta is having difficulties at

the moment,' said Ragnetrude sharply. 'How do you expect her to have a *good day* with that Baron to catch?'

Her father had always been rather absent-minded, and it took him a little while to remember. 'Oh yes, of course, the inquiry. That wretched serial killer – have you discovered his identity?'

'Yes,' said Roberta. She would have been so proud to reveal her discovery to her real father.

'Do tell us about it,' said Ragnetrude, with intense curiosity.

The pigeons had stopped cooing. The avatar of her father didn't draw a breath. The second hand of the clock above the door stood still.

'The tracers are the killer. They are merging together, taking human form and acting as executioner.'

There was a moment of complete silence.

'Of course,' murmured the entity Ragnetrude. 'That's why I failed to grasp his essence.'

'*Pede poena claudo*,' quoted Roberta's resuscitated father, who like the original was fond of Latin quotations.

'The punishment follows the crime, limping,' Roberta translated. 'Or you could say, long after the event.'

'Those clever little tracers were created by the College of Sorcery,' Ragnetrude pointed out. 'Do you realize that you witches and sorcerers are directly responsible for all these deaths?'

'No,' protested Roberta. 'There's something else going on. It's to do with the Records Office. And Fould.'

'Ah yes, of course. The Intriguer.' The clock struck one. 'Come along, time for lunch. The casserole won't wait.'

Roberta knew she had only to project her thoughts upwards to leave. But she sat there with her plate in front of her, marvelling with girlish naivety as the replica of her father described the minor events of the day. She had decided to regard what was going on around her as a kind of waking dream. Ragnetrude did not see it the same way. She didn't want to leave her visitor with pleasant memories, and thought this the right moment to make her suffer a little.

'You think we're dead, don't you?' she said in detached tones. 'You think we were carried away by the Great Flood?' She placed her hand over her husband's. 'I can tell you one thing: the earth has not yet welcomed us in.' The entity smiled. Roberta's father said nothing. 'Or that hedgehog of yours either, by the way, though it's quite some time since I felt his little claws scratch my surface.' She turned to her husband. 'You remember Hans-Friedrich, the telepathic hedgehog?'

'Yes, yes,' said the man, his mind elsewhere.

'Of course, that doesn't mean anything. He could have drowned.'

Roberta knew that Ragnetrude wasn't lying, because for a moment they had been thinking in unison. She wanted to ask more questions, but now the entity expelled her. The sorceress felt herself being projected upwards, and next moment she was back in the garden of Major Gruber's house, with the rain drumming on her umbrella. A pale dawn was breaking, her feet were frozen, but a little voice was singing away in her head, in her stomach and in her heart: 'Mama and Papa did not return to the earth. They really didn't.'

'The fact that Ragnetrude has failed to see them doesn't mean that your parents are still alive,' said Rosemonde, filling Roberta's cup to the brim as if to back up what he said. 'To be sure of that, you'd have to find and question the other four entities present at the dawn of the world. As far as I know no one has ever done such a thing.'

Morgenstern gave Rosemonde a defiant glance. Pichenette, standing behind the Professor of History, had been listening intently to the witch's account. In future he was going to be very careful about walking across gardens.

'At the same time, it's certainly encouraging,' admitted Rosemonde.

'Oh, let's change the subject,' said Roberta, and a fraught silence fell between the two of them.

'I am reminded of an edifying story by the fact that the killer and the tracers are one and the same,' began Pichenette, looking at them. 'My tale is set in India during the rule of the Maharajahs. We are in Jodhpur, in the year of grace 1873 . . .'

Rosemonde and Morgenstern were only half listening, and left him to indulge his enthusiasm. 'So the tracers are behind this lethal game,' said the Professor thoughtfully. 'The wind was the right trail to follow.'

'And so was the trail leading to the Records Office and the mystery gene. It was the pipes coming out of the back of the Community building that sent the surface wind blowing over Basle at certain fixed days and hours.'

Pichenette was continuing his story for the benefit of a selection of spices arranged on Major Gruber's mantelpiece. 'Three men in the prime of life were strangled in their sleep by hands of impossible size. The hands of a giant. The hands of a monster. Rumour ran riot in Jodhpur. A gigantic monkey was said to be spreading terror through the city . . .'

Roberta drank her coffee in little sips. 'This is good.'

'It's Egyptian.'

'Egypt again? Isis isn't among your former conquests, is she?'

Rosemonde, who almost never blushed, did so now. He made use of the joker that Roberta had already played. 'Let's change the subject,' he said evasively.

'. . . and the country's top tiger hunters were invited to

Jodhpur. They marked off a zone to the north of the city where they were sure the creature must be lying low. The hunt began. The Maharajah signalled the start by sounding a trumpet which, according to the palace historian, had once belonged to Saladin in person . . .'

Roberta finished her cup of coffee. 'I'm going to the College. I shall call for an extraordinary general meeting. As soon as possible. Today.'

'We could organize it for noon,' suggested Rosemonde, 'and then I can take the opportunity to explore Barnabite's observatory.'

'Did you go into the garden?'

'I have what I need, don't worry.'

Pichenette, facing the window, and no doubt seeing not the curtain of rain but the Brahmaputra flowing on into the fathomless eternal night, was still declaiming. 'At long last the beast's lair was discovered. When the Jodhpur police chief discovered a pair of gloves made from carefully hollowed-out bear's paws, he put them on and became a demon with incredible strength. He killed three men in trying to escape. Finally he was overpowered. The killer and the policeman charged with arresting him, although they were the same man, knew nothing about each other. We are told that Stevenson visited him in the Bentham asylum where he ended his days. No one knows whether his last breath was that of a man or a beast.'

Pichenette had finished. He turned round and was delighted to see Morgenstern and Rosemonde looking at him. They had actually been listening to his story! But neither of them seemed to want to applaud.

'Did you give him some kind of Egyptian brew to drink too?' asked Roberta, without taking her eyes off the strange phenomenon.

'No, but he says he's got his eyesight back.'

'Fancy that. You don't think he's lost a few of his mental powers in exchange?'

'My students are always a little odd after my introductory lecture. I put it down to something like the bends that divers get, on account of the depths.'

Roberta remembered how she too had found it difficult to sleep after hearing that very same lecture almost thirty years ago. And yet she knew even then that sorcery existed.

The rain had emptied the Great Court of its students. The University looked dismal and deserted. There was no one on supervision duty at the entrance to the School of Practical Studies, the anteroom of the College. Voices could be heard in the lecture hall at the end of the corridor. Roberta went over to the half-open door and ventured to cast a glance inside.

The staff of the School were gathered around a buffet lunch, and the noise level suggested that it was well under way. Jagrège, a specialist in Aztec civilization, was holding forth about the hieroglyph of Montezuma, which he had been privileged to see on a document in Archibald Fould's office three years earlier. He had never set eyes on that document again, despite repeated letters asking to see it. Some of the lecturers were discussing the night when Napoleon visited the pyramid of Cheops in Egypt. You could heard Old Norse spoken here, Chaldaean there.

'What's the party in aid of?' whispered Rosemonde, who had just come up behind her.

'Some kind of anniversary,' she deduced.

'Of the Deluge, the Fall of the Roman Empire or the final disappearance of Atlantis?'

They made their way into the library of the School of Practical Studies, which was of course empty. A soldiers' drinking song echoed down the corridor.

'You can tell there's a temple of Bacchus in the vicinity,' said Strudel, who had just joined them. 'Almost every time I'm here I find them opening bottles.'

Rosemonde pressed a switch hidden behind a hook. A door in a dark corridor leading on from the School looked as if it were blocked up, but it buzzed with the sound of an electric lock. Eleazar pulled it open, and it closed behind them as if it weighed a ton. They had just entered the precincts of the College of Sorcery.

They followed winding stairways and passages to reach the amphitheatre, where the oil lamps had been lit. The three spiralling tiers of seats symbolizing the three states of matter (solid, liquid and sublimated, working from the ground up to the sky) were half full. Roberta placed herself behind the speaker's lectern brought in for her.

The students were gathered around their respective teachers. Vandenberghe and Boewens were chatting on the lowest spiral. Lusitanus was dozing next to Plenck. Martineau wasn't there. Roberta had left a message for him at the Community Building, but was told that he was in a meeting on the top floor. As for Rosemonde, he had stationed himself by the exit from the amphitheatre, and was biding his time.

Barnabite and Banshee were the last to arrive and installed themselves on the highest point of the spiral, causing ripples to run through the compact body of their own students. The University clock chimed twelve. Lusitanus shook off his lethargy. Vandenberghe rose and waited for silence to fall.

'Witches, sorcerers and students! Our colleague has requested this extraordinary general meeting, and in the great tradition of the Sabbath we are here. She is granted the Devil's Minute during which no one may interrupt her.' The rector of the College placed one hand on the timer fixed to the wooden ramp in front of him. 'Roberta Morgenstern, the floor is yours.'

Everyone was looking at her, and Grégoire took advantage of this moment to slip out. Vandenberghe turned the timer upside down, and the first grains of sand fell into the lower container. Roberta knew that a minute would be too short for what she had to say anyway, so she went straight to the heart of the matter.

'We ourselves created the Baron of the Mists,' she immediately told the scholarly gathering, 'and we alone can stop him.'

Rosemonde went back along the corridor, past the celestial charts on its walls, crossed the Paracelsus Hall and opened the library door. Once inside, he made straight for the shelves where Hector Barnabite kept his precious *in verso* volumes. Barnabite and Banshee took a magic short cut to the sanctuary, and the book through which they passed couldn't be far away.

An expert on the subject himself, he stroked the precious bindings. A work slipped into his hand. Rosemonde put it down on a desk: Dante's *Inferno* illustrated by Doré. The book opened at the right passage. The full-page engraving showed the author and Virgil hesitating on the threshold of the entrance to Hell.

Grégoire stepped over the line around the engraving and found himself in a two-dimensional world of half-colours. He made his way past the motionless shapes of the two travellers and through the gateway, without stopping to read the warning carved over the lintel, which he knew by heart anyway. The same scene awaited him on the other side, but with both the shadows and the composition inverted. He made his way past the negative images of Dante and Virgil, stepped over the edge of the picture, and emerged from the book.

There was a light on in Hector's crypt. The athanor furnace

was purring away in its corner. A thick white liquid was running through a spiral tube between two bubbling flasks. Rosemonde prudently closed the *in verso* as you might close a door. He climbed up from the crypt to the ground floor, along the corridor with its smell of goulash, and out into the garden. Rain was pouring down on the rampart of poisonous flowers.

The copper pipe that Roberta had mentioned disappeared under the densely grown flowers in the direction of the observatory. A barrier of dead insects and small rodents marked a border that must not be passed. The sweet, intoxicating scent of lilac and jasmine in this garden was as dangerous as the miasma of plague or cholera.

Rosemonde took an atomizer out of his pocket. He had filled it with a distillation of one of his medicinal plants, a ragwort, which had explored Banshee's plot in the witches' garden like a hard-working missionary. The ragwort had been an excellent spy, mingling its roots with those of the poisoned plants to remove a little of the toxic sap and transform their chemical constitution. Now to see if it worked.

Rosemonde sprayed himself with the atomizer, turned up his coat collar, drew his head down between his shoulders, cursing himself for leaving his umbrella behind in the College, and walked straight towards the trap, with full confidence in his method. The flower bed of bright purple sprinkled with white opened up in front of him, revealing a path that ran straight to the observatory. Rosemonde quickly made for the shelter of the flight of steps.

Copper carbonate seeping from the verdigris dome had left long, venomous tracks all down the windows, and they were black with dirt too. Although Rosemonde tried looking through a pane at close quarters through the frame of his hands, he could see nothing of the interior.

He opened the door; no one had taken the trouble to lock it.

Roberta's news was received with concerted and incredulous murmuring. Banshee rose, almost interrupting the Devil's Minute. On meeting Vandenberghe's reproving gaze she restrained herself. A quarter of the sand had already run through the glass. Roberta decided to continue in spite of everything and everyone.

She told them about the wind and the ducts behind the Records Office. She described the mysterious gene, linking it to the tracers and their ability to read DNA. She spoke of her encounter with the Baron, and the way he had vanished into thin air.

The minute was over. No one said anything, and Roberta seized her chance to carry on. 'The tracer manufacturing plant must be taken out of operation at once. We're launching a million killers into the air of the city every week.'

At last the audience emerged from its stupefaction, and its reactions showed which way any vote would go. The majority, with Banshee at their centre, were vociferous. The minority remained silent. In the midst of all this pandemonium Martineau turned up. Roberta gave him a little wave, which he returned with an apologetic smile. Then he sat down beside Lusitanus. Banshee had risen to her feet.

'Our dear sister Roberta is famous for her clairvoyance,' she began. 'And hers is indeed a bold theory. But the tracers are tiny. They wouldn't hurt a fly!'

'We are made up of atoms,' replied the witch, who had thought this aspect of the problem out for herself. 'They could assemble, they could become conscious—'

'Oh, brilliant!' Banshee interrupted her. 'Conscious dust-motes in human form! Frankly, this is pure science fiction.' Her voice was cutting. 'Anyway, it's unthinkable for us to stop the machinery in Records. The tracers are a godsend to the College. The Ministry pays us for the use of them. You said a million killers? I say a million dollars. They are at the very heart of the Charter which unites us with the Municipality. They ensure that we are left alone. What would happen if we suddenly refused to produce them?'

'The innocent citizens of Basle would stop dying,' replied Roberta.

The hubbub reached new heights, but fell silent when Otto Vandenberghe rose and moved his stooped figure over to the desk. Roberta made way for him with immense relief.

'Roberta Morgenstern has made serious allegations – too serious for us to shout at each other like fishwives!' thundered the old man. He still had an air of authority. 'She has made a proposition. We shall now take a vote to decide what is best to be done. Are you for or against stopping the operation of the plant in Records? The consequences for our own welfare could indeed be devastating. But if the tracers are killing people then it is up to us to do something about it.'

Banshee murmured, in honeyed tones, 'Couldn't we postpone this vote, Rector? I'm busy with something at the moment, and . . .'

'Your something can wait. Martineau! You and Monsieur Strudel go and find the urn for the ballot. And don't get lost on the way.'

Heated argument broke out again. Banshee kept looking at Roberta, as if measuring her up with a view to putting the evil eye on her in future. Let's hope she's forgotten about Grégoire, the sorceress said to herself. He hadn't come back yet, and she was beginning to feel anxious. Martineau and Strudel returned with the urn, which in fact was a plain black wooden ballot box. Banshee looked very discontented when she found out that they were going to vote by both ballot papers and a show of hands.

'This will take an hour,' she complained to Barnabite under her breath.

'Don't worry,' he replied. 'It will be some time before the sulphur reaches the matrix. And the golem is on guard.'

Banshee turned a glare that would have terrified a famished jackal on her colleague, and suggested to him, mouthing the words, 'Why not just take Morgenstern's place at the desk and tell the whole College what we're doing? I doubt if you'd keep your job as librarian very long.'

Barnabite went red and decided to keep quiet. Meanwhile, the urn was placed in the centre of the amphitheatre, voting papers were handed out, and the students were buzzing around their teachers like furious bees.

Morgenstern took her chance to ask Martineau what he had been doing since they parted on the jetty. He shrugged the question off and said, aggressively, 'What's all this about the tracers? Have you gone off your head?'

Roberta stared at him, astonished. Why was Clément speaking to her in this tone? 'What's up, dear boy? Don't tell me you're angry!'

'Of course I'm angry! And don't call me "dear boy",' he snapped, showing his teeth. He tried to calm down, but Roberta had never seen him in such a state before. 'Accusing the tracers is as bad as accusing the Minister himself,' he went on.

The sorceress had recovered from the first shock, and she was tired of being taken for an idiot. 'I congratulate you on your powers of analysis,' she retorted. 'Your mother is certainly right: a brilliant future with Security lies before you.'

Martineau wasn't letting go. He started out by praising Fould's integrity before putting forward his own theory, which was that of the great majority: the Baron came from the Historic Quarter.

'So just how would the gypsies make that wind blow?' asked Roberta.

'With their windmills. Did you see the number of windmills on the roofs of the Historic Quarter? They use them as ventilators. It's obvious.'

Hardly knowing what argument to use against such a woolly-minded theory, she let him go on.

'And didn't the Queen of the Gypsies give her support to the outgoing Mayor? The immigrant vote could make all the difference. Are Count Palladio's former protégés so very far from sorcery themselves? I mean, they found you that telepathic hedgehog.'

'Yes, indeed,' she agreed. 'If the wind doesn't come from above then it comes from below. That's only logical.'

Martineau looked pleased to see her falling in with his views. So Roberta Morgenstern was showing a little sense at last! It was a shock when she said brusquely, 'You've become putty in the hands of the hierarchy, which saddens me. Is there as much air as all that in your head? You once wanted to fly to the moon, and now it looks as if you're aiming no higher than the roof of the Community Building!'

The voting interrupted this conversation. In his corner seat, Martineau took advantage of the inevitable pause to quell his anger. Once the votes were counted he'd tell his former partner the bad news in person. She was asking for it, and he had no reason to wait now.

Grégoire did not have such sharp, catlike eyes as Roberta, and the jumble of objects he saw gave him few clues. But gradually the observation instruments of the astronomer Tycho Brahe, brought with him into exile from Uraniborg, emerged from the darkness. Barnabite had piled them at the sides of the room to clear some of the restricted space.

Armillary spheres stood on top of each other, meridians stood side by side, parallactic rulers were stacked all anyhow in dilapidated pigeon-holes. A telescope lay between two brass astrolabes. Three clocks showing three different times stood in front of a model of the Zodiac from which entire constellations were missing.

The golem was on guard in a corner of this astronomical rubbish dump. It walked towards Rosemonde, who saw it coming but did not move. The colossus spread its red clay arms to crush the intruder. Now Rosemonde moved, and faster than the golem. He plunged his hand into its clay mouth and took out the phylactery which acted as the creature's consciousness. The golem stopped dead, arms still spread wide.

Rosemonde unrolled the parchment and ran his eye over the two hundred and twenty-one combinations of mystic signs that Barnabite had written to give the creature life. He found the one which gave the order to kill any intruder, erased it, and put the phylactery back. The being quivered, lowered its arms, and stood aside to let the visitor pass.

The copper pipe which crossed the garden ran level with the floor in here, leading up to a machine as tall as a cupboard. At its heart was a translucent tank with a complicated device holding it in place. It looked like a giant egg mounted in a metal framework of ornate Celtic design. Regular, silent flashes of light shot through it, like the lightning of a hot thunderstorm in a summer night sky.

The copper pipe branched out into a dozen ramifications which penetrated the base of the egg. Other channels, made of glass, carried fluids away. The golem was following Rosemonde. The explosions of colour were growing in intensity and cast patterns on the golem, making it look like a melancholy clown.

A yellowed piece of cardboard was tied with string to

a control panel on the side of the device. Rosemonde recognized the symbols for the elements of matter invented by John Dalton, one of the fathers of atomic theory. Most of the signs were crossed out or blocked out; the others represented sulphur, potassium, magnesium and iron. Rosemonde was interested by the egg. Its walls were like rock crystal, and coloured shapes coiled and scrolled inside it, presenting the image of a nebula being born, faint and dull, but active.

The pulsing accelerated. A human form emerged from the gassy swirls. It was still incomplete, but attached to life by a few frail filaments. Its heart set off tiny explosions of light. The huddled shape was sprinkled with gold dust. The internal organs were only dark patches with blurred edges, but the embryo's eyes were wide open. And they were looking at the Professor of History.

A violent jolt shook the baby. It stretched, fell feebly back, and stretched again. Rosemonde, deeply moved, felt that he should do something, but the golem placed a clammy hand on his shoulder to reassure him.

'Hic,' said the clay being.

Rosemonde understood what the golem was telling him, and they both kept watch on the baby until its hiccups died down.

'Roberta Morgenstern's motion has been rejected by seventy-two votes to twenty-seven,' announced Otto Vandenberghe. 'The manufacturing plant in Records will not cease operating.' Applause echoed through the high spiral tiers of seating. 'Quiet, please! Thank you. Let me remind you that the inauguration of Paris Street, which the College of Sorcery has helped to construct, takes place tomorrow in the Historic Quarter. You're all invited. On which note, and for time eternal, may all the horrors of darkness be with you!'

This rhetorical flourish had made no sense at all since the College signed the White Charter and stopped holding Black Sabbaths, but Vandenberghe had never really shaken off a certain nostalgia for tradition. He struck the desk with a small mallet, and the meeting was over. The three spirals emptied. Roberta was looking anxiously out at the corridor when Banshee planted herself in front of her.

'I'm sure your intentions are very praiseworthy,' she hissed. 'But I advise you to go no further. I mean, who'd believe you? Everyone will think you're mad. And if what you say were really true, do you think Archibald Fould would let the tracers kill his fellow citizens?'

'Yes, as a matter of fact I do.'

Banshee flinched, as if shocked by her colleague's frankness. 'So that's your notion! You are speaking of the Minister of Security!'

'And the man who already sees himself as Mayor. A killer at large is a useful asset if you can arrest him a few days before the polls open, don't you think? Unless the Baron of the Mists is intended for some purpose other than just winning votes?'

Banshee frowned. Barnabite was fidgeting impatiently behind her like a vampire at the approach of dawn. 'I was in the middle of an experiment,' he said. 'I have to go back to my laboratory.'

'Go on, then! You don't need a nanny.'

The alchemist didn't wait, but set off towards the library. He met Rosemonde coming out of it, his coat soaked and his shoes covered with mud. Banshee looked at the Professor suspiciously as he approached.

'Have you been out in the rain? Did you by any chance give us all the slip?'

Rosemonde was crushing a delicate jasmine flower in his fingers. On seeing it, Banshee registered his silent response and turned pale. She gave him and Roberta a look that would have turned a gorgon to stone, and set off after Barnabite down the corridor lined with celestial charts. The stars trembled as she passed.

'She suspects something now,' said the sorceress.

'I like confusing people. And now I know what they're up to.'

Here Martineau joined them, with an inscrutable look on his face. 'Listen, I won't be working under your orders on the trail of the tracers,' he told Roberta. 'In fact I won't be working under your orders *at all*. Archibald Fould has officially put me in charge of the case. You'll be obeying *my* orders from now on.'

'What did you say?'

'I – I said I'm in charge of the case.'

'You're in charge of the case?'

'I shall do all I can to arrest that monster,' he promised. Looking around him, he dropped his voice to a whisper, although by now the amphitheatre was almost empty. 'And to find out what Banshee and Barnabite are up to with the golem. It's connected with the Baron. The gypsies have always had links with the Kabbalah. Monsieur Rosemonde will back me up there, I'm sure.'

The Professor of History said nothing. Contrary to Martineau's expectations, Roberta seemed to be taking the news rather well.

'Congratulations,' she told the investigator. 'Please thank the Minister for me. He gives me more of a free hand than I had already.'

'What – what do you mean?'

'You have your own office now, I imagine?'

'You bet!' he said proudly. 'With a great view of Basle!'

Roberta slipped her arm into Grégoire's and told the newly promoted head of the CID, in a tone usually reserved for condolences, 'Then my letter of resignation will be on your desk this evening. Goodbye, Monsieur Martineau.'

The Snake in the Grass

Archibald Fould kept it a close secret, but he was a fervent believer in reincarnation. He would have given much to know who or what had died on Earth at the exact moment of his conception. He rather hoped it was a pit viper, a cousin of the rattlesnake which does not announce its presence by rattling.

Heavy rain carried on the wind beat against the large window of his office. The term Deluge was now being officially employed. The water within the dam of the lagoon was rising fifty centimetres every day. At this rate the low-lying parts of Basle would be submerged in less than two weeks. That did not prevent the Minister from feeling very pleased with himself. Very pleased indeed.

The Baron of the Mists had given his most spectacular and bloodthirsty performance of all under the Barometer. The rain and the monster worked together to keep fear alive in the hearts of the people of Basle. Prisoners of their terrible situation, his fellow citizens would soon be ready to accept the grand project he planned to put before them. Lord Mayor Fould the First allowed himself a jubilant and icy chuckle.

The interphone jolted him out of his dreams. He pressed the winking green button which indicated the internal line. 'Yes?'

It was his secretary. 'I have the editor in chief of the *Mainland News* on the line, sir, and . . .'

'And he's in a hurry. I know. Tell him I'll dictate you my bulletin. His typesetters can wait a few minutes longer.'

It was necessary to sum up the situation. Fould pressed the yellow button.

'Aye, aye, sir,' replied his chief of militia, who had been trained in the British style.

'What are the latest figures for the victims of the Barometer incident?'

'Twenty-one dead, fifty injured. Most of the dead were heart attacks. And a few people crushed to death, not counting the man who was torn apart.'

'And all this in broad daylight in front of twenty thousand witnesses,' lamented Fould with considerable pleasure. 'What does the latest opinion poll say?'

'Out of a thousand people questioned, 92.6% are frankly worried, 6.5% are on the brink of panic, and 0.9% don't know.'

'The Baron is the focus of anxiety, I suppose?'

'And the rain. The figures tend to show that the two are linked. Replies to the new question about the Baron's origin are revealing. Shall I go on?'

'Do.'

The Minister took a cigarette out of a silver case with his initials on it, lit it, and listened to the results of the opinion poll given by the chief of militia.

'2.5% think he's a creature from outer space, 3.2% believe he's a lagoon pirate, but 56.8% of the people of Basle are pointing the finger at the Historic Quarter. And incidentally, new demonstrations are planned for today.'

'Close off the Quarter,' Fould told him. 'I'm going there myself for the inauguration ceremony.'

'But sir, we can't guarantee your security!'

'I *am* Security,' Fould reminded him wearily.

He pressed the yellow button to cut the connection. In one week's time, the first round of the elections is held, he thought. In two weeks' time the low-lying areas are under water and the second round of the elections takes place, the heroic Fould expels the Baron of the Mists, orders the rain to stop falling, and becomes master of Basle.

And to do all that he needed to have the baby ready.

He pressed the red button. The secure line made the office hum like a Faraday cage. Barnabite's amplified, metallic voice uttered a cheerful, 'Hi there!'

'Er, good day, Hector. How's the little creature doing?'

'The baby . . . can you hear me there? Let's see . . .'

The Minister had been to the alchemist's lair only once, but he could picture him consulting his list of primal elements taken from Fulton, from Morton, who knew where else?

'The calcium took all right. There are still four elements to go. Potassium and—'

'Oh, for goodness' sake, hand me the phone!'

The Minister shivered at the sound of Carmilla Banshee's voice. He couldn't wait for the day when he would be able to speak to her in that tone himself.

'Calling from your eyrie in Security, I hope?'

'No one can hear us,' Fould reassured her. 'How far on are you with the project?'

'Another four elements to go, and I should warn you that they're not the easiest elements to acquire.'

'Couldn't your Frankenstein have helped himself under the Barometer? I mean, twenty-one bodies – what more do you want?'

'We can take only a single element at a time. And Frankenstein was the name of the scientist, not the monster he created.'

'All right, all *right*.'

'And we were told to be discreet, weren't we, Minister?'

'So you need four more deaths.'

'And the next has to be a slow death,' Banshee said.

'Slow? I know when the Baron kills, but not how!' he protested. 'Why a slow death?'

'Well, the next stage is to integrate potassium, which easily catches fire in the open air. But terror fixes the elements, partially solidifying them. If the victim sees his death coming – oh, I'm not about to give a politician a lecture on alchemy. I might as well play the Jew's harp in deep space. It has to be a slow death, full stop.'

Fould did not reply at once. He took a pamphlet out of his inside jacket pocket. *A Study of the Surface Winds Passing Through Basle*. The title page showed a delicately engraved compass rose. How lucky that Martineau had mentioned it to him the very day after poor Obéron Gruber's death – peace be to his ashes minus one primordial element. Amen. His secret visit to Archives two weeks earlier to get hold of the pamphlet had paid off, and the packet of thunderbolt herb pressed upon him by Banshee had been particularly good at removing all signs of his presence there.

He opened the invaluable pamphlet at the monthly timetable of the wind and its unexplained manifestations. The Baron was going to offer them only three opportunities over the next two weeks. Three, not four.

'Well?' said Banshee impatiently.

'Will your golem be free around twelve noon today?'

'Twelve noon again! Why? Do you want to invite it to lunch?'

'That'd be rather early for lunch. No, I had something more like an aperitif in mind. In the Historic Quarter.'

There was a pause at the other end of the line.

'Whereabouts in the Quarter is the Baron going to show up?'

'I can't tell you for certain. My sources are not exact on that point. But be on your guard. That's the only good advice the Minister of Security can give you.'

'And the same to you, my good man,' croaked Banshee before hanging up.

Fould pressed the red button, and the humming of the secure line stopped. Matters were moving faster than he had expected, but at least they were going the way he wanted. Was he taking a risk in attending the inauguration of Paris Street? His own DNA profile in Records was locked away, untouchable, impossible to modify. On the other hand, and thanks to his forethought, all the gypsies' profiles were being updated. The Baron would be spoilt for choice.

He pressed the yellow button. There was a click. At the other end of the line, the chief of militia was standing to attention. 'All present and correct, sir.'

'Has Roberta Morgenstern been in the Community Building since the day before yesterday?'

Clément Martineau had come to report a few hours after the scene of panic in the central square, and had told a very attentive Archibald Fould about the execution, how he and the sorceress, in hiding at the jetty, had seen what happened there, and how she then chased off after the Baron of the Mists . . . She had an annoying tendency to get too close to their purveyor of corpses, thought Fould. Well, Martineau had not voiced the slightest objection when he said he was going to sack her. Now he must take sterner measures.

'No, sir,' the chief of militia confirmed. 'I'm told she phoned, but she hasn't been here for a couple of days.'

'Remove her name from the team and cancel her safe-conduct pass. Until the Baron is behind bars,' said Fould, smiling at this impossible image, 'we must clamp down on any breach of discipline.'

Clamping down was second nature to the military man. 'Do you want her followed by the tracers?' he suggested with enthusiasm.

'Why not? Yes, good idea. Have her followed.'

Fould pressed the yellow button. It was time for him to flex his muscles and go into overdrive as mayoral candidate. He pressed the green button.

'Yes, sir?' said his secretary.

'You can send the *Mainland News* the third press release.'

'You mean the one where . . .' The secretary hesitated. 'The one where you mention the end of the world, and . . .'

'And promise to save Basle from the forces of darkness, yes, that one.' A thought crossed his mind. 'You don't doubt my ability to defeat the monsters who threaten our security, do you?'

'Me? Oh no, not for a moment, sir,' she replied with sincere feeling.

Archibald Fould pressed the green button again with a feeling close to exaltation. He imagined himself as a pit viper fighting an improbable dragon . . . Back to the green button for his secretary, who replied at once. 'Your press release is in the pneumatic post, sir.'

'Thanks. Bring in the visitor who's waiting to see me, my dear.'

'Yes, sir,' she whispered, wholly won over to the cause of her lord and master.

The double door padded with red velour opened to show the figure of Clément Martineau. Martineau had passed a bad night.

'Come on in, Clément. We have our work cut out for us.'

The young – very young – head of the CID handed his

Minister a letter. 'From Roberta Morgenstern. She wants you to accept her resignation.'

Fould read the letter, unable to believe his eyes. Wasn't the witch even going to give him the satisfaction of firing her? He countersigned her request, went out of his office and gave it to his secretary. 'A copy to the Mayor and one to Records,' he said.

Trembling with excitement, her cheeks red and her eyes bright, the young woman took the piece of paper.

Roberta was listening to the rain drumming down on the roof with the duvet pulled up to her nose. This was her first lie-in for ages, and she was making the most of it. Grégoire, who had got up to make breakfast, came back with a tray worthy of a four-star hotel. He put it down between them and lounged nonchalantly on the bed.

'You're an angel,' sighed Roberta, looking at what he had concocted. Rosemonde frowned. 'Though a fallen one, didn't you say?' she made haste to correct herself.

They began their breakfast in silence, but Roberta Morgenstern's silence never lasted long.

'How's our tame hack doing?'

'Wants to get started on a historical novel but hasn't picked the period yet. Pichenette, I suspect, is a bit of a crackpot.'

A piece of toast and half a mug of coffee later, Roberta exclaimed, 'Oh, I feel so wonderfully free! Goodbye CID! Goodbye all my worries!'

Rosemonde dunked his bread and butter in his coffee, which offended Roberta's sensibilities. She made no comment, but she did mutter, 'I've no objection to that couple reviving the golem – but hatching plots in cahoots with the Baron of the Mists is something else!' Rosemonde was spooning up the sodden remains of his bread and butter.

'Extracting the elements from corpses to bring a child into the world!' she continued. 'I'd never have expected that even of them.'

'We agreed to put all these puzzles aside for the next twenty-four hours, didn't we?' he reminded her.

'Sorry. You're right.' She finished her coffee, slurping noisily, which usually infuriated Grégoire, but he in his turn made no comment.

'Do you still want to go to the inauguration?' he asked.

'Oh yes, don't you? One thing's for sure, the wretched so-and-so' – here she made a face like Banshee – 'won't be there. She hates cheerful occasions. And as for that other so-and-so, *he* won't show himself in the Historic Quarter today. It's going to be Martineau's job to stir up bad feeling now.'

'We agreed not to say his name either until tomorrow morning.'

'Quite true,' said Roberta, putting the breakfast tray down beside the bed. 'Whatever am I thinking of?'

Leaning over to put her cup on the duvet, she let the quilt slide right down to her waist.

'Oh dear!' she said, one hand over her mouth, miming surprised innocence. She had taken advantage of Grégoire's absence to remove her pyjama top, and now she fluttered her eyelashes at the door, which closed without a sound. The quilt slipped all the way down to her feet. Her pyjama trousers had already joined the top. 'Shall we dance?' she suggested.

'On the bed?'

'In the bed.'

There wasn't all that much difference.

The key fitted itself slowly into the lock and turned, double-locking the door. The rain adjusted itself to keep time with them, beginning *moderato amoroso*.

★ ★ ★

A checkpoint had been set up at the bottom of the ramp leading to the Historic Quarter, and a dozen militiamen were guarding it. The wording on banners fixed to the railings proclaimed: 'Travellers Are Killers' and 'Gypsies Drink Blood!'

Grégoire and Roberta showed their papers to the militiamen, who let them pass. Small covered pony-traps were waiting on the other side of the checkpoint, and they got into the first available. The driver cracked his whip and they trotted off towards the Quarter, where the unfurled velarium looked like a gigantic marquee. The lagoon had invaded the waste land at the foot of the slope, restoring it to its original marshy state. A wooden footbridge had been set up over the sloping bank here.

Once they were under cover in the main street they put back the hood of the carriage. They turned right after Notre-Dame, passed through a carriage entrance flanked by two massive towers, and found themselves in Paris Street. The gypsy driver dropped them off and went back to pick up other visitors.

The place was not so much a street as a rectangular square surrounded by buildings with gables and covered wooden galleries, sturdy corbels and fantastic gargoyles. Ponies were being groomed in a stable under a small house with a thatched roof. Their fodder and droppings were scattered over the ground.

'The gypsies showing what they can do yet again,' commented Rosemonde, turning to appreciate the reconstruction. 'Let's join the party.'

About a hundred guests were circulating among tables set up outside the Great Gables, a replica of the house of Nicolas Flamel the famous alchemist. Strudel had done the catering. Hams, pâtés, filled rolls, terrines . . . he had provided a banquet fit for their surroundings. A cask of wine was enthroned in the middle of the dishes.

Roberta kissed the innkeeper. 'The Flamel vintage?' she asked.

'Improved since last time you tried it. I purified it with ether,' he told her, winking. He filled a glass from the tap fitted at the base of the cask. Roberta tasted the wine, winked back at him and, now decidedly pink-cheeked, joined Rosemonde and Vandenberghe, who were deep in discussion with the Mayor.

'Miss Morgenstern,' said the old man, bowing. 'I hear you've left the Criminal Investigation Department?'

'Goodness, was the news of my resignation important enough to reach you?'

'You're not just anyone, you know. And for a few more days at least, Monsieur Fould is one of my fifteen ministers. I must admit that I'm taking my chance to make life tough for him – from the administrative point of view, that is.' He shrugged his shoulders. 'I understand why you're leaving. I already know that my Minister of Security plans to see me back in private life too.'

'You can win this election,' Vandenberghe assured the Mayor.

'Well, yes, I shall get through the first round. But then what?' The Rector of the College did not reply. 'And I can tell you that I don't find the prospect of serving a city which is reverting to hatred and intolerance particularly attractive. That said, this wine is delicious, don't you think? I really feel as if I were in medieval Paris. Time travel on the spot – I love it. That smell of horse dung – all we need is plague and the cholera to make us believe in it.'

'You never said a truer word,' muttered the witch.

A dozen little pony-traps were driving into the square. Militiamen in civilian dress got out to post themselves at key positions in Paris Street, while the leading carriage drove up to the buffet. Fould and Martineau were sitting in the back of it, the former all smiles, the latter looking ill at ease. The Mayor made haste to drain his glass, grimacing, but not because of the wine.

'Please excuse me. Municipal obligations.' And he went to greet his Minister of Security.

'Was he expected to be part of the programme?' murmured Roberta, watching the two men shake hands.

'I don't think so,' said Rosemonde.

Vandenberghe joined them. 'We'd like to talk to you. By "we" I mean Amatas, Eleazar, I myself and our students. About the tracers. You're right, Roberta. We have to do something.'

She almost protested that she had given in her notice to the CID. But of course she was still on the staff of the College of Sorcery. 'If you like,' she said.

'At the pelota court,' said Rosemonde in an undertone. 'It'll be quieter there.'

'All right. In an hour's time then, at the pelota court in Mexico Street,' suggested Roberta, and Otto Vandenberghe left them.

'I'd say things are beginning to move fast,' commented Rosemonde, watching the old Rector passing on details of the secret meeting to his fellow conspirators. Then he turned to look. 'Ah, the Queen.'

This was the first time Roberta had seen the Queen of the Gypsies, who presided over the colony in the Historic Quarter. She was coming out of the house where the ponies stood in their stable, on her own and wearing a simple gold silk sari that left one shoulder bare. She had an olive complexion, black hair, and blue eyes that caught the light like clear water.

She made straight for the Mayor and welcomed him.

Then she joined Morgenstern and Rosemonde, with the Mayor beside her and Fould in tow. Martineau, standing to one side, was drinking a glass of Flamel and carefully avoiding the witch's eyes.

'Your Majesty,' said the Professor of History, bowing.

The Queen of the Gypsies was the very incarnation of Bohemia, old Spain, India and the Persia of the *Thousand and One Nights*. She had the casual grace of those princesses of the past who have been immortalized in brightly coloured miniatures and legendary tales.

'The reconstruction is a great success,' Rosemonde congratulated her.

'Yes, and much of it is due to you. Even though it's incomplete.'

Her voice was as tuneful as the Castalian spring of ancient myth. However, Fould, nit-picking as usual, asked, 'What do you mean, incomplete?'

'I was thinking of putting a pillory in the middle of the square, but that might have been misinterpreted by certain ill-informed journalists. I'm sure you'd agree, Minister.'

Fould went red. The Queen was already turning her back on him to ask Rosemonde, 'Would you be kind enough to show our honoured guests round the Great Gables? I'd like a word with Miss Morgenstern.'

'Of course.'

Grégoire moved away with Fould and the Mayor. A storm was brewing in Roberta's heart. She was imagining some relationship between the Queen and Rosemonde, and couldn't manage to put aside that sudden flame of jealousy – most unworthy of a disciple of Fire, so she contented herself with following the gypsy towards a corner of the square not far from where Martineau was lurking.

'Roberta,' he said when she was only a metre away.

'Aren't you joining the tour?' she asked. 'You should. Professor Rosemonde is a fascinating guide.'

'You're right. I will.' Martineau emptied his glass, put it down, and went off with a hangdog look.

Roberta called after him. 'By the way, did Strudel tell you that he purified the last vintage with ether?'

The new head of the CID didn't see what that had to do with him – just as, in turning round, he didn't see the waiter carrying a heavy tray with whom he collided head on. The witch joined the Queen, thinking that Strudel had added the ether with a generous hand, and quite right too.

The gallery of the half-timbered house led to a Venetian footbridge. Roberta had no time to look at the main road down below. The Queen went along a corridor that led to a red wooden door. The spiral staircase of the pagoda rose beyond this door, and a notice announced that the tea-room was closed for the day.

The top storey was open to the air. There were cushions on the floor, and the two women sat down opposite each other. The gypsy, watching Roberta, smiled. 'Are you still dancing the tango with the Professor of History?'

'When we have the energy. When events permit,' replied the witch, on the defensive.

'And do you manage to conjure up the – the apparition every time?'

'You mean the spirit?' Did the Queen just want to ask questions about their little metaphysical experiments? Well, Roberta and Grégoire had nothing to hide from the gypsies. She decided to be more forthcoming. 'It's more of a genie really. Grégoire Rosemonde is trying to compile a kind of catalogue of the entities conjured up by every kind of dance.

He intends to use it to prove that mankind invented the gods and not the other way around.'

'I see,' said the Queen, after a moment's reflection. 'And did the tango prove useful?'

'Yes, like the waltz and the calypso. And we hope for good results from the mambo, cha-cha and samba too.' The witch decided that she had a right to ask a question in her turn. 'All this hatred rising around you . . . how do you think it will end?'

'Hatred has pursued us for centuries,' replied the Queen. 'So many rumours have been spread about us. Travellers and people who live in houses have never got on well.'

Roberta felt a sudden urge to say frankly whose side she was on. 'I'm very fond of your people,' she said.

'I know. And you're fond of hedgehogs too, which is why I want you to be part of a project which, if the people of Basle continue going down this slippery slope, will soon have to be put into practice.'

'As you can see, the façade of the Great Gables is like a picture book telling a story.'

Leaving the buffet, Archibald Fould and the Mayor craned their necks to look at the low reliefs sunk into the façade like a stone jigsaw puzzle.

'The Eternal Father is over the main lintel, here's the Adoration of the Magi, and there you see the Flight into Egypt.'

'Rather conventional subjects for a man who called himself an alchemist,' said the Mayor.

'Discretion was essential for such activities. But look at the subjects beside the main themes: damned souls, dragons, crosses upside down. There's even a pair of angels standing on their heads on these capitals. This iconographical infection begins with the Father at the centre and spreads to the outer areas. For those who know how to read it, the façade of the Great Gables is a positive handbook of the Satanic arts.'

Fould approached one of the capitals, wondering if the stone might not in fact just have been fitted upside down by some incompetent gypsy builder. Seen the other way up, the angels would have been not crushed but in flight.

'And note the coat of arms of Nicolas Flamel,' Rosemonde continued.

'A hand holding some kind of case?' said the Mayor.

'A writing case. Flamel began his career as a member of the guild of scribes. Follow me, please, and be careful with the steps. They can be treacherous.'

By the time Martineau had apologized to the first waiter and then collided with a second, the other visitors had already disappeared into the house. Martineau made his way in. He managed the first step all right, the second not so well. The sight-seers in the Great Gables heard the sound of a fall, followed by a resounding oath.

'You absolutely must let me show you the Spring to Summer catalogue. They even have an ethnic collection, you know! "The Samarkand girdle adapts perfectly to your figure, while offering the soft luxury of wild silk and the thrill of the Oriental steppes," ' Roberta quoted from memory. She cast an expert glance at the rather well-rounded curves of the Queen of the Gypsies. 'It would suit you beautifully.'

'I've always been suspicious of mail-order catalogues. Don't they exaggerate a bit?'

'You haven't tried the Electrum model. Look at this.' And Roberta unbuttoned her top to show off the masterpiece.

'Doesn't it squeeze uncomfortably?

'I never felt more comfortable in my life. And it's not expensive, only 399 dollars.'

'Yes, I see. Perhaps I'll be tempted . . . I've had a touch of back-ache for several years. Do they make that model in wild silk too?'

'I'm not sure, but I could find out and maybe help you. I'm a good client, and I must have earned several reductions.'

Roberta did up her top again, telling herself that the Queen was charming – and a visionary too. For the proposition she had put a little while ago had left the witch speechless.

'Tell those you trust,' the Queen advised, 'but be careful. Fould's human tracers are everywhere. That snake in the grass won't be happy to see us escape him.'

'When are you planning to leave?'

'At the last minute. We still have a few technical details to work out, and they are quite important.'

Roberta rose, observing Don Quixote Martineau apparently fighting the windmill ventilators down below. Leave, she told herself, leave. She consulted her mental diary for any good reason to stay in Basle. There was nothing to keep her here for the next ten years. The CID was a thing of the past now. That still left the Professor of History. Would he be happy to resign his post at the College of Sorcery? She wasn't leaving without him, anyway.

Sirens howled from somewhere near the façade of the Palace of Westminster.

'The zurlas,' said the Queen. 'Always punctual.'

'What's up?' asked the witch, trying to spot the zurlas, whatever they were. All she could see was the sails of the windmills turning furiously in the east.

'Zurlas are wind instruments mounted on the roof-tops. They warn us when the whirlwind is on its way.'

'Whirlwind? What whirlwind?' The audible tension in Roberta's voice did not escape the gypsy.

'A violent whirlwind blows over the Historic Quarter on the day before the full moon every month. Is there a problem?'

The wind was turning the windmills all along the main street. It made the pagoda tremble on its base, and continued its wild career towards Little Prague.

The connection of the wind with the Baron of the Mists had not become public knowledge, but from the witch's expression, however, the gypsy guessed that something was ominously wrong.

'Where does the wind blow?'

'Towards the warehouses where we store the unused stage sets.'

'Is there any way of warning the people there?'

'We don't have telephones.'

'Then there's not a moment to lose. Come on!'

They ran down the nine floors of the pagoda and the three terraces of the Aztec pyramid on which it had been erected. A pony-trap was coming along the road. The Queen caught hold of the ponies' reins, forcing them to stop, and told the driver to give her his place. The witch scarcely had time to scramble in beside her.

'*Vayé! Vayé!*' cried the gypsy, cracking the reins. 'To the warehouses – quick!'

They crossed a large hall with a vaulted ceiling and climbed a narrow stairway to the floor above. Rosemonde followed a corridor paved with irregular hexagonal tiles and leading to a small room with a tapestry over the doorway. He drew it back with one hand. Light came in through bottle-glass window panes. There was something undeniably medieval about it.

'The treasure of the Great Gables,' he announced to the privileged visitors. Something flat covered with a blue velvet cloth was lying on a writing desk. 'Mind the beam,' warned Rosemonde. 'Nicolas Flamel was not a tall man.'

The Minister glanced nervously at his watch as he bent down to enter the room. Why had he let himself be taken on this stupid tour when the Baron might already have gone into action? He was annoyed to see Rosemonde let the tapestry fall into place behind them.

'The item kept here is one of the most precious possessions of the College of Sorcery,' declared the Professor, one hand on the desk. He raised the velvet cloth with the gesture of a conjuror. A thick book with a gilded cover and copper hinges came into view.

'A book,' said Fould.

Rosemonde corrected him. '*The* book. Flamel saw it in a dream, and bought it from a stranger years later for the sum of two florins. "A gilded book, extremely old and very large," as he himself described it, "its materials being made from the shoots and bark of tender young trees. The cover was of copper, engraved with strange characters and figures." '

'These figures are indeed very strange,' agreed the Mayor, leaning over the book.

'It contains the secret of the transmutation of the elements, which is at the heart of black magic. But Flamel never managed to discover what that secret was. The book was closed again, and closed it will remain until someone able to open it comes along.'

'You mean to say,' began the Mayor, 'that in all these years—?'

'No one has managed to open it.'

'Your story sounds like the tale of King Arthur and his magic sword in the stone.'

'You're closer to the truth than you may think. This book is our Excalibur, and we hope to take advantage of the present occasion in Paris Street to find the chosen person. For according to the legend, the book will open only under the hands of a scribe' – here Rosemonde looked at the Mayor of Basle – 'or the celebrant at a sacrificial ceremony.' And he glanced at the Minister of Security, whose cheeks flushed crimson. 'Mr Mayor? Over to you.'

The old man touched the metal cover, which was icy cold, and tried to open it, exerting slight pressure. It did not move a millimetre. Then Fould tried his luck, repeating the operation and trying as hard as he could, but also without success. The book remained hermetically sealed.

'Very interesting, I'm sure, but I have to go,' said the Minister brusquely, drawing back the tapestry. 'Thank you for the tour.' And he strode out into the corridor.

'I can understand why he wants to win at any price,' said the Mayor sympathetically. 'He's not a man who tolerates failure well.'

Rosemonde covered the book, drew the tapestry back in place, and accompanied the old man to the door. Meanwhile Martineau had been going in and out of empty rooms, up and down rickety staircases, looking for any witches or sorcerers who might be able to guide him through this impossible house – but no, he was well and truly lost.

'Yoohoo! Anyone there?'

He thought he heard a reply on the wind. Following it, he found himself in the dimly lit upper storey. The first beams just grazed his head. The next in line were more treacherous.

Sergei had not waited for the zurlas to give the warning before weatherproofing the hangars. He had started work early in the morning, padlocking sliding doors, locking high windows, making sure there was no opening that would let the whirlwind wreak havoc inside the three warehouses in his care. He was wedging a stout piece of wood firmly behind the last door when he remembered the metal foundry.

'The last of the *mujiks*, that's me,' he said crossly to himself, running that way.

The foundry was at the back of a long yard where the gypsies left trees before replanting them. The wind caught up with him just as he rushed inside. Bracing himself against the door, he managed to close it.

'Phew!' he breathed. 'Just in time.'

The blast furnace was not in operation, and stood there like a dismal, cold Moloch. At the back of the foundry a smelting cupola was heating up on a forge. The cupola was used for casting balustrades, door handles, harness, crosspieces, decorative hooks – and the pillory intended for Paris Street was beside it, mounted on a movable stand. The irons had been forged in place a little earlier. Sergei went over to admire the blacksmiths' work.

He never saw the tracers assume human form behind his back, but he heard a sound like an army of centipedes galloping over a metal surface. He hadn't even turned fully around when a black hand suddenly took him by the throat.

The carriage stopped outside the first warehouse. The Baron's path was marked by panels of corrugated iron torn away, crates turned upside down, dust swept to the roadsides.

'Don't try to follow me. Just make sure no one enters this area.'

'But what will you do if you come upon him?'

I have the ultimate weapon, thought Roberta. 'BodyPerfect,' she replied, winking.

She followed the Baron's trail to the yard, where broken branches and fallen leaves littered the ground. At the end of the yard stood a small dark building. Roberta programmed her Electrum girdle to one pulsation a minute. The door of the building was not locked, and she slipped inside. Laboured breathing could be heard beyond the blast furnace. She moved forward over the floor, which was covered with the dross from molten metal.

A man stood fettered in a pillory, and the Baron had one finger on his neck. Roberta guessed that he was analysing the victim's DNA and going back through his family tree from generation to generation, to find the punishment for the genetic brand he bore.

The BodyPerfect girdle pulsed. The sorceress began counting seconds. One . . . two . . . three . . . four . . . At fifty-five she would throw herself on the Baron. At sixty he would vanish into thin air.

The minute was almost over when a small green pea rolled between her feet and came to rest a few centimetres further on. Not a saponaria bath pearl, even if it looked very like one.

'Oh no,' cried Roberta, trying to run for it. But too late.

Archibald Fould had only to consult the liquid crystal screen of his vibration recorder to see that Morgenstern was moving rapidly east. He and his militiamen set off after her at once.

On reaching the warehouses they found the Queen and a handful of gypsies preparing to go to the witch's aid. The liquid crystal screen showed that Morgenstern was about a hundred metres south-east of their position. Fould sent some of his men in the opposite direction and left the others with the gypsies, with orders not to let them move. He followed the winking point of light on his screen to a dark building with its door wide open.

Yes, there was Morgenstern, spying on the Baron of the Mists as he went about his work. Fould opened his cigarette case without a sound, took out the retiarius seed and rolled it towards the sorceress. The little pea-like seed had hardly stopped when it began uncoiling and casting out its network of creepers. It wound around Roberta and pulled her heavily down on her back. Fould knew that the prickly creeper gave off a curare-based anaesthetic. He went over to the witch, not bothering to hide now, and crouched down beside her. She was watching him with glazed eyes, her lips contorted.

'You . . . can't . . . let . . . this happen,' she managed to say in a thickened voice.

'Go to sleep,' he advised her gently. 'Off you go to the land of dreams.'

And the sorceress gave in. The creeper, feeling the body it was holding tight relax, reabsorbed itself into its pea-like state. The Minister picked it up and returned it to his cigarette case as if nothing had happened. Taking out a cigarette, he put it between his lips.

So this is the historic Place de Grève of Paris, he thought, looking at the scene. The Baron had taken a crucible full of molten metal from the forge and was tipping it towards the man's mouth, which he was now holding open with two extra hands. The eyes of the victim, whose head was thrown back, were dilated by terror. A ghastly death, Banshee had wanted. Well, she'd get her wish.

Fould had seen horrors in his time, but he turned away at the last moment, and collided with something large and clammy. The golem. The red clay figure was two heads taller than the Minister, and was simply waiting for him to move. Fould took a couple of steps aside to let it pass. He managed to light his cigarette only at the third attempt.

The gypsy in the pillory had expired by the time the Baron put the crucible down on the floor, greeted the golem as an old acquaintance, and then dissolved in a swirl of black ash. The golem went over to the corpse and kissed its lips. Fould distinctly saw a bright flash of light move from one to the other. Potassium, he told himself. Then the golem went back into the garden with its heavy tread.

The Minister let five long minutes pass before raising the alarm on his vibration recorder. The militia arrived at speed. He pointed to the body in the pillory and then to the unconscious woman on the floor.

'Take her straight to jail,' he told them, 'and put her in solitary confinement. She's an accomplice of the Baron of the Mists. I shall deal with her case personally.'

At the same moment someone was scaling the façade of Number 42 Mimosa Street. The agile climber got in through an open window and made his way to the bedroom, where he crouched down and listened.

He could hear a very faint scratching sound, partly drowned by the rain, rising from the ground floor. Yet the house should have been empty. He went downstairs without making a single step creak, and glanced into the sitting room. Someone was writing at the desk.

'Pichenette? What on earth are you doing here?'

'Good heavens!' cried the journalist, spinning round.

The intruder wore a one-piece driving outfit, gloves and a brown leather cap. Dark glasses hid his eyes.

'Micheau? What a fright you gave me!'

The chauffeur took off his glasses and tilted his head to examine the little man. There was something different about the writer.

'You're not wearing glasses any more!'

'You're not a deaf mute any more!' cried Pichenette.

'Looks like we've both had miracle cures.'

'The main miracle is finding you here. I expected us to meet under the Barometer.'

'So did I, but the Minister had other ideas.'

'And he signed you a pass letting you act freely?'

'No, no, he's with the gypsies in the Historic Quarter. I've just dropped him off.'

Micheau, like Rosemonde a little earlier, studied the bookshelves. Pichenette watched him, chewing the end of his already badly eroded pencil.

'Don't tell me you still haven't found what you were looking for?'

'The day after the Major's death his files were sent to Archives,' explained Micheau, taking books off the shelves at random. 'They've all been burnt. But I heard one of the reservists saying that Gruber kept copies. Which must be somewhere in this house.' He looked inquiringly at Pichenette.

'No, I haven't found them. And I wish you luck, because if he classified his files the way he classified his library, you're not out of the woods yet!'

Micheau stepped back a couple of paces and looked at the shelves, hands on hips. He could see nothing odd about them himself. 'What do you mean?'

Pichenette rose to his feet and showed him, in succession, three books in three different places.

'Rainer Maria Rilke, *Complete Works*. Volume 1, prose. Volume 2, poetry. Volume 3, correspondence. Shelved just anywhere, no sense in it at all.'

But the three works were aligned on the same diagonal in the shelves. Micheau ran his hand down their spines from top to bottom. There was a click. A panel opened in the lower part of the bookshelves.

'As signposted by Cornet Christoph Rilke,' said the chauffeur, rather pleased with himself.

Pichenette was inspecting the mechanism with a happy smile while Micheau, on his knees, was removing the files from their hiding place. He put them on the desk and began looking at them at once. The writer scratched his forehead, his eyes going from the secret compartment to the desk, from the desk to the secret compartment . . .

'Ah, here we are!'

Micheau had taken out two sheets of paper pinned together. They were an account of the Major's last case but one: the interrogation of a pirate caught six months earlier in the act of theft with violence from a dealer in natural curiosities in the floating market. The number stamped in red ink on the upper left-hand corner of the report was 01–03, and a note from the prison authorities recording the pirate's admission completed the documentation.

'So he's in the municipal jail,' he muttered. 'In cell number . . . oh no, they don't give the number!'

'Let's have a look.' Pichenette consulted the document, at the same time satisfying his natural curiosity. 'Ah,' he told Micheau, with a wry smile, 'he's in the isolation cell at the very heart of the jail. It won't be easy to get him out of there.'

'It will be easier now I know where he is.' Micheau folded the report and slipped it into the pocket of his chauffeur's uniform. He leafed vaguely through the files and found a kind of personal diary, which he took just in case. It was time to leave. He took a blue capsule out of one pocket and held it between thumb and forefinger under Pichenette's nose.

'Come on, I'll drive you home.'

The writer made haste to pick up his fifteen projects for

novels and put them in a leather briefcase that had belonged to Major Gruber.

'Is that cowl really necessary?' he asked, looking at the capsule with distaste.

'I'm sure you're right.' Micheau put the capsule away again. 'Let's just act as if no one could spot us. Fould's bound to find you sooner or later. I'm sure he'll be delighted to make your acquaintance.'

'Oh, very well, very well.' Pichenette closed his eyes and mouth and pinched his nose. Micheau broke the capsule over his head. The material it contained flowed over his face, his clothes and his shoes, coating him all over with a shiny synthetic substance.

'Yuk!' he said, passing his tongue over his lips, which felt numb. The translucent film filtered both his voice and his breathing. 'It's disgusting.'

'We haven't yet found anything that works better than the cowl to keep the tracers from following.'

They left the house. The Ministry car was parked a little further along the road. The writer climbed in beside Micheau, who released the hand brake. They began coasting downhill. The rain beat down on the top of the car with a deafening sound.

'We'd be better off up there!' said Pichenette. Micheau, deep in his own thoughts, didn't reply. 'It never rains up above the clouds!' Still no reaction. 'You may not be dumb any longer, but you're still rather deaf!'

Micheau slowly turned his head to his passenger. Pichenette had seen that look before, on the face of a buccaneer in a South Seas tavern. He decided to keep quiet and immerse himself in his own thoughts . . . starting with a little visit to the room containing the four-poster bed, which unfortunately was empty.

'Sweetheart! Marinette!' he called.

Mata Hari still didn't put in an appearance. He waited, and then added enticingly, 'I have a little surprise for you! I'm wearing a cowl!'

The bead curtain moved slightly, but only very slightly, just enough to make the writer sigh.

Q. E. D.

' "Vote for me in the second round and I commit myself to the following five promises," ' Strudel read out. ' "First: to lower all taxes by thirty per cent during my first two years as Mayor." '

'No reason why he should deprive himself of the pleasure of promising the impossible,' commented Otto Vandenberghe.

' "Second," ' continued Strudel, ' "to provide security for all." '

'I'm surprised he didn't put that first,' remarked Suzy.

' "Third: to give special privileges to the original citizens of Basle. Outsiders will be escorted to the far side of the dam, and the accommodation thus left vacant will be allotted to citizens at present living in poor housing." '

'So the gypsies are to lose their civil rights,' Suzy added.

'This is where it begins to smell bad,' agreed Plenck.

' "Fourth: to render the Baron of the Mists harmless." A bit redundant, in view of Two. And finally, "Fifth . . ." '

'Yes, Eleazar?'

Strudel cleaned the lenses of his glasses, folded his copy of the *Mainland News* and then unfolded it again. No, his eyes had not deceived him.

' "And fifth, if you vote for me it will stop raining." '

'That takes the biscuit!' fulminated Vandenberghe. 'First

Fould will expel the monsters from Basle, then he'll command the elements. Now I've heard everything!'

'Machiavelli is trying to encroach on our own territory,' complained Lusitanus.

'Oh, does the rain obey us?' inquired Rosemonde in surprise. Up to now he had kept quiet. 'I had no idea.'

Silence fell over the other five people sitting together in the back room of the Two Salamanders.

'How on earth can three-quarters of the people of Basle have voted for him in the first round?' wailed Suzy.

'He casts a spell over them,' said Plenck. 'Vote for me and I'll give you the moon. And those idiots fell for it.'

Lusitanus, one forefinger raised to the ceiling, commented, 'As Rabelais said, "The people of Basle are so foolish, inquisitive and inept by nature that a juggler, a bearer of tittle-tattle, a mule with its bells or a player of the viol in the middle of a crossroads will attract a greater crowd than a man preaching the gospels." '

'Don't blame Basle on poor old Rabelais,' begged Vandenberghe.

'It's our friend Strudel's wine. For the last week I've felt I was living in Paris back in the time of lantern-bearers and shady alleyways where you had an equal chance of getting your throat cut or your pocket picked.'

'Monsieur Lusitanus!' said Vandenberghe, offended.

'Foolish the people of Basle may be, but if it goes on raining after what now looks like being Fould's victory they'll crucify him,' said Plenck.

'The Prevention of Natural Risks people don't expect any improvement in the next few days either,' said Lusitanus, baffled.

Eleazar poured them more black coffee and brought in some little cakes, but no one was very hungry this morning.

'Three gypsies have been murdered now,' Vandenberghe reminded them.

'Yes, that poor fellow in the foundry, the one found drowned in a sack five days ago, and the carpenter yesterday,' Plenck summed up. 'He died by strappado, dangling from the ministerial cable car. I did the autopsy on his remains.'

'We're still seeing historical methods,' Suzy put in. 'The sack dates back to the Romans. The strappado was practised all over Europe in the old days. As for the gypsy in the foundry, execution by pouring molten metal into the victim's mouth was traditional in Russia until 1672. They generally used lead.'

All present involuntarily tightened their jaws.

'And the tracers are definitely behind all this bloodshed,' said the Rector angrily. 'We have the evidence now, don't we, Plenck?'

'We have the evidence,' was all the forensic scientist said.

'Did you read that article on the gypsies?' asked Lusitanus. ' "Only getting their just deserts . . . The creature turning on its creators . . . Executioners die too." '

'Horrible,' said Vandenberghe from the corner where he was sitting.

'Let's look on the bright side,' said Rosemonde grimly. 'The workman Fliquart has been avenged, the incineration plant is working again, the streets are clean. And don't forget that the theory of the historically minded killer is now officially held by the authorities. You can't get into the Historic Quarter any more without a pass. The place is being turned into a ghetto,' he added.

'Horrible,' repeated Strudel.

'We have five days left before the second round of voting,' Vandenberghe reminded them. 'After that, with Fould in power, our hands will be tied.'

Eleazar raised an eyebrow and looked out at the main

room. Someone was approaching his inn. He rose, went over to the double-locked door and looked out through the spy-hole. A car had just parked beside the bronze equestrian statue outside the Two Salamanders. Martineau got out, crossed the road, tried to open the door, failed and went away again. Strudel returned to the back room.

'That was Martineau,' he said.

No one commented. 'Still no news of Roberta?' Vandenberghe asked Rosemonde.

'Still no news.'

'The Queen of the Gypsies was the last person to see her,' said Suzy. Alive, she added silently to herself.

'And our "new friends" know no more than we do?' said Plenck. 'You don't disappear just like that on a piece of mainland not much bigger than a pocket handkerchief!'

'We'll find her,' said Eleazar.

'Of course we'll find her, by St Anselm!' cried Vandenberghe, his voice shaking with anger. 'We're not leaving without Roberta, are we?'

'And now, ladies and gentlemen, *She's Leaving Home*. A melancholy little ditty from the Lonely Hearts Club Band. With a one – a two – a three.'

Roberta rubbed the ocarina on her grey prison dress and launched into the Beatles tune.

'In fact *too* melancholy,' she decided, stopping. 'What else can the Lonely Hearts Club Band offer?'

She flung herself wholeheartedly into a version of *Within You Without You* that sounded more Indian than the Taj Mahal itself, but again stopped after only a few bars. No one to hear her, no telepathic hedgehog in the offing, morale at a very low ebb . . . Roberta had to admit that she had just about exhausted her considerable powers of seeing life through rose-tinted spectacles.

Footsteps dragging, she went into the shower cubicle, sat down on the lavatory seat, and for the hundred-and-ninety-fourth time that day wondered what had been happening outside during the ten days of her solitary confinement in the municipal jail. Had Fould seized power? Was the Baron killing more people? Were her friends still alive?

A meal tray was passed through a flap at the bottom of the door three times a day. The lights came on and went off at fixed hours. Contact with anyone at all was impossible. The witch was cut off from the rest of the world.

She heard the sound of a key turning in the lock.

'But I had categorical orders,' said a fretful voice. 'No one's to go in.'

'Going to argue with the signature at the bottom of this document, are you?' Clearly the prison officer wasn't going to argue with anything at all. 'Archibald Fould has told me to question the suspect. Close the door after me, and never fear, I'm armed.'

'If you say so.'

The warder closed the door after the visitor, who walked into the apparently empty cell and over to the shower cubicle, calling softly, 'Louis, are you in there?'

Micheau felt a draught of air to his right and saw something reddish pass behind him at lightning speed. He was flung face down on the floor. It took him some seconds to realize what had happened. Morgenstern was holding his wrists in one hand and digging her knee into the small of his back, pinning him firmly to the ground.

'I can put your senses out of action one by one if I slightly increase the pressure on your spinal column,' she threatened. Then she hesitated. 'Micheau! Is that you?'

The chauffeur twisted his neck, to see that the prisoner held in isolation was none other than the former CID investigator. 'Morg— . . . Morgenstern! What – what are you doing here? Ouch!'

'Talking, too!'

She commandeered the official permit sticking out of the chauffeur's pocket and read it while he got up, groaning.

'Fould is sending you to interrogate the prisoner in solitary confinement,' she read out.

'I didn't know it was you,' he replied, massaging the nape of his neck. 'Anyway, that document's a fake.'

'Oh, I see. So Mister Micheau is a forger! Mister Micheau hides his game pretty well, I must say! Who is this Louis? And I advise you not to beat about the bush.'

Micheau dropped heavily on the witch's bed. 'Louis is my brother.'

'You mean your brother was imprisoned here?'

Micheau nodded.

Roberta, who was leaning against the wall and had her ocarina tied to one finger with a string, swung the instrument first one way and then another. 'I'm not really up to date with current events, but I do know that the previous occupant of this de luxe suite was the pirate arrested by Gruber in the floating market. And if a week in the cooler hasn't confused my brain completely, that means that you are—'

'Looking for my brother,' Micheau interrupted. 'And since I've found you we might as well leave together.'

He searched one of his pockets. Roberta watched him a little apprehensively. Could she trust a pirate? Well, she could certainly trust a pirate to get her out of here better than a militiaman.

'They're anxious about you up on the surface, you know.'

'They? Who do you mean? Friend or foe?'

'This College of Sorcery of yours – I'd never have suspected such a thing could exist in a town as dull as Basle.'

'You know about the College? How are they? How's Grégoire?'

'You'll soon see him if everything works out according to plan.'

Micheau had produced a blue capsule. Roberta was watching with great interest. 'Is that a cowl?'

Micheau knocked hard on the door. 'Officer!'

The door opened, and a timid-looking young man appeared. The pirate grabbed him by the collar, dragged him violently into the cell, and knocked him unconscious against one upright of the bed. Then he broke the capsule over the head of the motionless warder. The whole operation hadn't taken more than five seconds.

'Listen hard,' said Micheau. 'There are no cameras in the jail. Only the tracers keep watch on the prisoners. They won't see you leave.'

'They won't see me still in the cell either.'

'You could be in the shower, or doing your daily exercises, sweating too hard for them to pick you up.'

'OK, the shower, then. What about him?'

'It's the same for the warders too. The tracers will signal his disappearance in five minutes' time.'

'So I'm supposed to be in the shower with him, am I?'

The pirate crossed his arms, opened his mouth, and remained silent as he sought for an adequate answer.

'Oh, all right, let's get going,' said Roberta impatiently. 'We're wasting precious time.'

Micheau sighed noisily and broke a second capsule over the witch's head. The elastic substance covered her from head to foot. She passed her tongue over her numb lips.

'It feels like being covered with Vaseline.'

The pirate looked out into the corridor. No one in sight. 'Act as if your hands were bound,' he advised. 'And walk ahead of me. We'll look more convincing that way.'

They closed the cell door after them and climbed up through the Chrysanthemum, Periwinkle and Daisy floors of the prison building. They passed a dozen warders without attracting any attention and reached the exit, a simple airlock guarded by two armed militiamen. Roberta hunched her head down between her shoulders. But as the tracers were not setting off any alarms the militiamen did not react any more than the prison officers had. At last they were out. Micheau started the engine of the car parked just outside the prison.

'Get in,' he said in a tense voice. A minute later the square concrete building of the jail was far behind them.

'Well, I certainly owe you a debt,' the sorceress told her companion. 'This is the first time I've escaped from jail, the first time I've rubbed shoulders with a pirate, the—'

'Every moment of our lives we're doing something for the first time,' said Micheau philosophically. 'Especially at the last moment.'

He was driving fast towards the lagoon, so far as she could see through the squealing ballet of the windscreen wipers and the rain that reduced visibility.

'So your brother was – or is – imprisoned in the jail. I suppose you infiltrated the Ministry to get him out. Is that why you recruited Pichenette?'

'You talk too much, Miss Witch. We'll have plenty of time to discuss all this once we're somewhere safe.'

'There isn't anywhere safe in Basle. And I need to catch up on ten days of conversation, so I'm sorry, but I just have to talk. Tell me how you managed to get into the Ministry of Security,' she demanded, hands flat on her thighs.

'Sent them my CV,' said the chauffeur, laconically.

'Trying to be funny?'

'Not at all. Good drivers are few and far between. Clément

Martineau has made it to head of the CID. I could have been Minister!'

'Very well, if that's the tone you're going to take I'll say no more,' said Roberta.

Micheau slowed down, lowering his window to look out. 'I'm lost in all this rain. Where are we?'

'Where are we going?'

'To the Historic Quarter.'

'Then you want the second on the right. After that it's downhill to the coastal road and we'll be there. The last time I went that way there was a checkpoint at the foot of the ramp, and the guards weren't very friendly. Maybe they're a little less lax than the prison warders, do you think?'

'Don't worry about that.' Micheau accelerated. 'What about you? What happened to you? How come I found you in the jail?'

'Well, it's a long story, but I don't mind telling you that— oh, watch out!'

Something massive and dark appeared on their left, making straight for their car. Roberta's head struck the inside of the door. Micheau got out, shouting, 'What bloody idiot is ramming us?'

Roberta followed him, legs slightly shaky. Another car had smashed into their left front wing. Curious passers-by were watching the scene. Micheau gave the car that had rammed him several violent kicks.

'There can't be more than fifty cars in this town, and I have to come across a useless idiot driver!'

The driver who had bumped into them got out of his own vehicle, scarlet in the face.

'Martineau,' muttered Roberta, rubbing her forehead.

'You?' said the young man, seeing the Ministry driver. He planted himself in front of Micheau, fists clenched, nostrils flaring. 'It was my right of way! You ought to have let me go first!'

'You were going hell for leather!' said the pirate. 'You want to observe the speed limits, you do. Sunday driver!'

Micheau then fell silent, compressing his lips. Martineau had taken a step backwards. 'Hm – weren't you a deaf mute last time we met?'

The young man's hand went to the pocket where Roberta knew he kept his gun. She intervened. 'Let's keep this civilized, shall we?'

He widened his eyes on seeing her. 'Roberta! But . . . I mean . . . are you all right?'

'Not too bad, dear boy, not too bad.'

'Where've you been? I've been looking for you for ten days. And how come—'

Micheau had come up to Roberta. 'The militia,' he whispered.

Seven militiamen had appeared from nowhere to surround them, weapons in their hands. The leader of the squad approached, speaking into the microphone attached to his shoulder. 'Unit 22 to Control. Collision between two cars at the junction of Böcklin Avenue and Bergstrasse. Three persons involved in the incident.'

'Control to Unit 22,' they heard the control room reply. 'Never mind that. There's been an escape from the municipal jail. All units recalled to search. The fugitive is a woman, red hair, small, around fifty—'

The militiaman moved away to listen to Roberta's description. Micheau noticed the mark on her forehead. 'Are you hurt?' he whispered.

'It's all right. Just a little bump.'

'Your cowl is tearing,' he added, mouthing the words.

The militiaman came back to them. The six other men did not move, but kept their guns pointing to the ground.

Martineau turned. 'My name is Clément Martineau, Police Number 6373, director of the CID,' the young man introduced himself, showing his card. 'These people are Monsieur Micheau and Roberta Morgenstern. We are – er – all on the CID staff.'

'Right,' said the militiaman, without taking Martineau's card. 'Don't move. Help is on the way.'

The leader turned. The militia were blocking his path. Micheau sighed. The radio crackled. 'Control to Unit 22. You mentioned three people involved in the accident. The tracers see only two. Confirm, please.'

'Now we're done for,' grunted Micheau, retreating towards his car.

The militia leader turned. He could count to three, and he knew he hadn't been seeing things. There was a problem somewhere. 'Hey, you!' he said, pointing his gun at the pirate.

Roberta felt her cowl tearing from top to bottom. It fell at her feet like a transparent second skin.

'Control to Unit 22,' the radio crackled again. 'The tracers now see three people. It's OK. I repeat, everything OK. Carry out the previous order.'

The leader waited a few seconds before lowering his gun. He turned and walked away. Micheau made haste to get behind the wheel again. The engine was still running. He hoped the car could get them as far as the lagoon.

'Hey, you're not just going off like that, are you?' protested Martineau.

The militiamen were now some thirty metres away. The radio bawled, 'Control to Unit 22! The tracers have found the escaped prisoner. She's right behind you. I repeat, the escaped woman prisoner is right behind you.'

Roberta flung herself into the car as Micheau put it into reverse. They dragged Martineau's car along with them for several metres, and then managed to disengage from it with much metallic clanging. Shots were fired. The windscreen shattered.

'Hell-hounds!' muttered the pirate. 'They might at least have fired a shot across our bows first.'

He stepped on the gas and drove down Bergstrasse, which wound its zigzag way towards the lagoon. Roberta was clinging to the passenger door on her side. More bursts of firing cracked through the air. In the rear-view and wing mirrors they saw three large black shapes in pursuit of them.

'It's Martineau again!'

'And two vehicles with caterpillar tracks. They're not fast enough to catch up with us, but I'm not sure how we're going to get past the checkpoint now!'

'By flying?'

Micheau mounted the pavement to avoid two pedestrians crossing the road. Roberta saw their bodies, blurred by speed, swerve aside as they approached. The car got back on the slippery road surface, skidded, and collided head on with a tram coming up the slope. It then whirled round like a top and continued on its way. Martineau had gained ground on them.

The road turned sharply to the right. Micheau braked, tyres squealing. Martineau followed ten seconds later. The fugitives had driven straight into a building site where a house was being demolished. They had hit the first set of struts. The three gutted storeys of the building above crashed down. A cloud of dust rose, cutting the road in two.

Martineau slammed on his brakes and got out of his car. The tracked vehicles stopped behind him. The militia spread out around the scene of the disaster.

'Unit 22 to Control,' called the militiamen's leader into his radio. 'The fugitives can do no more harm. I repeat, they can do no more harm.'

'I don't believe it!' groaned Martineau, looking at the rubble.

The response from Control was immediate. 'Confirmation to Unit 22. The tracers are silent. They can't see them any more. We're sending you reinforcements at once.'

The militia were already getting security tape in place to keep curious onlookers away.

'Control to Unit 22. The CID investigator with you is wanted back at the Community Building. I repeat . . .'

The squad leader looked round for Police Number 6373, but he had disappeared, and so had his car.

And meanwhile Micheau and Morgenstern had boarded the Number 4 tram, each paying the quarter-dollar fare. They wore cowls again. Roberta dared not think of the number of bruises that would soon be covering her body. She swore to herself that she would never again let herself be pushed out of a vehicle being driven full speed by a deaf mute, even a fake deaf mute.

Sirens howled at the other end of the street, but seemed to be getting no closer. 'We've thrown them off,' she breathed.

'Yes, but this tram is going at snail's pace, and my pass won't be any good now.'

'We'll think of something. Oh no! Look! Not him!'

Martineau was indeed driving along beside the tram. He had seen Roberta and was waving to her.

'He's pleased to see me,' she said, touched.

This time the sirens were coming closer.

'That fool will get us sent back to jail! We must do something!'

The pirate strode up to the front platform and pushed the driver off into the road. He took hold of the speed regulator and turned the wheel several times. The tram accelerated violently. A woman inside shrieked.

'Get them out!' shouted Micheau.

The tram was swaying this way and that. Roberta, who was strap-hanging, announced, 'This is a tram-jacking! Co-operate and no harm will come to you! Everyone out!' she added, with a savage smile.

The six passengers flocked to the rear platform like so many frightened sheep.

'Keep your heads well down,' the sorceress advised them, 'and don't think, just jump!'

Fortunately there were no pregnant women, old people or children among them. Furthermore, Roberta suspected that these pale-faced passengers had been on their way down to the coastal road to rubberneck at the sight of the Historic Quarter being threatened by the rising waters, so she did not hesitate to create herself a demonic mask with smoking nostrils and eyebrows enhanced by flames, just to get them moving a little faster. The passengers jumped out and rolled over on the wet, gleaming road, uttering strangled cries.

Roberta went back to the pirate as they passed the last stop but one on the line, going much faster than the security norm for public transport. 'Ever been a tram driver too?' she asked, shouting to make herself heard.

'In another life!' was Micheau's not very reassuring reply.

The tramlines described a graceful left curve. The tram took it at full speed with a crunch of white-hot metal. They felt themselves flung over to the right, and then fell back heavily before the tram went on, faster than ever. They were making straight for the coastal road and the tram terminus, where a crowd was gathering to watch the rising water.

'Suppose we braked?' suggested Roberta.

Clenching his jaw, Micheau took a lever that emerged from the floor in both hands and pulled. Two large showers of sparks accompanied them on their way for a moment. There was a loud click.

'I don't think we have a brake any more,' he said.

They were about to go over the coastal road and crash a hundred metres below. A delightful prospect, thought Morgenstern. Micheau, leaning over the side of the tram, was looking underneath the engine.

'It's a Mékarski system!' he said, straightening up.

'So?'

'It works by compressed air!'

'So?' repeated Roberta, whose vocabulary was dwindling as fast as her hopes of survival.

The sightseers scattered as they saw the runaway tram making for them. Now there was only the coastal road, the void, and the top of the velarium just coming into view. Micheau had opened a panel beside the wheel to reveal a large red push-button.

'What are you doing?'

'The sea-wolf dies at sea or not at all!'

He pushed the button. The compressed air in the tanks under the tram was suddenly let out. The acceleration brought them up against the side of the vehicle. They saw themselves, as if in a dream, leaving the tramlines and the slope itself, crossing the coastal road, flying over the velarium . . . Micheau pushed the sorceress out of the tram. Roberta's one thought was: how dare he?

The velarium caught her as the tram continued on its way and finally plunged into the lagoon. She slid, rolled, turned, bounced on the gigantic slope of the fabric and stopped at the edge, above the pontoons where goods were unloaded. She couldn't tell up from down any more, she was chewing the ends of her hair, but she was alive.

A few metres away Micheau was clinging to the edge of the velarium. He scrambled down from it like a circus acrobat, went to find a ladder and helped Roberta down. Once on the quayside she found that she was tottering just a little.

'Any more cheery fun on the programme?' she asked in a husky voice.

'Oh yes,' said Micheau, apparently very pleased with his high-wire number. 'You'll like this bit.'

He set off for the Savoy, which was moored not far off. Telling herself that she was totally crazy, Roberta followed. Micheau pushed open the revolving door of the floating grand hotel, crossed the lobby and made for the billiard room. The cues were in their racks, the balls were in the pockets on the green baize cloth. There was a mournful look about the place. Micheau lifted a phone standing on a counter-top and said into it, 'We're here. You can come and get us.'

He rang off, and went back to the sorceress.

'Who can come and fetch us? Some extraterrestrial in his space-ship?'

'You're never very far from the truth.'

The floor quivered. The ceiling lights vibrated. The whole Savoy Hotel roared. A gulf opened up between two tables just in front of them, which rose vertically on top of a black column three metres wide and ten metres high. The column rose to the ceiling with a steady roar, and stopped. Micheau went over to it and caught hold of the first rung of the ladder which allowed you to climb down the side.

'Watch out, they're slippery,' he warned the sorceress.

They climbed down the submarine's superstructure and took refuge inside. The vessel plunged below the lagoon again. The floor and the billiard tables closed above it with a perfect hermetic seal.

'Your visitor has arrived, sir.' The secretary's voice suddenly rose to a shrill pitch. 'No — I won't let you! You have no right! Ouch!'

The office door was flung open to reveal Carmilla Banshee in a state of high excitement.

'Thank you,' said Fould down the interphone.

'Archie!' exclaimed the witch, as if they hadn't seen each other for years. 'You seem to be on good form.'

'You too,' he said, hastily putting a cigarette in his mouth in case she had some deranged idea of kissing him.

Banshee put her bag down on the Minister's desk, ignoring the files that lay there. She produced a bottle of champagne and two glasses. 'Tantantara!' she cried, and set about opening the bottle with wild abandon, twisting off the wire muzzle and pushing off the cork to open it as noisily as possible. She filled the glasses, put one in Fould's hand, and said, by way of a toast, 'To the Baron of the Mists!'

She drank her glass straight down and immediately refilled it. As for the Minister, he was inspecting the columns of bubbles rising to the surface of the clear, golden liquid. He would always be suspicious of his accomplice in black magic. Together with retiarius plants, thunderbolt grasses and pumpkins capable of destroying hot-air balloons, poisons must be among her favourite weapons. He put his glass down without tasting it.

'We agreed to meet on the eve of the second round of the elections,' he reminded her.

Banshee came closer and whispered in his ear, 'I must tell you a secret: the water's rising faster than expected.'

'I know that!' he snapped. 'At least we'll be rid of the Historic Quarter and its inhabitants all the sooner.'

'And by the same token Little Prague.'

'That'll be no great loss. Once I'm Mayor you won't have to hide out in such insalubrious accommodation.'

Banshee was looking hard at him. So there was a problem. Fould said, casually, 'Surely all we have to do is move the matrix? Under escort. We can install it here in this very office, away from prying eyes.'

'How simple life is going to be when you're in charge, my dear Archie! We do have a problem, though: the matrix *can't* be moved. We're not dealing with some gross fat human mother who may waddle along at only a kilometre an hour but will get there in the end. Do you think the Creator was racing about the place during the six days it took him to make the world? Here's the elephants, let's turn a somersault! Here come the gastropods, let's run the hundred metres!'

'I didn't know you were a church-goer.'

'I'm perfectly serious.'

Fould tried to hide his delight. So time was running short? She was afraid their project might not come to a successful conclusion? For once, he had a head start on the ambitious Carmilla Banshee.

'Do you still need any elements?' he asked straight out.

'Only one, iron. You might have followed it all more closely.'

'Oh.' He bit his lip. 'That's inconvenient. The Baron won't manifest himself again before the second round of voting.'

Banshee almost exploded, restrained herself, thought about it, and then exploded all the same. '*What* did you say?' She kicked the desk hard.

'It's no use getting worked up,' he said, trying to calm her down. 'You're damaging municipal property.'

'It's no use getting worked up? Then everything we've done so far has been no use either! You can wave goodbye to your fine ambitions. Vote for me and it will stop raining, wasn't that your line? Oh, make yourself a cap of giant paperclips, why don't you? Dance and sing on top of your wretched tower block here! We'll see how much good that does.'

Her anger subsided, and she forced herself to think. They couldn't stop now. The child meant far too much to her. 'Unless . . .' she said.

'Unless what?'

'Unless we see about finding a last victim for ourselves.'

'We really are on the same wavelength.' The Minister picked up a file from beneath the witch's bag and took out a set of prison records. The photographs, full face and profile, showed a man of about thirty with bright eyes and a tanned complexion. He wore a ring in his left ear.

'A pirate arrested just over six months ago in the floating market for violence to a stallholder. He's waiting on the Chrysanthemum floor of the municipal jail to hear his fate.'

'Chrysanthemums are usually flowers for the dead, aren't they?'

'That's right. The Chrysanthemum floor is Death Row. Although the citizens of Basle don't know it yet, I've just reintroduced capital punishment.' Banshee widened her eyes. 'The execution will be announced in the *Mainland News* tomorrow,' the Minister of Security went on.

'Surely there's been no capital punishment in Basle for centuries? Leaving aside the Baron's efforts, of course.'

'The City Council, in an extraordinary general meeting held last night, gave me all powers needed to calm the population.'

'What about the Mayor?'

'He's of no importance now. Not that he knows it yet either.' And Fould was not erring through personal pride.

'You think the people of Basle will follow you?'

'They're like the Carthaginians who threw their children into the maw of the god Baal to make it rain, except that this is the other way around. And we're not going to sacrifice any poor little innocents, only that pirate scum. No one will shed any tears over him, believe me.'

This devil of a man could be right, she told herself. 'When does the execution take place?'

'We don't have any time to lose, do we? I've fixed it for the day after tomorrow at nine in the morning. The scaffold will be erected in the central square above an open manhole cover. The pirate's head will fall through it and straight into the hands of your golem, unseen by anyone. The golem will extract the iron we need, and we can finish the job.'

'You think of everything.' Carmilla perched on the desk, flung a leg in the air and tipped her head back, uttering a kind of moan which may have been meant to be erotic. 'I can't wait for the day after tomorrow!' she chuckled. 'Especially now that waste of space Morgenstern isn't around to put a spoke in our wheels. Here's to you! Here's to us!' She waved her champagne glass in the air. 'Here's to the city we shall soon have back on the tracks again.'

In fact Fould had heard an hour before that Morgenstern had escaped with the help of Micheau, but he had decided to keep this information to himself. According to the latest report their tram had plunged into the lagoon. Whatever way she went, the important thing was for her to disappear.

'Cheers,' he said before finally sipping his champagne.

'My brother found this submarine near the Thor Fault in the shallows of the North Sea,' explained Micheau. 'It's an old Soviet Navy Victor III class sub. An antique. But it's taken some good prizes at sea in its time.'

The control room was exactly what Roberta might have imagined: green screens, a tangle of pipes, winking lights, latent claustrophobia. The whole vessel shook, creaked and groaned like an enormous metal stomach in the throes of indigestion.

'Course set to four straight ahead, going down to two knots,' announced the pilot, concentrating on his manoeuvre.

'Get the engines up to five. I'm in a hurry to reach our hideout.'

Roberta was trying to take up as little room as possible. A man with several knife scars on his face entered the control room, looked at her as if she were some kind of curious animal, and asked Micheau, who was studying the sonar, 'Who's she?'

'This lady was in the cell where I'd been told Louis was imprisoned,' said Micheau, without turning round.

'And you brought her back here? Oh, this is too much!'

Micheau swung round and jabbed his forefinger into the man's chest. 'Until my brother's back on board this ship – and he will be back, that's the promise I made to the whole crew and not just you, Labrèche – until he's back I'm in command. Our blood ties require it. Anything else you want to say?'

The two pirates faced each other in a silence broken only by the beeping of the machinery. Then Labrèche lowered his eyes and left the control room, muttering. All the same, Roberta could have sworn they were on the point of murdering each other.

'Welcome to the wonderful world of the Lagoon Brothers,' Micheau told her. 'Want to see where we're going?'

She nodded vigorously. He brought the periscope down, lowered the handles to the horizontal position, and let her look through. At first all she could see was blue water with massive dark shapes in it. Then she recognized the old houses on the banks of what had once been the river bed of the Rhine. The imperial bridge, still standing although it was submerged, came into sight straight ahead. They passed under it as a shoal of fish traced a silvery ring around its one great arch.

'Amazing,' she breathed.

The great bulk of the Münsterkirche appeared on their right. The submarine moved along beside the former cathedral, brushing past its flying buttresses. Then it performed a half-turn and positioned itself to face the great rose window. The tip of the spire that was still intact emerged from the lagoon a little higher up.

'In position,' announced the pilot.

'Move forward, then,' Micheau commanded.

The prow of the Victor III slid to the centre of the rose window, and they entered the cathedral. The submarine rose a few metres and its engines stopped. The periscope slipped back into its housing. Micheau was already climbing the ladder. Roberta, who had seen lights, people and galleries outside, joined him on the superstructure without delay.

The water lapped level with the upper windows of the cathedral. Wooden walkways lit by garlands of electric bulbs ran along the two sides of the nave. There was a floating village on a pontoon in the choir. The village stretched on down the arms of the transept.

'Welcome to our Basle hideout,' announced the pirate, grinning broadly.

The sailors moored the submarine to rings fitted into the pink sandstone walls. A gangplank was lowered from the hull, and they crossed it to the first gallery, where people were coming and going: men, women and children. Roberta, taking in every detail, wondered if she had suffered a nasty knock on the head when she saw Plenck coming towards her.

'Good, just the man I need!' said Micheau, seeing him. 'I'll hand Miss Morgenstern over to you. We'll see each other later when you're all here. I have things to do.'

Micheau went off towards the choir with Labrèche on his heels. The forensic surgeon hugged Roberta. 'Where've you been? We were frantic with anxiety.'

'How's Grégoire? Is he here?'

'He's going to join us later this afternoon, but don't worry, he's fine. We've been hard at work while you were away, you know. You were quite right: the tracers are the killers. I'll show you how they operate.'

The tiny pink, pale blue and silver globules moved in complex undulations in the three translucent blister containers. The body of each tracer bristled with a multitude of filaments swaying gently in the atmospheric solution. Some of them had pincers. Others were spiral in form. Others again were flexible with no protuberances, and looked like whiplashes.

Roberta moved away from the microscope and rubbed her eyes to dispel the monstrous image. The pirates' laboratory was in the Old Basle City Council Chamber. A copy of Holbein's *Danse Macabre*, the original of which was in the crypt, occupied the wall behind them.

'Claude Renard tells me there are many other underwater hideouts all over the world, sometimes entire submerged cities that are still inhabited,' Plenck told her enthusiastically.

'Claude Renard?'

'Micheau's pirate name. They're extraordinarily well equipped. This microscope with its three eyepieces costs a small fortune. I tried to get one for the Museum last year, but believe it or not, my request was turned down for lack of funds.'

The hall was divided in two by a large bullet-proof sheet of glass three inches thick. The study instruments were on one side, the side where they stood, and dangerous substances on the other. The tracer that Plenck was examining was imprisoned in a cube measuring one square millimetre.

'How did you get in touch with them?'

'Through Grégoire. Look at this little miracle. We could never observe it as well on the surface, what with all the contamination in the atmosphere: foraminifera, dust, pollen, tardigrada, rotifera, scales from butterfly wings and all that.'

An assembly line occupied most of the surface of the table, leading to a large container full of blue capsules. Roberta picked one up between her thumb and forefinger.

'This is where they make the cowls,' said Plenck, still riveted to his eyepieces.

Roberta replaced the capsule and bent over the microscope herself. The tracer put out one of its longest filaments as if waving to them.

'Hello to you too,' said the forensic scientist cheerfully.

'Exactly what have you discovered, Plenck?' asked Roberta, who had not forgotten what they were dealing with.

The scientist stepped back and rubbed the bridge of his nose to restore himself to an appearance of proper gravity. 'Have you ever had a chance to see one so close before?' he asked.

'In a way, yes. Well, several. But not in this form.'

'Let me give you a quick guided tour. A tracer consists of three shells filled with separate oily globules. The pink ones are its intelligence, its memory. That's where it stores the data from Central Filing and Records. The blue globules are its vital organs. Lungs, digestive system and all that.'

'What do they eat?'

'Air. Light. Tiny creatures smaller than themselves – oh, don't ask me! As for the silver globules – we'll come back to them later, but first let's look at the filaments. There are three kinds. The smooth ones are for locomotion. The hooked ones are – well, for hooking. The most interesting are the spiral filaments.'

'Which are the longest, and in the majority,' the sorceress noticed.

'Those are the transmitters that allow them to communicate with each other.' Plenck put his hands into two flexible gloves fitted through the glass pane and manipulated a pair of pincers very carefully, placing a second cube on top of the first. 'I'm putting two of our little friends in together,' he explained. 'Now I'll open their cages. Watch carefully.'

The image seen through the lens became opaque and agitated. Once it was calm again, Roberta saw that the two tracers were closely intertwined. Their transmitter filaments were touching at the ends, the hooked filaments were forming solid nodules. The whiplash locomotors were disposed around the new entity, which now had six swellings. Those containing the silvery granules were in direct touch, and globules were passing from one tracer to the other in both directions.

'You see what they're doing?'

'Anyone would think they were making love. It's disgusting!'

'They're exchanging with each other. Merging. Doing molecular division in reverse. Now there's only one. I sedated them mildly so that you could watch them do it, otherwise it's instantaneous.'

'And that's how the Baron takes shape?'

'Yes.' Plenck crossed his hands over his stomach. 'In short, the tracers are intelligent, autonomous social beings.'

'Like ants.'

'Brighter than ants. Let's go on to the second part of our demonstration.'

Plenck put the gloves on again, took a pipette and placed a drop of blood on the cube. Roberta saw the double tracer moving its filaments upwards. The silvery swelling touched the drop, absorbed a little of it and moved away. The pink globules became agitated.

'They're analysing it,' said Plenck.

The membrane holding the two coherent entities opened and closed several times.

'Now they're thinking.'

The spiral antennae moved out in all directions.

'They're calling their friends to their aid. They've spotted a hereditary brand! Time for the Baron to act. Just for the record, that blood is Martha Werber's.'

Roberta felt an itching sensation run through her body. Seeing her automatically scratch her forearm, Plenck smiled. She rose and walked up and down the room. The *danse macabre* was followed by Death in her mind's eye, sickle raised, eye-sockets empty.

'Why did they start killing?'

'Because we let them. Because they're busy little creatures. Because a certain number of factors coincided.' Plenck swivelled his lab chair from right to left, watching the sorceress as she walked to and fro. 'You know their history? They first appeared after the Great Flood, carried on the wind, no one really knows exactly when – or where they came from either.'

'And the College discovered them because of the Little Prague sanctuary.'

'Yes, where everything ends up. My illustrious predecessor at the Museum was the first to study the creatures and understand their capacity to observe and transmit information. Those were troubled times. Order had to be re-established, and the authorities knew about our own existence too.' He took a deep breath. 'We gained municipal immunity through the tracers. They were obedient, willing, and wonderfully malleable. Proper little militiamen in the making. Anyway, once we'd worked out the necessary nutrient fluids and built the manufacturing plant in Records, mass production began.'

'You're talking about thirty years ago.'

'Forty. Tracers began working for Security ten years before the date officially given.'

Roberta remembered the men running to the zoo,

shouting about the monster threatening their children. That had indeed been forty years ago.

'At the time no one saw the link between the Baron Mark One and those migratory particles,' Plenck went on. 'Who'd have thought they'd be able to form a kind of, well, collective consciousness and use it to imitate us?'

'Why did they lie low so long?'

'They were persecuted. No one wanted to see them in the Baron's shape, so they put aside their wish to be like us. And they gave us forty years of good, loyal service. Then came the administrative event which revived the Baron of the Mists.'

'The merger between the genetic data and the biographical data.'

'Yes. Before that, all they knew about us was our individual DNA codes. Now they were presented all of a sudden with the image of a whole society: its civil structure, its births and deaths and relationships. The potions we had devised for them told them to keep watch, raise the alarm and protect society. The tracers themselves added a duty to pursue inquiries, make arrests and carry out executions.'

'Yet they were acting within quite a strict legal framework. The fluids keep them under control, don't they?'

'Remember, only those citizens of Basle whose profiles were being modified have been victims of the Baron of the Mists. The tracers have been dipping into the reservoir of administrative limbo. And they've done pretty well,' continued Plenck, admiringly.

'Let's go back to their method, shall we?' said Roberta. 'They come together at fixed times and places, following the wind. They attack some poor soul, setting themselves up as judge, jury and executioner. But why condemn people for their ancestors' crimes?'

'As you may imagine, I asked myself the same question.'

'Have they no idea of the passage of time?'

'Their life expectancy is one lunar month, and like us they have an internal clock with a built-in countdown. I've an idea of what happens, but it's rather way-out and difficult to check. And it brings us back to the gypsies again, although strictly speaking they have nothing to do with any of this.'

'Come on, Plenck, let's hear your theory!'

The forensic surgeon was not unwilling to explain his idea. 'Well, the gypsies who arrived in Basle just over two years ago came from Palladio's Historic Cities and apparently from different periods, even if those periods were purely fictional,' he reminded her. 'Each city had its own calendar. With the best of intentions the authorities preserved those calendars unchanged, finding ways to make them correspond to the municipal calendar. That way the registers of citizens of Basle to which the tracers should never have had access include people born in the reign of François I of France, others married in the Aztec year of the Thunderbird, and so on,' he explained. 'When you have a brain no bigger than a micron it must be easy to get your time schemes mixed up.'

'You mean they got confused because of the Historic Cities?'

'I'd go further: I'd say that's why operations in Records broke down. A system that wasn't originally designed for it couldn't manage to fit those different periods together.'

At that moment Grégoire Rosemonde opened the Council Chamber door. He stopped dead on seeing Roberta.

'So it was true!' he breathed.

They flung their arms round each other and remained closely embraced. Well, I don't know, thought Plenck, one finger to his temples, are we really so very different from the tracers?

The news from the mainland was uncertain and disturbing. The pirates had picked up an order to the militia from Fould calling for the central square to be well guarded in two days' time. The Victor III submarine, after making two trips between the Münsterkirche and the Savoy Hotel, had also brought back from the Historic Quarter rumours of a forthcoming public execution. No one in the pirate hideout could really believe it. Fould surely wouldn't be mad enough to set the people of Basle against him that way.

Vandenberghe joined Plenck, Roberta and Grégoire early that evening, bringing several crates of Strudel's Flamel vintage which disappeared behind the bar, for a tavern had been set up around the great organ. The upper parts of its pipes emerged from the water below. Strudel, who was organizing his move, had been unable to come himself. Boewens was stranded in mainland Basle too. Meanwhile neither Micheau nor Pichenette put in an appearance.

In the little world of the Lagoon Brothers, nightfall was invariably accompanied by a party which often turned into a long drinking session. This evening's party, so far as the buccaneers could remember, was worthy of an Equatorial crossing. A three-piece band (bandoneon, zither and tambourine) provided background music. The Flamel was heady stuff. They all sang, laughed, and banged the table with tankards full of liquids highly unsuitable for consumption by anyone wishing to stay sound in body and above all in mind.

One table took only a distant interest in the general merriment. Its occupants were discussing serious matters.

'Fould has drawn up a blacklist, and we're on it,' said Vandenberghe. 'He has control of the press and the militia. If the voters don't give him power next Sunday then he's going to take it by force. And he will, without the slightest difficulty.'

'This is absolutely astonishing,' said Roberta, skimming through the electoral promises made by the Minister while she was in jail. 'Is he really going to stop the rain and save the world?'

'According to him, anyway,' muttered Plenck.

'And the people of Basle have nothing to say about that?'

'They're going to wait and see.'

'Meanwhile, the Historic Quarter is cordoned off,' Rosemonde told them.

'Surely it's been cordoned off for some time, hasn't it?' said Vandenberghe, surprised.

'The difference is that you can go in all right now but you can't come out again, and the rising water level isn't going to change that.'

The shocking image of the citizens of Basle standing up on the coastal road to watch the gypsies drown came into all their minds.

'I could stuff him,' suggested Plenck. '*Ministrum securitum*, very fine specimen, hard-nosed, shiny fur.' He was putting the last touch to the drawing of a tracer on which he had been working for a good half-hour. 'Portrait of the killer, or one of its constituent elements,' he said.

Taking the drawing, Roberta felt that itchy sensation in her forearms again. She quickly handed it to Vandenberghe, who passed it on. It had just finished going round the table when a pirate in a grey three-cornered hat, walking with a limp, joined them uninvited.

'Evening, all! My name's Ironleg,' he introduced himself. 'So here's to your health, landlubbers!'

They drank a toast, the Rector with some reserve, but evidently the pirate was going to join their discussion whether or not it was confidential.

'I suggest we vote by a show of hands,' Vandenberghe went on. 'That'll be quicker. Point number one: are we still all agreed to leave Basle? Those in favour raise their hands.'

The response was unanimous. The pirate who called himself Ironleg added his own opinion. 'I certainly see your point. That town is a whole new Basle game these days.' And he roared with laughter at his own joke. Vandenberghe cast him an irritated glance.

'About a hundred other people – family members, sympathizers – have expressed a wish to come with us,' he said. 'We shall have to organize a way to get them out.' He brought the flat of his hand down on the table and added, looking at the witch, 'Point number two: should the tracers be rendered harmless? Those in favour raise their hands.'

Once again the vote was unanimous.

'We shall have to sabotage the manufacturing plant in Records,' said Rosemonde.

Plenck, whose work of art was back in his own hands, folded it and slipped it into the funnel of the oil lamp on the table. The drawing caught fire, and the warm updraught of air scattered it in scraps above their heads.

'We'll see about that later,' said Vandenberghe, who had no idea just how they were going to do it. 'Point number three, the baby. Oh dear me, yes, the baby.' He rubbed his eyes. 'What are we going to do about the baby?' For Rosemonde had told the conspirators what Banshee and Barnabite were up to. 'Could we envisage eliminating it?'

'Eliminating it?' exclaimed Rosemonde. 'If you'd actually seen it, as I have, you wouldn't speak of *eliminating* it.'

'That's for sure,' said the pirate Ironleg. 'We care for babies like the apple of our eye. You should speak better of an innocent child, sir!'

Searching his jacket, the pirate brought out a tobacco pouch, tipped a considerable quantity of gunpowder into his tankard, stirred it well and took a gulp that brought fire to his cheeks. Vandenberghe, watching him, had put his head in his hands, wishing he could just ignore this human bomb sitting at their table.

'Very well then,' he summed up. 'We destroy the system in Records, we leave Basle, and we let the baby live.'

'We destroy the system in Records, we leave Basle, and we take the baby with us,' Rosemonde corrected him.

Everyone around the table stared at the Professor of the History of Sorcery. No one said anything at all.

'Oh, and do we take the golem too?' asked Plenck. 'I wouldn't mind studying it.'

'The golem will turn against its creator and be destroyed,' said Vandenberghe. 'That's how its reincarnations always end up.'

'I've certainly seen some tough guys during my travels,' said the pirate, 'but my word, you lot beat all records for ruthless boarding of the enemy.'

'Couldn't have put it better myself,' said the Rector, clinking his glass of Flamel against the pirate's tankard, but cautiously, for fear of an explosion.

The music grew louder. Conversation got going again. Roberta felt she needed a change of air.

'Come along,' said Rosemonde. 'Let's go for a little walk.'

They left the smoke-filled tavern and followed a gallery that sloped slightly upwards towards the intersecting ribs of the vault, leaving behind them the sound of the party echoing through the nave.

'What about a little stroll in the forest?' suggested Rosemonde.

'You mean there's a *forest* up here?'

An opening had been made in the vault. They went through it, and found themselves inside the roof structure of the Münsterkirche. Entire trees had been cut to size, carved and then assembled to hold up the roof itself. Small lamps lit up these fantastic beams. Up above Roberta could hear people snoring and grunting, and a few chuckles.

'The hammocks are up there. We can sleep in one of them.'

The forest creaked. Roberta felt as if the cathedral were moving, and pressed close to Grégoire.

'Don't worry. The water can't get in.'

'I'm a little scared all the same,' she said in a small voice.

'Let's go right up and look at the view of Basle.'

They went over to a rudimentary lift which hoisted them up to fresh air at the top of the spire. Water was lapping around it scarcely two metres below. Roberta could only guess at the city lights beyond the rain pouring down on the lagoon.

'I shall have to fetch my things,' she said. 'And my photos. And Beelzebub.'

'I've been feeding him while you were gone.'

'That was very kind of you, though having to go on a diet wouldn't hurt him.'

'And what about your mynah bird?'

'My mynah bird . . .' She leaned against Rosemonde, took his hands in hers, and breathed in the invigorating air above the lagoon with pleasure. 'Oh, Grégoire, how I've missed you! I was so scared of losing you!'

'I felt the same, my dear.'

It was a romantic moment, but questions were coming thick and fast in Morgenstern's ever-wakeful mind. 'Plenck says it was your idea to approach the pirates?'

'You're not in the CID any more, you know.'

'All the same, I didn't know I was sharing my life with a potential outlaw.'

Knowing her strong opinions, Rosemonde decided he had better explain himself. 'The pirates are simply tradesmen in the floating market. They're the sole suppliers of Lachryma Christi wine, fresh shellfish and gourmet cheeses.'

'How old are you?' Roberta suddenly asked.

It was a question she didn't remember ever having put to him before. And it must be a matter of some importance, because he didn't reply, or rather he replied evasively. 'Oh, I've given up counting the passing years.'

He kissed her affectionately on the forehead, right on the bump which was a souvenir of the collision with Martineau's car.

'Ouch!' Dozens of little twinges ran through her body again. If only she had a tube of castorium here!

'I have some magic ointment with me,' he told her. 'Let's find a hammock and I'll see to your injuries.'

'You don't know your age and you can read my thoughts? Who *are* you, Grégoire Rosemonde?'

The Professor of History did not reply. Taking the witch's hand, he led her into the heart of the forest along a path that he alone knew.

The Play is Over

Ernest Pichenette got out of the tram, put up his umbrella, and climbed the steps to the Palace of Justice. Once in the waiting room he folded his umbrella again, hung it over his forearm, and consulted the plan that Morgenstern had drawn for him.

'The evidence cupboard isn't easy to find,' she had warned him.

'You mean it isn't much in evidence,' the writer had replied, thinking himself very witty. Once again his joke fell flat.

'Can I help you?'

A militiaman with the safety catch off his gun had just accosted him. The militia had been patrolling every nook and cranny of the city since the previous evening. Indeed, thought Pichenette once he had recovered from his first moment of alarm, it was odd that this man wasn't in the central square waiting for the big show to begin on the scaffold.

'I'm looking for Gallery J7,' he replied, hoping the militiaman wouldn't notice the cowl covering him and making him look rather like a glow-worm.

The man pointed out the gallery and walked away. Pichenette went on into the Palace, found Gallery J7 and stopped at a door which could indeed have a cupboard behind it, as Roberta had said.

Here we go, he thought.

There was no indication that the items of evidence accumulated by investigators since the founding of the CID were really in here. Pichenette opened the door and found himself face to face with Marcelin. The witch had given an accurate description of the archivist, who was cleaning his nails with a paperclip. He narrowed his eyes when he saw the visitor take a large book out of a plastic bag and hold it out to him.

'The street atlas of Old Basle!' exclaimed Marcelin, with the air of a man discovering treasure.

'Roberta Morgenstern asked me to return it to you. With many thanks.'

Marcelin rose and said warmly, thrusting out his chest, 'Sir, you are a good citizen! Allow me to shake you by the hand!'

Pichenette took Marcelin's hand in his own and replied, in the same measured tones, 'Thank you too, and by the same token, sweet dreams.'

The archivist had no time to express his surprise at this peculiar wish. The anaesthetic syringe pricking his palm made him drop back into his chair with a blissful smile. There's nothing about an inert civil servant to attract a tracer's attention, Pichenette told himself, pulling the needle out of the man's hand while taking care not to prick himself. He put it in his pocket and went in search of what he had come for.

Evidence taken from those caught in the act to be found under 01 to 03, he said to himself. So where was the drawer for the current year?

He climbed a set of steps and found the right drawer at the very top. It contained only a single large envelope. Pichenette took it out, surprised to find it so heavy, climbed back down the steps and opened it. He removed the piece of evidence that Micheau had asked him to bring back.

It was only a piece of rock, a kind of quartz, vaguely oval in shape and with green and blue glints in it. This lump of mineral was what Louis Renard, known to mainland dwellers only as an anonymous pirate, had tried to steal from a stallholder, and he had used it in trying to knock out Gruber – Louis, who was due to have his head cut off in half an hour's time. Why, the journalist wondered, why were two of the most famous of the lagoon pirates ready to risk so much in order to get their hands on it?

Pichenette put the piece of quartz back in its envelope, stuffed the envelope into his overcoat pocket, and left the room, not without making sure that Marcelin was sitting comfortably in his chair.

'Goodbye and thanks,' he said, closing the door very quietly so as not to wake him.

This was his day of glory, the day that would go down in the history books as marking the beginning of the reign of Archibald Fould! The second round of the election would do no more than confirm him in power via the democratic route. For the Minister had only to look at the crowded square to know in advance that he had already won.

A ring of militiamen guarded the guillotine. A pathway had been left clear from the scaffold in the centre of the square to the street along which the hearse carrying the condemned man would come. All around the square, umbrellas formed a huge black and grey carapace.

The outgoing Mayor, his supporters, and a group of lawyers headed by Werner Boewens, Suzy's father, had tried to whip up public opinion against the execution. But the public wouldn't go along with them. Opinion polls showed that the people of Basle wanted to see the pirate dead, and the Minister, as their elected leader-to-be, was merely responding to their expectations.

'How many are there?' he asked his militia captain, who was on watch behind him.

'At least a hundred thousand, sir,' said the officer proudly.

The executioner – a real flesh-and-blood executioner – had been brought in at great expense by a Pelican DeLuxe vessel from Rocky Mountains State, one of the last places on mainland earth which still had capital punishment. It was usually done by electric chair, as the man had told Fould the previous evening, adding that all the same there was a quaint Old World touch about the guillotine which he rather fancied.

The guillotine itself came from the Ile de France. According to the antique dealer who had sold it to them for a wickedly high price, while also trying to flog them three Scottish battleaxes and two Iron Maidens from Nuremberg, the blade was brand new. The Minister wondered why.

The lever tipped the rocker device forward. The hole for the victim's head closed. The blade fell towards the ground. The three sounds as the guillotine was tested silenced the crowd, and they raised their umbrellas. Three knocks, as if to signal the start of a theatrical performance, thought the Minister, watching the executioner reassemble the mechanism. It was obviously in perfect working order.

Observing it all from the City Hall balcony, he felt he was watching a great spectacle, a play fit for this city, and he would be its author, director and principal actor. Act I, Scene 1: the hearse from the municipal jail stops on the edge of the square, the condemned man, in red shirt and black trousers, climbs out and goes along the corridor lined with militiamen, his tread firm, his head held high, to the plaudits of the people of Basle as they jostle each other for a sight of him.

'Shall we intervene?' asked the militia captain nervously.

'On no account.'

The crowd, a living, moving entity, an enormous animal without a head or tail, was a whole separate organism. And wasn't the Baron, who consisted of millions of tracers, its perfect embodiment? The frightened city of Basle wanted a culprit. It wasn't about to prevent the execution from taking place.

The pirate climbed to the platform of the scaffold, casting a scornful glance at the crowd swarming below. He doesn't lack courage, the Minister admitted to himself. The booing died away. Were they falling under the victim's spell? Fould picked up the microphone from the arm of his chair, rose to his feet and called, 'Fellow citizens!'

The umbrellas turned towards the City Hall balcony.

'It is not lightly that I see capital punishment carried out on this day, dismal as it already is. But we cannot allow the forces of Evil to threaten our civil liberties!' The crowd fidgeted, but did not dispute this obvious truth. 'We are not just executing a pirate today, we are executing Piracy. Tomorrow, in the same way, the blade will cut off not the head of the Baron of the Mists but the head of Crime itself!'

The crowd roared its approval. Fould calmed the noise with a gesture. He was no longer just a man, or a pit viper, or a Minister of Security . . . and the title of Mayor isn't impressive enough, he told himself. We'll get that changed on Monday.

'Let us strike the Beast at once, let us cut off its head, and then – ah, then you will see the demons take flight and the skies smile upon us.'

He flung his arms wide and closed his eyes. The people of Basle held their breath.

'In two days' time you go to the polls to elect a new Mayor. I promised you that if you voted for me the rain would stop.' He let several seconds pass for theatrical effect. 'I lied to you!'

Some protests were heard. There was total incredulity.

'No, even *before* you vote for me it will stop raining!'

The crowd began to chant the Minister's name louder and louder. 'Fould! Fould! Fould! Fould!'

He made the V for victory sign, wondering all the same if he wasn't going a little too fast . . . but after all, this pirate would certainly provide the iron for the baby today.

'And in any case the play is over!' he snarled, pointing his thumb downwards in the ancient Roman manner.

The executioner, who was just waiting for this signal, made the pirate lie down on the platform of the guillotine, fitted the frame into place on the nape of his neck, placed his hand on the lever working the blade . . .

And at this precise moment the first explosion came. A green, pistachio-coloured cloud hid the Central Pharmacy and spread in the air over the crowd, which started running away in all directions, yelling. The militia captain flung himself on Fould, who pushed him away violently. 'Get down there and command your men, you fool!' the Minister ordered. 'It's down there something's happening.'

The next explosions around the square channelled the panic towards the street, where most of the militia were posted. Meanwhile, pink foam emerging voraciously from open manhole covers added further confusion to the scene. What with the green explosions as well, the spectacle Fould had staged was now like a monstrous happening somewhere between kitsch and abstract art.

The explosions stopped. The firemen arrived to disperse the foam. Inert bodies came into sight on the tarmac. Several disorientated militiamen were turning round in circles. The executioner, still at his post with a large cap of pink bubbles on top of his head, was looking around as if he had lost something.

The pirate in the red shirt had vanished into thin air.

'Three cheers for Louis! Hip hip hooray!'

The crew of the Victor III submarine had their captain back. The brothers were reunited. The pirates had thwarted Fould and trampled his extremist ambitions. Rivers of alcohol were flowing in the transept of the Münsterkirche.

Roberta had seen Pichenette return from his excursion to the upper reaches of Basle with a large envelope in his hands. She would have loved to know just what he had found in the evidence cupboard, but the Renard brothers had got in first. They took Pichenette off for a private conversation and reappeared half an hour later. By now the members of the College staff were at their usual table in the tavern in the transept. Eleazar had a companion: a gypsy girl called Leila. He blushed whenever their eyes met.

'The militia don't insist on seeing a pass any more if you want to go down to the Historic Quarter,' said Rosemonde. 'But it keeps your identity papers, and once you've passed the railings you're officially an outlaw.'

'We're all outlaws now,' Lusitanus reminded him. 'And according to the *Mainland News*, which is telling the truth for once, the water will flood the low-lying districts tomorrow.'

'Well, that's convenient,' remarked Leila. 'Since tomorrow's when we're leaving anyway.'

She took the innkeeper's hand, turned it over and traced the lines of luck, love and life on his palm. Strudel, peony-red in the face, was breathing noisily. Vandenberghe went on.

'Luckily we can get up into the city through the sewer manhole covers. And the cowls enable us to move freely.'

'We just have to avoid getting caught,' Roberta reminded him. 'How far advanced are preparations for the move?'

'There are about a hundred people in Paris Street already, and we expect as many more again.'

'Everything we really need from the College will be packed up by noon tomorrow,' added Lusitanus. 'And what we take will be replaced by worthless replicas so as to lull suspicion.'

'Personally I'd have liked to carry the entire amphitheatre off,' said Rosemonde, 'but Banshee would never have been deceived.'

'You didn't come across her?'

'Not once. She must have moved in with Barnabite.'

'Cold goulash for breakfast. What a lovely life,' said Roberta, teeth clenched.

'Are you still planning to take the baby with us?' Plenck asked Grégoire.

'What else can we do? I mean, could *you* envisage leaving a child in that unnatural creature's clutches?' exclaimed the Professor of History in heated tones.

'All right, I agree with you,' Plenck said soothingly. 'So Banshee is far from being the model mother every baby deserves. But there's a problem.'

Rosemonde, although he looked forbidding, kept quiet and waited for the forensic scientist to explain.

'Judging by that list you saw in the observatory, together with the number of elements still missing, given the number of people killed between then and now and assuming I can still count up to four, the baby isn't ready. Louis Renard was to have been the last victim. So it wouldn't be just a case of snatching an innocent child from an unfit foster-mother but from its incubator. The baby may not be viable yet.'

A dreadful silence fell around the table.

'Plenck's right,' Vandenberghe backed him up. 'It's not for us to take such a decision.'

Rosemonde looked at the Rector with an exceptionally distressed expression.

'For the moment, anyway,' Vandenberghe added forcefully. 'For the moment.' He turned to Roberta, and went on. 'We've saved the branches we really need from our trees of sorcery. They'll be replanted in the gardens of the Historic Quarter. The garden plots are under glass, yours included. It wasn't all that easy to move them, but the gypsies were very helpful.'

'That *Orchidia carmilla* is going to feel very lonely on its own,' commented the sorceress.

'And we're still far from ready,' added Vandenberghe. 'We have to guide the emigrants to the right place, fetch our magic books . . .'

'My conjurors are stowed away in the cartons,' said Strudel, his hand still in Leila's. 'But I have all my kitchen things to pack.'

A cheerful, noisy company approached their table. 'And these are our friends from the College of Sorcery!' announced Claude Renard, introducing them to his brother, who had exchanged his red shirt for a bright emerald-green waistcoat.

He bowed, hand on heart. 'Louis Renard owes you a debt of honour,' he told the company at large. Then he took a chair and sat down between Morgenstern and Rosemonde. Claude remained standing. Ten or so pirates with determined expressions were watching them, arms crossed.

'It was a pleasure. And those green explosions were so pretty,' Roberta assured him. She had been present at the scene next to Werner and Suzy Boewens, well hidden by her cowl, of course. 'They went beautifully with my pink saponaria foam.'

'We can tell you how to make them if you like,' offered Louis Renard.

'And we'll tell you our own secret in return.'

Pirate and sorceress studied each other in silence. Louis

leaned forward, a cunning look on his face. 'Claude tells me you're thinking of attacking the Records Office.'

'Yes,' said Rosemonde, attracting his attention. 'We intend to destroy the plant that manufactures the tracers in the basement of the Community Building.'

Louis Renard narrowed his eyes. 'Then my crew will go with you. And my brother's too, no doubt?' He glanced inquiringly at Claude, and received his silent approval.

'We could certainly do with your help to keep the militia occupied while I sabotage the Ministry of Security,' continued Rosemonde, looking hard at Louis Renard.

Slowly, Roberta turned to the Professor of History. Had no one else heard what he'd just said? He was planning to attack the Records Office on his own – would no one protest?

'Oh, that's easy enough,' said Louis, bringing his hand down on the table to seal the bargain. 'We'll create a diversion.' He turned to Roberta. 'I'm told you once worked for the Criminal Investigation Department?'

'Once' was barely two weeks in the past – but for the sorceress, who nodded her head, it was an eternity.

'What happened to that man in grey who arrested me? I had good reason to dislike him, but he had a certain style – which those human machines the militia entirely lack. How's he doing?'

'Gruber's dead,' said Roberta, surprised to find she could reply so equably to that question. 'Fould had him killed.'

'Really? Archibald Fould may soon be Mayor, but he'll never move as fast as the blade of my sword,' said the pirate, with an assurance that would have done Minister Fould himself proud. He rose, saluted them, and moved away with his brother and a bodyguard of pirates.

'The Renards are quite a couple,' said Plenck.

'Do you think they look like each other?' asked Lusitanus.

'Not really,' said Vandenberghe judiciously, 'but there are brothers and brothers. Speaking of which, have you by any chance seen Ironleg? I'd have liked to invite him to our table . . . Ah, there he is!' The old sorcerer whistled through his fingers. 'Hey there, Ironleg, old boy! Come and join us, and the next round of drinks is on the College of Sorcery!'

The cable car moved away from the Community Building and rose into the air. Fould summoned up his courage and tapped out a number on his mobile. Banshee answered even before it had finished ringing.

'The water's rising and we still don't have the iron!' she shouted. 'I suppose you're happy?'

Fould held the mobile away from his ear. 'What's done can't be undone,' he said. 'And the Baron won't show up before Monday.'

Which meant not before the second round of the election. He was going to be minus a corpse, the baby would still be incomplete, he wouldn't be able to order the rain to stop falling and he wouldn't be elected . . .

'How can you be so sure of that?' snapped Banshee.

'I just know, that's all.'

'Oh, never mind all the mystification! Time is short, Archie. Tell me about your secret source of information.'

Reluctantly, the Minister revealed the existence of the pamphlet about the winds which Clément Martineau had discovered in the first place. Banshee laughed raucously on hearing how Fould, the big boss, always knew where the Baron would strike next. So he had only to consult the work of a meteorologist whose name hadn't even gone down in history! How pathetic! And how lucky that she had devised Plan B in case the execution failed. As indeed it had, in spades!

'Listen, Archie dear, have you any idea of the date of birth of the Baron of the Mists?'

'What are you getting at?' It was a question that the Minister had never asked himself in quite those terms. As he saw it, the killer was immaterial, a creature made of ephemeral dust without any genuine existence. But Banshee was right: the Baron's conscious mind was born of the merger with Central Filing, and the Filing Department had been on standby since the first breakdowns. So the killer tracers had been expelled from the machinery in the Records Office at the same time. They must be of the same generation.

'And the tracers are expelled once a week?' Banshee persisted.

'They generate only at the main lunar phases. You know that as well as I do,' said Fould angrily, tired of all this talking in riddles.

'And their life-span is only twenty-nine days, a lunar month?'

'So?'

'So I asked a simple question: when was the Baron of the Mists born?'

'The first murder was on 30th March, a Sunday. The merger with Filing took place the previous Friday. Our tracers were expelled on the evening of the next day, the Saturday.'

'Which means the Baron was born on Saturday 29th March, at the new moon. What day will it be tomorrow?'

'27th April.'

'And our baby will be how old?'

'Twenty-nine days.' Fould sighed. He had just taken her point. 'All right. So the Baron of the Mists dies tomorrow. I forgot to take that into account. Which means that my pamphlet is worthless now. You want to put an announcement in the Deaths column of the *Mainland News*?'

'Idiot! Idiot! Idiot!' snapped Banshee angrily. 'Can't you see beyond the end of your own nose? Haven't you ever wondered where the tracers go to die?'

Fould looked at the tower blocks of the city, blurred in the rain, standing like sentinels on both sides of the Ministerial cable car. 'No,' he admitted in a small voice.

'They die here in the sanctuary. The grey dust on the ground of Little Prague is nothing but the remains of dead tracers, my friend. That's how the College found out about them.'

'Which means that tomorrow . . .'

'Tomorrow the Baron will be in Prague one way or another, and we're going to give him a little present.'

'Present?'

'A goodbye present. I was thinking of a lamb.'

It took Fould a moment to understand that she was speaking metaphorically.

'The victim's profile would have to have been modified,' he said.

'I'll leave the technical details to you. Pick a young victim – the iron will be better quality. Male or female, it doesn't matter which. And while you're about it, choose someone whose death would suit you.' The wind began blowing hard, with violent gusts battering the cabin of the cable car. 'You *are* calling from the office, aren't you?' asked Banshee suspiciously.

'Yes,' Fould lied. 'Can't you hear the interference?' The wind and rain were producing a convincing crackle. 'Suppose he refuses our present?' he asked.

'He can't go against his true nature. And if he doesn't want it, well, we'll lend a hand ourselves.'

'Tomorrow?' asked Fould.

'At nightfall. You'll be there.'

It was an order, not a question. The witch was leading the

dance in this last figure, and Fould was obliged to fall in with her violent, staccato step.

'By the way, we know the baby's sex,' she said, throwing him a sop.

'Is it a boy?' he asked excitedly.

'See you tomorrow. Six in the evening, at Hector Barnabite's place.'

She hung up just as the cable car entered the tower of the Ministry of War building. The doors of the cabin opened. Fould set off along the red carpet unrolled for his arrival and tapped a second number into his mobile. The lamb whom he had in mind answered on the third ring. The number three, the theatrically minded Minister noticed. Things were moving again!

A gypsy had come from the cellars of the Little Ladies' café at the foot of the Municipal Mausoleum to find Suzy Boewens. The tunnel running out of the cellars joined the main sewer five hundred metres further on. There they boarded a large flat-bottomed barge going along the underground river. They overtook a dozen similar barges laden with furniture, cardboard cartons and refugees. A whole gypsy army was waiting at the exit from the sewer under the overhanging coastal road, very close to the velarium and in full view of the crowd of citizens of Basle that had gathered slightly higher up. The empty barges left again to collect more cargoes of goods and people.

The gypsy guided Suzy to Paris Street. The College's new base in Miracles Court was noisy, cheerful and colourful. Carriages kept arriving to be unloaded. Amatas Lusitanus cast spells on the heaviest furniture to lighten its weight. Otto Vandenberghe, standing on an upturned crate, was trying to impose some kind of order on all the racket.

'Suzy! Here you are at last!' he cried, seeing her arrive.

'Everything in the way of lab benches, magic books, alchemical retorts and chimeras in the Louvre tower over that way,' he added. 'We'll sort it out later. Now, Suzy, what can I do for you?'

'I'm looking for Roberta.'

'She's settling into . . . into . . .' He consulted a list. 'Into the Poets' Garret. That half-timbered house. Take it easy with our apothecarium,' he told a group of girls carrying the long chest as if it were a battering ram. 'That's valuable property, my dears, that's very valuable property.'

The four floors of the house known as the Poets' Garret had been converted into apartments. Doors stood wide open. Morgenstern and Rosemonde had settled in at the very top, said the cheerful students. Their names were sellotaped to the door, and an amazing rainbow-shaped workbench had been dumped in front of it. When Suzy rang the bell Roberta opened it.

'What a lovely surprise, Suzy! Do come in.'

There were packing cases everywhere, but one corner of the main room had been comfortably furnished with an architect's table and cushions flung at random on a sofa.

'You'll be comfortable in here,' said Suzy.

'Three handsomely decorated rooms, hearths big enough to roast an ox, exposed beams, Tuscan tiles on the floor. And a fine view over Venice, Paris, London and Mexico! Yes, this place is quite something. Why don't we sit down?'

Beelzebub, lurking between two cushions, climbed out and got on his mistress's lap. Roberta picked him up and moved him to the other end of the sofa. 'He's moulting, making a present of his fur to all and sundry. Really, it's too much!'

Suzy still said nothing, and Roberta added, 'Have you decided?'

'Yes. I'm staying. I can't do anything else.'

'Are you sure?'

'In a couple of days' time Basle will be living under a tyrant's rule. My clients are going to need a good lawyer.'

Roberta smiled. 'You mean your Siamese twins?'

'Well, Fould is perfectly capable of beheading one of them and saying his twin died of a broken heart.'

Brave girl, thought the sorceress. She wished she had made an effort to get to know Suzy better before leaving Basle. Beelzebub returned to the attack, winding around his mistress's legs and purring. Taken by surprise, Roberta let him carry on, and turned to check that the mynah bird, still asleep on its perch, wasn't missing any feathers. How come her naturally contrary cat had suddenly turned so cuddly? She couldn't make it out.

'When do you leave?' asked Suzy.

'Tomorrow evening. The operation will begin late in the afternoon at a dozen key points. May I offer you some good advice? Stay at home and make sure you have a cast-iron alibi.'

'I'll do just that.'

Suzy tried to stroke the cat, who growled at her. In retaliation she fleetingly assumed the mask of a large dog and barked, just once. Beelzebub fled into the next room, mewing pitifully. The lawyer reverted to her own grave, pretty face, but a tawny light lingered in her eyes.

'Very impressive,' Roberta congratulated her. 'How are you doing with the Ether? Are you getting on all right?'

'That's one reason why I came to see you. Did you know my mother has set up a centre for listening in on phone conversations, in case it's useful to any future resistance movement?'

'Otto did mention it. So at least we'll still be in contact.'

'Well, they've already picked up a conversation between Fould and Banshee. Here's the transcript.' Suzy offered two sheets of paper, which Roberta read with great interest. The pirated exchange between the cable car and Little Prague merely confirmed the suspicions they already had of what the Minister and the witch were up to.

'So Plenck was right: they need one more corpse.'

'And there's something else,' said Suzy. 'Clément – I mean Martineau – he called me just now. He invited me to go and see his new house. It has a garden,' she added. 'I declined.'

'Poor fellow,' said Roberta, not sure if she was really sorry for him.

'I wasn't being absolutely straight with him,' Suzy admitted. 'He unloaded a whole lot of nonsense on me, but I was sounding him out at the same time through the Ether. I mean, once you start it's difficult to stop.'

'Don't apologize. I'm just the same way with chocolate meringues.'

'I – I saw his feelings for me,' said the young woman.

'Strong feelings,' suggested the sorceress, cautiously.

'Totally ridiculous feelings, you mean! But that's not the problem. I felt a kind of anxiety about the Baron of the Mists in his mind. So for purely professional reasons I explored it.'

'And?'

'His mentor Archibald Fould has entrusted a mission to him. It was all about some mysterious contact who, said Fould, apparently knows the Baron's identity and is ready to reveal it to someone from Security tomorrow evening in Little Prague. He asked Martineau to go and meet this person.'

Roberta turned pale, and looked at the sheets of paper on the sofa. 'Clément – oh no! Not him!' she faltered, shaking her head.

'His profile has been modified, hasn't it?' said Suzy.

'By me, before I filed his family tree in sorcery.'

'And he had the brand?'

The family tree was in Rosemonde's cupboard with the contorted figures carved on it. She had only to get it out and unroll it to see the X gene come up again and again, from the founder of the dynasty right to the present day.

Roberta was horrified.

'So they've decided on their sacrificial lamb,' said Suzy in hollow tones.

Many Events But Few Words

The rain had come through the velarium and was pouring down on the Historic Quarter. Eleazar was just finishing putting up the Two Salamanders inn sign above the guardroom allotted to him when a large drop of water splashed on the end of his nose. He turned the screwdriver a couple of times and took refuge indoors.

The water had carried away the pontoon allowing people in the Historic Quarter to reach the ramp, and had invaded the main street. It would be hard for anyone to navigate the main sewer now. There was no going back for the sorcerers, gypsies and pirates or their families.

Eleazar looked at the room, rapidly assessing the work he still had to do: he must carve the runes against intoxication on those beams, pin up his collection of conjurors on the wall, test the fire-power of his new cooker . . .

He leaned his elbows on the counter. A glass of spruce liqueur nestled in the palm of his hand. He thought of friends who were leaving and others who were staying, and drank a silent toast to each and every one of them.

To the pirates, who were no doubt preparing for the assault at this moment. Ten simultaneous attacks in ten parts of the city, all to be carried out within a little less than two hours from now. It would be magnificent.

To the gypsies putting the final touch to their preparations for departure.

To Leila.

'You'll love the lagoon – it's so beautiful,' his little fortune-teller had assured him before planting a hazelnut-flavoured kiss on his lips.

Eleazar would join her in the garden that formed the prow when they cast off. Who cared that he had always lived on the mainland, and didn't think he would have very good sea legs?

To his friends of the College. To Otto, who had moved into Nicolas Flamel's house as the Guardian of the Book. To Lusitanus, perched on a roof-top somewhere to interrogate the sky. To Plenck, who had installed his collection of stuffed animals in the tower of the College of Lisieux. To Roberta. To Suzy, who was staying. To Grégoire, who was about to take so many risks.

'I know the layout of the place,' the Professor of History had said. 'I've actually worked for the Records Office, and my pass is still valid.' He had shown it to them. 'I'll join you once I've sabotaged the machinery.'

No one around the table could fault this reasoning. Roberta had simply taken Rosemonde's hand in her own and held it as long as possible.

The inn rose a few centimetres on the water. The movement of the swell had been minimized, but Eleazar could feel it distinctly, even standing on his own two feet. This foretaste of life on the lagoon brought him back to practical details.

Had he forgotten anything important, he wondered? Going behind the bar, he opened a carton. Bavarian tankards all present and correct, ditto pewter bowls, ditto spices.

But there was something else he mustn't forget, he knew there was. He picked up his list with growing anxiety.

Spices present and correct, Major Gruber's urn . . . He opened a carton, then a second carton, then a third. Major Gruber's urn . . .

He explored the shambles that was the kitchen, but he found nothing.

'You cretin!' he told himself, furious with his own stupidity. 'You've gone and left the Major's ashes in Basle!'

Grégoire Rosemonde had put on a cowl at the door of the Little Ladies' café. It gave him an hour to reach the Community Building without being picked up by the tracers. First he wanted to take one last look at his amphitheatre. The College of Sorcery was on his way to the Community Building, so he dropped in.

The University, like the rest of the city, was seized by a kind of apathy. Rosemonde met not a living soul on his way to the rotunda with its three spiral tiers of seats. He picked up a piece of white chalk from the groove under the blackboard and drew a question mark. All these years spent exploring the mysteries, he thought nostalgically, and most of them still unsolved.

He left the amphitheatre and went on to Barnabite's library. It too was empty, but the volume of Dante was open at the crucial passage. Like the two travellers at the gateway to the Inferno, Grégoire hesitated.

He had only to go through this door, climb the stairs from Hector's crypt, go to the observatory and then . . .

'Plenck is right,' Roberta had said. 'If the baby still has one element missing we can't risk taking it out of its incubator.'

Rosemonde turned on his heel, feeling a dull fury rising within him. He went back through the University and on to the Community Building, ignoring the rain and the passers-by, who could be counted on the fingers of one hand, as well as the militiamen, who were present in far greater numbers and gave the impression that the city was under curfew.

His anger did not die down until he was in the central square where the sinister scaffold stood. A large pool of black water surrounded it, lapping against the façades of some of the buildings. Rosemonde skirted the pool and went up a little shopping street. The place was cold and dismal. The only lighted window belonged to a children's toyshop displaying a dolls' house, a tin toy circus, and a little train-set with intricate mechanisms. A devil mask superimposed itself on the reflection of his own face.

Rosemonde opened the door. The bell fitted to it rang, a perky sound. A boy of no more than ten was counting the day's takings.

'I'm closing in five minutes,' he said. 'But you can look round if you like.'

Rosemonde explored the display, and struck lucky on top of some shelves of soft toys. His find was a brown teddy bear with a white front. The boy told him it cost fifteen dollars. Rosemonde paid, and once out in the street he felt the same sense of urgency come over him again. The pirates would be going into action in barely half an hour's time. He must be down in the basement of the Records Office before that. He lengthened his stride.

Reaching the street where the old Two Salamanders inn stood, he stood back against a wall covered with election posters showing Fould, Fould and Fould again. A checkpoint had been set up a dozen metres away, with three militiamen turning everyone away from the Administrative Quarter. He was just getting out his Records Office pass when a low voice called his name. 'Monsieur Rosemonde? Psst! Hey, Grégoire!'

The voice came from an alley as black as a moonless night.

'Eleazar?' The innkeeper stepped out into the light. 'What are you doing here?'

'The Major's ashes . . . I . . . I left them at the inn,' he faltered, looking desperate. 'And they'll never let me in there.'

'You mean you came to fetch them? You must go back to Paris Street at once!'

'Yes, but the Major . . .'

'I'll see to the Major. Give me your keys.' Eleazar held them out to him. 'Go back, and hurry, understand?'

The Professor watched the bulky shape move away. Then he strolled casually up to the checkpoint. The militiaman studied his Records Office pass.

'I'm a historian,' he explained. 'I work in the Doubtful Imprints Department.'

This was strictly true. Three years earlier he had drawn up a comprehensive file on a certain Count Palladio, the only known pluricentenarian registered in mainland records, before passing his information on to Roberta to help her solve the case of the Killers' Quadrille.[1]

'And there's a doubtful imprint that can't wait?' said the man sarcastically.

'The strange and the sinister don't observe office hours,' said Rosemonde philosophically.

The militiaman handed back his pass. 'The perimeter's guarded, and the lads are a little jumpy this evening, but you can go through.'

'Thanks. Good night.'

Rosemonde moved away and went into the Two Salamanders. The Major's urn was on the counter. He tipped the ashes into a napkin, tying its corners into a neat bundle and stowing it away under his coat with the teddy bear.

[1] See *Dance of the Assassins*.

Leaving the inn, he walked on for ten minutes at a brisk pace before climbing the steps to the Community Building.

The porter on duty opened it for him. There were no militiamen guarding the way to the manufacturing plant. Rosemonde had only to cast a quick spell to persuade the porter that he hadn't seen him and was still alone in the Community Building. Then he went down to the basement, moving like a shadow.

Suzy Boewens had refused Clément's invitation. She said she had better things to do.

I'm head of the CID, Martineau told himself. I'm not going to spend my life running after that stuck-up little madam! If she changes her mind she'll have to ask *me*. Then she'll find out what it feels like to be turned down.

He was on board his little boat, and had been navigating between the roofs of the flooded houses until he could tie up to a gable end with a carved stork on it. He followed the road leading to St John Nepomuk – not that it was a road any more, but a ravine, with the ground washed away in places and making strange gurgling sounds. The houses on each side of the road seemed about to collapse.

The gargoyles of Prague Cathedral were spouting jets of dirty water. The young man dodged them and entered the building. There was no sound apart from the wind blowing high in the roof. And there wasn't enough light. He groped his way forward between the pillars, afraid of colliding with something or falling down a hole. That would be just his luck!

He reached the foot of the steps leading to the Daliborka. His last visit had been a month ago. A new moon would rise this evening, a new moon with its cargo of dreams, its procession of nightmares, its promise of flying. He carefully climbed the steps and stopped at the top. Nothing in the tower had changed. The *prie-dieu* was still lying in the corner where Banshee had pushed it over, with a cobweb slung between it and the table. So the impassive, industrious spiders were still spinning away.

He put out his hand. He had taken off his moonstone ring for fear of being swept up into the air. He felt the lunar attraction caress him, warm him, tug his arm upwards. The crystal song of lunar sirens tempted him – 'One more step, join us. You are expected, O lord of the white moon.'

'No!' he moaned, his throat tight with fear. He went down the steps backwards, his back wet with sweat. When he reached the transept he was staggering slightly, but he soon got control of himself. Footsteps echoed through the church. He took out his six-shooter and listened. Whoever else was in here wasn't trying to hide. Was it the informer? The investigator made his way between two stone tombs and went back up the nave, moving cautiously from pillar to pillar so as to come up on the other person from behind. He retreated into the side aisle.

The contact he was expecting to meet turned out to be a small person with a kind of cape flung over its shoulders. It was carrying a flowered shopping bag which struck the young man as familiar.

'Hands up!' ordered Martineau, taking the safety catch off his gun.

The other person turned round. 'Oh, put that toy away, Martineau. You could hurt someone.'

'Morgenstern?'

The sorceress walked towards her former protégé and stopped a couple of paces away. There was a touch of defiance in her eyes. He was still pointing the gun at her.

'Don't tell me you'd be capable of shooting me down?'

'I'd be capable of arresting you,' he replied, his lips

quivering and his mind confused. 'The tracers warned us of your presence in the Historic Quarter. Go back and don't show your face here again, or I'll have to turn you in to the militia.'

'Planning to carry me all the way to the coastal road, are you? That's enough fooling about, Martineau. Listen, Fould has set a trap for you. You must get out of here.'

She knelt down to search her shopping bag.

'Don't move!' he said, his voice shaking hysterically. This time Roberta took the threat seriously.

'I've brought you an Electrum girdle,' she explained quietly. 'It arrived this morning. I think it ought to fit you.'

'A *girdle*? What are you doing here anyway?'

'I've come to save your life, you young idiot.'

Martineau hesitated. 'I'm giving you one last chance to leave,' he repeated.

The witch lost patience. 'I suppose it was Fould who sent you here to meet someone he described as an informer?'

'You – you mean the informer is you?'

'No, no, it's the Baron of the Mists.'

'The Baron of the Mists is working as an informer for the Ministry of Security?'

Roberta was glad to see that Martineau's simple-minded side still showed through his outer layer of conformism. She took the girdle out of her shopping bag and tossed it to him.

'Put that on. Your boss needs one last victim, and he's picked you. For all we know the Baron is eavesdropping on our interesting conversation at this very moment, and he'll . . .'

The organ of St John Nepomuk uttered a plaintive note and then fell silent.

'. . . he'll soon let us know it,' she finished, straining her eyes to look into the dark.

The wind chose this moment to rise.

Grégoire Rosemonde reached the machinery down in the basement of Records easily enough. The manufacturing procedure, which was normally under strict supervision, was operating on automatic mode. The plant was deserted.

The pressure gauges of the settling tanks showed that the next generation of tracers would soon be born. Rosemonde climbed up to the catwalk above the assembly line as the tanks began bubbling. The virgin tracers were on their way to the statistician, to absorb knowledge in the form of electronic data.

Rosemonde overtook them. On his way to the Two Salamanders he had worked out a way to sabotage the mechanism. Kneeling down, he grasped the wheel set in the channel linking the statistician to the boilers above the nutrient solutions, and turned it several times.

Sirens howled. Flashes of light, visible through the metal flaps of the device, swept through the statistician. Red lights winked on and off all over the place. Still turning the wheel, Rosemonde was enjoying himself. The place reminded him of the lurid atmosphere of Gehenna. Then the flashes stopped. The wheel jammed. The trap in the duct that let the tracers pass through opened.

Taking out the napkin containing Major Gruber's ashes, he held its knotted corners above the opening and undid it by mental projection.

'Over to you, Major,' he said.

The duct swallowed up the cloud of grey dust.

Rosemonde closed the trap, came down from the catwalk and made for the exit, while tracers raced towards the boilers behind him, to find only clogged nutrient solutions there. There was the sound of a dull explosion, followed by sinister grinding noises. The statistician fell apart, spitting out a volley of flashes that hit the walls. For a moment the whole production line looked like an incandescent spider collapsing in on itself. Then it exploded with a crash like thunder.

He had been born to serve. To serve mankind and its idea of justice.

He had burned those complex creatures, quartered them, drowned them, torn them apart, impaled them and set insects on them. Creatures as complex as himself. Human beings are merely composite existences, layer upon layer of generations linked by a thin thread of blood, his consciousness told him. His task was far from done. There were many guilty souls still walking the streets of Basle. But he was coming to the end of his allotted time. The being who had been known as the Baron of the Mists was approaching the moment of death.

Like his brothers who had preceded him, he had let the wind carry him to Little Prague, which itself gave a good idea of what death was like, and had taken refuge in the heights of that disturbing building the cathedral. He had been waiting up in the bell tower, watching his hands. Death, he knew, would begin at the extremities before reaching the ventricles of his carbon-based heart.

The Baron was resigned, but he was aware of events in the city. The atmosphere was saturated with electrical warnings. Danger. Invasion. Attack. Pirates. Green clouds surrounded the Municipal Mausoleum, the Palace of Justice, the central square, the Fortuny quarter, the floating market . . . Pollution. Terrorism. Diversions. No victims, but a militia which didn't know what to do next.

The Baron did not move. He was tired. His work was done. It was up to others now.

Even more alarming reports reached him from the Community Building, and he almost returned there. The new generation of tracers had been destroyed. Sons and daughters put to the sword. Babies strangled. A hecatomb. The end of a world. Vengeance.

Still the Baron did not move. He was tired and his work was over.

But death was slow in coming. He made one last round of St John Nepomuk – and suddenly saw the two humans who had been condemned to death. They might have come there on purpose to meet him!

The woman was the witch who had knocked him unconscious in the Pharmacy. As for the man, he had known him ever since the case of that incompetent soothsayer who escaped the stake. His two missions were to punish and to protect. He had never felt as much at peace with himself as in the incineration plant, punishing the guilty man with one hand, protecting the innocent with the other.

But the innocent man turned out not to be innocent at all. The brand was there in his blood. His profile was now being updated, which meant that the Baron could see it. It gave him a free hand to deal with the case immediately.

Roberta Morgenstern tried to intercept him, but the Baron swerved to avoid the electric shock before it reached him. She returned to the attack. A kick sent her flying into the nave.

The man was holding a gun. He fired, of course. Six shots, and while he fired them the Baron studied Martineau at his leisure, trying to pinpoint his crime. The brand was very clear, almost graphic. But he had to go all the way back to the forty-fourth page of the man's genetic history to find its origin.

Martineau had been midwife, acrobat, soothsayer. He had also been an architect, a builder of temples, libraries and tombs. The great work of the founder of the line had been a library, the most fabulous edifice of its time, commissioned by the rulers of Alexandria, who had imprisoned him in a windowless room inside the building so that the secret of its construction should die with him. His only crime was to have created a masterpiece.

The Baron saw him as clearly as he saw his descendant. The man was held captive in a cavern with a sandy floor, lit by a brazier, hurling imprecations at his jailers in a forgotten language. And he had disappeared into thin air without paying his debt to justice. The brand had been passed on down his line. Someone must pay that debt.

Then Morgenstern counter-attacked. The Baron had completely forgotten her. The electric shock was terrible. He felt dislocated, scattered, as if caught in the data-saturated storm that had given him birth. Morgenstern and Martineau were running for the door. He summoned up the last of his strength, despite the pain piercing him, and in two bounds he had barred their way.

He caught the man in two arms, four arms, six arms. He didn't have time to wall him up like his ancestor and watch him die. Only the end of the process mattered. He decided to obey his instinct and ignore historical verisimilitude: he took the form of what he really was.

Three enormous swellings, as tall as the church porch and bristling with twining filaments, surrounded Martineau and began squeezing. Only the young man's head could be seen outside the gigantic tracer. The longest of the whiplash filaments, sharp as steel, rose towards the stone vault to come down again and cut it off.

Death was approaching.

He must efface the brand, eliminate this stain on humanity. Those were the monster's last thoughts.

The blade fell, as merciless as a sentence against which there is no appeal.

★ ★ ★

Rosemonde had no difficulty getting back into the Records Office lobby, but he couldn't hope to get out of it. The militia were there already on the far side of the mosaic floor, firing point blank at him. He ran for the first lift, with bullets whistling over his head and striking the concrete. His plan was to reach the top floor of Security.

The lift took him up to the sixty-eighth floor, the highest floor of the Records Office Technical Services department. The other three lifts were coming up towards him, crammed with militia. Rosemonde took the stairs up to the sixty-ninth floor and set off to look for the ministerial lift. He was going along the CID corridor when militiamen appeared at the far end of it. He made his way into the first room on the right and blanked out the door behind him.

He was in a conference room with a skylight instead of a ceiling, a well of light going up to the roof. He scrambled up on the desk, but the skylight was still out of reach. He could hardly ask a militiaman to give him a leg up.

Detonations echoed out in the corridor. The walls trembled. Rosemonde looked at the desk, the skylight, and Victor the skeleton who was watching him, seated in the corner from which he had not moved since the Minister of Security's last meeting here.

'Would you be kind enough to lend me a hand?' asked the Professor of History. Some heavy object was being brought to bear against the wall, which was already showing cracks.

Victor rose, climbed on the desk himself, crouched down, spread out his finger-bones to make a stepping stone for Rosemonde, who clambered up on them, reached the skylight and opened it with his shoulder. Pushing off from the skeleton's shiny skull, he found himself outside, shut the skylight again, and began climbing down the fire escape fitted into the concrete cliff.

Victor readjusted his skull and his finger-bones, sat down at the desk and waited. The wall was breached. The militia rushed into the room, and on seeing him stopped. He waved his arms in welcome. Tough as the militiamen were they ran for it, yelling. Overcome by panic himself, Victor looked behind him and thought he saw a monster in his own shadow. He followed the fugitives as fast as his tibias would carry him, shouting, 'Wait for me! Don't leave me here! I'm so scared.'

Since a skeleton has no vocal cords, these remarks were expressed by incomprehensible and terrifying clicks of his jaws.

The golem entered the observatory without knocking. Fould, Barnabite and Banshee, all of them very pale, looked at it.

'Well?' said the witch impatiently.

Hector went over to the motionless creature, examined the insides of its clay hands, and then, standing on a small stool, its mouth.

'Nothing.'

'What? No iron?' exclaimed Banshee.

'Pinocchio here has failed,' said the Minister of Security ironically.

The baby, a delicately featured little girl, turned slowly in the matrix. Her legs were folded up in the foetal position, but her head was straight on her neck. She was looking at Fould, who smiled at her. She did not react.

'Can she live without iron?'

'Yes, but at what price?' asked the sorceress.

'We must try to find someone else,' begged Barnabite. 'Or something else. Even a large animal would do.'

'The hunting season's over,' Banshee cut him short. 'The water's lapping at your doorstep, Hector. Your house will be flooded tonight.'

'Why go looking for suitable prey in the forest when we have it here already?' asked the Minister, in a tone which turned the atmosphere to ice. He was holding a small hand gun, aiming it between the two sorcerers. The golem did not move.

'What are you doing?' asked Hector, thinking that Fould was aiming at Banshee.

'Taking iron anywhere I can get it.'

The witch stepped aside. Fould's gun was turned on the sorcerer.

'Sorry, Hector,' she apologized. 'But we really do need that element. You could say that once it's been integrated, you'll be with us all through this adventure in a way, right to the very end.'

Fury crimsoned the cheeks of the deceived alchemist. He didn't even think of running for it.

'By St Wenceslas!' he swore. 'You'll pay for this, Carmilla.'

Just as he was pulling the trigger, Fould saw something massive and reddish brown looming in front of him. He emptied almost the whole magazine into the golem. The clay creature knocked him down with a powerful blow of its fist before disappearing into the garden. Barnabite was no longer there.

'Devil take that brute,' said the Minister angrily, getting up. Large marks of red clay stained his 5000 dollar suit.

'Hector! We don't mean you any harm!' cried Banshee, turning to the garden.

'Very diplomatic!' said Fould sarcastically, joining her. 'I'm sure that'll bring him back to apologize for not shutting the door behind him.'

'Oh, be quiet!'

Fould shrugged his shoulders, and felt his jaw. 'How could we have foreseen that the golem would save his life?' he complained.

'If we could have foreseen everything I'm sure we'd never have got into this business together.'

They were facing each other. The matrix in the background radiated spectral light.

'We won't get the iron now,' he reminded the witch, gun in hand and ostensibly pointing at her. There was still one bullet to be fired, and they both knew it.

'We shall have to bring her into the world now with or without iron,' he went on implacably.

She could tear his head off, but how would she extract the iron without the golem's aid?

'Move over,' she told him, stationing herself in front of the control panel. The temperature indicators looked good. 'So long as the baby's strong enough,' she muttered. 'If not . . .'

If not then she would tear the Minister's head off just to calm her nerves. She switched off the inlet tap and turned the wheel a dozen times. Then she moved away from the matrix.

'Put your gun away. You won't be needing it now.'

The nutrient fluid was sucked into the base of the matrix. The baby closed her eyes and curled up. Without the optical magnifying effect of the liquid, she was only a tiny shape at the bottom of the transparent egg. Banshee opened it and felt the child's neck.

'The heart's beating.'

Fould bent down and picked up the baby. She weighed so little – she was so cold.

'Fetch that blanket,' he said sharply.

Banshee did as she was told, and put the thermal blanket round the baby, who was beginning to move. Her eyes slowly opened. They were black, incredibly black. Her mouth opened. Air rushed into her lungs. Her chest rose.

The Minister of Security had no experience of fatherhood, and he wished he had the use of his hands so that he could put them over his ears. But as a responsible adult he suffered what he had to. The new-born baby's cry struck him full in the face.

Rosemonde had just made his way into Archibald Fould's den when he stopped, ears pricked like a cat's.

'Welcome to Earth, little Lilith,' he said.

Sounds reached him from the light-well and the anteroom. But the Minister's retreat was as well locked as a strongbox, which slowed him down slightly. He took the teddy bear out from under his coat and squeezed its chest as he approached the most imposing piece of furniture in the room, an art deco desk which looked like a huge dark wooden paperweight on top of the nightmare of the Records Office.

His thumbs were working away at the bear's little white woolly front. He could feel a heart beating very faintly in its chest. Rosemonde put the teddy bear on the desk, propping it against the lamp.

'You must take great care of Lilith,' he told the teddy. 'Protect her like the apple of your eye.' The bear had turned its head and was looking at him. 'I'll come back for her soon. Very soon. And when I do I shall need you. Understand?'

The toy nodded.

'And now, hush!' said Rosemonde, a finger to his lips.

The teddy bear flopped over on one side. Once again it was the lifeless cuddly toy he had bought in a shop in Basle. Rosemonde looked out of the window. Green smoke was drifting over the city. The velarium was stretched above the Historic Quarter. Little Prague was keeping its secrets.

Dull thuds in the anteroom told him that the militia had brought in the heavy artillery. The roof, he thought, preparing a spell to break the glass. He must trust Pichenette to get him out of this tight spot. He must hope and wait.

Martineau was asleep. Someone was calling to him. He didn't want to wake up. His nose was pinched hard. He let out a yell of pain and jumped to his feet.

'So how's your head?' Morgenstern was looking at him, hands on her hips, red hair tousled. Fragmentary images came back to him. The Baron materializing in front of him, the monstrous creature stifling him in its dreadful heart, the whiplash filament rising . . .

A black star like the impact of a meteorite ran from his feet to the centre of the nave.

'You weren't dreaming, Clément. The Baron is dead.'

'Dead?' he repeated, brushing down his jacket, which was covered with sticky grey particles. Indeed, the young man was grey from head to foot.

'A natural death. And we'd better get out of here this minute if we don't want to join him.'

'What's happened?'

'A baby has been born,' Roberta explained calmly. 'A little girl. Never mind who she is. The power of her first cry set off a major earth tremor. As a result of which St John Nepomuk is about to collapse any minute.'

Martineau stared at the witch, stupefied. 'What?'

A keystone up in the vault came away and crashed into the choir of the cathedral, making the detective understand the precarious nature of their situation more clearly than if Roberta had gone on explaining at length. The part of the transept containing the Daliborka fell to the ground, raising a wall of dust.

They ran out and raced down the potholed road to the boat moored to its gable. Once aboard, Martineau rowed hard to put distance between the submerged roofs and themselves. Low rumbling sounds came from the islet on which Little Prague stood.

'You saved my life,' he admitted, once they were out of danger.

In a way Roberta herself regretted the past. But in an hour's time she would be far from Basle. There was no time to make friends again now. In the future, perhaps. 'I'll ask you just two things,' she said.

'Yes?'

'First, drop me off on the quayside of the Historic Quarter.'

The young man started the engine. The motorboat took them over to the deserted quay, drew in beside it, and Roberta jumped out.

'What's the second thing?' he asked, handing her bag to her.

He was a pitiful sight with his soaked suit, bowed shoulders and general hangdog look. Perhaps he hadn't really changed after all, the sorceress thought.

'If you ever feel like flying to the moon another time without stopping off on the top floor of the Community Building then let me know, Martineau. I'd be glad to see you again. And don't hang around here in this cockleshell of yours, or I'll have to fish you out of the water once more.'

He followed the little woman with his eyes until she disappeared under the velarium. Then he moved away, skirting the Savoy. Why would she have to fish me out of the water, he wondered, making for the Fortuny quarter. I mean, it's ages ago that those Viking spells almost drowned me!

Fould and Banshee were on the steps of the observatory, looking at the curtain of rain. The Minister was still holding the baby, who had stopped crying.

316

'Suppose she loves cold showers, then what?' he inquired, looking at the sky.

'Then we'll have to admit failure.'

Fould searched his pocket with one hand and brought out his mobile.

'What are you doing?'

He did not reply, but tapped out a number and put the phone to his ear. 'Yes, it's me. What? No, I'd switched it off. The pirates, you say? They've taken the tower block by storm?' He snorted noisily, but managed to keep calm. 'Well, if they're still in there, I want you to arrest them – or wipe them out, it's up to you. Give your men a bit of fun. No, no, that's all right, friend. That's normal. Right, are the loudspeakers still working? Connect me, then.'

The wind raised one corner of the blanket over the baby's face. The Minister was horrified to see blood trickling from both nostrils. The child's eyes were hollow, and she was breathing with difficulty.

'Basle is listening to you,' his militia captain assured him.

Fould put the blanket back in place and made his final campaign speech.

'Fellow citizens! This is Archibald Fould, Minister of Security, addressing you! I promised you the rain would stop falling before tomorrow, and there'd be no new flood to fear! I shall now keep my promise.' He walked out into the garden in the rain, to the edge of the bed of poisonous flowers. 'I order the elements to leave us in peace and depart from . . .'

'Here's the moment of truth,' murmured Banshee, behind him.

With his mobile jammed between his chin and his shoulder-blade, he took the baby in both hands, let the blanket drop to his feet, and held her up naked in the pouring rain.

'Now!'

317

The baby struggled, but Fould held on firmly. The blood flowing from her nostrils coloured her little stomach pale pink. She shrieked again. The rain suddenly stopped falling.

'Yes!' cried the witch.

The clouds blew aside, revealing a sky the colour of a blood orange, and were swept towards the horizon. A huge roar arose from the city. Fould handed the baby to Banshee, who made haste to dry her off. He was holding his mobile again, and laughing uproariously, like tens of thousands of the people of Basle.

'Yes,' he shouted into the phone. 'Yes. It's stopped. I'll see you tomorrow, my friends. I'll see you at the ballot boxes.'

And he rang off, to the sound of fanatical and joyous plaudits.

'At least no one can accuse me of getting elected on a platform of false promises,' he said happily, looking at the sky where the storm had been stopped in its tracks by the baby's furious yell.

His mobile rang, disrupting this beautiful moment. Fould hesitated to answer, and his features darkened when he heard what his militia captain had to tell him.

'What? Are you sure? How long, did you say?' He rang off and rushed into the observatory. 'Banshee!'

She was cradling the baby, who was whimpering, exhausted by the effort she had made.

'The dam's been breached!' he exclaimed. 'And its collapse has brought a tidal wave heading straight for us!'

The witch was transfigured. With the baby in her arms, she was rocking gently back and forth. She smiled at the child who, although worn out, made an effort to return her smile.

'A tidal wave, eh?' she said, to the baby. 'Quick, let's get away from that nasty wavy-bavy. What about it, Morgan, my little love? Shall we get out through Uncle Hector's bookie-wookie?'

She tickled the end of the baby's nose. The child watched, taken aback, and then sneezed, spraying tiny droplets of blood over the blanket.

'Morgan?' said Fould, rather annoyed not to have been consulted. 'You haven't forgotten her father's identity, I hope? If he doesn't like the name he may hold it against you.'

Banshee looked wearily at the Minister. 'Morgan is the perfect name for her. If you have a better idea, go on, I'm listening.'

'Oh, I don't know... we could always call her Administrationa?'

The exchange continued in this vein, with the two of them suggesting some ten names. Lilith, on Banshee's lap, told herself that life was not going to be easy in the company of these two human beings, who seemed to be united for worse rather than better.

'Fold back the velarium!'

The canvas was folded back to the perimeter of the Historic Quarter, which for the first time in weeks unveiled its terraces, roof-tops, windmills and gardens to the people of Basle gaping at it from the coastal road. Their booing, which had been interrupted by the miracle of St Archibald, resumed with fresh vigour.

The Queen of the Gypsies, sitting cross-legged on the top floor of the pagoda, which faced the lagoon, could communicate with her key lookout posts by means of a semaphore system on the lower levels. But for now she was simply listening to Earth, Air, Fire, Water and the Ether, each of which was bringing her news in its own way from this part of the world.

She turned her head east, and saw the baby passing by at

this very moment, close to two motionless travellers in muted colours. She looked west, and saw Martineau bringing his boat in to the foot of the Fortuny towers. Right ahead of her, Roberta was returning to the garden in the prow. To the north, behind her and much higher up, Grégoire was scanning the clear sky and smoking a cigarette. There was a fine view from the roof of the Community Building, but none the less he was beginning to get impatient.

The clairvoyant Queen opened her eyes and looked at her own partly submerged Quarter.

'Bring in the gangplanks!' was the second order.

The semaphore signallers on the second floor waved their flags. Latecomers hurried over the Venetian footbridges. Behind her, she heard the shouts of the people of Basle, who were expecting to see the immigrant quarter founder at the foot of their beloved city. The dull roar of the tidal wave could be heard now.

'Close the Quarter!'

The countless mechanical devices hidden within the buildings began to move. The façades along the main street drew closer together, protrusions neatly filling indentations. The low reliefs representing Huitizilopochtli fitted into the Byzantine leads of St Mark's Cathedral. The statues of Notre-Dame and Versailles embraced. The porch of the Palace of Westminster closed up like an oyster. The Historic Quarter was hermetically sealed and ready to move out into the lagoon.

A white crest appeared on the horizon. The wave was taller than the Queen had imagined, and coming on faster.

'Cast off!'

The whole Quarter swayed. The citizens of Basle, thinking they were watching the beginning of its final collapse, applauded loudly. The Queen was keeping an eye on the Savoy Hotel, which was going to act as a tug and pull them out of the mud. The pirates were men of their word. The floating grand hotel moved away from its moorings, ropes stretched taut. The superstructure of the Victor III, which had come up in the billiards room, was pulling the whole Historic Quarter out into the lagoon.

The tidal wave, almost twenty metres tall, reached the spire of the Münsterkirche and submerged it in an explosion of spray.

'Every man for himself, and hang on to anything you can!' was the fourth and somewhat contradictory order to precede a brief state of chaos.

The pirates disengaged from the Savoy just before the wave struck it full on. The grand hotel turned and capsized at once. The Historic Quarter rose, like a gigantic raft, from the garden of the prow to Little Mexico. Then the wave continued on its way towards the coastal road, where the shouting had changed its tone. The onlookers were running for their lives.

What a pity, thought the Queen, relieved to see that her floating town had passed its test by tidal wave. They'll never see anything finer.

For from their exile from the Historic Cities to the process of fitting the Quarter out as a ship, from their agreement with the pirates to the sabotage of the dam, from welcoming the College on board to this new departure, everything could be summed up in a single word. The high priestess rose to her feet, spread her arms wide and gave the signal for them to leave. '*Vayé!*'

The three gypsies stationed on the sixth to eighth floors of the pagoda waved their flags on three sides of the building. The windmills were turned to face the coastal road as the wave battered it. Their sails began turning faster and faster. The Queen felt their power driving the great raft on towards the breach that had been made in the dam. Gradually they gained speed. A wake formed behind them. Basle was fading away in the distance.

At the front of the garden in the prow Eleazar Strudel was leaning over dangerously close to the water, his arms crossed, with little Leila clinging to his plump stomach to keep him from falling in.

'Yoohoohoohoo!' he was shouting at the top of his voice, intoxicated with joy and the speed they were making. 'We're kings of the world! We're masters of the universe!'

What on earth could Ernest be doing, Rosemonde wondered in annoyance, crushing out his third cigarette end before shredding it and scattering it to the four winds of Basle.

The Historic Quarter had already cast off, and he still couldn't see anything coming. But at last the characteristic throb of the *Albatross*'s engines reached his ears. The airship appeared behind the Black Mountain, making for him as fast as its propellers would take it, in fact a little too fast for his liking.

The trapdoor giving access to the roof was flung open. The first militiamen surged on to the roof, firing at random. But the prow of the *Albatross* was already gliding past one of the walls of the Community Building. Rosemonde took a run, jumped into the air, and with an agile bound landed on the deck of the ship. By the time he joined Pichenette in the cabin, the tower of the Security Building was already far behind them.

'You kept me waiting long enough,' he told the pilot.

'Well, the *Albatross* was guarded. And the batteries were only half charged. And I'm not used to driving this sort of armoured vehicle. What do we do now? Follow the gypsies and the pirates?'

Rosemonde went over to the ship's rail and looked at the lagoon three hundred metres below the hull. The Historic

Quarter passed through the breach in the dam and out into open water. He could see the submarine ahead of him like a long black bobbin.

'Hold our present course. We put in at the next mainland port, and then we're going back to Basle.'

'What?'

'There's one last little person who has to come with us.'

'If you ask me,' said Pichenette, on the verge of losing his temper, 'going back to Basle for "some little person" is taking humanitarianism too far!'

Rosemonde laid a hand on the journalist's shoulder. Images that might have terrified an ogre passed before Pichenette's eyes. He immediately immersed himself in his charts to find a mainland port where they could land.

Epilogue

The gypsies had found shelter in the free port of Vallombrosa, in what had once been called Tuscany. The high hills, planted with cypress and olive trees, stood out against a sky the colour of lapis lazuli. Otto Vandenberghe and Roberta Morgenstern were walking in the garden at the prow. Multi-coloured ribbons tied to the may trees waved in the breeze.

'I suppose when you say a thing like that, Roberta, you have definite proof. Good heavens – this is no light matter!'

'Read it. You'll have a clearer idea then.'

Roberta gave him Major Gruber's diary, open at the page in question, and went over to the ship's rail. Louis Renard's Victor III lay at anchor near the coast. His brother's submarine was in dry dock. The pirates were singing at their work, and the sorceress thought she knew the tune, but the wind and the distance meant that she couldn't identify it. Otto joined her, giving her back the diary without comment.

'When Archibald Fould sent Major Gruber to Mexico to trap Palladio, he told him to bring back a sample of the Devil's DNA. Gruber picked up a cigarette end impregnated with saliva. And he never heard any more about it. That's what he writes in there. All the same, it's a disturbing coincidence, don't you think?'

'Was this notebook part of his estate?'

'Well, yes and no. It was in his house. Micheau – I mean Renard – found it in Mimosa Street when he was searching through the Major's files.'

'So you're saying they may have brought the Devil's baby into the world,' murmured Vandenberghe, tugging at his beard.

'Did you see the extent of the child's powers? The skies themselves obeyed it. The Ether's been in a state of total confusion since Fould stopped the rain. Suzy still isn't clear about it, but she's sure of one thing: an exceptional being has come into the world. Personally I think the baby is behind all this. I'd bet my poncho on it.'

'Oh, don't do a thing like that. You wouldn't be the same without your poncho.' Otto pulled a face. 'So Fould and Banshee are playing with fire – hell-fire – and they're getting results, too. Elected with ninety-nine per cent of the vote! Machiavelli can't compete!'

They were walking along an avenue of jacarandas planted by the gypsies the day before.

'You're thinking of Grégoire,' guessed the Rector of the College. 'Don't worry about him. The Queen saw him leave.'

'But she hasn't seen him come back.'

'He's a resourceful man. And if any of us is an expert on the Devil, it's our Professor of the History of Sorcery. He'll be back, if only out of a sense of professional duty. Well, I must be off. The Benedictine fathers here say they'd like to try their luck at opening the Book, and they're waiting for me at the Great Gables. Do you think the Chosen One could be in monastic robes?'

Vandenberghe roared with laughter and left Roberta to her own thoughts. She pulled the folds of her poncho closer and went down to the quay of the Historic Quarter. A dinghy was about to set off for the Victor III, and the sorceress asked the man in it to take her over too. They crossed the stretch of water, and she clambered up on the deck of the submarine, where a dozen pirates were at work repainting it. None of them took any notice of her.

Roberta felt the ocarina in the pocket of her jodhpurs. She hadn't played it since she was in the municipal jail. She had no chance of finding her telepathic hedgehog now, so far from Basle.

One of the pirates was singing as he painted the superstructure with anti-rust.

Roberta frowned. Surprising to hear that lad humming a Beatles song, she told herself. Another pirate on the other side of the superstructure took up the song – it was the one about the yellow submarine. Moving forward, Roberta heard a third voice join in along with the first two. This one came from the lookout post. Roberta clambered up on the superstructure, taking care not to catch her feet in her poncho. The third singer was painting the tube of the periscope. A fourth voice down inside the vessel struck up the submarine song too. Roberta could make it out, rather distorted.

I must be dreaming, the sorceress murmured.

She went down to the pilot's cabin, stopped and listened. She located the fourth voice in the stern of the vessel. ' 'Scuse me, 'scuse me,' she apologized, hurrying that way so as not to lose the precious clue.

She passed a ship's cook who was whistling the same familiar tune. A little way off a cabin boy was playing percussion on some pipes with an adjustable spanner.

The pirates suddenly stopped for a break, allowing Roberta to open up her mind.

'Hans-Friedrich!' she cried, recognizing the hedgehog's thought processes.

She didn't need the Beatles and their yellow submarine now. The telepathic hedgehog was guiding her the right way as surely as a beacon. She plunged into the depths of the ship, making her way to the compartment containing the propeller shaft, where the temperature was warmest. Behind her, the whole crew was singing again.

She found the hedgehog in a corner where old rags were stored. He quivered with pleasure when she hugged him. 'Hans-Friedrich! My poppet! I've missed you so much.'

She picked up the Gustavson, supporting his little paws, and held him out in front of her. He looked scrawny and rather sheepish.

'You could have let me have news of you! I've been worried to death.' She listened to the hedgehog's reply. 'You had no choice? What do you mean, you had no choice?'

The hedgehog explained. Roberta narrowed her eyes. She bent down, put the proud father on the floor, and delicately raised the rags protecting the litter. There were his eight babies snuggled up to the mother hedgehog, who gave her husband's old friend a rather curt greeting.

'Lots of little Gustavsons,' Roberta sighed, dropping a kiss on both parental snouts. 'Wonderful! Didn't you both do well!'

A kind of frenzy had come over the submarine. It was now just one huge musical resonator. Half the pirates were singing at the tops of their voices about the yellow submarine, while the others, using anything that came to hand as a percussion instrument, were beating out the wrong rhythm: 'Pom-ti-pom, ti-pom ti-pom.'

'Hans-Friedrich, dear, I don't think these gentlemen have quite the right tempo,' said Roberta, frowning.

She took out her ocarina, rubbed it on her poncho and raised it to her lips.

DANCE OF THE ASSASSINS

Hervé Jubert

**Welcome to the future.
Welcome to nineteenth-century London:
a theme park re-created for tourists.
But it's not just tourists visiting this
historical virtual city . . .
Jack the Ripper, too, has returned.**

Roberta Morgenstern and her intrepid assistant Clément Martineau are hot on the assassin's trail. Their mission will lead them from medieval Paris to Montezuma's Mexico, as they trace the steps of a criminal mastermind – and confront the Devil himself.